LAKE

OF THE

LONG

SUN

Tor books by Gene Wolfe

Castle of Days
Castleview
The Death of Doctor Island
Endangered Species
Free Live Free
Nightside the Long Sun
Pandora by Holly Hollander
Seven American Nights
Soldier of Arete
Soldier of the Mist
Storeys from the Old Hotel
There Are Doors
The Urth of the New Sun

LAKE

OF THE

LONG

SUN

———■———

Gene Wolfe

A TOM DOHERTY ASSOCIATES BOOK

NEW YORK

LAKE OF THE LONG SUN

Copyright © 1994 by Gene Wolfe

A Tor Book
Published by Tom Doherty Associates, Inc.
175 Fifth Avenue
New York, N.Y. 10010

Tor® is a registered trademark of Tom Doherty
Associates, Inc.

Library of Congress Cataloging-in-Publication Data

Wolfe, Gene.
    Lake of the long sun / Gene Wolfe.
        p.   cm. — (The Book of the long sun ; bk. 2)
    ISBN 0-312-85494-3
    I. Title.   II. Series: Wolfe, Gene. Book of the
long sun ; bk. 2.
    PS3573.052L35   1994
    813'.54—dc20   93-37001
                                                CIP

First edition: January 1994

Printed in the United States of America

0 9 8 7 6 5 4 3 2 1

For Dan Knight, who will understand more than most

GODS, PERSONS, AND ANIMALS MENTIONED IN THE TEXT

N.B. In Viron, biochemical males are named for animals or animal products: Auk, Blood, Crane, Musk, and Silk bear names of this type. Biochemical females are named for plants (most frequently flowers) or plant products: Chenille, Mint, Orchid, Rose. Chemical persons, both male and female, are named for metals or minerals: Hammerstone, Marble, Sand, Schist.

Aquila, a young eagle being trained by Musk.

Arolla, a woman who has left Orchid's.

Auk, a housebreaker, a friend of Silk's, devoted to Mint, a large and powerful man with a heavy jaw and prominent ears. Called "Hackum" by Chenille.

Bass, the bully who maintains order at Orchid's.

Bellflower, one of the women at Orchid's.

Maytera *Betel,* once one of the sibyls at the manteion on Sun Street, now deceased.

Bittersweet, a member of Incus's circle of black mechanics.

Blood, a crime lord, the de facto owner of Silk's manteion and Orchid's yellow house. Tall, heavy, balding, and red-faced; about fifty-five.

Chenille, one of the women at Orchid's. She is probably
nineteen, is tall and athletic, and has dyed her hair
the fiery shade of her name-flower. Called "Jugs" by
Auk.

Chervil, a young middle-class woman from Viron, wife of
Coypu.

Coypu, a young middle-class man from Viron, husband
of Chervil.

Chiquito, a parrot once owned by Mamelta's parents.

Doctor *Crane,* Blood's private physician, a small, fussy
man with an iron-gray beard.

Dreoilin, Iolar's favorite daughter.

Echidna, a major goddess, consort of Pas, mother of the
gods, and chief goddess of fertility. Particularly
associated with snakes, mice, and other crawling
creatures.

Feather, a small boy at Silk's palaestra.

Fulmar, a member of Incus's circle of black mechanics.

Councillor *Galago,* a member of the Ayuntamiento and
its expert on diplomacy and foreign affairs.

Gib, the big man who maintains order in the Cock. A
friend of Auk's.

Patera *Gulo,* a young augur.

Corporal *Hammerstone,* a soldier in Viron's army.

Hare, Musk's assistant.

Hierax, a major god, the god of death and patron of the
fourth day of the week. Particularly associated with
carion birds, jackals, and (like Tartaros) with black
animals of every kind.

Hoppy, a derogatory name for a Guardsman.

Horn, the leader of the older boys at Silk's palaestra.

Hyacinth, a beautiful courtesan controlled by Blood.

Patera *Incus,* Remora's prothonotary, a small, sly man
with buck teeth. His hobby is black mechanics.

Iolar, a Flier.

Kalan, a thief killed by Auk.

Kit, a small boy who attends Silk's palaestra.

Kypris, a minor goddess, the goddess of love. Particularly associated with rabbits and doves.

Councillor *Lemur,* the Secretary of the Ayuntamiento and thus the de facto ruler of Viron.

Councillor *Loris,* a member of the Ayuntamiento, its presiding officer in Lemur's absence.

Mamelta, a sleeper wakened by Mucor and freed by Silk.

Maytera *Marble,* now a sibyl of Silk's manteion, junior to Rose but senior to Mint; she is over three hundred years old, and nearly worn out.

Marrow, a greengrocer.

Maytera *Mint,* the junior sibyl at Silk's manteion.

Molpe, a major goddess, the goddess of music, dancing, and art, of the winds and of all light things, patroness of the second day of the week. She is particularly associated with songbirds and butterflies.

Mucor, Blood's adopted daughter; she is about fifteen, capable of asomatous travel, and something akin to a devil.

Musk, Blood's steward and lover.

Nettle, Horn's sweetheart.

Olive, a sleeper.

Colonel *Oosik,* the commander of the Third Brigade of the Civil Guard of Viron.

Orchid, madame of the yellow house on Lamp Street. Orpine's mother.

Oreb, Silk's pet night chough, a large black bird with scarlet legs and a crimson beak.

Orpine, Orchid's daughter, stabbed by Chenille.

The *Outsider,* the minor god who enlightened Silk.

Pas, the father of the gods and ruler of the Whorl, which he built. The god of sun and rain, of mechanisms and much else, pictured with two heads.

He is particularly associated with cattle and birds of
prey.
Phaea, a major goddess, the goddess of food and healing
and patroness of the sixth day of the week. She is
particularly associated with swine.
Patera *Pike*, an augur, Silk's predecessor at the manteion
on Sun Street, now deceased.
Poppy, one of the women at Orchid's, small, dark, and
pretty.
Councillor *Potto*, a member of the Ayuntamiento and its
expert on law enforcement and espionage,
round-faced and deceptively cheerful-looking.
Patera *Quetzal*, the Prolocutor of Viron and as such the
head of the Chapter. Addressed as "Your
Cognizance."
Patera *Remora*, coadjutor to Quetzal. Tall and thin, with
a long, sallow face and lank black hair. Addressed as
"Your Eminence."
Maytera *Rose*, the senior sibyl at Silk's manteion, largely
a collection of prosthetic parts. Over ninety.
Sargeant *Sand*, a soldier in the army of Viron.
Private *Schist*, a soldier in the army of Viron.
Scleroderma, the butcher's wife. She sells meat scraps as
food for pets and is sometimes called "the cats' meat
woman." Short and very fat.
Scylla, a major goddess, the goddess of lakes and rivers,
and the patroness of the first day of the week and of
Silk's native city of Viron; particularly associated with
horses, camels, and fish; pictured with eight, ten, or
twelve arms.
Patera *Silk*, augur of the old manteion on Sun Street; he
is twenty-three, tall and slender, with disorderly
yellow hair.
Commissioner *Simuliid*, a key bureaucrat in the

government of Viron, tall and very fat, with a thick black mustache.

Sphigx, a major goddess, the goddess of war and courage, and the patroness of the seventh day of the week; particularly associated with lions and other felines.

Councillor *Tarsier,* a member of the Ayuntamiento and its expert on architecture and engineering.

Tartaros, a major god, the god of night, crime, and commerce, and the patron of the third day of the week; particularly associated with owls, bats, and moles, and (like Hierax) with black animals of every kind.

Teasel, a girl at Silk's palaestra.

Thelxiepeia, a major goddess, the goddess of magic, mysticism, and poisons, and the patroness of the fifth day of the week; particularly associated with poultry, deer, apes, and monkeys.

Villus, a small boy at Silk's palaestra.

Vulpes, an advocate of Limna.

Chapter 1

THEY HAD SCIENTISTS

Silence fell, abrupt as a shouted command, when Patera Silk opened the door of the old, three-sided manse at the slanted intersection where Sun Street met Silver. Horn, the tallest boy in the palaestra, was sitting bolt upright in the least comfortable chair in the musty little sellaria; Silk felt sure he had dropped into it hastily when he heard the rattle of the latch.

The night chough (Silk had stepped inside and shut the door behind him before he remembered that he had named the night chough Oreb) was perched on the high, tapestried back of the stiff "visitor's" chair.

" 'Lo, Silk," Oreb croaked. "Good Silk!"

"And good evening to you. A good evening to you both. Tartaros bless you."

Horn had risen as Silk entered; Silk motioned for him to sit again. "I apologize. I'm terribly sorry, Horn. I truly am. Maytera Rose told me she meant to send you to talk to me this evening, but I forgot all about it. So much has been—O Sphigx! Stabbing Sphigx, have pity on me!"

This last had been in response to sudden, lancing pain in his ankle. As he limped to the room's sole comfortable chair, the one in which he sat to read, it occurred to him that its seat was probably still warm; he considered feeling the cushion to make sure, rejected the idea as embarrassing to Horn, then (propping himself with Blood's lioness-headed walking stick) laid his free hand on the seat anyway out of sheer curiosity. It was.

"I sat down there for a minute, Patera. I could see your bird better from there."

"Of course." Silk sat, lifting his injured ankle onto the hassock. "You've been here half the night, no doubt."

"Only a couple hours, Patera. I sweep out for my father while he empties the till and—and—locks the money up."

Silk nodded approvingly. "That's right. You shouldn't tell me where he keeps it." He paused, recalling that he had intended to steal this very manteion from Blood. "I wouldn't steal it, because I'd never steal anything from you or your family; but you never know who may be listening."

Horn grinned. "Your bird might tell, Patera. Sometimes they take shiny things, that's what I've heard. Maybe a ring or a spoon."

"No steal!" Oreb protested.

"I was thinking of a human eavesdropper, actually. I shrove an unhappy young woman today, and I believe there was someone listening outside her window the whole time. There was a gallery out there, and once I felt certain I heard the boards creak when he shifted his weight. I was tempted to get up and look, but crippled as I am at present, he would've been gone before I could have put my head out of the window—and back again, no doubt, the moment I sat down." Silk sighed. "Fortunately she kept her voice quite low."

"Isn't listening like that a major offense against the gods, Patera?"

"Yes. Not that he cares, I'm afraid. The worst part of the whole affair is that I know the man—or at least, I'm beginning to know him—and I've liked what I've seen of him.

There's a great deal of good in him, I feel certain, though he tries so hard to conceal it."

Oreb fluttered his sound wing. "Good Crane!"

"I didn't mention his name," Silk told Horn, "nor did you hear any name."

"No, Patera. Half the time I can't make out what that bird's saying."

"Fine. Perhaps it would be even better if you had as much difficulty understanding me."

Horn colored. "I'm sorry, Patera. I didn't want to—It wasn't because—"

"I didn't mean that," Silk explained hastily. "Not at all. We haven't even begun to talk about that yet, though we will. We must. I merely meant that I shouldn't even have mentioned shriving that woman. I'm much too tired to keep a proper watch on my tongue. And now that Patera Pike has left us—well, I still have Maytera Marble to confide in. I'd go mad, I think, if it weren't for her."

He leaned forward in the soft old chair, struggling to concentrate his surging thoughts. "I was going to say that though he's a good man, or at least a man who might be good, he has no faith in the gods; yet I'm going to have to get him to admit he listened, so I can shrive him of the guilt. It's sure to be difficult, but I've been examining the matter from all sides, Horn, and I can see no way to evade my duty."

"Yes, Patera."

"I don't mean this evening. I've been entirely too busy this evening, and this afternoon, too. I saw . . . something I can't tell you about, unfortunately. But I've been thinking about this particular man and the problem he presents ever since I came in. Seeing that blue thing on the bird's wing reminded me."

"I was wondering what that was, Patera."

"A splint, I suppose you'd call it." Silk glanced at the clock. "Your mother and father will be frantic."

Horn shook his head. "The rest of the sprats'll tell them where I went, Patera. I told them before I left."

"By Sphigx, I hope so." Silk leaned forward and drew up his injured leg, pushed down his stocking, and unwound the chamois-like wrapping. "Have you seen one of these, Horn?"

"A strip of leather, Patera?"

"It's much more than that." Silk tossed it to him. "I want you to do something for me, if you will. Kick it hard, so that it flies against the wall."

Horn gawked.

"If you're afraid you'll break something, throw it down hard three or four times. Not here on the carpet, I think. Over there on the bare boards. Hard, mind."

Horn did as he was told, then returned the wrapping to Silk. "It's getting hot."

"Yes, I thought it would." Silk rewound it about his aching ankle and smiled with satisfaction as it tightened. "It isn't just a strip of leather, you see, although it may be that its exterior actually is leather. Inside there's a mechanism, something as thin as the gold labyrinth in a card. When that mechanism is agitated, it must take up energy. At rest, it excretes a part of it as heat. The remainder emerges as sound, or so I was told. It makes a noise we can't hear, I suppose because it's too soft or perhaps because it's pitched too high. Can you hear it now?"

Horn shook his head.

"Neither can I, yet I could hear sounds that Patera Pike could not—the squeaking of the hinges on the garden gate, for example, until I oiled them."

Silk relaxed, soothed by the wrapping and the softness of his chair. "These wonderful wrappings were made in the Short-Sun Whorl, I imagine, like glasses and Sacred Windows, and so many other things that we have but can't replace."

"They had scientists there, Patera. That's what Maytera Rose says."

Oreb croaked, "Good Crane!"

Silk laughed. "Did he teach you to say that while he was treating your wing, you silly bird? Very well, Doctor Crane's a scientist of sorts, I suppose; he knows medicine at least, which is more science than most of us know, and he let me borrow this, though I must return it in a few days."

"A thing like that must be worth twenty or thirty cards, Patera."

"More than that. Do you know Auk? A big man who comes to sacrifice on Scylsdays?"

"I think so, Patera."

"Heavy jaw, wide shoulders, big ears. He wears a hanger and boots."

"I don't know him to talk to, Patera, but I know who you mean." Horn paused, his handsome young face serious. "He's trouble, that's what everybody says, the kind who knocks down people who get in his way. He did that to Teasel's father."

Silk had taken out his beads; he drew them through his fingers absently as he spoke. "I'm sorry to hear it. I'll try to speak to him about it."

"You'd better keep away from him, Patera."

Silk shook his head. "I can't, Horn. Not if I'm to do my duty. In fact, Auk's precisely the sort of person I must get close to. I don't believe that even the Outsider— And it's too late for that in any case. I was going to tell you that I showed this wrapping to Auk, and he indicated that it was worth a great deal more. That isn't important, however. Have you ever wondered why so much knowledge was left behind in the Short-Sun Whorl?"

"I guess the ones that knew about those things didn't come to our whorl, Patera."

"Clearly they did not. Or if they did, they can't have settled here in Viron. Yet they knew many things that would be very valuable to us, and certainly they would have had to come if Pas had instructed them to."

"The Fliers know how to fly, Patera, and we don't. We saw one yesterday, remember? Just after the ball game. He was pretty low. That's what I'd like to know. How to fly like they do, like a bird."

"No fly!" Oreb announced.

Silk studied the voided cross dangling from his beads for a moment, then let the beads fall into his lap. "This evening I was introduced to an elderly man who has a really extraordinary artificial leg, Horn. He had to buy up five broken or worn-out legs to build it, but it's an artificial leg such as the first settlers had—a leg that might have been brought from the Short-Sun Whorl. When he showed it to me, I thought how marvelous it would be if we could only make things like that now for Maytera Rose and Maytera Marble, and for all the beggars who are blind or crippled. It would be marvelous to fly, too, of course. I've always wanted to do it myself, and it may be that they are the same secret. If we could build wonderful legs like that for the people who need them, perhaps we could build wonderful wings as well for everyone who wanted to have them."

"That would be great, Patera."

"It may come to pass. It may yet come to pass, Horn. If people in the Short-Sun Whorl could teach themselves to do such things . . ." Silk shook himself and yawned, then rose with the help of Blood's stick. "Well, thank you for coming by. It's been a pleasure, but I'd better go up to bed."

"I was supposed—Maytera said—"

"That's right." Silk put away his beads. "I'm supposed

to punish you. Or lecture you, or something. What was it
you did that made Maytera Rose so angry?"

Horn swallowed. "I was just trying to talk like you do,
Patera. Like in manteion. It wasn't even today, and I won't
do it again."

"Of course." Silk settled back into his chair. "But it *was*
today, Horn. Or at least, today was one of several such days.
I heard you before I opened the door. I sat down on the
step for a minute to listen, in fact. You imitated me so well
that for a while I actually thought that your voice was my
own; it was like hearing myself. You're very good at it."

"Good boy," Oreb croaked. "No hit."

"I won't," Silk told the bird, and it lurched through the
air to his lap, then hopped from his lap to the arm of the
chair, and from the arm to his shoulder.

"Maytera Rose hits us sometimes, Patera."

"Yes, I know. It's very courageous of her, but I'm not at
all certain it's wise. Let's hear you again, Horn. Out on the
step, I couldn't hear everything you said."

Horn muttered, and Silk laughed. "I couldn't hear you
that time, either. Surely I don't sound like that. When I'm
at the ambion, I can hear my bray echo from the walls."

"No, Patera."

"Then say it again, just as I would. I won't be angry, I
promise you."

"I was only . . . You know. Like the things you say."

"No talk?" Oreb inquired.

Silk ignored him. "Fine. Let me hear it. That's what you
came to talk about, and I feel sure it will be a valuable
corrective for me. I tend to get above myself, I'm afraid."

Horn shook his head and stared at the carpet.

"Oh, come now! What sorts of things do I say?"

"To always live with the gods, and you do it any time
you're happy with the life they've given you. Think about
who's wise and act like he does."

"That was well said, Horn, but you didn't sound in the least like me. It's my own voice I want to hear, just as I heard it on the step. Won't you do that?"

"I guess I've got to stand up, Patera."

"Then stand, by all means."

"Don't look at me. All right?"

Silk shut his eyes.

For half a minute or more there was silence. Through his eyelids, Silk could detect the fading of the light (the best in the manse) behind his chair. He welcomed it. His right forearm, torn by the hooked beak of the white-headed one the night before, felt hot and swollen now; and he was so tired that his entire body ached.

"Live with the gods," his own voice directed, "and he does live with the gods who consistently shows them that his spirit is satisfied with what has been assigned to him, and that it obeys all that the gods will—the spirit that Pas has given every man as his guardian and guide, the best part of himself, his understanding and his reason. As you intend to live hereafter, it is in your power to live here. But if men do not permit you, . . ."

Silk stepped on something that slid beneath his foot, and fell with a start to the red clay tiles.

". . . think of wisdom only as great wisdom, the wisdom of a prolocutor or a councillor. That itself is unwise. If you could talk this very day with a councillor or His Cognizance, either would tell you that wisdom may be small, a thing quite suited to the smallest children here, as well as great. What is a wise child? It is a child who seeks out wise teachers, and hears them."

Silk opened his eyes. "What you said first was from the Writings, Horn. Did you know it?"

"No, Patera. It's just something I've heard you say."

"I was quoting. It's good that you've got that passage by heart, even if you learned it only to make fun of me. Sit down. You were talking about wisdom. Well, no doubt I must have spouted all that foolishness, but you deserve to learn better. Who are the wise, Horn? Have you really considered that question? If not, do so now. Who are they?"

"Well . . . you, Patera."

"NO!" Silk rose so abruptly that the bird squawked. He strode to the window and stood staring out through the bars at the ruts of Sun Street, black now under a flood of uncanny skylight. "No, I'm not wise, Horn. Or at least, I've been wise for a moment only—one moment out of my whole life."

He limped across the room to Horn's chair and crouched before it, one knee on the carpet. "Allow me to tell you how foolish I have been. Do you know what I believed when I was your age? That nothing but thought, nothing except wisdom, mattered. You're good at games, Horn. You can run and jump, and you can climb. So was I and so did I, but I had nothing but contempt for those abilities. Climbing was nothing to boast of, when I couldn't climb nearly as well as a monkey. But I could think better than a monkey—better than anyone else in my class, in fact." He smiled bitterly, shaking his head. "And that was how I thought! Pride in nonsense."

"Isn't thinking good, Patera?"

Silk stood. "Only when we think rightly. Action, you see, is the end that thought achieves. Action is its only purpose. What else is it good for? If we don't act, it's worthless. If we can't act, useless."

He returned to his chair, but did not sit down. "How many times have you heard me talk about enlightenment, Horn? Twenty or thirty times, surely, and you remember very well. Tell me what I said."

Horn glanced miserably at Oreb as though for guidance, but the bird merely cocked his head and fidgeted on Silk's shoulder as if eager to hear what Horn had to say. At last he managed, "It—it's wisdom a god sort of pours into you. That doesn't come from a book or anything. And—and—"

"Perhaps you'd do better if you employed my voice," Silk suggested. "Stand up again and try it. I won't watch you if it makes you nervous."

Horn rose, lifting his head, rolling his eyes toward the ceiling, and drawing down the corners of his mouth. "Divine enlightenment means you know without thinking, and that isn't because thinking's bad but because enlightenment is better. Enlightenment is sharing in the thinking of the god."

He added in his normal voice, "That's as close as I can come, Patera, without more time to remember."

"Your choice of words might be improved upon," Silk told him judiciously, "but your intonation is excellent, and you have my speech mannerisms almost pat. What is of much, much more importance, nothing that you said was untrue. But who gets it, Horn? Who receives enlightenment?"

"People who've tried to live good lives for a long time. Sometimes they do."

"Not always?"

"No, Patera. Not always."

"Would you believe me, Horn—credit me fully without reservation—if I told you that I myself have received it? Yes or no."

"Yes, Patera. If you say so."

"That I received it only yesterday?"

Oreb whistled softly.

"Yes, Patera."

Silk nodded, mostly to himself it seemed. "I did, Horn, and not through any merit of mine. I was about to say that you were with me, but it wouldn't be true. Not really."

"Was it before manteion, Patera? Yesterday you said you wanted to make a private sacrifice. Was it for that?"

"Yes. I've never made it, and perhaps I never will—"

"No cut!"

"If I do, it won't be you," Silk told Oreb. "Probably it won't be a live animal at all, although I'm going to have to sacrifice a lot of them tomorrow, and buy them as well."

"Pet bird?"

"Yes, indeed." Silk lifted Blood's lioness-headed stick to shoulder height; Oreb hopped onto it, turning his head to watch Silk from each eye.

Horn said, "He wouldn't let me touch him, Patera."

"You had no reason to touch him, and he didn't know you. All animals hate the touch of a stranger. Have you ever kept a bird?"

"No, Patera. I had a dog, but she died."

"I was hoping to get some advice. I wouldn't want Oreb to die—although I'd imagine that night choughs are hardy creatures. Hold out your wrist."

Horn did, and Oreb hopped onto it. "Good boy!"

"I wouldn't try to hold him," Silk said. "Let him hold you. You can't have had many toys as a child, Horn."

"Not many. We were—" Suddenly, Horn smiled. "There was one. My grandfather made it, a wooden man with a blue coat. It had strings, and if you did them right, you could make him walk and bow."

"Yes!" Silk's eyes flashed, and the tip of the lioness-headed stick thumped the floor. "That's exactly the sort of toy I mean. May I tell you about one of mine? You may think I'm straying from the topic, but I won't be, I promise you."

"Sure, Patera. Go ahead."

"There were two dancers, a man and a woman, very neatly painted. They danced on a little stage, and when I wound it up, music played. And they danced, the little

woman quite gracefully, and the little man somersaulting
and spinning and cutting all sort of capers. There were
three tunes—you moved a lever to choose the one you
wanted—and I used to play with it for hours, singing songs
I'd made up for myself and imagining things for him to say
to her, and for her to say to him. Silly things, most of them,
I'm afraid."

"I understand, Patera."

"My mother died during my last year at the schola,
Horn. Possibly I've already told you that. I'd been cram-
ming for an examination, but the Prelate called me into his
chambers again and told me that after her last sacrifice I
would have to go home and remove my personal belongings. Our house—her whole estate, but it was mostly the
house—went to the Chapter, you understand. One signs an
agreement before one enters the schola."

"Poor Silk!"

He smiled at the bird. "Perhaps, though I didn't think
so at the time. I was miserable on account of my mother's
death, but I don't believe that I ever felt sorry for myself. I
had books to read, and friends, and enough to eat. But now
I really am wandering from the subject.

"To hurry back to it, I found that toy in the back of my
closet. I had been at the schola for six years, and I doubt
that I'd so much as laid eyes on the toy for years before I
left. Now here it was again! I wound it up, and the dancers
danced once more, and the music played exactly as it had
when I was a little boy. The tune was 'First Romance,' and
I'll never forget that song now."

Horn coughed. "Nettle and me talk about that sometimes, Patera. You know, when we're older."

"Nettle and I," Silk corrected him absently. "That's
good, Horn. It's very good, and you'll both be older much
sooner than you imagine. I'll pray for you both.

"But I had intended to say that I cried then. I hadn't at

her rites; I hadn't been able to, not even when her casket was put into the ground. But I did then, because it seemed to me that for the dancers no time at all had passed. That they couldn't know that the man who wound them now was the boy who had wound them the last time, or that the woman who had bought them on Clock Street was dead. Do you follow what I'm saying, Horn?"

"I think so, Patera."

"Enlightenment is like that for the whole whorl. Time has stopped for everyone else. For you, there is something outside it—a peritime in which the god speaks to you. For me, that god was the Outsider. I don't think I've said much about him when I've talked to the palaestra, but I will be saying a great deal about him in the future. Maytera Mint said something to me this afternoon that has remained with me ever since. She said that he was unlike the other gods, who take council with one another in Mainframe; that no one save himself knew his mind. Maytera Mint has great humility, but she has wisdom, too. I must remember not to let the first blind me to the second."

"Good girl!"

"Yes, and great goodness, too. Humility and purity."

Horn said, "About enlightenment, Patera. Yours, I mean. Is that why somebody's writing things about you getting to be caldé?"

Silk snapped his fingers. "I'm glad you mentioned that—I had intended to ask you about it. I knew I'd forgotten something. Someone had chalked, 'Silk for caldé,' on a wall; I saw it on the way home. Did you do that?"

Horn shook his head.

"Or one of the other boys?"

"I don't think it was one of us sprats at all, Patera. It's on two places. There on the slop shop, and then over on Hat Street, on that building Gosseyplum lives in. I've looked at them both, and they're pretty high up. I could do it without standing on anything and I think maybe Locust could, but he says he didn't."

Silk nodded to himself. "Then I believe you're correct, Horn. It was because I've been enlightened. Or rather it's happened because I told someone about it, and was overheard. I've told several persons now, yourself included, and perhaps I shouldn't have."

"What was it like, Patera? Besides everything stopped, like you said?"

For several tickings of the clock on the mantel, Silk sat silent, contemplating for the hundredth time the experience he had by this time revolved in his mind so often that it was like a water-smoothed stone, polished and opaque. At last he said, "In that moment I understood all that I'll ever truly need to know. It's erroneous, really, for me to call it a moment, when it was actually outside time. But I, Horn,"—he smiled—"I am inside time, just as you are. And I find that it takes time for me to comprehend everything that I was told in that moment that was not a moment. It takes time for me to assimilate it. Am I making myself clear?"

Poor Horn nodded hesitantly. "I think so, Patera."

"That may be good enough." Silk paused again, lost in thought. "One of the things I learned was that I'm to be a teacher. There's only one thing that the Outsider wishes me to do—I am to save our manteion. But it is as a teacher that he wishes me to do it.

"There are many callings, Horn, the highest being pure worship. That isn't mine; mine is to teach, and a teacher has to act as well as think. The old man I met this evening— the man with the wonderful leg—was a teacher, too; and yet he's all action, all activity, as old as he is, and one-legged, too. He teaches swordfighting. Why do you think he is as he is? All action?"

Horn's eyes shone. "I don't know, Patera. Why?"

"Because a fight with swords—still more, with azoths— affords no time for reflection; thus to be all action is a part of what he has to teach. Listen carefully now. *He has thought about that.* Do you understand? Even though fighting with a sword must be all action, teaching others that kind of fighting requires thought. The old man had to think not only about what he was to teach, but about how he could best teach it."

Horn nodded. "I think I understand, Patera."

"In the same way, Horn, you must think about imitating me. Not merely about how I can be imitated, but about what to imitate. And when to do it. Now go home."

Oreb flapped his sound wing. "Wise man!"

"Thank you. Go, Horn. If Oreb wishes to go with you, you may keep him."

"Patera?"

Silk rose as Horn did. "Yes. What is it?"

"Are you going to study swordfighting?"

For a moment Silk considered his reply. "There are more important things to learn than swordfighting, Horn. Whom to fight, for example. One of them is to keep secrets. Someone who holds in confidence only those secrets he has been told not to reveal can never be trusted. Surely you understand that."

"Yes, Patera."

"And there is more to be learned from any good teacher than the subject taught. Tell your father and mother that I didn't keep you so late in order to punish you, but through carelessness, for which I apologize."

"No go!" Fluttering frenziedly, Oreb half flew and half fell from Horn's shoulder to the lofty back of the tapestried chair. "Bird stay!"

Horn's hand was already on the latch. "I'll tell them we were just talking, Patera. I'll say you were teaching me

about the Outsider and a lot of other things. It'll be the
truth."

Oreb croaked, "Good-bye! Bye, boy!"

"You foolish bird," Silk said as the door closed behind
Horn, "what have you learned from all this? A few new
words, perhaps, which you will misapply."

"Gods' ways!"

"Oh, yes. You're very wise now." Although it was still
warm, Silk unwound the wrapping. After beating the hassock with it, he wrapped it around his forearm over the
bandage.

"Man god. My god."

"Shut up," his god told him wearily.

He had thrust his arm into the glass, where Kypris was
kissing it. Her lips were as chill as death, but it was a death
he welcomed at first. In time he grew frightened and struggled to withdraw it, but Kypris would not release it. When
he shouted for Horn, no sound issued from his mouth.
Orchid's sellaria was in the manse, which did not seem odd
at all; a wild wind moaned in the chimney. He remembered
that Auk had foretold such a wind, and tried to recall what
Auk had said would happen when it blew.

Without relinquishing her grip on his arm, the goddess
revolved, her own arms upraised; she wore a clinging gown
of liquid spring. He was acutely conscious of the roundness
of her thighs, the double globosity of her hips. As he
stared, Blood's orchestra played "First Romance" and Kypris became Hyacinth (though Kypris still) and lovelier
than ever. He kicked and tumbled, his feet above his head,
but his hand clasped hers and would not be torn from it.

He woke gasping for breath. The lights had extinguished
themselves. In the faint skylight from a curtained window,
he saw Oreb hop out and flap away. Mucor stood beside his

bed, naked in the darkness and skeletally thin; he blinked; she faded to mist and was gone.

He rubbed his eyes.

A warm wind moaned as it had in his dream, dancing with his ragged, pale curtains. The wrapping on his arm was pale too, white with frost that melted at a touch. He unwound it and whipped the damp sheet with it, then wound it about his newly painful ankle, telling himself that he should not have climbed the stairs without it. What would Doctor Crane say when he told him?

The whipping had evoked a spectral glow from the lights, enough for him to distinguish the hands of the busy little clock beside his triptych. It was after midnight.

Leaving his bed, he lowered the sash. Not until it was down did he realize that he could not have seen Oreb fly out—Oreb had a dislocated wing.

Downstairs, he found Oreb poking about the kitchen in search of something to eat. He put out the last slice of bread and refilled the bird's cup with clean water.

"Meat?" Oreb cocked his head and clacked his beak.

"You'll have to find some for yourself if you want it," Silk told him. "I haven't any." After a moment's thought he added, "Perhaps I'll buy a little tomorrow, if Maytera cashed Orchid's draft, or I can myself. Or at least a fish—a live one I could keep in the washtub until whatever's left over from the sacrifices runs out, and then share with Maytera Rose. And Maytera Mint, of course. Wouldn't you like some nice, fresh fish, Oreb?"

"Like fish!"

"All right, I'll see what I can do. But you have to be forthcoming with me now. No fish if you're not. Were you in my bedroom?"

"No steal!"

"I didn't say that you stole," Silk explained patiently. "Were you there?"

"Where?"

"Up there." Silk pointed. "I know you were. I woke up and saw you."

"No, no!"

"Of course you were, Oreb. I saw you myself. I watched you fly out the window."

"No fly!"

"I'm not going to punish you. I simply want to know one thing. Listen carefully now. When you were upstairs, did you see a woman? Or a girl? A thin young woman, unclothed, in my bedroom?"

"No fly," the bird repeated stubbornly. "Wing hurt."

Silk ran his fingers through his strawstack hair. "All right, you can't fly. I concede that. Were you upstairs?"

"No steal." Oreb clacked his beak again.

"Nor did you steal. That is understood as well."

"Fish heads?"

Silk threw caution to the winds. "Yes, several. Big ones, I promise you."

Oreb hopped onto the window ledge. "No see."

"Look at me, please. Did you see her?"

"No see."

"You were frightened by something," Silk mused, "though it may have been my waking. Perhaps you were afraid that I'd punish you for looking around my bedroom. Was that it?"

"No, no!"

"This window is just below that one. I *thought* I saw you fly, but I really saw you hop out the window and drop down into the blackberries. From there it would have been easy for you to get back here into the kitchen through the window. Isn't that what happened?"

"No hop!"

"I don't believe you, because—" Silk paused. Faintly, he had heard the creak of Patera Pike's bed; he felt a pang

of guilt at having awakened the old man, who always la-
bored so hard and slept so badly—although he had
dreamed (only dreamed, he told himself firmly) that Pike
was dead, as he had dreamed, also, that Hyacinth had
kissed his arm, that he had talked to Kypris in an old yellow
house on Lamp Street: to Lady Kypris, the Goddess of
Love, the whores' goddess.

Shaken by doubt, he went back to the pump and
worked its handle again until clear icy water gushed into
the stoppered sink, splashed his sweating face again and
again, and soaked and resoaked his untidy hair until he was
actually shivering despite the heat of the night.

"Patera Pike is dead," he told Oreb, who cocked his
head sympathetically.

Silk filled the kettle and set it on the stove, starting the
fire with an extravagant expenditure of wastepaper; when
flames licked the sides of the kettle, he seated himself in the
unsteady wooden chair in which he sat to eat and pointed
a finger at Oreb. "Patera Pike left us last spring; that's
practically a year ago. I performed his rites myself, and
even without a headstone, his grave cost more than we
could scrape together. So what I heard was the wind or
something of that sort. Rats, perhaps. Am I making myself
clear?"

"Eat now?"

"No." Silk shook his head. "There's nothing left but a
little maté and a very small lump of sugar. I plan to brew
myself a cup of maté and drink it, and go back to bed. If
you can sleep too, I advise it."

Overhead (above the sellaria, Silk felt quite certain)
Patera Pike's old bed creaked again.

He rose. Hyacinth's engraved needler was still in his
pocket, and before he had entered the manse that evening
he had charged it with needles from the packet Auk had
bought for him. He pulled back the loading knob to assure

himself that there was a needle ready to fire, and pressed down the safety catch. Crossing the kitchen to the stair, he called, "Mucor? Is that you?"

There was no reply.

"If it is, cover yourself. I'm coming up to talk to you."

The first step brought a twinge of pain from his ankle. He wished for Blood's stick, but it was leaning against the head of his bed.

Another step, and the floor above creaked. He mounted three more steps, then stopped to listen. The night wind still sighed about the manse, moaning in the chimney as it had in his dream. It had been that wind, surely, that had made the old structure groan, that had caused him—fool that he was—to think that he had heard the old augur's bed creak, squeak, and readjust its old sticks and straps as Patera rolled his old body, sitting up for a moment to pray or peer out through the empty, open windows before lying down again on his back, on his side.

A door shut softly upstairs.

It had been his own, surely—the door to his bedroom. He had paid it no attention when he had put on his trousers and hurried downstairs to look for Oreb. All the doors in the manse swung of their own accord unless they were kept latched, opening or shutting in walls that were no longer plumb, cracked old doors in warped frames that had perhaps never been quite right, and certainly were not square now.

His finger was closing on the trigger of the needler; recalling Auk's warning, he put his fingertip on the trigger guard. "Mucor? I don't want to hurt you. I just want to talk to you. Are you up there?"

No voice, no footfall, from the upper floor. He went up a few more steps. He had shown Auk the azoth, and that had been most imprudent; an azoth was worth thousands of cards. Auk broke into larger and better defended houses than this whenever he chose. Now Auk had come for the azoth or sent an accomplice, seen his opportunity when the kitchen lights kindled.

"Auk? It's me, Patera Silk."

There came no answering voice.

"I've got a needler, but I don't want to have to shoot. If you raise your hands and offer no resistance, I won't. I won't turn you over to the Guard, either."

His voice had energized the single dim light above the landing. Ten steps remained, and Silk climbed them slowly, his progress retarded by fear as much as pain, seeing first the black-clad legs in the doorway of his bedroom, then the hem of the black robe, and at last the aged augur's smiling face.

Patera Pike waved and melted into silver mist; his blue-trimmed black calot dropping softly onto the uneven boards of the landing.

Chapter 2

LADY KYPRIS

Neither Silk nor Maytera Marble had remembered mutes, yet mutes appeared an hour before Orpine's rites were to begin, alerted by the vendor who had supplied the rue. Promised two cards, they had already gashed their arms, chests, and cheeks with flints by the time the first worshipers arrived, and were the very skiagraph of misery, their long hair fluttering in the wind as they rent their sooty garments, howled aloud, or knelt to smear their bleeding faces with dust.

Five long benches had been set aside in the front of the manteion for the mourners, who began to arrive by twos and threes some while after the unrestricted portion of the old manteion on Sun Street was full. For the most part they were the young women whom Silk had seen the previous afternoon at Orchid's yellow house on Lamp Street, though there were a few tradesmen as well (dragooned, Silk did not doubt, by Orchid), and a leaven of rough-looking men who could easily have been friends of Auk's.

Auk himself was there as well, and he had brought the ram he had pledged. Maytera Mint had seated him among the mourners, her face aglow with happiness; Silk assumed that Auk had explained to her that he had been a friend of the deceased. Silk accepted the ram's tether, thanked Auk

with formal courtesy (receiving an abashed smile in return), and led the ram out the side door into the garden,
where Maytera Marble presided over what was very nearly
a menagerie.

"That heifer's stolen several mouthfuls of my parsley,"
she told Silk, "and trampled my grass a bit. But she's left
me a present, too, so that I'll have a much nicer garden
next year. And those rabbits—oh, Patera, isn't it grand!
Just look at all of them!

Silk did, stroking his right cheek while he deliberated
the sacred sequence of sacrifice. Some augurs preferred to
take the largest beast first, some to begin with a general
sacrifice to the entire Nine; that would be the white heifer
in either case today. On the other hand, . . .

"The wood hasn't arrived yet. Maytera insisted on going
herself. I wanted to send some of the boys. If she doesn't
ride back on the cart . . ."

That was Maytera Rose, of course, and Maytera Rose
could scarcely walk. "People are still coming," Silk told
Maytera Marble absently, "and I can stand up there and
talk awhile, if necessary." He would (as he admitted after
a moment of merciless self-scrutiny) have welcomed an
excuse to begin Orpine's rites without Maytera Rose—and
to complete them without her, for that matter. But until
the cedar came and the sacred fire had been laid, there
could be no sacrifices.

He reentered the manteion just in time to witness the
arrival of Orchid, overdressed in puce velvet and sable in
spite of the heat, and somewhat drunk. Tears streamed
down her cheeks as he conducted her to the aisle seat in the
first row that had been marked off for her; and though he
felt that he ought to be amused by her unsteady gait and
clattering jet beads, he discovered that he pitied her with
all his heart. Her daughter, shielded by a nearly invisible
polymer sheet from the dampness of her sparkling couch

of ice, appeared by comparison contented and composed.

"The black ewe first," Silk found himself muttering, and could not have explained how he had reached his decision. He informed Maytera Marble, then stepped through the garden gate and out into Sun Street to look for Maytera Rose's cartload of cedar.

Worshipers were still trickling in, faces familiar from scores of Scylsdays, and unfamiliar ones who were presumably connected in some fashion to Orpine or Orchid, or had merely heard (as the whole quarter appeared to have heard) that rich and plentiful sacrifices would be offered to the gods today on Sun Street, in what was perhaps the poorest manteion in all Viron.

"Can't I get in, Patera?" inquired a voice at his elbow. "They won't let me."

Startled, Silk looked down into the almost circular face of Scleroderma, the butcher's wife, nearly as wide as she was high. "Of course you can," he said.

"There's some men at the door."

Silk nodded. "I know. I put them there. If I hadn't, there would have been no places for the mourners, and a riot before the first sacrifice, as likely as not. We'll let some of them stand in the side aisles once the wood arrives."

He took her through the garden gate and locked it behind them.

"I come every Scylsday."

"I know you do," Silk told her.

"And I put something in whenever I can. Pretty often, too. I almost always put in at least a bit."

Silk nodded. "I know that, too. That's why I'm going to take you in through the side door, quietly. We'll pretend that you brought a sacrifice. Hurriedly he added, "Although we won't say that."

"And I'm sorry about the cats' meat, that time. Dumping it all over you like that. It was a terrible thing to do. I was just mad." She had waddled ahead of him, perhaps because she did not want to meet his eyes; now she stopped to admire the white heifer. "Look at the meat on her!"

He could not help smiling. "I wish I had some of your cats' meat now. I'd give it to my bird."

"Have you got a bird? Lots of people buy my meat for their dogs. I'll bring you some."

He took her in through the side door as he had promised, and turned her over to Horn.

By the time that he had mounted the steps to the ambion, the first shoulderload of cedar was coming down the center aisle. Maytera Rose seemed to materialize beside the altar to supervise the laying of the fire, and the trope restored Patera Pike—almost forgotten in the bustle of preparations that morning—to the forefront of Silk's mind.

Or rather, as Silk told himself firmly, Patera's ghost. There was nothing to be gained by denial, by not calling the thing by its proper name. He had championed the spiritual and the supernatural since boyhood. Was he to fly in terror now from the mere mention of a supernatural spirit?

The Charismatic Writings lay on the ambion, placed there by Maytera Marble over an hour ago. On Phaesday he had told the children from the palaestra that they could always find guidance there. He would begin with a reading, then; perhaps there would be something there for him as well, as there had been on that afternoon two days ago. He opened the book at random and silenced the assembled worshipers with his eyes.

"We know that death is the door to life—even as the life we know is the door to death. Let us discover what counsel the wisdom of the past will provide to our departed sibling, and to us."

Silk paused. Chenille (her fiery hair, illuminated from

behind by the hot sunshine of the entrance, identified her at once) had just stepped inside the manteion. He had told her to attend, he recalled—had demanded that she attend, in fact. Very well, here she was. He smiled at her, but her eyes, larger and darker than he remembered them, were fixed on Orpine's body.

"Let us hope that they will not only prepare us to face death, but better fit us to amend our lives." After another solemn pause, he scanned the page. " 'Everyone who is grieved at anything, or discontented, is like a pig for sacrifice, kicking and squealing. Like a dove for sacrifice is he who laments in silence. Our one distinction is that it is given us to consent, if we will, to the necessity imposed upon us all.' "

A wisp of fragrant cedar smoke drifted past the ambion. The fire was lit; the sacrifices might proceed. In a moment Maytera Marble, in the garden, would see smoke rising through the god gate in the roof and lead the black ewe out onto Sun Street and into the manteion through the main entrance. Silk gestured to the brawny laymen he had stationed there, and the side aisles began to fill.

"Here, truly, is the counsel we sought. Soon I will ask the gods to speak to us directly, should they so choose. But what could they tell us that would be of better service to us than the wisdom that they have just provided to us? Nothing, surely. Consider then. What is the necessity laid upon us? Our own deaths? That is beyond dispute. But much, much more as well. We are every one of us subject to fear, to disease, and to numerous other evils. What is worse, we suffer this: the loss of our friend, the loss of our lover, the loss of our child."

He waited apprehensively, hoping that Orchid would not burst into tears.

"All of these things," he continued, "are conditions of our existence. Let us submit to them with good will."

Chenille was seated now, next to the small, dark Poppy. Studying her blank, brutally attractive face and empty eyes, Silk recalled that she was addicted to the ocher drug called rust. It had stimulated Hyacinth, he remembered; presumably different people reacted differently, and it seemed likely that Hyacinth had not taken as much.

"Orpine lies here before us, yet we know that she is not here. We will not see her again in this life. She was kind, beautiful, and generous. Her happiness she shared with us. What her sorrows were we cannot now learn, for she did not trouble others with them but bore their burden alone. That she was favored by Molpe we know, for she died in youth. If you wonder why a goddess should favor her, consider what I have just said. Riches cannot buy the favor of the gods—everything in the whorl is already theirs. Nor can authority command it; we are subject to them, not they to us, and so it shall forever be. We of this sacred city of Viron did not greatly value Orpine, perhaps; certainly we did not value her as her merits deserved. But in the eyes of the all-knowing gods, our valuations mean nothing. In the eyes of the all-knowing gods she was precious."

Silk turned to address the grayish glow of the Sacred Window behind him. "Accept, all you gods, the sacrifice of this fair young woman. Though our hearts are torn, we—her mother" (there was a sudden hum of whispered questions among the mourners) "and her friends—consent."

The mutes, who had remained silent while Silk spoke, shrieked in chorus.

"But speak to us, we beg, of the times to come. Of hers as well as ours. What are we to do? Your lightest word will be treasured. Should you, however, choose otherwise . . ." He waited silently, his arms outstretched. As always, there was no sound from the window, no flicker of color.

He let his arms fall to his sides. "We consent still. Speak to us, we beg, through our other sacrifices."

Maytera Marble, who had been waiting just inside the Sun Street door, entered leading the black ewe.

"This fine black ewe is presented to High Hierax, Lord of Death and Orpine's lord hereafter, by Orchid, her mother." Silk drew his sacrificial gauntlets and accepted the bone-hilted knife of sacrifice from Maytera Rose.

Maytera Marble whispered, "The lamb?" and he nodded.

A stab and slash almost too quick to be seen dispatched the ewe. Maytera Mint knelt to catch some of the blood in an earthenware chalice. A moment later she splashed it upon the fire, producing an impressive hiss and a plume of steam. The point of Silk's knife found the joint between two vertebrae, and the black ewe's head came off cleanly, still streaming blood. He held it up, then laid it on the fire. All four of the hoofs followed in quick succession.

Knife in hand, he turned again toward the Sacred Window. "Accept, O High Hierax, the sacrifice of this fine ewe. And speak to us, we beg, of the times that are to come. What are we to do? Your lightest word will be treasured. Should you, however, choose otherwise . . ."

He let his arms fall to his sides. "We consent. Speak to us, we beg, through this sacrifice."

Lifting the ewe's carcass to the edge of the altar, he opened the paunch. The science of augury proceeded from certain fixed rules, though there was room for individual interpretation as well. Studying the tight convolutions of the ewe's entrails and the bloodred liver, Silk shuddered. Maytera Mint, who knew something of augury too, as all the sibyls did, had turned her face away.

"Hierax warns us that many more are to walk the path that Orpine has walked." Silk struggled to keep his voice expressionless. "Plague, war, or famine await us. Let us not say that the immortal gods have permitted these evils to strike us without warning." There was an uneasy stir among the worshipers. "That being so, let us be doubly thankful to the gods, who graciously share their meal with us.

"Orchid, you have presented this gift, and so have first claim upon the sacred meal it provides. Do you want it? Or a part of it?"

Orchid shook her head.

"In that case, the sacred meal will be shared among us. Let all those among us who wish to do so come forward and claim a portion." Silk pitched his voice to the laymen at the Sun Street entrance, although their continued presence went far to answer his question. "Are there more outside? Many more?"

A man replied, "Hundreds, Patera!"

"Then I must ask those who share in the sacred meal to leave at once. One additional person will be admitted for each who leaves."

At every sacrifice that Silk had previously performed, those who came to the altar had gotten no more than a single thin slice. This was his chance to indulge his charitable nature, and he did—an entire leg to one, half the loin to another, and the whole breast to a third; the neck he passed to one of the women who cooked for the palaestra, a rack to an elderly widow whose house was not fifty strides from the manse. The twinges in his ankle were a small price to pay for the smiles and thanks of the recipients.

"This black lamb I myself offer to Tenebrous Tartaros, in fulfillment of a vow."

The lamb dispatched, Silk addressed the Sacred Window. "Accept, O Tenebrous Tartaros, the sacrifice of this lamb. And speak to us, we beg, of the times that are to come. What are we to do? Your lightest word will be treasured. Should you, however, choose otherwise . . ."

He let his arms fall to his sides. "We consent. Speak to us, we beg, through this sacrifice."

The black lamb's entrails were somewhat more favorable. "Tartaros, Lord of Darkness, warns us that many of us must soon go into a realm he rules, though we shall emerge again into the light. Those of you who will are welcome to come forward and claim a portion of this sacred meal."

The black cock struggled in Maytera Marble's grasp, freeing and flapping its wings, always a bad sign. Silk offered it entire, filling the manteion with the stink of burning feathers.

"This gray ram is offered by Auk. Since it is neither black nor white, it cannot be offered to the Nine, singly or collectively. It can, however, be offered to all the gods or to some specific minor god. To whom are we to offer it, Auk? You'll have to speak loudly, I'm afraid."

Auk rose. "To that one you're always talking about, Patera."

"To the Outsider. May he speak to us through augury!" Suddenly and inexplicably Silk was overjoyed. At his signal, Maytera Rose and Maytera Mint heaped the altar with fragrant cedar until its flames reached beyond the god gate and leaped above the roof.

"Accept, O Obscure Outsider, the sacrifice of this fine ram. And speak to us, we beg, of the times that are to come. What are we to do? Your lightest word will be treasured. Should you, however, choose otherwise . . ."

He let his arms fall to his sides. "We consent. Speak to us, we beg, through this sacrifice."

The ram's head burst in the fire as he knelt to examine the entrails. "This god speaks to us freely," he announced after a protracted study. "I do not believe I have ever seen so much written in a single beast. There is a message here for you personally, Auk, by which I mean that it carries the sign of the giver. May I pronounce it now? Or would you prefer that I impart it to you in private? I would call it good news."

From his place on a front bench, Auk rumbled, "Whatever you think best, Patera."

"Very well then. The Outsider indicates that in the past

you have acted alone, but that time is nearly over. You will stand at the head of a host of brave men. They and you will triumph."

Auk's mouth pursed in a silent whistle.

"There is a message here for me as well. Since Auk has been so forthright, I can do no less. I am to do the will of the god who speaks, and the will of Pas as well. Certainly I will strive to do both, and from the manner in which they are written here, I believe that they are one." Silk hesitated, his teeth scraping his lower lip; the joy that he had felt a moment before had melted like the ice around Orpine's body. "There is a weapon here as well, a weapon aimed at my heart. I will try to prepare." He drew a deep breath, fearful, yet ashamed of his fear.

"Lastly, there is a message for all of us: When danger threatens, we are to find safety between narrow walls. Does anyone know what that may mean?"

Though his legs felt weak, Silk rose and scanned the sea of faces before him. "The man sitting near Tartaros's image. Have you a suggestion, my son?"

The man in question spoke, inaudibly to Silk.

"Would you stand, please? Let us hear you."

"There's old tunnels underneath of the city, Patera. Fallin' down in places, an' some's full of water. My bunch hit one last week, diggin' for the new fisc. Only they had us to fill it in so nobody'd get hurt. Pretty narrow down there, an' everything shiprock."

Silk nodded. "I've heard of them before. They could be a place of refuge, I suppose, and they may well be what is meant."

A woman said, "In our houses. There's nobody here that has a big house."

Orchid turned in her seat to glare at her.

"In a boat," suggested a man on the other side of the aisle.

"Those are all possibilities as well. Let us keep the

Outsider's message in mind. I feel certain that its meaning will be made apparent to us when the time comes.''

Maytera Marble was standing at the back of the mante- ion with a pair of doves. Silk said, "Auk has first claim on the sacred meal. Auk? Do you wish to claim all or a portion of it, my son?''

Auk shook his head, and Silk swiftly divided the ram's carcass, casting its heart, lungs and intestines into the altar fire when everything else was gone.

Maytera Marble held one dove while Silk presented the other to the Sacred Window. "Accept, O Comely Kypris, the sacrifice of these fine white doves. And speak to us, we beg, of the times that are to come. What are we to do? Your lightest word will be treasured. Should you, however, choose otherwise . . .''

He let his arms fall to his sides. "We consent. Speak to us, we beg, through this sacrifice.''

A single deft motion severed the head of the first dove. Silk consigned it to the flames, then held the fluttering, crimson and white body so that the blazing cedar was sprayed with blood. At first he thought the staring eyes and open mouths of the mourners and the throng who had come to worship or in hope of sharing Orpine's mortuary sacrifices no more than a reaction to something that had happened at the altar. Perhaps his gauntlets or his robe had taken fire, or old Maytera Rose had fallen.

Maytera Marble saw the Sacred Window blaze with color, and heard an indistinct voice. A god spoke, as Pas had in Patera Pike's time. She fell to her knees, and in so doing involuntarily freed the dove she had been holding. It shot toward the roof, and then, seeming almost to ride the sacred flames, rose through the god gate and was gone. An unshaven man in the second row, seeing her upon her knees, knelt too. In a moment more, the bespangled, brilliantly dressed young women who had come with Orchid were kneeling, too, nudging one another and tugging at the skirts of those who still sat transfixed. When Maytera Marble raised her head at last to see, for what would almost certainly be the final time in her life, the swirling colors of present divinity, Patera Silk was beside her, his hands lifted in supplication.

"Come back!" Silk implored the dancing colors and that gentle thunder. "Oh, come back!"

Maytera Mint saw the goddess's face clearly and heard her voice, and even Maytera Mint, who knew so little of the world and wished to know less, knew that both exceeded in beauty any mortal woman's. They were also very much like her own, and seemed to become more so as she looked, until at last, moved by reverence and superabundant modesty, she closed her eyes. It was the greatest sacrifice that she had ever made, though she had made thousands, of which five at least had been very great indeed.

Maytera Rose was the last of the three sibyls to kneel, out of no lack of reverence, but because kneeling involved certain body parts with which she had been born—parts that were now in a strict sense dead, though they still functioned and would continue to function for years to come. Echidna had blinded her to the gods, the goddess's just punishment, and so she saw and heard nothing, though the holy hues danced again and again across and down the Sacred Window. In the deep tones of the divine voice, tones that she found herself comparing to those of a cello, she occasionally caught a word or a phrase. Young Patera Silk (who was always so careless, and never more careless than when dealing with matters of the greatest importance) had dropped the knife of sacrifice, the knife that Maytera Rose had cleaned and oiled and sharpened now for almost a century, still dyed with the dove's blood. Stretching, Maytera Rose retrieved it. Its bone handle had not cracked; its blade did not even seem to have been soiled by its brief contact with the floor, though she wiped it on her sleeve as a precaution. Absently, she tested the point against the tip of her thumb as she listened and sometimes made out, or nearly made out, a short sentence played by an orchestra too wonderful for this poor whorl, this whorl which was, like Maytera Rose herself, worn out and worn away, past its time which had never come, too old, though it was not even as old as Maytera Marble and though it was so much nearer to death. Cellos of the woods of Mainframe, flutes of diamond. Maytera herself, old Maytera Rose who was so tired that she no longer knew that she was tired, had once played the flute. She had not thought of her flute since the shame of blood. Pain's eaten it away, she thought, tortured it to silence, though once it sounded sweetly, oh, so sweetly, at evening.

Somehow old Maytera Rose sensed that this goddess was not Echidna. Thelxiepeia, maybe, or even Scalding Scylla. Scylla was another favorite of hers, and this was Scylsday, after all.

The voice was stilled. Slowly, the colors faded like the beautiful and complex tinctures of river-washed stones, which fade to nothing as the stones dry in the sunshine. Still on his knees, Silk bowed, his forehead touching the floor of the sanctuary. A murmur rose from the mourners and worshipers and soared until it was like the roaring of a storm. Silk glanced over his shoulder at them. One of the rough-looking men sitting with Orchid appeared to be shouting as he shook his fist at the Sacred Window, his eyes bulging and his face purple with some emotion at which Silk could only guess. A lovely young woman with curls as black as Orchid's beads was dancing in the center aisle to a music played for her alone.

Silk stood and limped slowly to the ambion. "All of you are entitled to hear—"

His voice seemed nonexistent. His tongue and lips had moved, and air had passed them, but no trumpeter could have made himself heard above the din.

Silk raised his hands and looked at the Sacred Window again. It was a shimmering gray, as empty as if no goddess had ever spoken through it. Yesterday in the yellow house on Lamp Street, the goddess had told him that she would speak to him again soon, repeating *soon*.

She kept her word, he thought.

Almost idly it occurred to him that the registers behind the Sacred Window would no longer be empty, as he had always seen them. One would show a single one, now; the other would display the length of the goddess's theophany, in units that no living person understood. He wanted to look at them, to verify the reality of what he had just seen and heard.

"All of you are entitled to hear—" His voice sounded weak and reedy, but at least he could hear it.

All of you are entitled to hear yourselves speaking when you could not hear yourselves at all, he thought. All of you are entitled to know how you felt and what you said to the goddess, or wanted to say—though most of us never will.

The tumult was subsiding now, falling like a wave on the lake. Strongly, Silk told himself, from the diaphragm. They had praised him for this at the schola.

"You are entitled to know what the goddess said, and the name that she gave. It was Kypris; and that is not a name from the Nine, as you know." Before he could stop himself, he added, "You are entitled to know as well, that Kypris has previously appeared to me in a private revelation."

She had told him not to speak of that, and now he had;

he felt sure that she would never forgive him, as he would never forgive himself.

"Kypris is mentioned seven times in the Writings, where it is said that she always takes an interest in—in—in young women. Women of marriageable age, who are young. No doubt she took an interest in Orpine. I feel sure she must have."

They were almost quiet now, many listening intently; but his mind was still whelmed by the wonder of the goddess, and barren of cohesive thought.

"Comely Kypris, who has so favored us, is mentioned upon seven occasions in the Chrasmologic Writings. I think I said that before, though some of you may not have heard it. White doves and white rabbits are to be offered her, which was why we had those doves. The doves were supplied by her mother—I mean by Orpine's mother, by Orchid."

Providentially, he remembered something more. "In the Writings she is honored as the most favored companion of Pas among the minor gods."

Silk paused and swallowed. "I said you were entitled to hear everything that she said. That is what is called for by the canon. Unfortunately, I cannot adhere to that canon as I would wish. A part of her message was directed to the chief mourner alone. I must deliver that in private, and I'll try to arrange to do that as soon as I am finished here."

The sea of faces stirred. Even the mutes were listening with wide eyes and open mouths.

"She—I mean Comely Kypris—said three things. One was the private message that I must deliver. She said also that she would prophesy, in order that you would believe. I don't think there's anyone here who does not, not now. But possibly some of us might question her theophany later. Or possibly she intended our whole city, all of us in Viron.

"Her prophesy was this: there will be a great crime, a successful one, here in Viron. She spreads her mantle above the—the criminals, and because of it they will succeed."

Shaken and trying frantically to collect his wits, Silk fell silent. He was rescued by a man sitting near Auk, who shouted, *"When?* When'll it be?"

"Tonight." Silk cleared his throat. "She said it would be tonight."

The man's jaw snapped shut, and he stared about him.

"The third was this: that she would come again to this Sacred Window, soon. I asked her—you must have heard me, some of you. I implored her to come back, and she said she would, and soon. That—that's everything I can tell you now."

He saw Maytera Marble's bowed head, and sensed that she was praying for him, praying that he would somehow receive the strength and presence of mind that he so clearly needed. The knowledge itself strengthened him.

"And now I must request that the chief mourner come up here. Orchid, my daughter, please join me. We must retire to—to a private place, in order that I can deliver the goddess's message to you."

He would take her out the side door and into the garden, and thinking of the garden reminded him of the heifer and the other victims. "Please remain where you are, all of you. Or leave if you like, and let others join in the sacred meal. That would be a meritorious act. As soon as I have conveyed the goddess's message, we will proceed with Orpine's rites."

He had left Blood's lioness-headed walking stick behind the Sacred Window; he retrieved it before they started down the stair to the side door. "There are seats in the arbor, outside. I have to take off this thing around my leg and—and beat it against something. I hope you won't mind."

Orchid did not reply.

It was not until he stepped out into the garden that Silk realized how hot it had been in the manteion, near the altar fire. The whole place seemed to glow; the rabbits lay on their sides gasping for breath, and Maytera Marble's herbs were wilting almost visibly; but to him the hot, dry wind felt cool, and the burning bar that was the midday sun, which should have struck him like a blow, seemed without force.

"I ought to have something to drink," he said. "Water, I mean. Water's all we have. No doubt you should, too."

Orchid said, "All right," and he led her to the arbor and limped into the kitchen of the manse, pumped and pumped until the water came, then doused his head in the gushing stream.

Outside again, he handed Orchid a tumbler of water, sat down, and filled another for himself from the carafe he had brought. "It's cold, at least. I'm sorry I don't have wine to offer you. I'll have some in a day or two, thanks to you; but there wasn't time this morning."

"I have a headache," Orchid said. "This's what I need." And then, "She was beautiful, wasn't she?"

"The goddess? Oh, yes! She was—she's lovely. No artist—"

"I meant Orpine." Orchid had emptied her tumbler; as she spoke she held it out to be refilled, and Silk nodded as he tilted the carafe.

"Don't you think that was one reason why this goddess came? I'd like to think so anyhow, Patera. And it might be true."

Silk said, "I had better give you the goddess's message now—I've already waited too long. She said that I was to tell you that no one who loves something outside herself can be wholly bad. That Orpine had saved you for a while, but that you must find something else to save you now. That you must find something new to love."

Orchid sat silent for what seemed to Silk a long while. The white heifer, lying beneath the dying fig tree, moved to a more comfortable position and began to chew her cud. The people waiting in Sun Street, on the other side of the garden wall, were chattering excitedly among themselves. Silk could not understand, though he could easily guess, what they were saying.

At last she murmured, "Does love really mean more than life, Patera? Is it more important?"

"I don't know. I think it may be."

"I would've said I loved a lot of other things." Her mouth twisted in a bitter grin. "Money, just for starters. Only I gave you a hundred cards for this, didn't I? Maybe that shows I don't love it as much as I thought."

Silk groped for words. "The gods have to speak to us in our own language, a language that we are always corrupting, because it's the only one we understand. They, perhaps, have a thousand words for a thousand different kinds of love, or ten thousand words for ten thousand; but when they talk to us, they must say 'love,' as we do. I think that at times it must blur their meaning."

"It won't be easy, Patera."

Silk shook his head. "I never imagined it would be, nor do I think that Kypris believed it would. If it were going to be easy, she wouldn't have sent her message, I feel sure."

Orchid fingered her jet beads. "I've been wondering why somebody—Kypris or Pas or whatever—didn't save her. I think I've got it now."

"Then tell me," Silk said. "I don't, and I would like to very much."

"They didn't because they did. It sounds funny, doesn't it? I don't think Orpine loved anybody except me, and if I'd died before she did . . ." Orchid shrugged. "So they let her go first. She was beautiful, better looking than I ever was. But she wasn't as tough. I don't think so, anyhow. What do you love, Patera?"

"I'm not certain," Silk admitted. "The last time that we talked, I would have said this manteion. I know better now, or at least I think I do. I try to love the Outsider—I'm always talking about him, just as Auk said—but sometimes I almost hate him, because he has given me responsibility, as well as so much honor."

"You were enlightened. That's what somebody told me on the way here. You're going to bring back the Charter and be caldé yourself."

Silk shook his head and rose. "We'd better go inside. We're keeping five hundred people waiting in that heat."

She patted his shoulder when they parted, surprising him.

When the last sacrifice had been completed and the last morsel of the sacred meal that it had provided parceled out, he cleared the manteion. "We will lay Orpine in her casket now," he explained, "and close the casket. Those who wish to make a final farewell may do so on the way out, but everyone must leave. Those of you who will accompany the casket to the cemetery should wait outside on the steps."

Maytera Rose had left already, to wash his gauntlets and the sacrificial knife. Maytera Mint whispered, "I'd rather not watch, Patera. May I . . . ?"

He nodded, and she hurried off to the cenoby.

The mourners were filing past, Orchid waiting so as to be last in line. Maytera Marble said, "Those men will carry it, Patera. That's why they were here. Yesterday I happened to think that there would have to be someone, and the address was on the draft. I sent a boy with a note to Orchid."

"Thank you, Maytera. As I've said a thousand times, I don't know what I'd do without you. Have them wait at the entrance, please."

Chenille was still in her seat. "You should go, too," he told her, but she appeared not to have heard him.

When Maytera Marble returned, they lifted Orpine's body from its bed of ice and laid it in the waiting casket. "I'll help you with the lid, too, Patera."

He shook his head. "Chenille wishes to speak with me, I believe, and she won't as long as you're here. Go to the entrance, please, Maytera, where you won't overhear us if we keep our voices down." To Chenille he added, "I'm going to fasten the lid now. You can talk to me while I do it, if you like."

Her eyes flickered toward him, but she did not speak.

"Maytera must remain, you see. There must be two of us, so that each can testify that the other did not rob the body or molest it." Grunting, he lifted the heavy lid into place. "If you stayed to ask whether I've confided anything that you told me in your shriving to anyone else, I have not. You probably won't believe this, but I've actually forgotten most of it already. We make an effort to, you see. Once you've been forgiven, you're forgiven; that part of your life is over, and there's no point in our retaining it."

Chenille remained as before, staring straight ahead. Her wide, rounded forehead gleamed with perspiration; while Silk studied her, a single droplet trickled into her left eye and out again, as though reborn as a tear.

The casket builder had provided six long brass screws, one for each corner. They were hidden, with the screwdriver from the palaestra's broom closet, under the black cloth that draped the catafalque. Holes had been bored to receive each screw. As Silk got them out, he heard Chenille's slow steps in the aisle and glanced up. She was looking toward him now, but her motions seemed almost mechanical.

He told her, "If you'd like to say good-bye to Orpine, I can remove the lid. I haven't started the first screw yet."

She made an inarticulate noise and shook her head.

"Very well, then." He forced himself to look down at his work. He had not realized she was so beautiful—no, not even when they had sat talking in her room at Orchid's. In the garden, he had begun to say that no artist could paint a face half so lovely as Kypris's. Now it seemed to him that the same thing might almost be said of Chenille, and for a moment he imagined himself a sculptor or a painter. He would pose her beside a stream, he thought, her face up-tilted as though she were watching a meadowlark. . . .

He sensed her proximity before he had tightened the first screw. Her cheek, he felt certain, was within a span of his ear. Her perfume filled his nostrils; and though it was in no way different from any other woman's, and stronger than it ought to have been, though it was mingled with perspiration, the inferior scents of face and body powders, and even the miasma of a woolen gown that had been stored for most of this protracted summer in one of the battered old trunks he had seen in her room, he found it intoxicating.

As he drove the third screw, her hand came to rest on his own. "Perhaps you'd better sit down," he told her. "You're not supposed to be in here, actually."

She laughed softly.

He straightened up and turned to face her. "Maytera's watching. Have you forgotten? Go and sit down, please. I have no desire to exert my authority, but I will if I must."

When she spoke, it was with mingled wonder and amusement. She said, *"This woman's a spy!"*

Chapter 3

COMPANY

Though he had been in the old cemetery often, Silk had never ridden the deadcoach before—or rather, as he told himself sharply, the deadcoach had been Loach's wagon. They always walked behind it in procession, as custom demanded, on the way there; and Loach nearly always invited him to ride back to the quarter, sitting beside Loach on the weathered gray board that was the driver's seat.

This was a real deadcoach, however, all glass and black lacquered wood, with black plumes and a pair of black horses, the whole rented for a staggering three cards from the maker of Orpine's casket. Silk, who had scarcely been able to limp along by the time they reached the cemetery, had been relieved when the liveried driver had offered him a ride, and utterly astonished to find that the deadcoach seat had a back, both seat and back stylishly upholstered in shiny black leather, like a costly chair. The seat was very high as well, which afforded him a fresh perspective on the streets through which they passed.

The driver cleared his throat and spat expertly between his horses. "Who was she, Patera? Friend of yours?"

"I wish I could say she was," Silk replied. "I never met her. Her mother's a friend, however, or so I hope. She paid for this fine coach of yours, as well as a great many other things, so I owe her a great deal."

The driver nodded companionably.

"This is a new experience for me," Silk continued, "my second in three days. I'd never ridden in a floater; but I did the day before yesterday, when a gentleman very kindly had one of his take me home. And now this! Do you know, I almost like this better. One sees so much more from up here, and one feels—I really can't say. Like a councillor, perhaps. Is this what you do every day? Driving like this?"

The driver chuckled. "An' curry the horses, an' feed an' water, an' muck out an' so on an' such like, an' takin' care of the coach. Waxin' an' polishin', an' keepin' everythin' clean, an' greasin' the wheels. Them that rides in back don't complain more'n once. Mebbe less. But their relations does, sayin' it sounds so dismal an' all. So I keeps 'em greased, which ain't nearly so hard as all the waxin' an' washin'."

"I envy you," Silk said sincerely.

"Oh, it's not no bad life, long as you rides up front. You get the rest of the day off, do you, Patera?"

Silk nodded. "Provided that no one requires the Pardon of Pas."

The driver extracted a toothpick from an inner pocket. "But if somebody does, you got to go, don't you?"

"Certainly."

"An' before we ever loaded her in, you'd done for how many pigeons an' goats and such like?"

Silk paused, counting. "Altogether, fourteen including the birds. No, fifteen in all, because Auk brought the ram he'd pledged. I had forgotten it for a moment, although its entrails indicated that I—never mind."

"Fifteen, an' one a ram. An' you done for the lot, an' read 'em, an' cut 'em up, I bet."

Silk nodded again.

"An' marched out to the country on that bad leg, readin' prayers an' so forth the whole way. Only now you get to pull your boots off, unless somebody's decided to leave. Then you don't. Have a easy time of it, don't you, you augurs? 'Bout like us, huh?"

"It isn't such a bad life," Silk said, "as long as one gets to ride back."

They both laughed.

"Somethin' happen in there? In your manteion?"

Silk nodded. "I'm surprised that you heard about it so quickly."

"They were talkin' 'bout it when I got there, Patera. I ain't religious. Don't know nothin' 'bout gods an' don't want to, but it sounded interestin'."

"I see." Silk stroked his cheek. "In that case, what you know is fully as important as what I know. I know only what actually transpired, while you know what people are saying about it, which may be at least as important."

"What I was wonderin' was why she come after nobody for so long. Did she say?"

"No. And of course I could not ask her. One does not cross-examine the gods. Now tell me what the people outside the manteion were saying. All of it."

It was practically dark by the time the driver reined up in front of the garden gate. Kit and Villus, who had been playing in the street, were full of questions: "Did a goddess really come, Patera?" "A real goddess?" "What'd she look like?" "Could you see her really good?" "To talk to?" "Did she tell things, Patera?" "Could you tell what she said?" "What'd she say?"

Silk raised his hand for silence. "You could have seen her, too, if you'd come to our sacrifice as you should have."

"They wouldn't let us." "We couldn't get in."

"I'm very sorry to hear that," Silk told them sincerely.

"You would have seen Comely Kypris just as I did, and most of the people who attended—there must have been five hundred, if not more—could not. Now listen. I know you're anxious to have your questions answered, just as I would be in your place. But I'm going to have to talk a great deal about the theophany in the next few days, and I don't want to go stale. Besides, I'll have to tell all of you in the palaestra, in a lot of detail, and you'll be bored if you have to listen to all of it twice."

Silk crouched to bring his own face to the level of the quite dirty face of the smaller boy. "But, Kit, there's a lesson in this, for you especially. Only two days ago, you asked me whether a god would actually come to our Window. Do you remember that?"

"You said it would be a long time, but it wasn't."

"I said it might be, Kit, not that it would be. You're fundamentally quite right, however. I did think it would be a long time, probably decades, and I was badly mistaken; but the thing I wanted to point out was that when you asked your question all the other students laughed. They thought it was very funny. Remember?"

Kit nodded solemnly.

"They laughed as though you'd asked a foolish question, because they thought it a foolish question. They were even more mistaken than I, however; and that must be plain even to them now. Yours was a serious and an important question, and you erred only in asking of someone who knew very little more than you did. You must never let yourself be turned aside from life's serious and important questions by ridicule. Try not to forget that."

Silk fumbled in his pocket. "I want you boys to run an errand for me. I'd go myself, but I can hardly walk, much less run. I'm going to give you, Villus, five bits. Here they are. And you, Kit, three. You, Kit, are to go to the greengrocer's. Tell him the vegetables are for me, and ask him to give you whatever is best and freshest, to the amount of three bits. You, Villus, are to go to the butcher. Tell him I want five bits worth of nice chops. I'll give each of you," Silk paused, ruminating, "a half bit when you bring me your purchases."

Villus inquired, "What kind of chops, Patera? Mutton or pork?"

"We will let him decide that."

Silk watched as the two dashed off, then unlocked the garden gate and stepped inside. The grass had been sadly trampled, just as Maytera Marble had said; even in the last dying gleam of day that was apparent, as was the damage to Maytera's little garden. He reflected philosophically that in a normal year the last produce from the garden would have come weeks before in any event.

"Patera!"

It was Maytera Rose, leaning from a window of the cenoby and waving, an offense for which she would have reprimanded Maytera Marble or Maytera Mint endlessly.

"Yes," Silk said. "What is it, Maytera?"

"Did they come back with you?"

He hobbled to the window. "Your sibs? No. They were going to walk back together, so they said. They should be here soon."

"It's past time for supper," Maytera Rose asserted. (The assertion was manifestly untrue.)

Silk smiled. "Your supper should be here shortly, too, and may Scylla bless your feast." He turned away, still smiling, before she could question him further.

There was a package wrapped in white paper and tied with white string on the kitchen doorstep of the manse. He picked it up and turned it over in his hands before opening the door.

Oreb, who from the scattered drops had been drinking from his cup, was on the kitchen table. " 'Lo, Silk."

"Hello, yourself." Silk got out the paring knife.

"Cut bird?"

"No, I'm going to open this. I'm too tired—or too lazy—to pick apart these knots, but if I cut them I should be able to save most of the string anyway. Did you kill that rat I threw away, Oreb?"

"Big fight!"

"I suppose I ought to congratulate you, and thank you as well. All right, I do." Unwrapping the white paper exposed a collection of odorous meat scraps. "This is cat's meat, Oreb. Having had a bucket of it dumped on my head once, I'd know it anywhere. Scleroderma promised us some, and she's made good her promise already."

"Eat now?"

"You may, if you wish. Not me. But you ate a good deal of that rat you killed. Don't tell me you're still hungry!"

Oreb only fluttered his wings and cocked his head inquiringly.

"I'm not at all sure that so much meat is good for you."

"Good meat!"

"As a matter of fact it isn't." Silk pushed it toward the bird. "But if I keep it, it will only get worse, and we have no means of preserving it. So go ahead, if you like."

Oreb snatched a piece of meat and managed to carry it, half flying and half jumping, to the top of the larder.

"Scylla bless your feast, too." For the two thousandth time it occurred to Silk that a feast blessed by Scylla ought logically to be of fish, as the Chrasmologic Writings hinted it had originally been. Sighing, he took off his robe and hung it over the back of what had been Patera Pike's chair. Eventually he would have to carry the robe upstairs to his bedroom, brush it, and hang it up properly; and eventually he would have to remove the manteion's copy of the Writings themselves from the robe's big front pocket and restore it to its proper place.

But both could wait, and he preferred that they should. He started a fire in the stove, washed his hands, and got out the pan in which he had fried tomatoes the day before, then filled the old pot Patera Pike had favored with water from the pump and set it on the stove. He was contemplating the kettle and the possibility of maté or coffee when there was a tap at the Silver Street door.

Unbarring it, he took from Villus a package similar to the one he had found on the step, though much larger, and fumbled in his pocket for the promised half bit.

"Patera . . ." Villus's small face was screwed into an agony of effort.

"Yes, what is it?"

"I don't want nothing." Villus extended a grimy hand, displaying five shining bits, small squares sheared from so many cards.

"Are those mine?"

Villus nodded. "He wouldn't take 'em."

"I see. But the butcher gave you these chops anyway; you certainly didn't wrap this package. And now, since he would not accept money from me—I shouldn't have told you to tell him the meat was for me—you feel that you should not either, as a boy of honor and piety."

Villus nodded solemnly.

"Very well, I certainly won't make you take it. I owe your mother a bit, however; so give four back to me and give the fifth to her. Will you do that?"

Villus nodded again, handed over four bits, and vanished into the twilight.

"These chops are neither yours nor mine," Silk told the bird on the larder as he closed the Silver Street door and lifted the heavy bar back into place, "so leave them alone."

Large as his pan was, the chops filled it. He sprinkled them with a minute pinch of precious salt and set the pan on the stove. "We are made plutocrats of the supernatural," he informed Oreb conversationally, "and that to a degree that's almost embarrassing. Others have money, as Blood does, for example. Or power, like Councillor Lemur. Or strength and courage, like Auk. We have gods and ghosts."

From the top of the larder, Oreb croaked, "Silk good!"

"If that means you understand, you understand a great deal more than I. But I try to understand, just the same. Plutocrats of the supernatural do not need money, as we've seen—though they get it, as we've also seen. Strength and courage hasten to assist them." Silk dropped into his chair, the cooking fork in one hand and his chin in the other. "What they require is wisdom. No one understands gods or ghosts, yet we have to understand them: Lady Kypris today, Patera at the top of the stairs last night, and all the rest of it."

Oreb peered over the edge of the larder. "Bad man?"

Silk shook his head. "You may perhaps object that I've omitted Mucor, who is not dead and thus cannot be a ghost, and certainly is not a god. She behaves almost exactly like a devil, in fact. Which reminds me that we have those too, or one at any rate—that is to say, poor Teasel has or had one. Doctor Crane thinks she was bitten by some sort of bat, but she herself said it was an old man with wings."

The chops were beginning to sputter. Silk got up and prodded one experimentally with his fork, then lifted another to study its browning underside. "Speaking of wings, what do you say we begin with the simplest puzzle? I mean yourself, Oreb."

"Good bird!"

"I dare say. But not so good that you can fly with that bad wing, though I saw you do it last night just before I saw Mucor, and watched her vanish. That is suggestive—"

"Patera?" Steel knuckles rapped the door to the garden.

"Just a moment, Maytera, I have to turn your chops." To Oreb, Silk added, "I didn't include Mucor because I won't call what she does supernatural. I freely admit that it appears to be. I may be the only man in Viron who would scruple to call it that."

With the fork still in his hand, he threw wide the door.

"Good evening, Maytera. Good evening, Kit. May all the gods be with you both. Are those my vegetables?"

Kit nodded, and Silk accepted the big sack and laid it on the kitchen table. "This seems like a great deal to get for three bits, Kit, as high as prices are now. And there are bananas in there, too—I smell them. They're always very dear."

Kit remained speechless. Maytera Marble said, "He was standing in the street, Patera, afraid to knock. Or rather, I think he may have knocked very softly, and you failed to hear him. I took him into the garden, but he wouldn't give up that huge bag."

"Very properly," Silk said. "But, Kit, I wouldn't bite you for bringing me vegetables, particularly when I asked you to do it."

Kit extended a grubby fist.

"I see. Or at least, I think I may. He wouldn't take the money?"

Kit shook his head.

"And you were afraid that I'd be angry about that—as to tell the truth I am, somewhat. Here, give it to me."

Maytera Marble inquired, "Who wouldn't take your money, Patera? Marrow, up the street?"

Silk nodded. "Here, Kit. Here's the half bit that I promised you. Take it, close the gate after you, remember what I told you, and don't be afraid."

"I'm afraid," Maytera Marble announced when the boy

was gone. "Not for myself, but for you, Patera. They don't like anyone to be too popular. Did Kind Kypris promise to protect you? What will you do if they send the Guard for you?"

Silk shook his head. "Go with them, I suppose. What else could I do?"

"You might not come back."

"I'll explain that I have no political ambitions, which is the simple truth." Silk drew his chair nearer the doorway and sat down. "I wish I could invite you in, Maytera. Will you let me bring the other chair out for you?"

"I'm fine," Maytera Marble said, "but your ankle must be very painful. You walked a long way today."

"It's not really as bad as it was yesterday," Silk said, feeling the wrapping. "Or perhaps I'm getting a second wind, so to speak. A great many things happened Phaesday, and they took place very fast. First there was the very great thing I told you about while we were sitting in the arbor during the rain, then Blood's coming here, then meeting Auk and riding out to Blood's villa, hurting my ankle, and talking to Blood. Then on Sphixday, bringing the Pardon of Pas to poor little Teasel, Orpine's death and an exorcism, and Orchid's wanting to have Orpine's final sacrifice here. I wasn't accustomed to so much happening so rapidly."

Maytera Marble looked solicitous. "No one could expect you to be, Patera."

"Last night I was just beginning to find my feet, if I may put it like that, when several other things took place. And today, Kypris favored us—the first manteion in Viron to be so favored in over twenty years. If—"

Maytera Marble interrupted him. "That was wonderful. I'm still trying to come to terms with it, if you know what I mean, trying to integrate it into my operating parameters. But it just—you know, Patera, this business with Marrow, for instance. I saw 'Back to the Charter!' painted on the side of a building. And then this, at our manteion. Do be careful!"

"I will," Silk promised. "As I was trying to explain, I've gotten my mental equilibrium back. I've done what you said you were trying to do—gotten all of it worked into my operating whateveryoucallums, my way of thinking. While we were following the deadcoach, I had time to sort things out. It gave me an opportunity to weigh my own impressions against the Writings as I read them. Do you recall the passage that begins, 'Sovereign nature, which governs the whole, will soon change all the things you see, and from their substance make other things, and again still other things from the substance of them, in order that the whorl may be ever new'?

"In the context of her last sacrifice, it meant no more than that Orpine would grow up again as grass and flowers, of course. And yet, that passage struck home to me particularly, as though it had been put there for me, specifically, to read today. I wish I could learn to say things to other people that would affect them half as much as that passage affected me. I realized as I read it that the peaceful life here that I'd imagined I had, the life that I'd hoped would continue without interruption and almost without incident until I was old, had been nothing of the sort—that it had been no more than the current state of things in an endless flux of states. My final year in the schola, for example—"

"Did you say something about those chops being for me when I knocked, Patera? You meant that they would save me all the work of preparing the main course, and I appreciate it very much. They smell delicious. I feel certain Maytera Rose and Maytera Mint will enjoy them immensely."

Silk sighed. "You're telling me it's time to turn them again, aren't you?"

"No, Patera. Time to take them up—to put them on a platter. You've turned them once already."

He hobbled off to the stove. Oreb had been at the cat's meat while he had been talking with Kit and Maytera Marble; it was scattered over the table, with addenda on the floor. The undersides of the chops were a deep, golden brown. Silk piled them on the largest plate in the cupboard, draped them with a clean cloth, and carried them to Maytera Marble on the other side of the threshold.

"Thank you very, very much, Patera." She peeped beneath the cloth. "Oh, my! Aren't they marvelous! You've saved at least three for yourself, I hope."

Silk shook his head. "I had chops last night when Auk bought my dinner, and I really don't care for meat."

She made him a tiny bow. "I must hurry off before they get cold."

"Maytera?" He hobbled after her, down the graveled path toward the cenoby. The burning line of the sun was completely obscured by the shade now; the night air hung still and dry and hot, like one driven by fever to the border of death.

"What is it, Patera?"

"You said those chops smelled delicious. Do things—does food really smell good to you, Maytera? You can't eat it."

"But I can cook it, and I do," she reminded him gently, "so naturally I know when something smells good."

"I was thinking only of Maytera Rose, and that was wrong of me. I should have gotten something all three of you could enjoy." Silk paused, groping futilely for words that would not be inadequate. "I'm really terribly sorry, and I'll try to find a way to make up for it."

"I *do* enjoy this, Patera. It gives me great pleasure to be the one to take this good food to my sibs. Now please go back to the manse, where you can sit down. I hate seeing you in pain."

He hesitated, wanting to say more, nodded, and turned back. Turning seemed to twist his ankle inside the rapidly loosening wrapping, bringing pain so sharp he nearly cried out. Wincing, he grasped the arbor, then a convenient limb of the little pear tree.

There was a distant knock.

He would have halted to listen if he had not been halted already. Another knock, a trifle louder, and beyond question from his left, from Sun Street. The front door of the manse was on Sun Street—the cenoby had no door on Sun Street at all.

He meant to shout for the visitor to wait, but he did not shout, immobilized with surprise. A shadow (very faint because the lights there had darkened almost to extinction) had flitted across the curtains of his bedroom. Someone up there was going to answer that knock—someone, so at least it seemed, who had watched him limp down the path in pursuit of Maytera Marble.

All of the manse's windows facing the garden were wide open. Through them he heard the swift rattle of feet on the crooked stairs; and then, unmistakably, the bar being lifted from the door on Sun Street and the creaking of the hinges as that door opened; there was an indistinct murmur of voices—not friendly voices, or so they sounded.

It was strange how little pain his ankle gave him now. He opened the sellaria door as quietly as he could, but both turned to face him at once, one smiling, one glaring.

"Here he is," Chenille announced. "You can tell him yourself, whatever it is."

Musk snarled and shoved her aside. Catlike, he stalked across the sellaria to seat himself in Silk's reading chair.

Silk cleared his throat. "Although I have no desire to

appear inhospitable, I must ask both of you what you're doing here."

Musk sneered; Chenille endeavored to look demure, almost successfully. "I wasn't—really I wasn't—up to walking that far behind the deadcoach. Not in these sham shoes. And Orchid hadn't said we had to go to the grave. She just said for us to come to Orpine's rites, and I'd done it. Some of the others didn't even come."

Silk said, "Go on."

"That was all that you said I had to do, too. I mean, to come and pray, and I'd done it."

"Women are not to set foot in this manse," Silk told her harshly. Musk was sitting in his chair, and he refused as a matter of principle to take one of the others. "Excuse me for a moment."

In the kitchen, his pot of water was boiling vigorously; he added a good-sized split to the firebox and found Blood's walking stick in a corner.

When he stepped back into the sellaria, Chenille said, "You say that I'm not supposed to be in here, but I didn't know that. I wanted to talk to you back in your manteion, when you were fastening down the lid of the coffin, but it didn't seem like the best time or the best place, with that chem woman watching us. I was going to wait for you there, but you never came back. After a couple hours, I went into your garden looking for a drink of water and found this cute little house. I played with your pet bird for a while, and then . . . Well, I'm afraid I lay down and went to sleep."

Silk nodded, half to himself. "I know you use rust, and you must drink heavily sometimes, too. When you were telling me you had a good memory yesterday during the exorcism, you said that you hadn't had a drop that day. Were you drinking here?"

"I wouldn't bring a bottle to Orpine's funeral!"

Musk snickered. He had drawn his knife and was scraping his fingernails.

"Perhaps not," Silk conceded. "And if you had, I would have seen it, unless it was a very small one. But you would have brought money, and there are a dozen places within an easy walk that would sell you beer or brandy, or anything else you wanted."

Musk said, "How much did Orchid give you?"

"Ask her. She knows you, and no doubt she's afraid of you—most women seem to be. I'm sure she'll tell you."

"A lot, that's what I heard. Lots of flowers and enough livestock to keep every god in Mainframe fed for a week. That much. This whore's in your bed and you're scratching to pump what she's there for, you putt."

Chenille ran her hands down her gown. "Look at me, I'm dressed. Would I be dressed?"

Silk rapped the floor with Blood's walking stick. "This is senseless! Be quiet, both of you. Chenille, you say you wish to talk with me. I tried to talk to you this afternoon in the manteion, but you would not reply."

She had a trick of staring down at his feet with a half smile, as if she found his scuffed black shoes amusing; he had a sudden presentiment that he could come to know it only too well. "Explain yourself," he said, "or leave at once."

"I couldn't talk with you just then, Patera. I had so much thinking to do! That was why I waited. You know, to make amends, kind of like Musk said. Only I want to talk to you too, when we're alone."

"I see. And what about you, Musk? Have you come for a private talk, as well? I warn you, I have some sharp things to say to you."

Musk's face showed a flicker of surprise; for an instant the point of his knife paused in its patrol of his nails. "I can tell you now. Blood sent me."

Silk nodded. "So I had assumed."

"He gave you how long? Four weeks? Some dog puke like that?"

Silk nodded. "Four weeks, at the end of which I was to produce a substantial sum; when I did so, we were to confer again."

Musk rose as lithely as one of the beasts Mucor called lynxes. He held his knife level, its blade flat and its point aimed at Silk's chest, reminding Silk forcibly of the warning he had read in the entrails of Auk's ram. "That doesn't go, not anymore. You get a week for everything. One week!"

From the top of the dusty cabinet of curios beside the stair, Oreb croaked, "Poor Silk?"

"We had an agreement," Silk said.

"You want to see what your shaggy agreement's worth?" Musk spat at Silk's feet. "You got a week for everything. Maybe. Then we come."

"Bad man!"

The long knife flashed the length of the sellaria, to stick quivering in the wainscotting over the cabinet. Oreb gave a terrified squawk, and one black feather drifted toward the floor.

"You got yourself a turd bird," Musk whispered, "to make us dimber hornboys, didn't you? Well, up lamp! There's not a hawk I'd feed your turd bird to, and if you're warm to keep it you'd better teach it to shut its flap."

Chenille grinned. "If you're going to throw knives at him, you'd better be good enough to hit him. Missing's not so impressive."

Musk swung at her, but Silk caught his wrist before the blow landed. "Don't be childish!"

Musk spat in his face, and the carved hardwood handle of the walking stick caught Musk beneath the jaw with the hard, incisive rap of a mason's maul. Mask's head snapped back; he staggered backward, smashing a small table as he fell.

"Ah!" It was Chenille, her eyes bright with excitement, and her face intent.

Musk lay still for a second or two that seemed a great deal longer; his eyes opened, gazing for a protracted moment at nothing. He sat up.

Silk raised the stick. "If you've a needler, this is the time to pluck it."

Musk glowered at him, then shook his head.

"All right. Was that your message? That I have a week in which to pay Blood his twenty-six thousand?" With his free hand, Silk got his handkerchief and wiped Musk's spittle from his face.

Scarcely parting his lips, Musk rasped, "Or less."

Silk lowered the walking stick until he could lean on it. "Was there anything else?"

"No." Laboriously, Musk got to his feet, a hand braced against the wall.

"Then I have something to say to you. Orpine's rites were held today. You knew her, clearly, and both of you were working for Blood, directly or indirectly. You knew that she had died. You did not attend her rites, nor did you provide a beast for sacrifice. When her grave was closed, I asked Orchid whether she had received any expression of regret from you or Blood. She said very forcibly that she had not. Do you dispute that?"

Musk said nothing, though his eyes flickered toward the Sun Street door.

"Did you send anything or say anything? Don't try to go just yet. I don't advise it."

Musk met Silk's stare with his own.

"Possibly you believed that Blood had said something or done something in both your names. Was that it?"

Musk shook his head, the faded lights of the sellaria gleaming on his oiled hair.

"Very well then. You are a member of our human race. You have shirked your human duty, and it is mine to remind you of it—to teach you how a man acts, if you don't know it already. The lesson won't be quite so easy next time, I warn you." Silk strode past him to the Sun Street door and opened it. "Go in peace."

Musk left without a word or a backward glance, and Silk closed the door behind him. As he was fitting the bar into place, he felt Chenille's swift kiss on the nape of his neck. "Don't do that!" he protested.

"I wanted to do it, and I knew you wouldn't let me kiss your face. He did have a needler, you know."

"I surmised it. So do I. Won't you please sit down? Anywhere. My ankle hurts, and I can't sit until you do."

She took the stiff wooden chair in which Horn had sat the night before, and Silk dropped gratefully into his usual seat. Crane's wrapping was noticeably cold now; he unwound it and flogged the hassock with it. "I've tried doing this more often," he remarked, "but it doesn't seem to have much effect. I suppose this thing's got to cool before it will heat up again."

Chenille nodded.

"You said that you wished to speak with me. May I ask you a question first?"

"You can ask," Chenille told him. "I don't know if I'll be able to answer it. What is it?"

"When we were in the manteion—when I was securing the lid of Orpine's casket—you indicated that she had been a spy, and refused to speak again when I asked what you meant. A few minutes ago, I was warned by one of our sibyls that I was at risk because a few people in our quarter seem to be trying to thrust me into politics. If I have performed the funeral rites of a spy, and when it becomes known, my risk will be substantially increased, and thus—"

"I didn't, Patera! Orpine wasn't a spy. I was talking about myself—talking like I was somebody else. It's a bad habit I have."

"About *yourself?*"

She nodded vigorously. "You see, Patera, until then I hadn't really realized what was happening—what I'd been doing. Then while I was sitting through the funeral it was like I'd been struck by lightning. It's really awfully hard to explain."

Silk rewrapped his ankle. "You've been spying on our city? On Viron? Don't try to evade or prevaricate, please, my daughter. This is an extremely serious matter."

Chenille stared at his shoes.

After a long moment had passed, Oreb poked his head over the edge of the curio cabinet. "Man go?"

"Yes, he's gone," Chenille said. "But he may come back, so you have to be careful."

The night chough bobbed his head and began to wrestle with Musk's knife, tugging the pommel with his beak, then perching on the handle and pushing against the wainscotting with one scarlet foot. Chenille watched, apparently amused—though perhaps, Silk thought, merely glad of any distraction.

He cleared his throat. "I said that I wanted to ask you just one question, and have already asked several, for which I apologize. You indicated that you wanted my advice, and I said, or at least I implied, that you might have it. What is it you wish to discuss?"

"That's it," she said, turning from the busy bird to Silk. "I'm in trouble, just like you said. I'm not sure how much you're in, Patera, but I'm in one shaggy lot more. If the Guard ever finds out what I've been doing, I'll most likely be shot. I've got to have a place to stay where he can't find me, to start with, because if he does I'll be in that much deeper. I don't know where I can stay, but I'm not going back to Orchid's tonight."

"He?" For an instant Silk shut his eyes; when he opened them again, he asked, "Doctor Crane?"

Chenille's eyes widened. "Yes. How did you know?"

"I didn't. It was nothing more than a guess, and now I suppose I should be gratified because I was right. But I'm not."

"Was it because he came to my room yesterday while you and I were talking?"

Silk nodded. "For that and other reasons. Because he gave you a dagger, as you told me yesterday. Because he saw you first, out of all the women at Orchid's, and sometimes gave you rust. He might have examined you before the others simply as a favor to you, so that you could go out sooner, as you implied when I asked about it yesterday. But it seemed clear that it could also have been because he expected to get something of value from you; and information of some sort was one possibility."

Silk paused, rubbing his cheek. "Then too, you had that dagger concealed on your person when you encountered Orpine. Most women who carry weapons carry them at night, or so I've been told; but Blood, at least, expected you back at Orchid's for dinner. Later you yourself told me that you expected to work very hard at Orchid's in the evening."

"Women like me that have to go out nightside need some kind of weapon, Patera, believe me."

"I do. But you weren't going to be out after dark, so you were going into some other danger, or thought you were. That the man who had given you your dagger was the man who was sending you into danger seemed a reasonable guess. Do you want to tell me where you were going?"

"To take a— No. Not yet, anyhow." She leaned forward, sincere and deeply troubled, and at that moment he would have sworn she was ignorant of her own beauty. "All this is wrong. I mean it's right—all the facts are right—but it doesn't seem like it really was. It makes it seem like I'm really from another city. I'm as Vironese as you are. I was born right here, and I used to sell watercress around the market when I wasn't much bigger than that stool you got your foot up on."

Silk nodded, wondering whether she realized how much he wanted to touch her. "I believe you, my daughter. If you wish me to know the truth, however, you must tell me. How did it appear to you at the time?"

"Crane was a friend, just like I said yesterday. He was nice, and he brought me things, when he didn't have to. You remember about the bouquet of chenille? Little stuff like that, but nice. Most of the girls like him, and sometimes I gave him a free one. He's got a thing for big girls. He sort of laughs about it."

Silk said, "He's sensitive about his height; he told me so the first time we met. It may be that a tall woman makes him feel taller. Go on."

"So that's how it's been with us ever since I moved into Orchid's place. He didn't say, I want you to do some spying, so promise to sell out your city and I'll give you a uniform. We were talking a couple months ago, four or five of us in the big room when Crane was there. There were jokes about what he does when he looks us over. About the checkups. You know the kind of thing?"

"I don't," Silk admitted wearily, "though I can readily imagine."

"Somebody let it drop that a commissioner had been in, and Crane kind of whistled and asked who hooked him. I said it was me, and he wanted to know if he gave me much of a tip. Then later, when he was looking me over, he wanted to know if this commissioner happened to mention the caldé."

Silk's eyebrows shot up. "The caldé?"

"That's the way I felt, Patera. I said no, he didn't, and I thought the caldé was dead. Crane said, yeah, sure, he is. But when we were done and I was getting dressed, he said that if this commissioner or anybody else ever said anything about the caldé or the Charter, he'd like for me to tell him about it, or if he said anything about a councillor. Well, he had said something about councillors—"

"What was it?" Silk asked.

"Just that he'd gone out to the lake to see a couple of them, Tarsier and Loris. I went oh! and ah! the way you're supposed to, but I didn't think it sounded like it was very important. Crane just sort of stopped when I told it. You know what I mean?"

"Certainly."

"Then when I was dressed and going out, he was coming out of Violet's room and he passed me this folded up paper. He stuck it—you know, Patera—right down here. When I was alone I pulled it out and looked, and it was a bearer draft for five cards, signed by some cull I never even heard of. I thought probably it was no good, but I was going up that way anyhow, so I took it to the fisc and they gave me five cards for it, no who are you or how'd you get hold of this at all. Just like that, five cards slap on the counter." Chenille paused, waiting for his reaction. "How often do you think I snaffle a dimber five-card tip like that, Patera?"

He shrugged. "Since you've entertained a commissioner, once a month, perhaps."

"Not counting that one, I've got two in my whole life and that's lily. At Orchid's the cully's forked ten bits to get in and look at the dells, and then he's got to pay me a card—I've got to split with Orchid—unless it's somebody like that commissioner. He gets in free and gets it free, because nobody wants trouble. The best of everything and keep telling him how good he is, and usually he don't tip, either. From the ones that pay, I get a card like I said. That's for all night if they want it. So if the first one does and he won't tip, I clear half a card for the whole night."

Silk said, "I know people who don't get half a card for a week's hard work."

"Sure you do. Why do you think we do it? But what I'm saying is that in a good week, with tips, I might clear four or five. Maybe six. Only if it is, next week'll be two or three every time. So here I've got as much as I'd make in a good week, just for telling Crane something this commissioner said. Real candy! You're going to tell me I should've known, but I didn't think much about it back then, and that's lily." Chenille paused again, as if anticipating an accusation.

Silk murmured, "So that was how it began. What about the rest, my daughter?"

"Since then I've passed along maybe six or eight other things and taken things to a couple people for him dayside. Then if a commissioner or maybe a colonel—somebody like that, you know?—comes in, I'm really nice to them and I don't work them for tips and presents or anything like the other dells would. It's got to where they ask for me when I'm not around."

The night chough stirred uneasily on top of the curio cabinet, his head cocked inquiringly and his long, crimson beak half open.

"So ever since I saw Orpine on ice, I've been thinking." Chenille drew her chair nearer Silk's and lowered her voice. "You've got to fork twenty-six thousand to Blood if you want to hang onto this place? That's what Musk said."

Silk's head inclined less than a finger's width.

"All right, then. Why don't you—why don't you and me get it from Crane, Patera?"

"Man here," Oreb warned them. "Out there."

Chenille glanced up at him apprehensively.

"There now," Oreb insisted. "No knock."

Chapter 4

THE PROCHEIN AMI

Silk rose as silently as he could, irresistibly reminded of his failure to surprise Musk and Chenille earlier. Leaving Blood's walking stick beside his chair, he crossed the room to the Sun Street door, snatched the heavy bar out of its fittings and (retaining the bar in his left hand for use as a weapon if necessary) jerked the door open.

The tall, black-robed man waiting in the street beyond the step did not appear in the least surprised. "Did my presence here—ah—disturb you, Patera?" he inquired in a reverberant, nasal voice. "I strove to be discreet and—um—unobtrusive. Do you follow me? Subdued, eh? Not so skillful about it, perhaps. I'd reached your door before I heard the—ah lady's voice."

Silk leaned the bar against the wall. "I know that it's somewhat irregular, Your Eminence—"

"Oh, no, no, no! You have your reasons, I'm certain, Patera." The black-robed man bowed from the waist. "Good evening, my dear. Good evening, and may every god be with you this night." He favored Silk with a toothy smile that gleamed even in the glimmering light from the sky-lands. "I took great care to stand well out of the—ah—zone of—um—listening, Patera. Audibility? Earreach. Beyond the—ah—carry of the lady's voice. I could hear voices, I confess, save when a cart passed, if you follow me. But not one word you said. Couldn't make out a single thing, hey?" He smiled again. "Sweet Scylla, bear witness!"

Silk left the manse to stand upon its doorstep. "I'm exceedingly sorry that I was so abrupt, Your Eminence. We heard—I should say we were told—"

"Perfectly proper, Patera." One hand flipped up in a gesture of dismissal. "Quite, quite correct."

"—that there was someone outside, but not who—" Silk took a deep breath. "Your business must be urgent, or it wouldn't have brought you out so late, Your Eminence. Won't you come in?"

He held the door, then barred it again when the black-robed man had entered. "This is our sellaria, I'm afraid. The best room we have. I can offer you water and—and bananas, if you'd like some." He recalled that he had not yet explored Kit's sack. "Perhaps some other sort of fruit, as well."

The black-robed man waved Silk's fruit away. "You were advising this young lady, weren't you, Patera? Not shriving her, I hope. Not yet at least, though I didn't understand a word. I'd recognize the—ah—cadence of the Pardon of Pas, or so I fancy, having performed it so many, many times myself. The litany of Sacred Names, hey? Speak here for Great Pas, for Divine Echidna, for Scalding Scylla, and the rest. And I heard nothing like that. Nothing at all."

Chenille, who had followed Silk to the door and stood behind him in the doorway, inquired, "You're an augur, too, Patera?"

The black-robed man bowed again, then held up the voided cross he wore; its gold chain gleamed like the Aureate Path itself in the dingy little sellaria. "I am indeed, my dear. One quite, quite capable of discretion, or I should not be where I am today, eh? So you've nothing to fear, not that I overheard a single word you said."

"I'm confident that I can trust you implicitly, Patera. I was about to say that Patera Silk and I are liable to be quite some time. I can go somewhere else and come back in an hour or two—however much time you estimate that you may require."

Silk stared at her, astonished.

"Such a lady as you, my dear? In *this* quarter? I would not—ah—will not hear of it. Not for a single instant! But perhaps I might have a word with Patera now, eh? Then I'll be on my way."

"Of course," Chenille told him. "Please disregard me completely, Your Eminence."

He was more than half a head taller than Silk (though Silk was nearly as tall as Auk) and at least fifteen years his elder. Thin, coal-black hair spilled down his forehead; he tossed his head to keep it out of his eyes as he spoke. "It is Patera Silk, hey? I don't believe I've had the—ah—pleasure, Patera. I'm a perfect stranger, eh? Or nearly. Near as makes no matter. I wish it weren't so. Wish that—ah—that we met now as old acquaintances, eh? Though I did you a bad turn, eh? Couple of years ago. I admit it. I acknowledge it. No question about it, but I've got to do what's best for the Chapter, eh? The Chapter's our mother, after all, and bigger than any man. I'm Remora."

He turned his smile on Chenille. "This young beauty may prefer to maintain an—ah—ah—discreet anonymity, eh? That might be the prudent course, hey? However she prefers, and no offense taken."

Chenille nodded. "If you don't object, Patera."

"No, no, indeed not." Remora's hand waved negligently. "Indeed not. Why I—ah—advise it myself."

Silk said, "You attended my graduation, Your Eminence. You were on the dais, to the right of our Prelate. I don't expect you to remember me."

"Oh, but I do! I do! Won't you sit, my dear? I do indeed, Silk. You received honors, after all, eh? Never forget the sprats that get those. You were quite the huskiest cub the old place could show that year. I recall remarking to Quetzal—the Prolocutor, my dear, and I ought to have said His Cognizance. Remarking afterward that you ought to have gone into the arena, eh? So we—ah—ah—sent you there. Yes, we did! Merely a jest, to be sure. I was—um—I am responsible. My fault, all of it. That you were sent here, I mean. To this quarter, this manteion. I suggested it." With a sidelong glance at the wreckage of the table upon which Musk had fallen, Remora lowered his lanky body into Silk's reading chair. "I urged it—sit down, Patera—and dear Quetzal quite agreed."

"Thank you, Your Eminence." Silk sat. "Thank you very much. I couldn't have gone to a better place."

"Oh, you don't mean it. I can't blame you. Not at all, eh? Not at all. You've had a miserable time of it. I—ah—we know that, Quetzal and I. We realize it. But poor old—um—your predecessor. What was his name?"

"Pike, Your Eminence. Patera Pike."

"Quite right. Patera Pike. What if we'd sent poor old Pike one of those rabbity little boys, eh? Killed and eaten him on the first day, in this quarter, eh? You know it now, Patera, and I knew it then. So I suggested to Quetzal that we send you, and he saw the logic of it straight off. Now here you are, hey? All alone. Since Pike left for—ah—purer climes? You've done a fine, fine job of it, too, Patera. An—ah—exceptional job. I don't think that's too strong an expression."

Silk forced himself to speak. "I would like to agree, Your Eminence." The words came singly and widely spaced, as heavy as waystones. "But this manteion has been sold. You must know about that. We couldn't even pay taxes. The city seized the property; I assume that the Chapter was notified, though I was not. The new owner will certainly close the manteion and the palaestra, and he may well tear them both down."

"He's worked hard, my dear," Remora told Chenille. "You don't live in the quarter, eh? So you can't know. But he has. He has."

Silk said, "Thank you, Your Eminence. You're very kind. I wish, though, that there were no need for your kindness. I wish I had made a success of this manteion, somehow. When I thanked you for assigning me here, I wasn't being polite. I don't really love this place—these cramped old, run-down buildings and so forth, though I used to try to make myself believe I did. But the people— We have a great many bad people here. That's what everyone says, and it's true. But the good ones have been tried by fire and remained good in spite of everything that the whorl could throw against them, and there's nothing else like them in the whorl. And even the bad ones, you'd be surprised—"

At that moment, Oreb fluttered into Chenille's lap with Musk's knife in his beak.

"Hey? Extraordinary! What's this?"

"Oreb has a dislocated wing," Silk explained. "I did it by accident, Your Eminence. A physician put the bone back in the socket yesterday, but it hasn't healed yet."

Remora waved Oreb's woes aside. "But this dagger, hey? Is it yours, my dear?"

Chenille nodded without a trace of a smile. "I threw it to illustrate a point that I was making to Patera Silk, Your Eminence. Now Oreb's kindly returned it to me. He likes me, I think."

Oreb whistled.

"*You* threw it? I don't want—ah—intend to appear skeptical, my dear—"

Chenille's hand flicked in the direction of the cabinet, and the wainscotting above its top boomed like a kettle-drum. With its blade half buried in oak, Musk's knife did not even vibrate.

"Oh! O you gods!" Remora rose and went to examine the knife. "Why, I'd never— This is really most—ah—um—most . . ." He grasped the hilt and tried to pull the knife out, but was forced to work it back and forth. "There's only the single scar here, one—um—hole in the wood."

"I thought Patera Silk would prefer that I mark his wall as little as possible," Chenille told him demurely.

"Hah!" Remora gave a snort of triumph as he succeeded in freeing the knife; he returned it with a profound bow. "Your weapon, my dear. I knew that this quarter is said to be—ah—rough? Tough. Lawless. And I observed the broken table. But I hadn't realized . . . Patera, my—ah—our admiration for you was already very great. But it's—um—mine's now, well . . ." He seated himself again. "That's what I was about to remark, Patera. You may possibly imagine that we—um—Quetzal and I—"

His attention shifted to Chenille. "As this good augur knows, I am His Cognizance's—ah—prochain ami, my dear. Doubtless you are already familiar with the—ah—um—locution. His adjutant, as they would say it in the Guard. His coadjutor, hey? That's the—ah—formal official phraseology, the most correct usage. And I was about to say that we have been following Patera's progress with attention and admiration. He has had difficulties. Oh, indeed! He has encountered obstacles, eh? His has been no easy field to plow, no—um—quiet pasture, this manteion, poor yet dear to the immortal gods."

Chenille nodded. "So I understand, Your Eminence."

"He ought to have come to us for—ah—assistance, eh?

He ought to have appealed, frankly and forthrightly, to His Cognizance and to me. Ought to have laid his case before us, so to speak. Do you follow me? But we, still more, hey? We still more ought to have proffered our assistance without any of that. Yes, indeed! Proffered the ready assistance of the Chapter, and—ah—more. Much more. And much sooner than this."

"I couldn't get in to see you," Silk explained somewhat dryly. "Your prothonotary kindly informed me that a crisis was occupying all your attention."

Remora wheezed. "Doubtless one was, Patera. Frequently it seems that my sole task, my—ah—entire duty consists of wrestling with an unending—um—onrushing and—ah—remorseless torrent of continually worsening crises."

Blowers roared to the west, louder and louder as an armed Civil Guard floater roared along Sun Street. Remora paused to listen.

"It's our—ah—invariable policy with young augurs, Patera, as you must understand, to—ah—permit them to try their wings. To observe their first flights, as it were, from a distance. To thrust them rudely from the nest, if I may say it. You follow me? It is an examination you have passed very—um—creditably indeed."

Silk inclined his head. "I'm gratified, Your Eminence, although thoroughly conscious that I'm not entitled to such praise. This may be the best opportunity I'll have, however, to report—I mean informally—the very great honor that was accorded to our troubled manteion today by the—"

"Troubled did you say, Patera? This manteion?" Remora smiled all difficulties away. "It has been—ah—um—well, sold, as you say. But the sale is only a legality, eh? You follow me? A mere contrivance or—ah—stratagem of old Quetzal's, actually. The new owners—ah. The name is—the name . . ."

"Blood," Silk supplied.

"No, that's not it. Something more common, hey?"

Chenille murmured, "Musk?"

"Quite, quite correct. Musk, indeed. Rather a foolish name, hey? If I may put it so. Infants do not, as a rule, smell half so—ah—sweet. But this Musk has paid your taxes. That's how he got it. You follow me? For the taxes and some trifling amount over. These buildings are in need of—ah—refurbishing, eh? As you pointed out yourself, Patera. We'll let him do it, hey? Why not? Let him bear the expense, and not the burse, eh? Eventually he'll donate everything to us again. Give it all back to the Chapter, eh? A meritorious act."

Chenille shook her head. "I doubt—"

"We have ways, my dear, as you'll see. Dear old Quetzal has, most particularly. He's very good at it. His—ah—um—consequence as the Prolocutor of the Chapter. And his influence with the Ayuntamiento, eh? He has plenteous—ah—standing there even yet, never doubt it. An arsenal of pressures that he—ah—that we can, and will, exert in any such an eventuality as—ah—this present instance. As yours here on Sun Street, Patera."

Silk said, "Musk is no more than the owner of record, Your Eminence. Blood controls this property, and Blood is threatening to tear down everything."

"Doesn't matter. Doesn't matter. You'll see, Patera." Remora flashed his toothy smile again. "It will not occur—ah—come to pass. No fear. No fear at all. Or if it should, the old structures will be replaced with better ones. That would be the best way, eh? Rebuilt in a better style, and upon a more—ah—commodious scale. I must remember to speak to Quetzal about it tomorrow when he has had his beef tea."

Remora inclined his head toward Chenille. "He's quite fond of beef tea, is old Quetzal. Doubtless Patera knows. These things get bandied about, you know, among us. Like a bunch of—um—washerwomen, eh? Gossip, gossip. But dear old Quetzal should eat more, hey? I'm forever after him about it. A man can't live on beef tea and air, hey? But Quetzal does. Feeble, though."

He glanced at the clock above the sellaria's diminutive fireplace. "What I—ah—ventured out to inform you of, Patera Silk— You see, my dear, I'm terribly selfish. Yes, even after half a lifetime spent in the pursuit of—ah—sacrosanctity. I wished to inform him myself. Patera, you shall no longer labor alone. I said—um—earlier, eh? I assured you that your struggles had not gone unnoticed, hey? But now I can say more, as I—ah—most certainly shall. As I do. An acolyte, a youthful augur who only in the springtide of this very year completed his studies with honors—um. As you yourself did, Patera. I—ah—we are very aware of that. With a prize, I was about to say, for hierologics will arrive in the morning. You yourself shall know the joy of leading this promising neophyte down the very paths that you yourself have traversed with so much credit. You have two bedrooms, I believe, upstairs here? Please have the less—ah—vantaged prepared to receive Patera Gulo."

Remora rose and extended his hand. "It has been a great pleasure, Patera. A pleasure and an honor much, much too long delayed. And denied. Self-denial, indeed, and self-denial must have an end, hey?"

Silk rose with the assistance of Blood's walking stick, and they shook hands solemnly.

"My dear, I'm sorry to have disrupted your own interview with your—ah—spiritual guide. With this devout young augur. I do apologize. Our little tête-à-tête cannot have been of much interest to you, yet—"

"Oh, but it was!" Chenille's smile might well have been sincere.

"Yet it was brief at least. Ah—succinct. And now my blessing upon you, whatever your troubles may be." Remora traced the sign of addition in the air. "Blessed be you in the Most Sacred Name of Pas, Father of the Gods, in that of Gracious Echidna, His Consort, in those of their Sons and their Daughters alike, this day and forever, in the name of their eldest child, Scylla, Patroness of this, Our Holy City of Viron."

"The new owner," Silk informed Remora with some urgency, "insists that any moneys above the operating expenses of the manteion must be turned over to him. In light of what transpired today at sacrifice—Your Eminence simply cannot have remained unaware of it—"

Remora grunted as he set aside the heavy bar. "You have a good deal here in need of repair, Patera. Or replacement. Or—ah—augmentation. Items which this Musk will not—um—exert himself to rehabilitate. Your own—ah—um—wardrobe, eh? That would be a fair beginning. You might do—um—much. Many things. As for the rest, you tote up your own accounts, I take it? Doubtless you can discover many good uses for this—ah—merely presumptive surplus. And you have borrowed various sums, I believe. So I'm—ah—we, His Cognizance and I, have been given to understand."

The door clicked shut behind him.

Oreb whistled. "Bad man."

Chenille put out her arm, and the bird hopped onto it. "Not really, Oreb. Only a man deeply in love with his own cleverness."

A slight smile played about the corners of her mouth as she spoke to Silk. "All that for a single manifestation by a merely minor goddess. For one not numbered among the

Nine—didn't you say something like that in the manteion? I think I remember that."

Silk dropped the bar into place and turned to reply, but she raised a hand. "I know what you intend to say, Patera. Don't say it. My name is Chenille. That is to be a given, not subject to debate or qualification. You're to call me Chenille, even when we're alone. And you're to treat me as Chenille."

"But—"

"Because I am Chenille. You don't really grasp these things, no matter how much you may have studied. Now sit down. Your leg hurts, I know."

Silk dropped into his chair.

"There was something else you wanted to say—not that other, which isn't really true. What is it?"

"I'm afraid that it may offend you, but it isn't intended to offend." He hesitated and swallowed. "Chenille, you . . . you talk very differently at different times. Yesterday at Orchid's, you spoke like a young woman who had grown up in the streets, who couldn't read but who had picked up a few phrases and some sense of grammatical principles from better-educated people. Tonight, before His Eminence came, you used a great deal of thieves' cant, as Auk does. As soon as His Eminence arrived, you became a young woman of culture and education."

Her smile widened. "Do you want me to justify the way I speak to you, Patera? Hardly the request of a gentleman, much less a man of the cloth."

Silk sat in silence for a time, stroking his cheek. Oreb hopped from Chenille's wrist to her shoulder, then to the top of the battered library table next to Silk's chair.

At length Silk said, "If you had spoken to His Eminence as you spoke to me, he would have assumed that I had hired you for the evening or something of that kind. To save me from embarrassment, you betrayed your real nature to me. I wish I knew how to thank you properly for that, Chenille."

"You pronounce my name as though it were a polite lie. I assure you, it's the truth."

Silk asked, "But if I were to use another name—we both know which—wouldn't that be the truth as well?"

"Not really. Far less than you believe, and it would lead to endless difficulties."

"You're more beautiful tonight than you were in Orchid's house. May I say that?"

She nodded. "I wasn't trying then. Or not much. Not well. Men think it's all bones and makeup. But a lot is . . . Certain things I do. My eyes and my lips. The way I move. The right gestures. You do it too, unconsciously. Silk. I like to watch you. When you don't know I'm watching." She yawned and stretched until it seemed that her full breasts would split her gown. "There. That wasn't very beautiful, was it? Though he used to love it when I yawned, and kiss my hand. I did it sometimes. Just to give him pleasure. Such delight. Silk, I'm going to have to have a place to sleep tonight. I love your name, Silk. I've been wanting to say it all night. Most names are ugly. Will you help me?"

"Of course," he said. "I am your slave."

"Chenille."

He swallowed again. "I'll help you all I can, Chenille. You can't sleep here, but I feel sure we can find something better."

Suddenly she was again the woman he had met at Orchid's. "We've got to talk about that, but there are other things to talk about first. You do realize why that awful man came? Why you're getting an acolyte? Why that awful man and this Prolocutor are going to try to take your manteion back from Blood?"

Silk nodded gloomily. "I'm naive at times, I admit; but

not that naive. Once I was on the point of suggesting that he drop the pretense."

"He would have turned nasty, I'm sure."

"So am I." Silk drew a deep breath and exhaled with mingled relief and disgust. "That acolyte's being sent to keep an eye on me. I'd like to find out how he's spent the summer."

"You think he may be a protégé of Remora's? Something of that kind?"

Silk nodded. "He's probably been an assistant to his prothonotary. Not the prothonotary himself, because I've met him and his name isn't Gulo. If I can talk with some other augurs who were in the same class, they may be able to tell me."

"So you intend to spy on the spy." Chenille smiled. "At least your manteion's safe."

"I doubt that. In the first place, I don't have a great deal of confidence in His Cognizance's ability to manipulate Blood. Less, anyway, than His Eminence has, or says that he has. Everyone knows the Chapter doesn't have the influence in the Ayuntamiento that it once had, although Lady Kypris's theophany today may help considerably. And . . ."

"Yes? What is it now?" Chenille was stroking Oreb's back. Stretching out his neck, the bird rubbed her arm with his crimson beak.

"In the second, if they can manipulate Blood I won't be here much longer. I'll be transferred, most likely to some administrative position, and this Patera Gulo will take over everything."

"Um-hum. I'm proud of you." Chenille was still looking at the bird. "Then my little suggestion is still of interest to you?"

"Spying on Viron?" Silk gripped Blood's lioness-headed stick with both hands as if he intended to break it.

"No! Not unless you order me to do it. And, Chenille—you really are Chenille? Now?"

She nodded, her face serious.

"Then, Chenille, I can't allow you to continue to do it either. All questions of loyalty aside, I can't let you risk your life like that."

"You're angry. I don't blame you, Silk. Though it's better to be cold. He . . . You call him Pas. Someone said once that he was always in a cold fury. Not always, Silk."

She licked her lips. "It wasn't true. But almost. And he came to rule the whole—whorl. Our whorl, bigger than this. So fast. All in a few years. No one could believe it."

Silk said, "I don't think I'm very good at cold furies, but I'll try. I was going to ask what will happen if we succeed? Suppose that we get twenty-six thousand cards from Doctor Crane to hand over to Blood. I doubt that it's even possible, but suppose we do. What good would it do anybody except Blood?"

Silk fell silent for a time, his face in his hands. "I should want to do good to Blood, of course, as I should want to do good to everyone. Even when I broke into his house to try to make him give my manteion back, I did it in part to keep him from staining his spirit by converting the property to a bad purpose. But getting money for him that he doesn't need isn't going to do him any good, and it may even do him harm."

Oreb dropped onto Silk's shoulder, startling him into looking up; as he did, Oreb caught a lock of his straying hair and tugged at it.

"He knows what you're feeling," Chenille said quietly. "He would like to make you laugh, if he can."

"He's a good bird—a very good bird. This isn't the first time he's come to me of his own accord."

"You would take him with you, wouldn't you? Even if

you were sent to that administrative position? Silk. It isn't against some rule for augurs to keep pets?"

"No. They're permitted."

"So everything wouldn't be lost, even then." Chenille floated from her chair to slip behind his own. "I could . . . Supply some trifling comfort, too. Now, Silk. If you wish it."

"No," he repeated.

Silence refilled the little sellaria. After two minutes or more had passed, he added, "But thank you anyway. Thank you very much. What you said shouldn't make me feel better; but it does, and I'll always be grateful to you."

"I'll take advantage of your gratitude, you know."

He nodded soberly. "I hope you do. I want you to."

"You don't like girls like me."

"That isn't so." He fell silent for a moment to think about it. "I don't like what you do—the kinds of things that go on every night at Orchid's—because I know they do everyone involved more harm than good, and injure all of us eventually. I don't dislike you or Poppy or the others; in fact, I like you. I even like Orchid, and every god"—He would have stopped, but it was already too late—"knows I felt sorry for her this afternoon."

She laughed softly. "All the gods don't know. Silk. . . . One does. Two. You think those men don't marry because they have us. Most are married already, and shouldn't be."

He nodded reluctantly.

"You've seen how young most of us are. What do you think happens to us?"

"I've never considered it." He wanted to say that many probably perished like Orpine; but she had stabbed Orpine.

"You think we all turn into Orchids, or use too much rust and die in convulsions. Most of us marry, that's all. You don't believe me, but it's the truth. We marry some buck who always asks for us. Silk."

She was stroking his hair. Inexplicably he felt that if he were to turn around he would not see her; that these were the fingers of a phantom.

"You said you wouldn't. Silk. Because you wanted to see a god. To someone. Yesterday? And now?"

"Now I don't know," he admitted.

"You're afraid I'll laugh. You'll be clumsy. All men are. Silk. Patera. You're frightened of my laughter."

"Yes, I am."

"Would you kill me? Silk? For fear that I might laugh? Men do that."

He did not reply at once. Her hands were where Musk's had been, yet he knew they would bring no pain. He waited for her to speak again, but heard only the distant crackle of the dying fire in the kitchen stove and the rapid tick of the clock on the mantel. At last he said, "Is that why some men strike women, in love? So they won't laugh?"

"Sometimes."

"Does Pas strike you?"

She laughed again, a silver flood, whether at Pas or at him he could not have told. "No. Silk. He never strikes anyone. He kills . . . or nothing."

"But not you. He hasn't killed you." He was conscious again of her mingled perfumes, the mustiness of her gown.

"I don't know." Her tone was serious, and he did not understand.

Oreb whistled abruptly, hopping from Silk's shoulder to the tabletop. "She here! Come back." He hopped to the shade of the broken reading lamp, fluttering from there to the top of the curio cabinet. "Iron girl!"

Silk nodded and rose, limping to the garden door.

Chenille murmured, "I didn't mean, by the way, that we should spy on Viron *for* Crane. I don't think I'll be doing it anymore myself. What I meant to suggest was that we get your money from Crane."

She yawned again, covering her mouth with a hand larger than most women's. "He seems to have a lot. To control a lot, at least. So why shouldn't we take it? If you were the owner of this manteion, it would be awkward to transfer you, I'd think."

Silk gawked at her.

"Now you expect me to have an elaborate plan. I don't. I'm not good at them, and I'm too tired to think anymore tonight anyway. Since you won't sleep with me, you think about it. And I will, too, when I get up."

"Chenille—"

Maytera Marble's steel knuckles tapped the door.

"It's that mechanical woman of yours, like Oreb said. What is it they called them? Robota? Robotniks? There used to be a lot more."

"Chems," he whispered as Maytera Marble knocked again.

"Whatever. Open the door so she can see me, Silk."

He did so, and Maytera Marble regarded the tall, fiery-haired Chenille with considerable surprise.

"Patera has been shriving me," she told the sibyl, "and now I need someplace to stay. I don't think he wants me to sleep here."

"You . . . ? No, no!" Although it was impossible, Maytera Marble's eyes appeared to have widened.

Silk interposed, "I thought that you—and Maytera Rose and Maytera Mint—might put her up in the cenoby tonight. You have vacant rooms, I know. I was about to come over and ask. You must have read my mind, Maytera."

"Oh, no. I was just bringing back your plate, Patera." She held it out. "But—but . . ."

"You'd be doing me an enormous favor." He accepted

the plate. "I promise that Chenille won't give you any trouble, and perhaps you, and Maytera Rose and Maytera Mint, may be able to advise her in ways that I, a man, cannot—though if Maytera Rose is not willing, Chenille will have to stay elsewhere, of course. It's getting late, but I'll try to find a family that will open its home to her."

Maytera Marble nodded meekly. "I'll try, Patera. I'll do my best. Really, I will."

"I know," he assured her, smiling.

Leaning against the doorjamb with the plate in his hand, he watched the two women, Maytera Marble in her black habit and Chenille in her black gown, alike yet so very unlike as they walked slowly along the little path. When they had nearly reached the door of the cenoby, the second, lagging behind, turned to wave.

And it seemed to Silk at that moment that the face he glimpsed was not Chenille's, and not a conventionally good-looking face at all but one of breathtaking loveliness.

Hare was waiting outside the floater shed. "Well, it's finished," Hare said.

"Will it fly?"

Hare shrugged. He had noticed the bruise on Musk's jaw, but was too wise to mention it.

"Will it *fly?*" Musk repeated.

"How'd I know? I don't know anything about them."

Musk, a head shorter, advanced a step. "Will it fly? This's the last time."

"Sure." Hare nodded, tentatively at first, then more vigorously. "Sure it will."

"How the shag do you know, putt?"

"He says it will. He says it'll lift a lot, and he's been making them for fifty years. He ought to know."

Musk waited, not speaking, his face intent, his hands hovering near his waist.

"It looks good, too." Hare took a half step backward. "It looks real. I'll show you."

Musk nodded almost reluctantly and motioned toward the side door. Hare hurried to open it.

The shed was too new to have the creeping greenish sound-activated lights that the first settlers had brought with them or, just possibly, had themselves known how to make. Beeswax candles and half a dozen lamps burning fish oil illuminated its cavernous interior now; there was a faint, heavy odor from the hot wax, a fishy reek, and dominating both a stronger and more pungent smell of ripe bananas. The kite builder was bent above his creation, adjusting the tension of the almost invisible thread that linked its ten-cubit wings.

Musk said, "I thought you said it was finished. All finished, you said."

The kite builder looked up. He was smaller even than Musk; but his beard was gray-white, and he had the shaggy brows that mark the penultimate season in man's life. "It is," he said. His voice was soft and a trifle husky. "I was trimming."

"You could fly it now? Tonight?"

The kite builder nodded. "With a wind."

Hare protested, "She won't fly at night, Musk."

"But this. This'll fly now?"

The kite builder nodded again.

"With a rabbit? It'll carry that much?"

"A small rabbit, yes. Domestic rabbits get very large. It wouldn't carry a rabbit that big. I told you."

Musk nodded absently and turned to Hare. "Go get one of the white ones. Not the littlest one, the next to littlest, maybe. About like that."

"There's no wind."

"A white one," Musk repeated. "Meet us on the roof."

He motioned to the kite builder. "Bring it and the wire. Anything you're going to need."

"I'll have to disassemble it again, then reassemble it up there. That's going to take at least an hour. Could be more."

"Give me the wire," Musk told him. "I'll go up first. You stay down here and hook it up. I'll pull it up. Hare can show you how to get up there."

"You haven't let out the cats?"

Musk shook his head, went to the bench, and got the reel. "Come on."

Outside, the night hung hot and still. No leaf stirred in the forest beyond the wall.

Musk pointed. "Stand right over there, see? Where it's three floors. I'll be up on that roof."

The kite builder nodded and went back to the floater shed to crank open the main door, three floaters wide. When he picked it up, the new kite felt heavy in his hands; he had not weighed it, and now he tried to guess its weight: as much as the big fighting kite he'd built when he was just starting, with the big black bull on it.

And that wouldn't fly in any wind under a gale.

He carried the new kite along the white stone path, then across the rolling lawn to the spot that Musk had pointed out. There was no sign of Hare and no dangling wire. Craning his neck, the kite builder peered up at the ornamental battlement, black as the bull against the mosaic gaiety of the skylands. There was no one there.

Some distance behind him, the cats were pacing nervously in their pen, eager for their time of freedom. He could not hear them, yet he was acutely conscious of them, their claws and amber eyes, their hunger and their frustration. Suppose that the talus were to free them without waiting for Musk's order? Suppose that they were free already, slinking through the shrubbery, ready to pounce?

Something touched his cheek.

"Wake up down there!" It was Musk's husky, almost feminine voice, calling from the roof.

The kite builder caught the wire and fastened the tiny
snap hook at its end to the kite's yoke, then stepped back
to admire his work as his kite swiftly mounted the dressed
stone, his kite like a man smaller and slighter than almost
any actual man, with a dragonfly's gossamer wings.

Hare was coming over the lawn with something pale in
his arms. The kite builder called, "Let me see that," and
trotted to meet him, taking the white rabbit from him and
holding it up by its ears. "It's too heavy!"

"This is the one he said to bring," Hare told him. He
retrieved the rabbit.

"It can't lift one that big."

"There's no wind anyhow. You coming up?"

The kite builder nodded.

"Come on, then."

Entering the original villa by a rear door, they climbed
two flights of stairs and clattered up the iron spiral that Silk
had descended two nights before; Hare threw open the
trap door. "We had a big buzzard up here," Hare said. "We
called him Hierax, but he's dead."

Somewhat out of breath, the kite builder felt obliged to
chuckle nonetheless.

They crossed the tiles and scrambled up onto the roof
of the wing, the kite builder holding the docile rabbit again
and passing it to Hare when Hare had attained the higher
roof, accepting a hand as he himself scrambled up.

Musk was sitting on the battlement, practically hidden
by the kite. "Show a little life. I've been waiting for an hour.
Are you going to have to run with it?"

"I'll hold the spool," the kite builder said. "Hare can
run with it. But it won't fly without a wind."

"There's wind," Musk told him.

The kite builder moistened his forefinger and held it up; there was indeed some slight stir here, fifty cubits above the ground. "Not enough," he said.

"I could feel it," Musk told him. "Feel it trying to go up."

"Naturally it wants to." The kite builder could not and would not conceal his pride in his craft. "Mine all do, but there's not enough wind."

Hare asked, "You want me to tie the rabbit on?"

"Let me see him." Musk, too, lifted the rabbit by its ears, and it squealed in protest. "This is the little one. You putt, you brought the little one."

"I weighed 'em. There's two lighter than this, I swear."

"I ought to drop it off. Maybe I ought to drop *you* off, too."

"You want me to get them? I'll show them to you. It'll only take a minute."

"What if it gets threshed and goes off? We haven't got any more this little. What'll we use in the morning?" Musk returned the rabbit to Hare.

"Two of them, by Scylla's slime. By any shaggy gods you want to name. I wouldn't lie to you."

"That's not a rabbit, it's a shaggy rat."

A passing breeze ruffled the kite builder's hair, like the fingers of an unseen goddess. He felt that if he were to turn quickly he might glimpse her: Molpe, goddess of the winds and all light things, Molpe, whose suitor he had been all his life. *Molpe, make your winds blow for me. Don't shame me, Molpe, who have always honored you. A brace of finches for you, I swear.*

Musk snapped, "Tie it on," and Hare knelt on the sun-soft tar, whipping the first cord around the unfortunate rabbit and tying it cruelly tight.

"Split along!"

"Cooler. I can't see a shaggy thing I'm doing here. We should've brought a lantern."

"So it can't fall out."

Hare rose. "All right. It won't." He took the kite from Musk. "Should I hold it over my head?"

The kite builder nodded. He had picked up the reel of wire; now he moistened his finger again.

"Want me to run down that way?"

"No. Listen to me. You have to run toward me, into the wind—into whatever wind there is, anyway. You're running so that the wind will feel stronger to the kite than it really is. If we're lucky, that false wind will lift it enough to get it up to where the wind really is stronger. Go down that way, all the way to the corner. I'll reel out as you walk down, and reel in as you run back. Any time the kite wants to lift out of your hands, toss it up. If it starts to fall, catch it."

"He's from the city," Musk explained. "They don't fly them there."

The kite builder nodded absently, watching Hare. "Hold it by the feet, as high as you can get it. Don't run until I tell you to."

"It looks real now," Musk said, "but I don't know if it looks real enough. It'll be daylight and sunshine, and they can see a shaggy scut better than we can. Only they don't always know real from fake. They don't think about it like we do."

"All right," the kite builder called. "Now!"

Hare ran, long-legged and fast, the kite's wings moving, stroking the air a trifle at every stride as though it would fly like a bird if it could. Halfway along the long roof he released it, and it rose.

Molpe! O Molpe!

At twice Hare's height it stalled, hung motionless for an instant, dipped until it nearly touched the roof, lifted again to head height, and fell lifeless to the tar.

"Catch it!" Musk screamed. "You're supposed to catch it! You want to bust its shaggy neck?"

"You're worried about your rabbit," the kite builder told him, "but you've got more, and you could buy a dozen tomorrow morning. I'm worried about the kite. If it's broken it could take two days to mend it. If it's broken badly, I'll have to start over."

Hare had picked up the kite. "The rabbit's all right," he called across the roof. "Want to try again?"

The kite builder shook his head. "That bowstring's not tight enough. Bring it here."

Hare did.

"Hold it up." The kite builder knelt. "I don't want to put it down on this tar."

"Maybe we could tow it behind one of the floaters," Hare suggested.

"That would be riskier even than this. If it went down, it would be dragged to rags before we could stop." By touch alone, he loosened the knot. "I wanted to put a turnbuckle in this," he told Musk. "Maybe I should have."

"We'll try it again when you've got it right," Musk said.

"There might be a wind in the morning."

"I'm going to fly Aquila in the morning. I don't want to be wondering about this."

"All right." The kite builder stood, wet his forefinger again, and nodded to Hare, pointing.

This time the enormous kite lifted confidently, though it seemed to the kite builder that there was no wind at all. Fifteen, twenty, thirty cubits it soared—then dipped—swooped abruptly with a terrified squeal from its passenger, and struggled to climb again, nearly stalling.

"If it gets down below the roof, the house'll kill the wind."

"Exactly right." The kite builder nodded patiently. "The very same thought had occurred to me earlier."

"You're pulling it down! What are you doing that for? It was going to fly that time."

"I need to slack off the lower bridle line," the kite builder explained. "That's the string going from the feet to the yoke."

To Hare he called, "Coming down! Catch it!"

"All right, that's enough!" Musk's needler was in his hand. "We'll try again in the morning. We'll try it again when there's more wind, and it had better fly and fly good when we do. *Are you listening to me, old man?*"

Hare had the kite now; the kite builder released the reel crank. "About that much." He indicated the distance with his fingers. "Didn't you see it dive? If it dove like that into this roof, or into the ground, it could be completely wrecked."

While Hare held the kite up, the kite builder loosened the lower bridle string and let it out the distance he had indicated. "I thought that I might have to do this," he explained, "so I left a little extra here."

Musk told Hare, "We won't risk it again tonight."

"Be quiet." The kite builder's fingers had stopped, the bridle string half-retied. Far away he had heard the murmur of the dry forest, the shaking of raddled old leaves and the rubbing a million dry twigs upon a million more. He turned his head blindly, questing.

"What is it?" Hare wanted to know.

The kite builder straightened up. "Go to the other corner this time," he said.

"It had better not break." Musk slipped his needler beneath his tunic.

"If it breaks, I'll be safe," the kite builder remarked. "You couldn't repair it, and neither could he."

"If it flies you'll be safer," Musk told him grimly.

Two chains and more away, Hare could hear their voices. "All right?"

Automatically the kite builder glanced down at his reel. The trees had fallen silent now, but he felt Molpe's phantom fingers in his hair. His beard stirred. *"NOW!"*

Hare held onto the huge kite until he was halfway across the roof, and loosed it with an upward toss. Immediately it shot up fifty, then sixty cubits; there it paused, as though gathering strength.

"Up," Musk muttered. "Away hawk!"

For a full two minutes, the kite soared no higher, its transparent wings almost invisible against the skylands, its human body as black as the shade, the rabbit a writhing dot upon its chest. At last the kite builder smiled and let out more wire. It climbed confidently, higher and higher, until it seemed that it would be lost among tessellated fields and sparkling rivers on the other side of the whorl. "Is that enough?" the kite builder asked. "Shall I bring it down?"

Musk shook his head.

Hare, who had joined them to watch the kite, said, "Looks good, don't it? Looks like the lily thing."

"I want my money," the kite builder told Musk. "This is what we agreed upon. I've built it, you've approved it, and it will carry a rabbit."

"Half now," Musk whispered, still watching the kite. "I don't approve until Aquila goes for it. I'm still not sure it's going to look right to her."

Hare chuckled. "Poor little bunny! I bet it don't even know where it's got to. I bet it's lonesome way up there."

Musk contemplated the distant rabbit with a bitter smile. "It'll get some company in the morning." The mounting wind fluttered his embroidered tunic and pushed a long strand of curling hair across his handsome forehead.

The kite builder said, "If you don't think that it will deceive your eagle, tell me what changes you'd like me to make. I'll try to have them finished by morning."

"It looks good now," Musk conceded. "It looks exactly like a real flier holding a rabbit."

In bed, tossing and turning, Silk drove the deadcoach through a dark and ruined dreamscape, the land of the dead still a land of the living. The wind was blowing and blowing, fluttering all the yellow-white curtains of all the bedroom windows, fluttering the velvet hangings of the deadcoach like so many black flags; like the slashed poster on Sun Street with old Councillor Lemur's eyes gouged out, his nose and his mouth dancing, dancing in the wind; like the kind face of old Councillor Loris cut away and blowing down the gutter; like Maytera Rose's wide black habit, heavy with hemweights and death but fluttering anyway while the tall black plumes bent and swayed, while the wind caught the black lash of Silk's dancing whip, so that when he intended to whip one black horse he whipped the other. The unwhipped black horse lagged and lagged, dogged and dogged it, snorted at the billowing yellow dust but was never whipped. He should have been for cheating his brother who sweated and lunged at the harness though his flanks were crusted with yellow dust that the white foam had already dyed black.

In the deadcoach Orpine writhed naked and white, Silk's old torn cotton handkerchief falling from her face, always falling but never fallen, always slipping but never slipped, though the wind whistled against the glass and carried dust through every crack. While whipping the wrong horse, always the wrong horse, Silk watched her clawing Chenille's dagger, saw her claw and pull at it though it was wedged between her ribs, saw her clawing like a cat at the red cat with the fiery tail, at the fine brass guard all faceted with file work. Her face beneath the slipping handkerchief was stained with her blood, forever the face of Mucor, of Blood's crazed daughter. There were sutures in her scalp and her brown hair was shaved away, her black hair shaved by Moorgrass, who had washed her body and shaved half her head so that the stitches showed and a drop of blood at each stitch though her full breasts leaked milk onto the black velvet. The grave awaited her, only the grave, one more grave in a whorl of graves where so many lay already watched over by Hierax, God of Death and Caldé of the Dead, High Hierax the White-Headed One with her white spirit in his claws because the second one had been a brain surgeon, for whom if not for her?

Nor did Silk, alone in the padded black-leather driver's seat, know what any of these things meant, but only that he was driving to the grave and was late as usual. He always came to a grave too late and too soon, driving nightside in a dark that was darker than the darkest night, on a day that was hotter than the hottest day, so that it burned the billowing dust as an artist's earths are burned in an artist's little furnace, glowing gold in the heat, the black plumes billowing while he whipped the wrong horse, a sweating horse that would die at the grave if the other did not pull too. And where would Orpine lie, with the dead black horse in her grave?

"Hi-yup!" he shouted, but the horses did not heed him, for they were at the grave and the long sun gone out, burned out, dead forever until it kindled next time. "Too deep," Chenille told him standing by the grave. "Too deep," the frogs echoed her, frogs he had caught as a boy in the year that he and his mother had gone to the country for no reason and come back to a life no different, the frogs he had loved and killed with his love. *"Too deep!"* and the grave was too deep, though its bottom was lined with black velvet so that the sand and the cold clay would never touch her. The cold, sinking waters of underground streams that were sinking every year it seemed would never wash Orpine, would not rot her back to trees and flowers, never wash off

Blood's blood nor wet the fiery cat with the black mouse in its jaws, nor the golden hyacinths. Never fill the golden pool in which the golden crane watched golden fish forever; for this was no good year for golden fish, nor even for silver ones.

"Too deep!"

And it was too deep, so that the yellow dust would never fill it and the velvet at the bottom was sprinkled with sparks that might flicker at last but hadn't flickered yet as Maytera Marble told him pointing, and by the light of that one there she was young again, with a face like Maytera Mint's and brown gloves like flesh covering her hard-working steel fingers.

"Too long!" he told the horses, and the one that never pulled at all lunged and plunged and put his back into it, pulling for all he was worth, though the wind was in his teeth and the night darker than any night could be, with never a patch of skylands showing. The long road underground was buried forever in the billowing dust and all this blowing brush.

"Too long!"

Hyacinth sat beside him on the padded leather seat; after a time he gave her his old, bloodstained handkerchief to cover her nose and mouth. Though the wind bayed like a thousand yellow hounds, it could not blow their creaking, shining, old deadcoach off of this road that was no road at all, and he was glad of her company.

Chapter 5

THE SLAVE OF SPHIGX

It was Molpsday, Silk reminded himself as he sat up in bed: the day for light-footed speed, and after work for singing and dancing. He did not feel particularly light-footed as he sat up, swung his legs over the side of his bed, and rubbed his eyes and his bristling jaw. He had slept—how long? Almost too long, but he could still join the sibyls in their morning prayers if he hurried. It had been the first good night's sleep he had gotten since. . . .

Since Thelxday.

He stretched, telling himself he would have to hurry. Breakfast later or not at all, though there was still fruit left and vegetables enough for half the quarter.

He stood, resolved to hurry, received a flash of pain in his right ankle for his effort, and sat down again abruptly.

Blood's lioness-headed stick was leaning against the head of the bed, with Crane's wrapping on the floor beside it. He picked up the wrapping and lashed the floor with it.

"Sphigx will be the goddess for me today," he muttered, "my prop and my support." He traced the sign of addition in the air. "Thou Sabered, Stabbing, Roaring Sphigx, Lioness and Amazon, be with me to the end. Give me courage in this, my hour of hardship."

Crane's wrapping was burning hot; it squeezed his ankle like a vise and felt perfectly wonderful as he trotted down the stairs to fill his washbasin at the kitchen pump.

Oreb was asleep on top of the larder, standing on one leg, his head tucked beneath his sound wing. Silk called, "Wake up, old bird. Food? Fresh water? This is the time to ask."

Oreb croaked in protest without showing his face.

There was still some of his old cage left, and a large, live ember from the fire that had cooked no vegetables last night. Silk laid half a dozen twigs across it, puffed, and actually rubbed his hands at the sight of the young flame. He would not have to use any precious paper at all!

"It's morning," he told the bird. "The shade's up, and you should be too."

There was no reply.

Oreb, Silk decided, was openly ignoring him. "I have a broken ankle," he told the bird happily. "And a stiff arm—Master Xiphias thought I was left-handed, did I tell you about that? And a sore belly, and a fine big black-and-blue mark on my chest where Musk hit me with the pommel of his knife." He arranged three small splits on top of the blazing, snapping twigs. "But I don't care one bit. It's Molpsday, marvelous Molpsday, and I feel marvelous. If you're going to be my pet, so must you, Oreb." He clanged shut the firebox and set his shaving water on the stove.

"Fish heads?"

"No fish heads. There hasn't been time for fish heads, but I believe there might be a nice pear left. Do you like pears?"

"Like pears."

"So do I, so it's share and share alike." Fishing out of the sink the knife he had used to slice his tomatoes, he wiped the blade (noticing with a pang of guilt that it was beginning to rust) and whacked the pear in half, then bit into his share, drained the sink, pumped more water, and splashed his face, neck, and hair. "Wouldn't you like to join us for morning prayers, Oreb? You don't have to, but I have the feeling it might be good for you." Picturing Maytera Rose's reaction to the bird he laughed. "It would be good for me, too, in all likelihood."

"Bird sleep."

"Not until you've finished your pear, I trust. If it's still here when I get back, I'll eat it myself."

Oreb fluttered down to the tabletop. "Eat now."

"Very wise," Silk commended him, and took another bite from his half, thinking first of his dream—it had been a remarkable dream, from what he remembered of it— then of the yellowish surgical catgut lacing Mucor's scalp. Had he seen that, or merely dreamed it? And then of Crane who was a doctor too, and had almost certainly implanted the horned cats in the mad girl's womb, doubtless two or even three at a time.

Upstairs, while he lathered and scraped, he remembered what Chenille had said about getting enough money from Crane to save the manteion. Ordinarily he would have discarded any suggestion as wild as that summarily, but Chenille was not Chenille—or at least, not Chenille solely—and no matter what she might say, there was no point in deceiving himself about that, though politeness, apparently, demanded a pretense. He had begged Comely Kypris to return, but she had done him one better: she had never left—or rather, merely left the Sacred Window to possess Chenille.

It was a great honor for Chenille, to be sure. For a moment he envied her. He himself had been enlightened by the Outsider, however, and that was a greater honor still. After that, he should never envy anyone else anything at all. Kypris was the whores' goddess. Had Chenille been a good whore? And was she being rewarded for it? She—or rather, the goddess—or perhaps both—had said she would not go back to Orchid's.

He wiped and dried his razor and inspected his face in the mirror.

Did that mean, perhaps, that Kypris loved them without loving what they did? It was an inspiring thought, and very possibly a correct one. He did not know nearly as much as he urgently needed to know about Kypris, just as he remained lamentably ignorant of the Outsider, though the Outsider had showed him so very much and Kypris had revealed something of herself last night—her relations with Pas, particularly.

Silk toweled his face and turned to the wardrobe for a clean tunic, recalling as he did that Patera Remora had as much as ordered him to buy himself new clothes. With the cards left from Orpine's rites, there should be no trouble about that.

Hyacinth had held his tunic for him, had helped him put it back on despite his injured arm. He found that instead of running downstairs to join the sibyls in the manteion he was sitting on his bed again with his head in his hands, his head swimming with thoughts of Hyacinth. How beautiful she had been, and how kind! How wonderful, sitting beside him as they drove to the grave. He would have to die—all men died—and so would she; but they need not die alone. With a slight shock he realized that his dream had been no idle phantom of the night but had been sent by a god, no doubt by Hierax, who had figured in it (that in itself was a nearly determinative signature) with Orpine's white spirit in his hands.

Filled with joy again, Silk stood and snatched a clean tunic from the wardrobe. Blood had called his bird Hierax, a deliberate blasphemy. He, Silk, had killed that bird, or at least had fought against it and caused its death. Hierax therefore had favored him—indeed, Hierax had been fa-

voring him ever since, not only by sending him a dream
filled with the god's symbols, but by giving him Orpine's
very profitable rites. No one could say Hierax had been
ungrateful!

The robe he had worn the day before was soiled now,
and badly spotted with dried blood; but there was no clean
robe with which to replace it. He got out his clothes brush
and whaled away, making the dust fly.

Men and women, made of mud (originally by the Outsider, according to one somewhat doubtful passage in the
Writings) turned to dust at last. Fell to dust only too
quickly, in all truth. The same sober thought had crossed
his mind toward the close of Orpine's rites, as he had been
driving the screws to fasten the lid of Orpine's casket.

And Chenille had interrupted him, rising like—
like . . . The comparison slipped away. He tried to recreate
the scene in his mind. Chenille, taller than many men, with
tightly curled fiery hair, big bones, flat cheeks, and large
breasts, wooden yet twitching in her plain blue gown.

No. It had been a black gown, as was proper. Had she
been wearing blue when he had seen her first, at Orpine's?
No, green. Almost certainly green.

Horn's toy! That was it. He had never seen it. (He
brushed harder than ever.) But he had seen toys like it,
jointed figures worked with four strings on a wooden cross.
Horn's had worn a painted blue coat, and Chenille had, at
first, moved like such a toy, as if the goddess had not yet
learned to work her strings well. She had talked no better
than Oreb.

Was it possible that even a goddess had to learn to do
new things? That was a fresh thought indeed.

But goddesses learned quickly, it seemed; by the time
Patera Remora had arrived she had been able to throw
Musk's knife better than Musk himself. Musk, who last
night had given him a scant week in which to redeem the

manteion. The manteion might not be worth preserving, but the Outsider had told him to save it, so save it he must.

Now here was the pinch at last. What was he going to do today? Because there was no time to waste, none at all. He must get more time from Blood today—somehow—or acquire most or all of that enormous sum.

He slapped his trousers pocket. Hyacinth's needler was still there. Kneeling, he pulled the cashbox from beneath his bed, unlocked it, and took out the azoth; with the azoth under his tunic he relocked the cashbox, replaced the key, and returned the empty box to its hiding place.

"Sabered Sphigx," he murmured, "remember your servants, who live or die by the sword." It was a Guardsman's prayer, but it seemed to him that it suited him at least as well.

Chenille was waiting in the garden when Silk, preceded by Maytera Rose and followed by Maytera Marble and little Maytera Mint, emerged from the side door of the manteion. Oreb called, "Good Silk!" from her shoulder and hopped over to perch on his; but Maytera Rose's back was to him, so that he missed her expression—if in fact she had noticed the living bird.

Maytera Marble said, "I thought of inviting you to join us, Chenille, but you were sleeping so soundly. . . ."

Chenille smiled. "I'm glad you didn't, Maytera. I was terribly tired. I peeked in on you later, though. I hope you didn't see me."

"Did you really?" Maytera Marble smiled in return, her face lifted and her head cocked slightly to the right. "You should have joined us then. It would have been all right."

"I had Oreb, and he was frightened. You had reached the anamnesis, anyway."

Silk nodded to himself. There was nothing of Kypris in Chenille's face now, and the already-hot sunshine was cruel to it; but Chenille would not know that term. He said, "I hope that Chenille wasn't too much of a bother to you last night, Maytera?"

"No, no. None at all. None. But you'll have to excuse me now. The children will be arriving before long. I have to unlock, and look over the lesson."

As they watched her hurry away, Chenille said, "I make her nervous, I'm afraid. She'd like to like me, but she's afraid I've corrupted you."

"You make me nervous, too, Chenille," Silk admitted. As he spoke, both of them noticed Maytera Mint, waiting with downcast eyes in the diffused shade of the arbor. Softening his voice, Silk inquired, "Was there something you wished to speak to me about, Maytera?"

She shook her head without looking up.

"Perhaps you wanted to say farewell to your guest; but to tell the truth, I'm not sure she won't have to stay with you and your sibs tonight, as well."

For the first time since Silk had met her, Maytera Mint actually startled him, stepping out of the shadows to stare up into Chenille's face with a longing he could not quite fathom. "You don't make me nervous," she said, "and that's what I wanted to say to you. You're the only grown-up who doesn't. I feel drawn to you."

"I like you, too," Chenille said quietly. "I like you very much, Maytera."

Maytera Mint nodded, a nod (Silk thought) of acceptance and understanding. "I must be fifteen years older than you are. More, perhaps—I'll be thirty-seven next year. And yet I feel that— Perhaps it's only because you're so much taller . . ."

"Yes?" Chenille inquired gently.

"That you're really my older sister. I've never had an older sister, really. I love you." And with that, Maytera Mint whirled with a swirl of black bombazine and hurried off toward the cenoby, swerved suddenly halfway down the path, and cut across the dry, brown lawn toward the palaestra, on the other side of the playground.

"Bye-bye!" Oreb called. "Bye, girl!"

Silk shook his head. "I would never have expected that. The whorl holds possibilities beyond my imagining."

"Too bad." Chenille sighed. "I have to tell you. To explain. Silk. Patera. We ought to be talking about the other thing. Getting money from Crane. But I . . . We've a problem. There with poor Maytera Mint. It's my doing. In a way."

Silk said, "I hope it's not a serious problem. I like her, and I feel responsible for her."

"So do I. Still, we may. We do, I know. Perhaps we could go back to your little house? And talk?"

Silk shook his head. "Women aren't supposed to enter a manse, although there are a whole string of exceptions—when an augur's ill, a woman may come in to nurse him, for example. When I want to talk with Maytera Marble, we do it here in the arbor, or in her room in the palaestra."

"All right." Chenille ducked beneath the drooping grape vines. "What about Maytera Mint? And the old one, Maytera Rose? Where do you talk to them?"

"Oh, in the same places." With a slight pang of guilt, Silk took the old wooden seat across from Chenille's; it was the one in which Maytera Marble normally sat. "But to tell you the truth, I seldom talk very long with either of them. Maytera Mint is generally too shy to reply, and Maytera Rose lectures me." He shook his head. "I should listen to her much more closely than I do, I'm afraid; but after five or ten minutes I can't think of anything except getting away. I don't intend to imply that either isn't a very good woman. They are."

"Maytera Mint is." Chenille licked her lips. "That's why

I feel bad. As I do. Silk. It was . . . Well, not *me*. Not Chenille."

"Of course!" Silk nodded vigorously. "She senses the goddess in you! I should've understood at once. You don't want her to tell—"

"No, no. She does, but it's not that. And she won't tell anybody. She doesn't know herself. Not consciously."

Silk cleared his throat. "If you feel that there may be some physical attraction—I'm aware that these things take place among women as they do among men—it would certainly be better if you slept elsewhere tonight."

Chenille waved the subject away. "It wouldn't matter. But it's not that. She doesn't want . . . She doesn't want anything. Anything from me. She wants to help. Give me things. I understand it. It's not . . . discreditable. Is that what you'd say? Discreditable?"

"I suppose it is."

"But all this . . . It doesn't matter. None of it. I'm going to have to tell you. More. I won't lie." Her eyes flashed. "I *won't!*"

"I wouldn't want you to," Silk assured her.

"Yes. Yes, you do, Silk. Silk. Possession, you . . . We talked about it last night. You think a god . . . Me? I mean Kypris. Or another one. That horrible woman with the snakes. You think we go into people. Like fevers?"

"I certainly would not have put it like that."

Chenille studied him hungrily through heavy-lidded eyes that seemed larger than they had been outside the arbor, dark eyes that glowed with their own light. "But you think it. I know. We . . . It goes in through the eyes. We gods aren't . . . Something you see? We're patterns. We change. Learning and growing. But still patterns? And I'm not Kypris. I told you that. . . . You thought I lied."

Oreb whistled. "Poor girl!"

And Silk, who had turned away from the frightful power

and craving of those dark eyes, saw that they had begun to weep. He offered his handkerchief, recalling that Maytera Marble had given him hers, here under the arbor, before he had gone to Blood's villa.

"I didn't. I don't. Not much. Not unless I've got to. And I'm not. But what you call possession— Kypris copied a part, just a little part of herself." Chenille blew her nose softly. "I haven't had one little sniff. Not since before Orpine's . . . This's what it does, Patera. Not getting it, I mean. Everything you look at you think, that's not rust, and everything's so sad."

"It will be over very quickly," Silk said, hoping that he was right.

"A week. Maybe two. I did it, one other time. Only . . . Never mind. I wouldn't. I won't now. If you had a whole cup full of rust and held it out for me to take as much as I wanted right now, I wouldn't take any."

"That's wonderful," he said, and meant it.

"And that's because of the pattern. The little piece of Kypris that she's put inside of me, through my eyes, in your manteion yesterday. You don't understand, do you? I know you don't."

"I don't understand about the patterns," Silk said. "I understand the rest, or at least I believe I do."

"Like your heart. Patterns of beats. Yes, yes, no, no, no, yes, yes. There's this thing behind everybody's eyes. I don't understand everything myself. The mechanical woman? Marble? Somebody too clever learned he could do it to them. Change programs in little ways. People made machines. Just to do that. So that people like Maytera Marble would work for them instead of for the State. Steal for them. He . . . Pas, you call him. He had people study it. And they found out that you could do something like it with people. It was harder. The frequency was much higher. But you could, and so we do. That was how it all began. Silk. Through the terminals, through their eyes."

"Now I am lost," Silk admitted.

"It doesn't matter. But it's flashes of light. Light no one else can see. The thuds, the pulses, making up the program, the god that runs in Mainframe. Kypris is the god, that program. But she closed her eyes. Mint did. Maytera Mint. And I wasn't through, it wasn't finished."

Silk shook his head. "I know this must be important, and I'm trying to understand it; but to tell you the truth, I have no idea of what you mean."

"Then I'll lie." Chenille edged toward him until her knees touched his. "I'll lie, so that you can understand, Patera. Listen to me now. I . . . Kypris wanted to possess Maytera Mint—never mind why."

"You're Chenille now."

"I'm always Chenille. No, that's not right. Lying, I'm Kypris. All right, then. I'm Kypris now, talking the way Chenille used to. Say yes."

Silk nodded, "Yes, Great Goddess."

"Fine. I wanted to possess Maytera Mint by sending my divine person flowing into her, through her eyes, from the Sacred Window. See?"

Silk nodded again. "Certainly."

"I knew you'd understand. If it was wrong. All right. It feels good, really good, so practically nobody ever shuts their eyes. They want it. They want more. They don't even blink, drinking it in."

Silk said, "It's wholly natural for human beings to want some share of your divine life, Great Goddess. It's one of our deepest instincts."

"Only she did, and that's what you've got to understand. She only got a piece of me—of the goddess. I can't even guess what it may do to her."

Silk slumped, stroking his cheek.

Oreb, who had deserted Silk's shoulder to explore the vines, muttered, "Good girl."

"Yes, she is, Oreb. That's one of the reasons this worries me so much."

"Good now!"

After half a minute of anxious silence, Silk threw up his hands. "I wouldn't have believed that a god could be divided into parts."

Chenille nodded. "Me either."

"But you said—"

"I said it happened." She put her hand upon his knee. "I wouldn't have thought it could. But it did, and it may make her different. I think it already has. I'm Chenille, but I feel like there's somebody else in here with me now, a way of thinking about things and doing things that wasn't here till yesterday. She doesn't. She has a part of Kypris, like you might have a dream."

"This is a terrible thing to say, I suppose, Chenille. But can it be undone?"

She shook her head, her fiery curls bouncing. "Kypris could do it, but we can't. She'd have to be in front of a terminal—a Sacred Window or a glass, it wouldn't matter—when Kypris appeared. Even then, there'd be something left behind. There always is. Some of Maytera Mint's own . . . spirit would go into Kypris, too."

"But *you're* Kypris," Silk said. "I know that, and I keep wanting to kneel."

"Only in the lie, Patera. If I were a real goddess, you couldn't resist me. Could you? Really I'm Chenille, with something extra. Listen, here's another lie that may help. When somebody's drunk, haven't you ever heard somebody else say it was the brandy talking? Or the beer, or whatever?"

"Yes, that's a very common saying. I don't believe that anyone intends it seriously."

"All right, it's kind of like that. Not exactly, maybe, but pretty close, except that it won't ever die in her the way brandy does. Maytera Mint will be like she is now for the rest of her life, unless Kypris takes herself back—copies the part that went into her, with all of the changes, and erases what was in her."

"Then the only thing that we can do is watch her closely and be, ah," (Silk felt a sudden rush of sympathy for Patera Remora) "try to be tolerant of the unexpected."

"I'm afraid so."

"I'll tell Maytera Marble. I don't mean that I'll tell her what you told me, but I'll warn her. Maytera Rose would be worthless for this. Worse, if anything. Maytera Marble will be wonderful, although she can't be in her own room at the palaestra and in Maytera's at the same time, of course. Thank you, Chenille."

"I had to say something," Chenille dabbed at her nose and eyes. "Now, about the money. I was thinking about that while you were in the manteion, because I'm going to need it. I'm going to have to find a new way to live. A shop? Something . . . And I'll help you all I can, Silk. If you'll go halves?"

He shook his head. "I must have twenty-six thousand for Blood, so that I can buy this manteion from him; so that has to come first. But you can have anything above that amount. Say that we somehow obtain one hundred thousand—though I realize that's an absurd figure. You could keep seventy-four thousand of it. But if we obtain only twenty-six, the entire sum must go to Blood." He paused to look at her more closely. "You're shivering. Would it help if I brought out a blanket from the manse?"

"It will be over in a minute or two, Patera. Then I'll be fine. I've got a lot more control of this than she did. I'm taking you up. On your offer? Have I said that? Your generous offer. That's what I ought to call it. . . . Have you thought of a plan? I'm good at . . . certain things? But I'm not a very good planner. Not really, Silk. Silk? And neither was she. Am I talking right now?"

"I would say so, although I don't know her well. I was hoping you had devised a plan, however. As Chenille, you're much more familiar with Crane than I, and you should have a much clearer conception of the espionage operation that you tell me he's conducting."

"I've tried to think of something. Last night, and then again this morning. The easiest thing would be to threaten to reveal what he's doing, and I've got this." She took an image of Sphigx carved of hard, dark wood from a pocket of her gown. "I was supposed to give it to a woman who has a stall in the market? That's where I was going when I—you know. It was why I got dressed so fast? Then it happened, and I stayed at Orchid's. You know why. And then there was the exorcism. Your exorcism, Silk? So by the time I got to the market it was closing? There was hardly anybody left, except the ones who stay all night. To watch whatever they sell? She'd already gone."

Silk accepted the devotional image. "Sphigx is holding a sword," he murmured, "as she nearly always does in these representations. She also has something square, a tablet, perhaps, or a sheaf of papers; perhaps they represent Pas's instructions, but I don't think I've ever seen them before." He returned the carving to Chenille.

"You would have if you'd seen this woman's stall. She always had three or four of them? Most of them were bigger than this. I'd give mine to her, and she'd say something like are you sure you don't want it? Very pretty and very cheap. And I'd shake my head and go away, and she'd put it on the board with the rest, just like I'd only been looking at it for a minute."

"I see. That stall might be worth a visit." Uncertain how far he could presume upon the goddess's patronage, he hesitated before casting the dice. "It's a shame you're not actually Kypris. If you were, you might be able to tell me the significance of—"

"Man come!" announced Oreb from the top of the arbor, and a moment later they heard a loud knock at the door of the manse.

Silk rose and stepped from under the vines. "Over here, Auk. Won't you join us? I'm glad to see you, and there's someone else here whom you may be glad to see."

Chenille called, "Auk? Is that you? It's me. We need your help."

For a moment, Auk gaped. "Chenille?"

"Yes! In here. Come sit with me."

Silk parted the vines so that Auk could enter the arbor more easily; by the time that he himself had ducked inside, Auk was seated next to Chenille. Silk said, "You know each other, clearly."

Chenille dimpled, and suddenly seemed no older than the nineteen years she claimed. "Remember day before yesterday, Patera? When I said there was somebody? Somebody younger than Crane? And I said I thought he might help me . . . us? With Crane?"

Auk grinned and put his arm around her shoulders. "You know, I don't think I ever saw you in the daytime, Chenille. You're a lot better looking than I expected."

"I've always known how . . . handsome? You are, Auk." She kissed him, quickly and lightly, on the cheek.

Silk said, "Chenille's going to help me get the money that I need to save this manteion, Auk. That's what we've been talking about, and we'd like your advice."

He turned his attention to her. "I should tell you that Auk has already helped me—with advice, at least. I don't think he'll mind my saying that to you."

Auk nodded.

"And now both you and I require it. I'm sure he'll be as generous with us as he has been with me."

"Auk has always been . . . very good to me. Patera? He always asked for me. Since . . . spring?"

She clasped Auk's free hand in her own. "I won't be at Orchid's anymore, Auk. I want to live someplace else, and not . . . You know. Always asking men for money. And no more rust. It was . . . nice. Sometimes when I was afraid. But it makes girls too brave? After a while it owns you. With no rust, you're always so down. Always so scared. So you take it, take more, and get pregnant. Or get killed. I've been too brave. Not pregnant. I don't mean that. Patera will tell you. Auk?"

Auk said, "This sounds good. I like it. I guess you two got together after the funeral, huh?"

"That's right." Chenille kissed him again. "I started thinking. About dying, and everything, you know? There was Orpine and she was so young and healthy and all that? Am I talking better now, Patera Silk? Tell me, and please don't spare my feelings."

Oreb poked his brightly colored head from the half-dead grape leaves to declare, "Talk good!"

Silk nodded, hoping that his face betrayed nothing. "That's fine, Chenille."

"Patera's helping me sound more . . . You know. Uphill? Auk. And I thought Orpine could be me. So I waited. We had a big talk last night, didn't we, Silk? And I stayed with the sibyls." She giggled. "A hard bed and no dinner, not a bit like Orchid's. But they gave me breakfast. Have you eaten breakfast, Auk?"

Auk grinned and shook his head. "I haven't been to bed. You heard what the goddess said yesterday, didn't you, Jugs? Well, look here."

Taking his arm from her shoulders and half standing, Auk groped in his pocket. When his hand emerged, it coruscated with white fire. "Here you go, Patera. Take it. It's not any shaggy twenty-six thousand, but it ought to bring three or four, if you're careful where you sell it. I'll tell you about some people I know." When Silk did not reach for the proffered object, Auk tossed it into his lap.

It was a woman's diamond anklet, three fingers wide. "I really can't—" Silk swallowed. "Yes, I suppose I can. I will because I must. But, Auk—"

Auk slapped his thigh. "You got to! You were the one that could understand Lady Kypris, weren't you? Sure you were, and you told us. No fooling around about having to get the word from somebody else first. All right, she said it and I believed it, and now I got to let her know I'm the pure keg, too. They're all real. You look at them all you want to. Get some nice sacrifices for her, and don't forget to tell her where they come from."

Silk nodded. "I will, though she will know already, I'm sure."

"Tell her Auk's a dimber cull. Treat him brick and he treats you stone." Taking Chenille's hand, Auk slipped a ring onto her finger. "I didn't know you were going to be here, but this's for you, Jugs. Twig that big red flare? That's what they call a real blood ruby. Maybe you scavy you seen 'em before, but I lay five you didn't. You going to sell it or keep it?"

"I couldn't ever sell this, Hackum." She kissed him on the lips, so passionately that Silk was forced to avert his eyes, and so violently that they both nearly fell from the little wooden bench. When they parted, she added, "You gave it to me, and I'm going to keep it forever."

Auk grinned and wiped his mouth and grinned again, wider than ever. "Sharp now. If you change your mind don't do it without me with you."

He turned back to Silk. "Patera, you got any idea what shook last night? I'd bet there was a dozen houses solved up on the Palatine. I haven't heard yet what else went on. The hoppies are falling all over themselves this morning." He lowered his voice. "What I wanted to talk to you about, Patera—what'd she say to you exactly? About coming back here?"

"Only that she would," Silk told him.

Auk leaned toward him, his big jaw outthrust and his eyes narrowed. "What words?"

Silk stroked his cheek, recalling his brief conversation with the goddess in the Sacred Window. "You're quite right. I'm going to have to report everything she said to the Chapter, verbatim, and in fact I should be writing that report now. I pleaded with her to return. I can't give you the precise words, and they aren't important anyway; but she replied, 'I will. Soon.' "

"She meant this manteion here? Your manteion?"

"I can't be absolutely—"

Chenille interrupted him. "You know she did. That's just what she meant. She meant that she was going to come right back to the same Window."

Silk nodded reluctantly. "She didn't actually say that, as I told you; but I feel—now, at least—that it must have been what she intended."

"Right . . ." Chenille had found a patch of sunlight that drew red fire from the ring; she watched it as she spoke, turning her hand from side to side. "But we've got to tell you about Crane, Auk. Do you know Crane? He's Blood's pet doctor."

"Patera might've said something last night."

Auk looked his question to Silk, who said, "I did not actually tell Auk, although I may have hinted or implied that I believe that Doctor Crane may have presented an azoth to a certain young woman called Hyacinth. Those cost five thousand cards or more, as you probably know; and thus I was quite ready to believe you when you suggested that it might be possible to extort a very large sum from him. If he did give such a thing to Hyacinth—and I'm inclined to think he did—he must control substantial discretionary funds." Compelled by an inner need, Silk added, "Do you know her, by the way?"

"Uh-huh. She does what I used to do, but she's working for Blood direct now, instead of Orchid. She left Orchid's a couple weeks, maybe, after I moved in."

Reluctantly, Silk dropped the gleaming anklet into the pocket of his robe. "Tell me everything you know about her, please."

"Some of the other dells know her better than I do. I like her, though. She's—I'm not quite sure how to put it. She's not always saying, well, this one's good but that one's bad. She takes people the way they come, and she'll help you if she can, even if you haven't always been as nice to her as you ought to be. Her father's a head clerk in the Juzgado. Are you sure you want to hear this, Silk?"

"Yes, indeed."

"And one of the commissioners saw her when she was maybe fourteen and said, 'Listen, I need a maid. Send her up and she can live at my house'—they had eight or nine sprats, I guess—'and she can make a little money, too, and you'll get a nice promotion.' Hy's father was just a regular clerk then, probably.

"So he said all right and sent Hy up on the Palatine, and you know what happened then. She didn't have to work much—no hard work, just serve meals and dust, and she started to get quite a bit of money. Only after a while the commissioner's wife got really nasty. She lived for a while with a captain, but there was some sort of trouble. . . . Then she came to Orchid's."

Chenille blew her nose into Silk's handkerchief. "I'm sorry, Patera. It's always like this if you haven't had any for a day or so. My nose will run and my hands will shake until

Tarsday, probably. After that everything ought to be all right."

For Auk's sake as well as his own, Silk asked, "You're not going to use rust anymore? No matter how severe your symptoms become?"

"Not if we're going to do this. It makes you too brave. I guess I said that. Didn't I? It's great to have a sniff or a lipful. . . . Some people do that too, but it takes more when you're scared practically to death. But after a while you find out that it was what you ought to have been scared of. It's worse than Bass or even Musk, and a lot worse than the cull that looked so bad out in the big room. Only by that time it's got you. It has me, and it has Hy, too, I think. Silk?"

He nodded, and Auk patted Chenille's arm.

"I know her, but now that I think about her, there's not a whole lot I know, and I've already told you most of it. Have you seen her?"

"Yes," Silk said. "Phaesday night."

"Then you know how good-looking she is. I'm too tall for most bucks. They like dells tall, but not taller than they are, or even the same. Hy's just right. But even if I was this much shorter, they'd still run after her instead of me. She's getting really famous, and that's why she works for Blood direct. He won't split with Orchid or any of the others on somebody that brings in as much as she does."

Silk nodded to himself. "He has other places, besides the yellow house on Lamp Street?"

"Oh, sure. Half a dozen, most likely. But Orchid's is one of the best." Chenille paused, her face pensive. "Hy was kind of flat-chested when I met her at Orchid's. . . . I guess that's something else Crane's given her, huh? Two big things."

Auk chuckled.

"From what you've said, she was born here in Viron."

"Sure, Patera. Over on the east side someplace? Or at

least that's what I heard. There's another girl at Orchid's from the same quarter."

Auk said, "Patera thinks she might be an informant. For you and him, now, I guess."

"And he'll want to pay her from my share," Chenille said bitterly. "Nothing doing unless I give the nod."

"That isn't what I meant at all. As Auk just told you, I believe that Hyacinth might help me against Blood; but I have no reason to believe that she would willingly help us against Crane, which is what we need at present. I ought to explain, Auk, that Chenille feels quite sure that Crane is spying on Viron, although we don't know for what city. Do we, Chenille?"

"No. He never said he was a spy at all, and I hope that I never said he did. But he is . . . he was hot to find out about all sorts of gammon, Auk. Especially about the Guard. He just about always wanted to know if any of the colonels had been in, and what did they say? And I still think the little statues are messages, Patera, or they've got messages inside them."

Sensing Auk's disapproval, she added, "I didn't know, Hackum. He was nice to me, so I helped him now and then. I didn't get flash till yesterday."

Auk said, "I wish I'd met this Crane. He must be quite a buck. You're going to wash him down, or try to, Patera? You and Jugs?"

"Yes, if washing someone down means what I suppose it does."

"It means you deal him out and keep the cards. You're going to try to bleed your twenty-six out of him?"

Chenille nodded, and Silk said, "Much more, if we can, Auk. Chenille would like to buy a shop."

"The easy out for him would be to lay you both on ice. You scavy that?"

"To murder us, you mean, or to have someone else do

it. Yes, of course. If Crane is a spy, he won't hesitate to do that; and if he controls money enough to present Hyacinth with an azoth, he could readily employ someone else to do it, I imagine. We will have to be circumspect."

"I'll say. I could name you twenty bucks who'd do it for a hundred, and some of 'em good. If this cull Crane's been working for Blood long—"

"For the past four years," Silk put in, "or so he told me that night."

"Then he'll know who to get about as good as I do. This Hy—" Auk scratched his head. "You remember when we had dinner? You told me about the azoth, and I told you I bet Crane's got a lock. Well, if he was after Jugs to tell him about colonels, this Hy would be a lot better from what you said about her. So that's the lock. She was staying out at Blood's place in the country, right? Does she ever come into town?"

"She seemed to be. She had a suite of rooms there, and the monitor in her glass referred to her as its mistress." Silk recalled Hyacinth's wardrobes, in which the monitor had suggested he hide. "She had a great deal of clothing there, too."

Chenille said, "She gets to the city pretty often, but I'm not sure where she goes . . . or when. When she does, there'll be somebody with her to watch her, unless Blood's gone abram."

Auk straightened up, his left hand on the hilt of the big, brass-mounted hanger he wore. "All right. You wanted my advice, Patera. I'll give it to you, but I don't think you're going to get it down easy."

"I'd like to have it, nevertheless."

"I thought you would. You run wide of this Hy, for now anyhow. Just finding her's liable to be dicey, and more than likely she'll squeak to this Crane buck straight off. Jugs says she didn't know she was spying. Maybe so. But if this Crane stood this Hy an azoth, you can bet the basket this Hy knows, and is trotting behind. If she was the only handle you had, I'd say go to it. But that's not the lay. If this Crane had Jugs telling him all about colonels and what they said, and this Hy doing the same, and that's what it sounds like, wouldn't he have maybe four or five others, too? Most likely at some of Blood's other kens. And when Jugs is gone—'cause she says she's going—won't he line up somebody else at Orchid's?"

Chenille suggested, "The best thing might be for me to go back to Orchid's after all. If I'd talk against Viron a little, he might let me help more. Maybe I could find out who the woman in the market is."

Silk explained, "There's a stallkeeper there who seems to be a contact of Crane's, Auk. Crane had Chenille carry images of Sphigx to her. Was it always Sphigx, Chenille?"

She nodded, her fiery curls trembling. "They always looked just like that one I showed you, as near as I can remember."

"Then see what happens to them," Auk suggested. "When the market closes, where does this mort go?"

"Good Silk!" Oreb dropped from the vines to light in his lap. "Fish heads?"

"Possibly," Silk told the bird, as it hopped onto his shoulder. "In fact, I think it likely."

He returned his attention to Auk. "You're quite right, of course. I've been thinking too much about Hyacinth. I'd hate to see Chenille return to Orchid's, but either of the courses that you suggest—and they're by no means mutually exclusive—would be preferable to approaching Hyacinth, I'm afraid, without some hold on her. When we learn a bit more, however, we should have such a hold. We'll be able to warn her that we know Crane's an agent of another city, that we have evidence that's at least highly suggestive,

and that we're aware that she's been assisting him. We'll
offer to protect her, provided that she'll assist us."

Chenille asked, "You don't think Crane's Vironese? He
talks like one of us."

"No. Mostly because he seems to control so much
money, but also because of something he once said to me.
I know nothing of spies or spying, however. Nor do you, I
think. What about you, Auk?"

The big man shrugged. "You hear this and that. Mostly
it's traders, from what they say."

"I suppose that practically every city must question its
traders when they return home, and no doubt some traders
are actually trained agents. I would imagine that an agent
well supplied with money would be like them—that is to
say, a citizen in the service of his native city—and probably
thoroughly schooled in the ways of the place to which he
was to be sent. An agent willing to betray his own city might
betray yours as well, surely; particularly if he were given a
chance to make off with a fortune."

Chenille asked, "What was it Crane said to you, Patera?"

Silk leaned toward her. "What color are my eyes?"

"Blue. I wish mine were."

"Suppose that a patron at Orchid's requested a companion with blue eyes. Would Orchid be able to oblige
him?"

"Arolla. No, she's gone now. But Bellflower's still there.
She has blue eyes, too."

Silk leaned back. "You see, blue eyes are unusual—here
in Viron, at any rate; but they're by no means really rare.
Collect a hundred people, and it's quite likely that at least
one will have blue eyes. I notice them because I used to be
teased about mine. Crane noticed them, too; but he, a
much older man than I, said that mine were only the third
he'd seen. That suggests that he has spent most of his life

in another city, where people are somewhat darker and blue eyes rarer than they are here."

Auk grinned. "They got tails in Gens. That's what they say."

Silk nodded. "Yes, one hears all sorts of stories, most quite false, I'm sure. Nevertheless, you have only to look at the traders in the market to see that there are contrasts as well as similarities."

He paused to collect his thoughts. "I've let myself be drawn off the subject, however. I was going to say, Auk, that although both the courses you suggested are promising, there is a third that seems more promising still to me. You're not at fault for failing to point it out, since you weren't here when Chenille provided the intimation.

"Chenille, you told me that a commissioner had been to Orchid's, remember? And that Crane was intensely interested when you told him that this commissioner had told you he had gone to Limna—you said to the lake, but I assume that's what was intended—to confer with two councillors."

Chenille nodded.

"That started me thinking. There are five councillors in the Ayuntamiento. Where do they live?"

She shrugged. "On the hill, I guess."

"That's what I'd always supposed myself. Auk, you must be far more familiar with the residents of the Palatine than either Chenille or I am. Where does, say, Councillor Galago make his home?"

"I always figured in the Juzgado. I hear there's flats in there, besides some cells."

"The councillors have offices in the Juzgado, I'm sure. But don't they have mansions on the Palatine as well? Or their own country villas like Blood's?"

"What they say is nobody's supposed to know, Patera. If they did, people would always be wanting to talk to them or throw rocks. But I know who's in every one of those houses on the hill, and it isn't them. All the commissioners have big places up there, though."

Silk's voice sank to a murmur. "But when a commissioner was to speak with several councillors, he did not go home to the Palatine. Nor did he merely ascend a floor or two in the Juzgado. From what Chenille says, he went to Limna—to the lake, as he told her. When one man is to speak with several, he normally goes to them rather than having them come to him, and that is particularly so when they're his superiors. Now if Crane is in fact a spy, he must surely be concerned to discover where every member of the Ayuntamiento lives, I'd think. All sorts of things might be learned from their servants, for example." He fell silent.

"Go on, Patera," Chenille urged.

He smiled at her. "I was merely thinking that since you told Crane about the commissioner's boast some months ago, he's apt to have been there several times by now. I want to go there myself today and try to find out who he's talked to and what he's said to them. If the gods are with me—as I've reason to believe—that alone may provide all the evidence we require."

She said, "I'm coming with you. How about you, Auk?"

The big man shook his head. "I've been up all night, like I told you. But I'll tell you what. Let me get a little sleep, and I'll meet you in Limna where the wagons stop. Say about four o'clock."

"You needn't put yourself out like that, Auk."

"I want to. If you've got something by then, I might be able to help you get more. Or maybe I can turn up something myself. There's good fish places there, and I'll spring for dinner and ride back to the city with you."

Chenille hugged him. "I always knew how handsome you were, Hackum, but I never knew how sweet you are. You're a real dimberdamber!"

Auk grinned. "To make a start, this's my city, Jugs. It's not all gilt, but it's all I got. And there's a few friends in the Guard. When you two have washed down this buck Crane, what do you plan to do with him?"

Silk said, "Report him, I'd think."

Chenille shook her head. "He'd tell about the money, and they'd want it. We might have to kill him ourselves. Didn't you augurs send sprats to Scylla in the old days?"

"That could get him tried for murder, Jugs," Auk told her. "No, what you want to do is roll this Crane over to Hoppy. Only if you're going to queer it, you'd be better off doing him. They'll beat it out of you, grab the deck and send you with him. It'd be a lily grab on you, Jugs, 'cause you helped him. As for the Patera here, Crane saw to his hoof and rode him to Orchid's in his own dilly, so it'd be candy to smoke up something."

He waited for them to contradict him, but neither did.

"Only if you go flash, if you roll him over to some bob culls with somebody like me to say Pas for you, we'll all be stanch cits and heroes too. Hoppy'll grab the glory while we buy him rope. That way he'll hand us a smoke smile and a warm and friendly shake, hoping we'll have something else to roll another time. I've got to have pals like that to lodge and dodge. So do you two, you just don't know it. You scavy I never turned up the bloody rags, riffling some cardcase's ken? You scavy I covered 'em up and left him be? Buy it, I washed him if he'd stand still. And if he wouldn't, why, I rolled him over."

Silk nodded. "I see. I felt that your guidance would be of value, and I don't believe that Chenille could call me wrong. Could you, Chenille?"

She shook her head, her eyes sparkling.

"That's rum, 'cause I'm not finished yet. What's this hotpot's name, Jugs?"

"Simuliid."

"I'm flash. Big cully, ox weight, with a mustache?"

She nodded.

"Patera and me ought to pay a call, maybe, when we get back from the lake. How's your hoof, Patera?"

"Much better today," Silk said, "but what have we to gain from seeing the commissioner?"

Oreb cocked his head attentively and hopped up into the grapevines again.

"I hope we won't. I want a look around, 'specially if you and Jugs go empty at the lake. Maybe those councillors live way out there like you say, Patera. But maybe, too, there's something out there that they wanted to show off to him, or that he had to show off to them. You hear kink talk about the lake, and if you and Jugs plan to fish for this Crane cull, you might want bait. So we'll pay this Simuliid a call, up on the hill tonight. Plate to me, bait to you, and split the overs."

Oreb hopped onto the back of the old wooden seat. "Man come!"

Nodding, Silk rose and parted the vines. A thick-bodied young man in an augur's black robe was nudging shut the side door of the manteion; he appeared to be staring at something in his hands.

"Over here," Silk called. "Patera Gulo?" He stepped out of the arbor and limped across the dry, brown grass to the newcomer. "May every god favor you this day. I'm very pleased to see you, Patera."

"A man in the street, Patera"—Gulo held up a dangling, narrow object sparkling with yellow and green—"he simply—we—he wouldn't—"

Auk had followed Silk. "Mostly topaz, but that looks like a pretty fair emerald." Reaching past him, he relieved Gulo of the bracelet and held it up to admire.

"This lady's Chenille, Patera Gulo." By a gesture, Silk indicated the arbor, "and this gentleman is Auk. Both are prominent laypersons of our quarter, exceedingly devout and cherished by all of the gods, I feel sure. I'll be leaving with them in a few minutes, and I rely on you to deal with the affairs of our manteion during my absence. You'll find Maytera Marble—in the cenoby there—a perfect fisc of valuable information and sound advice."

"A man gave it to me!" Gulo blurted. "Just a minute ago, Patera. He simply pressed it into my hand!"

"I see." Silk nodded matter-of-factly as he reassured himself that the azoth beneath his tunic was indeed there. "Return that to Patera Gulo, please, Auk.

"You'll find our cashbox under my bed, Patera. The key is underneath the carafe on the nightstand. Wait a moment." He took the diamond anklet from his pocket and handed it to Gulo. "Put them in there and lock them up safely, if you will, Patera. It might be best for you to keep the key in your pocket. I should return about the time that the market closes, or a little after."

"Bad man!" Oreb proclaimed from the top of the arbor. "Bad man!"

"It's your black robe, Patera," Silk explained. "He's afraid he may be sacrificed. Come here, Oreb! We're off to the lake. Fish heads, you silly bird."

In a frantic flurry of wings, the injured night chough landed heavily on Silk's own black-robed shoulder.

Chapter 6

LAKE LIMNA

"What was it you said, my son?" Silk dropped to one knee to bring his face to the height of the small boy's own.

"Ma says ask a blessing." His attention seemed equally divided between Silk and Oreb.

"And why do you wish it?"

The small boy did not reply.

"Isn't it because you want the immortal gods to view you with favor, my son? Didn't they teach you something about that at the palaestra? I'm sure they must have."

Reluctantly, the small boy nodded.

Silk traced the sign of addition over the boy's head and recited the shortest blessing in common use, ending it with, "In the name of their eldest child, Scylla, Patroness of this, Our Holy City of Viron, and in that of the Outsider, of all gods the eldest."

"Are you really Patera Silk?"

None of the half dozen persons waiting for the holobit wagon to Limna turned to look, yet Silk was painfully aware of a sudden stiffening of postures; Lake Street, although it was far from quiet, seemed somehow quieter.

"Yes, he is," Chenille announced proudly.

One of the waiting men stepped toward Silk and knelt,

his head bowed. Before Silk could trace the sign of addition, two more had knelt beside the first.

He was saved by the arrival of the wagon—long-bodied, gaily painted, surmounted by a jiggling old patterned canvas canopy, and drawn by two weary horses. "One bit," boomed the driver, vaulting from his post. "A bit to Limna. No credit no trade, everybody sits in the shade."

"I've got it," Chenille said.

"So do I," Silk told her in his most inflexible tone, and hushed several passengers who tried say that Patera Silk ought to ride free. When he pocketed Silk's bits, the driver said, "You'll have to get off if anybody complains about the bird," and was startled by a chorus of protests.

"I don't like this," Silk told Chenille as they found places on one of the long, outward-facing benches. "People have been writing things on walls, and I don't like that, either."

The driver cracked his whip, and the wagon lurched ahead.

" 'Silk for Caldé . . . ?' Is that what you mean, Silk? A good idea."

"That's right." He extracted his beads from his pocket. "Or rather, it's wrong. Wrong as concerns me, and wrong as it concerns the office of caldé. I'm not a politician, and no inducement that you could name would ever persuade me to become one. As for the caldéship, it's become nothing more than a popular superstition, a purely historical curiosity. My mother knew the last caldé, but he died shortly after I was born."

"I remember him. I think?"

Without looking at her, Silk told her miserably, "If you meant half what you've said, you can't possibly recall him, Comely Kypris. Chenille's four years younger than I am."

"Then I'm thinking about . . . someone else. Aren't you

worried? Silk? Traveling with somebody like me? All of these people know who you are."

"I hope that they do, Great Goddess, and that they're thoroughly disillusioned now—that without dishonoring my sacred calling I save my life."

A particularly vicious jolt threw Silk against the woman on his right, who apologized profusely. When he had begged her pardon instead, he began the prayer of the voided cross. "Great Pas, designer and creator of the whorl, lord guardian and keeper of the Aureate Path—" The path across the sky that was the spiritual equivalent of the sun, he reminded himself. Sacrifices rose to it, and so were brought in the end to Mainframe, where both the sun and the Path began, at the east pole. The spirits of the dead walked that glorious road, too, if not weighted with evil, and it was asserted in the Chrasmologic Writings that the spirits of certain holy theodidacts had at times abandoned the shapen mud of their corporeal bodies and—joining the crowding, lowing beasts and the penitent dead—journeyed to Mainframe to confer for a time with the god who had enlightened them. He himself was a theodidact, Silk reminded himself, having been enlightened by the Outsider.

He had finished the voided cross and (he counted them by touch) four beads already. Murmuring the prescribed prayers and adding the name of the Outsider to them all, he willed himself to leave his body and this crowded street and unite with the hastening traffic of the Aureate Path.

For an instant it seemed that he had succeeded, though it was not the sun's golden road that he saw, but the frigid black emptiness beyond the whorl, dotted here and there with gleaming sparks.

"Talking of writing on walls, Silk. Silk? Look there. Open your eyes."

He did. It was a poster, badly but boldly printed in red and black, so new that no one had yet torn it or scrawled an obscene drawing over it, which in this quarter probably meant that it had been up less than an hour.

STRONG YOUNG MEN
WILL BE WELCOMED IN
THE NEW PROVISIONAL RESERVE BRIGADE
Have YOU Wished to Become a GUARDSMAN?
The Reserve Brigade Will Drill Twice Weekly
Will Receive PAY and UNIFORMS
Will Receive FIRST CONSIDERATION
for
TRANSFER TO THE REGULAR FORMATIONS
Apply
THIRD BRIGADE HEADQUARTERS
Colonel Oosik, Commanding

"You don't think the kite tired him too much?"

It was not the first time Blood had asked the question, and Musk had tired of saying no. This time he said, "I told you. Aquila's a female." The huge hooded bird on his wrist baited as he spoke, whether at the sound of her name, or at that of his voice, or by mere coincidence. Musk waited for her to slake before he finished the thought. "Males don't get this big. For Molpe's sake listen sometime."

"All right—all right. Maybe a smaller one could fly higher."

"She can do it. The bigger they are, the higher they fly. You ever see a sparrow fly any higher than that bald head of yours?" Musk spoke without looking at the fleshy, red-faced man to whom he spoke, his eyes upon his eagle or on the sky. "I still think we should've let Hoppy in."

"If they bring it back, in a week they'll have done it themselves."

"They fly high, way up close to the sun. If we get one, he could come down anywhere."

"We've got three floaters with three men in each floater. We've got five on highriders."

With his free hand, Musk lifted his binoculars. Though he knew there was nothing there, he scanned the clear vacancy overhead.

"Don't point those things at the sun. You could blind yourself." It was not the first time Blood had said that, either.

"He could come down anywhere in the whorl. You heard where the kite came down, and it was on a shaggy string, for Molpe's sake. You think that it's got to be close to a road because you travel on them." It was a long speech for Musk. "If you'd hunted with my hawks a couple of times, you'd know different. Most of the whorl's not anywhere near any shaggy road. Most of the whorl's twenty, thirty, fifty stades from a shaggy road."

"That's good," Blood said. "What I'm afraid of is some farmer peeping to Hoppy." He waited for Musk to speak again; when Musk did not, he added, "They can't really get up near the sun. The sun's a lot hotter than any fire. They'd be burned to death."

"Maybe they don't burn." Musk lowered his binoculars. "Maybe they're not even people."

"They're people. Just like us."

"Then maybe they got needlers."

Blood said, "They won't carry anything they don't have to carry."

"I'm shaggy glad you know. I'm shaggy glad you asked them."

Aquila adjusted the position of one huge talon with a minute jingle of hawk bells as Musk lifted his binoculars again.

"There's one!" Blood said unnecessarily. "Are you going to fly her?"

"I don't know," Musk admitted. "He's a long ways off, the yard."

Blood trained his own binoculars on the flier. "He's coming closer. He's headed this way!"

"I know. That's why I'm watching him."

"He's high."

Musk struggled to speak in the bored and bitter tones he had affected since childhood. "I've seen them higher." The thrill of the hunt was upon him, as sudden as a fever and as welcome as spring.

"I told you about that big gun they built. They shot at them for a month, but shells don't go straight up there, and they couldn't get them high enough anyway."

Musk let his binoculars drop to his chest. He could see the flier clearly now, silhouetted against the silver mirror that was Lake Limna, mounting into the sky on the other side of the city.

"Wait for him to get closer," Blood said urgently.

"If we wait much longer, he'll be farther by the time she gets up there."

"What if—"

"Stand back. If she goes for you, you're dead." With his free hand Musk grasped the crown of scarlet plumes and snatched the hood. *"Away, hawk!"*

This time there was no hesitation. The eagle's immense wings spread, and she sprang into the air with a whirlwind roar that for a moment frightened even Musk, flying hard at first, laboring to gain the thermal from the roof, then lifting, rising, and soaring, a jet black, heraldic bird against the sun-blind blue of the open sky.

"Maybe the rabbit filled her up."

Musk laughed. "That baby bunny? It was the littlest we

had. That only made her strong." For the second time since they had met, he took Blood's hand.

And Blood, desperately happy but pretending that nothing had occurred, inquired as calmly as he could, "You think she sees him?"

"Shag yes, she sees him. She sees everything. If she went straight for him she'd spook him. She'll get above him and come down at him out of the sun." Unconsciously Musk rose upon his toes, so as to be, by the thickness of three fingers, nearer his bird. "Just like a goose. Just like he was a big goose. They're born knowing it. You watch." His pale, handsome face was wreathed in smiles; his devil's eyes glittered like black ice. "You just watch her, old cully shagger."

Iolar saw the eagle far below him to the north, and put on speed. The front, marked by a line of towering clouds, was interesting and might even be important; but the front was two hundred leagues off, if not more, and might never reach this parched and overheated region. The index was a hundred fifteen here, a hundred nine over much of the sun's length; with the seasonal adjustment—he checked the date mentally—a hundred and eighteen here.

He had forgotten the eagle already.

He was a small man by any standard, and as thin as his own main struts; his eyes were better than average, and most of those who knew him thought him introverted and perhaps a trifle cold-blooded. He seldom spoke; when he did, his talk was of air masses and prevailing winds, of landmarks by day and landmarks by night, of named solar reaches unrecognized (or only grudgingly recognized) by science, and of course of wings and flightsuits and instruments and propulsion modules. But then the talk of all fliers was like that. Because he was so near the ideal, both physically and mentally, he had been permitted three wives, but the second had left him after something less than a year. The first had borne him three nimble, light-boned children, however, and the third, five as cheerful and active as crickets, of whom the younger girl was his favorite, tiny, laughing-eyed Dreoilin. "I can see the wings of her," he sometimes told her mother; and her mother, who could not, always happily agreed. He had been flying for eighteen years.

His increased speed had cost him altitude. He upped the thrust again and tried to climb, but the temperature of the air was falling a bit, and the air with it in the daylight downdraft of the big lake. There would be a corresponding updraft once he got over land again, and he resolved to take it as high as it would take him. He would need every cubit of altitude he could scrape up when he reached those distant thunderheads.

He did not see the eagle again until it was almost upon him, flying straight down, the enormous thrust of its wings driving it toward the land below far faster than any falling stone until, at the last possible split second, it folded its wings, spun in the air, and struck him with its talons, double blows like those of a giant's mailed fists.

Perhaps it stunned him for a moment. Certainly the wild whirl of earth and sky did not disorient him; he knew that his left wing was whole and sound, that the other was not, and that his PM did not respond. He suspected that he had half a dozen broken ribs and perhaps a broken spine as well, but he gave little attention to those. With a superb skill that would have left his peers openmouthed, could they have witnessed it, he turned his furious tumble into a controlled dive, jettisoned the PM and his instruments, and had halved his rate of descent before he hit the water.

"Did you see that splash!" Chenille rose from her seat in the holobit wagon as she spoke, shading her eyes against the sunglare from the water. "There are some monster fish in the lake. Really huge. I remember—I haven't been out here since I was a little girl. . . . Or anyhow, I don't think I have."

Nodding, Silk ducked from under the canopy to glance at the sun. Unveiled by clouds moving from east to west, that golden blaze streaking the sky was—he reminded himself again—the visible symbol of the Aureate Path, the course of moral probity and fitting worship that led Man to the gods. Had he strayed? He had felt no willingness in himself to offer Crane in sacrifice, though a goddess had suggested it.

And that, surely, was not what the gods expected from an anointed augur.

"Fish heads?" Oreb tugged at Silk's hair.

"Fish heads indeed," he told the bird, "and that is a solemn promise."

Tonight he would help Auk rob Chenille's commissioner. Commissioners were rich and oppressive, battening upon the blood and sweat of the poor; no doubt this one could spare a few jewels and his silver service. Yet robbery was wrong at base, even when it served a greater good.

Though this was Molpsday, he murmured a final prayer to Sphigx as he returned his beads to his pocket. Sphigx above all would understand; Sphigx was half lioness, and lions had to kill innocent creatures in order to eat—such was the inflexible decree of Pas, who had given to every creature save Man its proper food. As he completed the prayer, Silk bowed very slightly to the ferocious, benevolent face on the handle of Blood's walking stick.

"We used to come here to pick watercress," Chenille said. "Way over on that side of the lake. We'd start out before shadeup and walk here, Patera. I don't know how many times I've watched for the water at the first lifting. If I couldn't see it, I'd know we had a long way to go yet. We'd have paper, any kind of paper we could find, and we'd wet it good and wrap our watercress in it, then hurry back to the city to sell it before it wilted. Sometimes it did, and that was all we had to eat. I still won't eat it. I buy it, though, pretty often, from little girls in the market. Little girls like I was."

"That's very good of you," Silk told her, though he was already planning.

"Only there isn't much these days, because so many of the best cress creeks have gone dry. I never eat it anyway. Sometimes I feed it to the goats, you know? And sometimes I just throw it away. I wonder how many of the ladies that used to buy it from me did the same thing."

The woman next to Silk said, "I make sandwiches. Watercress and white cheese on rye bread. I wash it thoroughly first, though."

Silk nodded and smiled.

"It makes a fine hot weather lunch."

Speaking across Silk, Chenille asked her, "Do you have friends here in Limna?"

"Relations," the woman said. "My husband's mother lives out here. She thinks the pure air off the lake is good for her. Wouldn't it be wonderful if our relations could be our friends, too?"

"Oh, wouldn't it, though! We're looking for a friend. Doctor Crane? A small man, around fifty, rather dark? He has a little gray beard . . . ?"

"I don't know him," the woman said grimly, "but if he's a doctor and he lives in Limna, my mother-in-law does. I'll ask her."

"He just bought a cottage here. So that he can get away from his practice, you know? My husband's helping him move in, and Patera's promised to bless it for him. Only I can't remember where it is."

The man on her left said, "You can ask at the Juzgado,

on Shore Street. He'll have had to register the transfer of deed."

"Is there a Juzgado here, too?" Chenille asked him. "I thought that was just in the city."

"Just a small one," the man told her. "Some local cases are tried there, and they hold a handful of petty prisoners. There's no Alambrera here—those with long sentences are sent back to Viron. And they take care of the tax rolls and property records."

By this time the holobit wagon they rode was trundling along a narrow, crooked, cobbled street lined with tottering two- and three-storied wooden houses, all with high, peaked roofs and many a weathered silver-gray from lack of paint. Silk and Chenille, with the man who knew about the Juzgado and the woman who made watercress sandwiches, were on the landward side of the long wagon; but Silk, looking over his shoulder, could catch occasional glimpses of dirty water and high-pooped, single-masted fishing boats between the houses.

"I haven't been here since I was just a sprat myself," he told Chenille. "It's odd to think now that I fished here fifteen years ago. They don't use shiprock like we do, do they? Or mud brick, either."

The man on Chenille's left said, "It's too easy to cut trees on the banks and float the logs to Limna."

"I see. I hadn't considered that—although I should have, of course."

"Not many people would," the man said; he had opened his card case, and he extracted a pasteboard visiting card as he talked. "May I give you this, Patera? Vulpes is my name. I'm an advocate, and I've got chambers here on Shore Street. Do you understand the procedure if you're arrested?"

Silk's eyebrows shot up. "Arrested? Molpe defend us! I hope not."

"So do I." Vulpes lowered his voice until Silk could barely hear him above the street noises and the squeaking of the wagon's axels. "So do we all, I think. But do you understand the procedure?"

Silk shook his head.

"If you give them the name and location of an advocate, they have to send for him—that's the law. If you can't give them a name and the location, however, you don't get one until your family finds out what's happened and engages somebody."

"I see."

"*And,*" Vulpes leaned in front of Chenille and tapped Silk's knee to emphasize his point, "if you're here in Limna, somebody with chambers in Viron won't do. It has to be somebody local. I've known them to wait, when they knew someone might be coming here soon, so as to make the arrest here for exactly that reason. I want you to put that in your pocket, Patera, so that you can show it to them if you have to. Vulpes, on Shore Street, right here in Limna, at the sign of the red fox."

At the word *fox,* the wagon creaked to a stop, and the driver bawled, "Everybody off! Rides back to Viron at four, six, and eight. You get 'em right here, but don't dare be late."

Silk caught him by the sleeve as he was about to enter the barn. "Will you tell me something about Limna, Driver? I'm not at all familiar with it."

"The layout, you mean?" The driver pinched his nostrils thoughtfully. "That's simple enough, Patera. It's not no great big place like Viron. The main thing you got to hang on to is where we are now, so you'll know where to go to catch your ride back. This here's Water Street, see? And right here's pretty close to the middle o' town. There's only three streets that amount to much—Dock, Water, and Shore. The whole town curls around the bay. It's shaped kind o' like a horseshoe, only not bent so much. You know what I'm tellin' you? The inside's Dock Street—that's where the market is. The outside's Shore Street. If you want to go out on a boat, Dock Street's the place, and I can give you a couple good names. If you want to eat, try the Catfish or the Full Sail. The Rusty Lantern's pretty good, too, if you got deep pockets. Stayin' overnight?"

Silk shook his head. "We'd like to get back to the city before dark, if we can."

"You'll want the six o'clock wagon, then," the driver said as he turned away.

When he had gone, Chenille said, "You didn't ask him where the councillors live."

"If neither you nor I nor Auk knew, it can't be common knowledge," Silk told her. "Crane will have had to discover that for himself, and the best thing for us to learn today may well be whom he asked. I doubt that he'll have ridden down on one of the wagons as we did. On Scylsday he had a hired litter."

She nodded. "It might be better if we split up, Patera. You high, and me low."

"I'm not sure what you mean by that."

"You talk to the respectable people in the respectable places. I'll ask around in the drinking kens. When did . . . Auk? Say he'd meet us here?"

"Four o'clock," Silk told her.

"Then I'll meet you right here at four. We can have a bite to eat. With Auk? And tell each other whatever we've learned."

"You were very skillful with that woman on the wagon," Silk said. "I hope that I can do half as well."

"But it didn't get us anything? Stick with the truth, Patera. Silk? Or close to it. . . . I don't think you'll be terribly good with the . . . other thing? What're you going to say?"

Silk stroked his cheek. "I was thinking about that on the

wagon, and it seemed to me that it will have to depend upon the circumstances. I might say, for example, that such a man witnessed an exorcism I performed, and since I haven't returned to the house that had been afflicted, I was hoping he could tell me whether it had been effective."

Chenille nodded. "Perfectly true. . . . Every bit of it. You're going to be all right. I can see that. Silk?" She had been standing close to him already, forced there by the press of traffic in the street; she stepped closer still, so that the nipples of her jutting breasts pressed the front of his tunic. "You don't love me, Patera. You wouldn't, even if you didn't think I belonged to . . . Auk? But you love Hy? Don't you? Tell me. . . ."

He said miserably, "I shouldn't. It isn't right, and a man in my position—an augur—has so little to offer any woman. No money. No real home. It's just that she's like the— There are things I can't seem to stop thinking about, no matter how hard I try. Hyacinth is one of them."

"Well, I'm her, too." Swift and burning, Chenille's lips touched his. By the time he had recovered, she was lost among porters and vendors, hurrying visitors and strolling, rolling fishermen.

"Bye, girl!" With his uninjured wing, Oreb was waving farewell. "Watch out! Good luck!"

Silk took a deep breath and looked around. Here at the end nearest Viron, Lake Limna had nurtured a town of its own, subject to the city while curiously detached from it.

Or rather (his first two fingers inscribed slow circles on his cheek), Lake Limna, in its retreat, had drawn a fleck of Viron with it. Once the Orilla had been the lakeshore—or Dock Street, as it was called here. To judge from its name, Shore Street had been the same in its day, a paved prelude to wharves, with buildings on its landward side that over-looked the water. As the lake had continued to shrink, Water Street, on which he stood, had come into being. Still later, twenty or thirty years ago, possibly, Water Street had been left behind like the rest.

And yet the lake was still immense. He tried to imagine it as it must have been when the first settlers occupied the empty city built for them at what was then its northern end, and concluded that the lake must have been twice its present size. Would there come a time, in another three centuries or so, when there was no lake at all? It seemed more likely that the lake would then be half its present size—and yet the time must surely come, whether in six hundred years or a thousand, when it would vanish altogether.

He began to walk, wondering vaguely what the respectable places the goddess wished him to visit were. Or at least which such places would be most apt to yield information of value.

Drawn by boyhood recollections of cool water and endless vistas, he followed a block-long alley to Dock Street. Here half a dozen fishing boats landed silver floods of trout, shad, pike, and bass; here cookshops supplied fish as fresh as the finest eating houses in the city at a tenth the price; and top-lofty inns with gaily painted shutters displayed signboards for those anxious to exchange the conveniences of Viron for zephyrs at the height of summer, and those who, in whatever season, delighted in swimming, fishing, or sailing.

Here, too, as Silk soon discovered, was the fresh poster that he and Chenille had seen before their holobit wagon had left the city, offering "strong young men" an opportunity to become part-time Guardsmen and holding out the promise of eventual full-time employment. As he read it through again, Silk recalled the darkly threatening entrails of the ewe. No one spoke as yet of war—except the gods. Or rather, he reflected, only the gods and this poster spoke of war to those who would listen.

The next-to-final line of the poster had been crossed

out with black ink, and the phrase *at the Juzgado in Limna* had been substituted; the new reserve brigade would station a company or two here at the lake, presumably—perhaps an entire battalion, if enough fishermen could be persuaded to enlist.

For the first time it struck him that Limna would make an excellent base or staging area for an army moving against the city, offering shelter for many if not all of the enemy troops, assurance against surprise from the south, a ready source of food, and unlimited water for men and animals. No wonder, then, that Crane had been interested to learn that the councillors were here, and that a commissioner had come to confer with them.

"Fish heads!" Oreb fluttered from Silk's shoulder to the ground, then ran with unexpected speed three-quarters the length of a nearby jetty to peck at them.

"Yes," Silk murmured to himself, "fish heads at last, and fish guts, too."

As he strolled down the jetty, admiring the broad blue purity of the lake and the scores of bobbing, heeling craft whose snowy sails dotted it, he meditated upon Oreb's meal.

Those fish belonged to Scylla, just as serpents belonged to her mother, Echidna, and cats of all kinds to her younger sister, Sphigx. Surging Scylla, the patroness of the city, graciously permitted her worshipers to catch such fish as they required, subject to certain age-old restrictions and prohibitions. Yet the fish—even those scraps that Oreb ate—were hers, and the lake her palace. If devotion to Scylla was still strong in the Viron, as it was though two generations had passed since she had manifested her divinity in a Sacred Window, what must it be here?

Joining Oreb, he sat down upon the head of a convenient piling, removed Crane's almost miraculous wrapping from his fractured ankle, and whipped the warped planks of the jetty with it.

What if Crane wished to erect a shrine to Scylla on the lakeshore in fulfillment of some vow? If Crane could hand out azoths as gifts to favored informers, he could certainly afford a shrine. Silk knew little of building, but he felt certain that a modest yet appropriate and wholly acceptable shrine could be built at the edge of the lake for a thousand cards or less. Crane might well have asked his spiritual advisor—himself—to select a suitable site.

Better still, suppose that Chenille's commissioner were the grateful builder—no one would question the ability of a commissioner to underwrite the entire cost of even a very elaborate structure. It would not be a manteion, since it could have no Sacred Window, but sacrifice might take place there. Fostered by a commissioner, it might well support a resident augur—someone like himself.

And Crane would have gone where Chenille's commissioner had gone, assuming that he had learned where that was.

"Good! Good!" Oreb had completed his repast; balanced upon one splayed crimson foot, he was scraping his bill with the other.

"Don't soil my robe," Silk told him. "I warn you, I'll be angry."

As he replaced Crane's wrapping, Silk tried to imagine himself the commissioner. Two councillors had summoned him to the lake for a conference, presumably a confidential one, possibly concerned with military matters. He would (Silk decided) almost certainly travel to Limna by floater; but he would—again, almost certainly—leave his floater and its driver there in favor of a mode of transportation less likely to attract attention.

To focus his thoughts as he often did in the palaestra, Silk pointed his forefinger at his pet. "He might hire a donkey, for example, like Auk and I did the other night."

A small boat was gliding toward the lakeward end of the jetty, a gray-haired man minding its tiller while a couple of boys hastily furled its single sail.

"That's it!"

The night chough eyed him quizzically.

"He would hire a boat, Oreb. Perhaps with a reliable man or two to do the sailing. A boat would be much faster than a donkey or even a horse. It would carry a secretary or a confidential clerk as well as the commissioner, and he could go straight to whatever point on the lake—"

"Silk good?" Oreb stopped preening the tuft of scarlet feathers on his breast to cock his sleek head at Silk. "All right?"

"No. Slightly wrong. He wouldn't hire a boat. That would cost him money of his own, and he might not feel that he could trust the men who sailed it for him. But the town must have boats—to keep the fishermen from fighting among themselves, for example—and whoever's governing it would fall all over himself hurrying to help a commissioner. So climb aboard, you silly bird. We're going to the Juzgado." After looking in several pockets, Silk found the advocate's visiting card. "On Shore Street. His chambers were on the same street as the Juzgado. Remember, Oreb? No doubt it's convenient when he has to hurry off to court."

As the door of the big shed opened, the old kite builder looked up in some surprise.

The small, gray-bearded man in the doorway said, "Excuse me. I didn't know you were in here."

"Just packing up to leave," the kite builder explained. For an instant he wondered whether Musk had thought that he might steal, and had sent this man to watch him.

"I heard about the kite. You built it? Everyone says it was a beautiful job."

"It certainly wasn't pretty." The kite builder tied a string around a sheaf of slender sticks. "But it was what they wanted, and it was one of the biggest I've ever done. The bigger they are, the higher they fly. To get up high, they have to lift a lot of wire, you know."

"I'm Doctor Crane," the bearded man said. "I should have introduced myself earlier." He picked up one of the fish-oil lamps and shook it gently. "Nearly full. Have you been paid yet?"

"Musk paid me, the full amount." The kite builder patted his pocket. "Not cards, a draft on the fisc. I suppose Blood sent you to see me out."

"That's right, before they left. They're all gone now, I think. Blood and Musk are, at any rate, the guards, and a few of the servants."

The kite builder nodded. "They took all the floaters. There were a couple in here. All the highriders, too. Am I supposed to talk to Blood before I leave? Musk didn't say anything about it."

"Not as far as I know." Crane smiled. "The front gate's open and the talus got fired, so you can go whenever you like. You're welcome to stay, though, if you want to. When they get back from wherever they've gone, Blood might have a driver run you home. Where did they go, anyhow? Nobody told me."

Scrabbling around for his favorite spokeshave, the kite discovered it under a scape of cloth. "To the lake. That's what some of them said."

Crane nodded and smiled again. "Then they'll be gone quite a while, I'm afraid. But you're welcome to wait if you want to." He closed the door behind him and hurried back to the villa. If he did not look now, he asked himself, when would he? He'd never have a better chance. The pantry

door stood open, and the door to the cellar stair was un-
locked.

The cellar was deep and very dark, and from what he
had gathered during friendly chats with the footmen, there
should be a wine cellar deeper yet. That might or might not
be the same as the subcellar a maid had mentioned. Halfway down the stairs, Crane stopped to raise his lamp.

Emptiness. Rusted, dust-shrouded machinery that
could not, almost certainly, ever be set in motion again.
And—

He descended the remaining steps and trotted across
the dirty, uneven floor to look. Jars of preserves: peaches in
brandy, and pickles. No doubt they'd come with the house.

Would they post a sentry at the entrance to the tunnels?
He had decided some time ago that they would not. The
door (if it was a door) would be locked, however, or barred
from below. Possibly hidden as well—located in a secret
room or something of that kind. Here, behind the ranks of
shelves, was another stair with, yes, footprints leading to it
still visible in the dust.

A short flight of steps this time, with a locked door at
the bottom. His pick explored the lock for half a minute
that seemed like five before the handle would turn to draw
back the bolt.

The creak of the hinges activated a light whose perpetual crawl had brought it near the peak of the low vault
overhead. By its foggy light, he saw wine racks holding five
hundred bottles at least; stacks of cases of brandy, agar-
dente, rum, and cordials; and kegs of what was presumably
strong beer. He moved several of the last and studied the
floor beneath them, then scanned the floor everywhere,
and at last tapped the walls.

Nothing.

"Well, well, well, a well," he murmured, "and a drink
for the plowman." Opening a squat, black bottle that had

clearly been sampled previously, he took a long swallow of pallid, fiery arrack, recorked the bottle, and made a last inspection.

Nothing.

He closed the wine cellar door silently behind him and twisted its handle clockwise, the muted squeal of the bolt recalling unpleasantly a small dog he had once watched Musk torment.

For a moment he considered leaving the door un-locked; it would save time and almost certainly be blamed—if in fact Blood's sommelier or anyone else ever discovered it—upon a careless servant. Caution, however, as well as extensive training, urged him to leave everything precisely as he had found it.

Sighing, he took out his picks, twisted the one that he had used to enter in the lock, and was rewarded by a faint click.

"You're very good at it, aren't you?"

Crane spun around. Someone—in the thick twilight of the cellar it appeared to be a tall, handsome, white-haired man—stood at the top of the short flight of steps looking down at him.

"You recognize me, I hope?"

Crane dropped his picks, drew, and fired in one single blur of motion, the rapid *crack, crack, crack* of his needler unnaturally loud in the confined space.

"You can't hurt me with that," Councillor Lemur in-formed him. "Now come up here and give it to me, and I'll take you where you've been trying to go."

"You had a commissioner come in this spring," Silk told the plump, middle-aged woman behind the heaped work-table. "You very kindly provided him with a small sailing vessel of some type." He gave her his most understanding smile. "I'm not about to ask you to provide me with a boat as well. I realize that I'm no commissioner."

"Last spring, Patera? A commissioner from the city?" The woman looked baffled.

At the precise moment that Silk became certain that he had forgotten the commissioner's name, he recalled it; he leaned closer to the woman, wishing he had asked Chenille for a more detailed description. "Commissioner Simuliid. He's an extremely important official. A large and" (Silk struggled to capture the prochain ami's perpetual note of prudence and confidentiality) "—an—um—portly man. He wears a mustache."

When the woman's expression remained blank, he added desperately, "a most becoming mustache, now, I would say, although perhaps—"

"Commissioner Simuliid, Patera?"

Silk nodded eagerly.

"It wasn't that long ago. Not spring. Two months ago, maybe. Not more than three. It was terribly hot already, I remember, and he had on a big straw hat. You know the sort of thing, Patera?"

Silk nodded encouragement. "Perfectly. I used to have one myself."

"And he had a stick, too. Bigger than yours. But he didn't want a boat. We'd have been glad to lend him one, if he had, so it wasn't that." The woman nibbled at her pen. "He asked for something else, and we didn't have it, but I can't remember what it was."

Oreb cocked his head. "Poor girl!"

"Yes, indeed," Silk said, "if she was unable to assist Commissioner Simuliid."

"I did help him," the woman insisted. "I know I did. He was quite satisfied when he left."

Silk strove to appear an augur who moved frequently in

the company of commissioners. "Certainly he didn't complain about you to me."

"Don't you know what he wanted, Patera?"

"Not what he wanted from you," he told the plump woman, "because I had been under the impression that he wanted a boat. There are some perfectly marvelous vistas all along the lakeshore, I understand; and I have been thinking that it would be a meritorious act for Commissioner Simuliid—or anyone—to erect an appropriate shrine to our Patroness on such a spot. Something tasteful, and not too small. The Commissioner may quite possibly have been thinking the same thing, from all that I know of him."

"Are you sure he wasn't offering to repair it, Patera? Or build an addition? Something like that? Scylla's got a beautiful shrine near here already, and some very important people from the city often go out there to, you know, think things over."

Silk snapped his fingers. "An addition! An attached aedicule for the practice of hydromancy. Why, of course! Even I ought to have realized—"

Oreb croaked, "No cut?"

"Not you, in any event," Silk told him. "Where is this shrine, my daughter?"

"Where—?" Suddenly the woman's face was wreathed in smiles. "Why, that's what Commissioner Simuliid wanted, I remember now. A map. How to get there, really. We don't have any maps that show the shrine, there's some sort of a regulation, but you don't need one. All you have to do is follow the Pilgrims' Way, I told him. West around the bay, then south up onto the promontory. It's quite a climb, but if you just go from one white stone to the next, you can't possibly miss it." The woman got out a map. "It's not on here, but I can show you. The blue is the lake, and these black lines are for Limna. Do you see Shore Street?

The shrine's right where I'm pointing, see? And this is where the Pilgrims' Way goes up the cliffs. Are you going to go up there yourself, Patera?"

"At the first opportunity," Silk told her. Simuliid had made the pilgrimage; that seemed practically certain. The question was whether Crane had followed him.

"And I thank you very much indeed, my daughter. You've been extremely helpful. Did you say that even councillors go there to meditate sometimes? An acquaintance of mine, Doctor Crane—you may know him; I believe he must spend a good deal of time out here at the lake—"

The woman shook her head. "Oh, no, Patera. They're too old, I think."

"Doctor Crane may have misinformed me, then. I thought he had gotten his information here, most likely from you. A small man with a short gray beard?"

She shook her head. "I don't think he's been in here, Patera. But I don't think the councillors really come. He was probably thinking of commissioners. We've had several of them, and judges and so on, and sometimes they want to go in a boat, only we have to tell them they can't. It's up on a cliff, and there's no path up from the water. You have to follow the Pilgrims' Way. You can't even ride, because of where there's steps cut into the rock. I suppose that must be why the councillors don't come, too. I've never seen a councillor."

Neither had he, Silk reflected as he left the Juzgado. Had anyone? He had seen their pictures—there had been a group portrait in the Juzgado, in fact—and Silk had seen the pictures so often that until he had actually considered it he had supposed that he had at some time or other seen the councillors themselves. But he had not, and could not recall having met anyone who had.

Simuliid had, however; or at least he had told Chenille he had. Not, presumably, at the shrine of Scylla, since the councillors never went there. In one of the eating places, perhaps, or on a boat.

"No cut?" Oreb wanted more reassurance.

"Absolutely not. A shrine isn't really the best place for sacrifice, anyway, although it's often done. A properly instructed person, such as myself, is more apt to visit a shrine to meditate or do a little religious reading."

Various political figures from the city often went to this lake shrine of Scylla's, according to the woman in the Juzgado. It seemed odd—politicians might make a show of belief, but he had never heard of one who seemed to have any genuine depth of religious feeling. The Prolocutor had little influence in the governance of the city these days, according to everyone except Remora.

Yet either Auk or Chenille—it had been Auk, surely— had called Simuliid, whom he had known by sight, oxweight or something of that sort. Had implied, at any rate, that he was a large and very heavy man. Yet Simuliid had made a pilgrimage to this shrine of Scylla's (or so it appeared) on foot, after the hot weather had begun. It seemed improbable in the extreme, particularly since he could not have met the councillors there.

Silk massaged his cheek as he walked, gazing idly into shop windows. It was quite conceivable that Commissioner Simuliid's boast to Chenille had been nothing more than a vainglorious lie, in which case Chenille had not earned her five cards, and any time that Crane might have spent here had been wasted.

But whether Crane had wasted his time or not, he did not appear to have traced Simuliid through Limna's Juzgado, as he himself had. It might even be that Crane had not traced him at all.

"Something's very wrong here, Oreb. We've a rat in the wainscotting, if you know what I mean."

"No boat?"

"No boat, no doctor, and no councillors. No money. No manteion. No ability, either—not a speck of whatever it was that the Outsider thought he saw in me." Although the immortal gods, as reason taught and the Writings confirmed, did not "think" that they saw things. Not really. Gods knew.

With no special purpose in mind, he had been strolling west along Shore Street. Now he found it obstructed by a sizable boulder, painted white and crudely carved with the many-tentacled image of Scylla.

He crossed to the center of the street to examine the image more closely and discovered a rhyming prayer beneath it. Tracing the sign of addition in the air, he appealed to Scylla for help (citing her city's need for the manteion and apologizing for his impetuosity in rushing off to the lake with so little reason to believe that there was anything to be gained) before reciting the prayer, somewhat amused to find that the great goddess's features, as depicted on the boulder, bore a chance resemblance to those of the helpful woman in the Juzgado.

Members of the Ayuntamiento never visited the shrine, she had said, though commissioners came quite often. Did she herself visit the shrine with any frequency, and thus see who came and who did not? Almost certainly not, Silk decided.

With a start, he realized that half a dozen passersby stood watching him as he prayed with head bowed before the image; when he turned away, a stocky man about his own age excused himself and asked whether he intended to make the pilgrimage to the shrine.

"That was one of the points on which I begged for the goddess's guidance," Silk explained. "I told a good woman only a few minutes ago that I would go as soon as I had the opportunity. It was a rash promise, of course, because it can be very difficult to judge what 'opportunity' signifies.

I have business here today, and so may be said to have none; but there is a remote chance that a pilgrimage to the shrine would further it. If that is so, I am clearly bound."

A woman of about the same age said, "You shouldn't even think of it, Patera. Not when it's this hot."

"Good girl!" Oreb muttered.

"This is my wife, Chervil," the stocky man told Silk. "My name's Coypu, and we've made the pilgrimage twice." Silk started to speak, but Coypu waved it away. "That place over there has cold drinks. If you hike up to the shrine today, you'll need all the wet stuff you can hold, and we'd like to buy you something. But if you'll let us, and listen to us, you probably won't go at all."

"Thirsty!"

Chervil laughed, and Silk said, "Be quiet, Oreb. So am I for that matter."

It was mercifully cool inside, and to Silk, stepping in from the sunlight, it seemed very dark. "They have beer, fruit juices—even coconut milk, if you haven't tried that— and spring water," Coypu told him. "Order whatever you like."

To the waiter who appeared as soon as they sat down, he said, "My wife will have the bitter orange, and I'll take whatever kind of beer's been in your cistern the longest."

He turned to Silk. "And you, Patera? Anything that you want."

"Spring water, please. Two glasses would be nice."

"We saw your picture on a fence," Chervil told him. "It can't have been more than five minutes ago—an augur with a bird on his shoulder, quite artistically rendered in chalk and charcoal. Over your head the artist had written, 'Silk is here!' And yesterday, back in the city, we saw 'Silk for Caldé.' "

He nodded grimly. "I haven't seen the picture with the

bird you mentioned, but I believe that I can guess who drew it. If so, I must have a word with her."

The waiter set three moisture-beaded bottles—yellow, brown, and clear—on their table, with four glasses, and marked their score on a small slate.

Coypu fingered the brown bottle and smiled. "There's always a crowd on Scylsday, and everything's pretty warm. These were probably let down then."

Silk nodded. "It's always cold underground. I suppose that the night that surrounds the whorl must be a winter's night."

Coypu shot him a startled glance as he opened his wife's orange juice.

"Haven't you ever thought of what lies beyond the whorl, my son?"

"You mean if you keep digging down? Isn't it just dirt, no matter how far down you go?"

Silk shook his head as he opened his own bottle. "The most ignorant miner knows better than that, my son. Even a grave digger—I talked with several of them yesterday, and they were by no means unintelligent—would tell you that the soil our plows till is scarcely thicker than the height of a man. Clay and gravel lie beneath it, and below them, stone or shiprock."

Silk poured cool water into a glass for Oreb while he collected his thoughts. "Beneath that stone and shiprock, which is not as thick as you might imagine, the whorl spins in emptiness—in a night that extends in every direction without limit." He paused, remembering, as he filled his own glass. "It is spangled everywhere with colored sparks, however. I was told what they were, though at the moment I cannot recall it."

"I thought it was just that the heat didn't reach down there."

"It does," Silk told him. "It reaches beyond the depths

of this cistern, and deeper than the wells at my manteion, which always yield cold water with sufficient pumping. It extends, in fact, to the outermost stone of the whorl, and there it is lost in the frigid night. If it weren't for the sun, the first as well as the greatest gift Pas gave to the whorl, we would all freeze." For a moment Silk watched Oreb drinking from his glass, then he drank deeply from his own. "Thank you both. It's very good."

Chervil said, "I wouldn't argue with Pas or you about the value of the sun, Patera, but it can be dangerous, too. If you really want to see the shrine, I wish you'd consider making your pilgrimage in the evening, when it's not so hot. Remember last time, Coypu?"

Her husband nodded. "We'd gone out last fall, Patera. We enjoyed the hike, and there's a magnificent view from the shrine, so we decided we'd do it again this year. When we finally got around to it the figs were getting ripe, but it wasn't as hot as it is now."

"Not nearly," Chervil put in.

"So off we went, and it got hotter and hotter. You tell him, sweetheart."

"He left the path," Chervil told Silk. "The Pilgrims' Way, or whatever you call it. I could see the next couple of stones ahead of us, but he was veering off to the right down this little—I don't know what they call it. This rocky little valley between two hills."

"Ravine?" Silk suggested.

"Yes, that's it. This ravine. And I said, 'Where are you going? That's not the way.' And he said, 'Come on, come along or we'll never get there.' So I ran after him and caught up with him."

They'll have a child in another year, Silk thought. He pictured the three of them at supper in a little courtyard, talking and laughing; Chervil was neither as beautiful nor

as charming as Hyacinth, yet he found that he envied
Coypu with all his heart.

"And it ended. The ravine. It just stopped at a slope too
steep to climb, and he didn't know what to do. Finally I
said, 'Where do you think you're going?' And he said, 'To
my aunt's.' "

"I see." Silk had drained his glass; he poured the rest of
the bottle into it.

"It took me a long time to get him back to the path, but
when I did I saw this man coming toward us, coming back
from the shrine. I screamed for him to help me, and he
stopped and asked what the matter was and made Coypu
go along a little bit farther to where there was some shade,
and we got him to lie down."

"It was the heat, of course," Silk said.

"Yes! Exactly."

Coypu nodded. "I was all mixed up, and somehow I got
the idea we were in the city, walking to my aunt's house. I
kept wondering what had happened to the street. Why it
had changed so much."

"Anyway, this man stayed there with us until Coypu felt
better. He said it was the early stages of heat stroke, and
that the thing to do was to get out of the sun and lie down,
and eat salty food and drink cold water, if you could. Only
we couldn't because we hadn't brought anything, and it
was way too high up for us to climb down to the lake. He
was a doctor."

Silk stared at her. "Oh, you gods!"

"What's the matter, Patera?"

"And yet some people will not believe." He finished his
water. "I—even I, who ought to know better if anyone
does—often behave as though there were no forces in the
whorl beyond my own feeble strength. I suppose I ought to
ask you this doctor's name, for form's sake; but I don't have
to. I know it."

"I've forgotten it," Coypu admitted, "although he stayed there talking to us for a couple of hours, I guess."

Chervil said, "He had a beard, and he was only a little taller than I am."

"His name is Crane," Silk told them, and signaled to the waiter.

Chervil nodded. "That was it. Is he a friend of yours, Patera?"

"Not exactly. An acquaintance. Would you like another, both of you? I'm going to get one."

They nodded, and Silk told the waiter, "I'm paying for everything—for our first drinks and these, too."

"Five bits if you want to pay now, Patera. You know anything about this Patera Silk, in the city?"

"A little," Silk told him. "Not as much as I should, certainly."

"Had a goddess in his Window? Supposed to be some sort of wonder worker?"

"The first is true," Silk said, "the second is not." He turned back to Coypu and Chervil. "You said Doctor Crane talked with you for some time. If I'm not presuming on our brief acquaintance, may I ask what he talked about?"

"He *is* Patera Silk," Chervil told the waiter. "Don't you see his bird?"

Silk laid six cardbits on the table.

Coypu said, "He wanted to know if my mother and father were in good health, and he kept feeling my skin. And what my grandmother'd died of. I remember that."

"He asked a lot of questions," Chervil said. "And he made me keep fanning him—fanning Coypu, I mean."

Oreb, who had been listening intently, demonstrated with his sound wing.

"That's right, birdie. Exactly like that, only I used my hat."

"I must get one," Silk muttered. "Get another, I should say. Fortunately I have funds."

"A hat?" Coypu asked.

"Yes. Even the commissioner was wearing—it doesn't matter. I don't know the man, and I don't wish to make you believe I do. I've done enough of that. What I should say is that before I start for the shrine, I want to buy a straw hat with a broad brim. I saw some in a shop window here, I know."

The waiter brought three more sweating bottles and three clean glasses.

Coypu told Silk, "Half the shops here sell them. You can get an ugly sunburn out on a boat on the lake."

"Or even swimming, because people mostly just sit on the rocks." Chervil laughed; she had an attractive laugh, and Silk sensed that she knew it. "They come here from the city because the lake's nice and cold, and they think they want that. But once they get into it they jump out pretty fast, most of them."

Silk nodded and smiled. "I'll have to try it myself one of these days. Do you remember any of Doctor Crane's other questions?"

"Who built the shrine," Coypu said. "It was Councillor Lemur, about twenty-five years ago. There's a bronze plate on it that says so, but the doctor must not have noticed it when he was out there."

Chervil said, "He wanted to know if Coypu was related. I don't think he knew what a coypu is. And whether we knew him, or any of them, and about how old they were. He said most of them became our councillors more than forty years ago, so they must have been pretty young then."

"I'm not sure that's right," Coypu told her.

"And if we knew how badly off some of the other cities were, and didn't we think we ought to help. I said that the first thing we ought to do was make sure everyone there got a fair share of their own food, because a lot of the trouble was because of people there buying up corn and waiting for higher prices. I said prices in Viron were high enough for me already without our sending rice to Palustria."

She laughed again, and Silk laughed with her as he put his unopened bottle of spring water into the front pocket of his robe; but his thoughts were already following the trail of white stones, the Pilgrims' Way stretching from Limna to Scylla's shrine—the holy place that both Doctor Crane and Commissioner Simuliid had visited—on the cliffs above the lake.

When he set off nearly an hour later, the sun seemed a living enemy, a serpent of fire across the sky, powerful, poisonous, and malign. The Pilgrims' Way shimmered in the heat, and the third white stone, upon which he sat in order to re-energize Crane's wrapping, felt as hot as the lid of a kettle on the stove.

As he wiped his forehead with his sleeve, he tried to recall whether it had been equally hot two or three months before, when Simuliid has made his pilgrimage, and decided that it had not. It had been hot—indeed it had been so hot that everyone had complained incessantly. But not as hot as it was now.

"This is the peak," he told Oreb. "This is the hottest that it will get all day. It might have been wiser to wait until evening, as Chervil suggested; but we're supposed to meet Auk this evening for dinner. We can comfort ourselves with the thought that if we can stand this—and we can—we can stand the worst that this sun can do and that from this moment on things can only get better. Not only will the way back be downhill, but it will be cooler then."

Oreb clacked his bill nervously but said nothing.

"Did you see the look on Coypu's face when I limped away from our table?" Silk slapped the wrapping against the side of the white-painted boulder one final time.

"When I told him I had a broken ankle, I was afraid he might try to keep me in Limna by main force."

As Silk stood up, he reflected that Simuliid's age and weight had probably been handicaps as great or greater than his ankle. Had he, like Crane, encountered pilgrims on the path? And if so, what had he told them?

For that matter, what should he himself, Patera Silk, from Sun Street, tell those he met; and what should he ask them? As he walked, he tried to contrive some reasonably truthful account that would permit him to ask whether they, too, had ever talked with Crane on the Pilgrims' Way, and what Crane had said to them, all without revealing his own purpose.

There was no occasion for it. Though well marked (as the woman in the Juzgado had said), the path was deserted, steep, and stony, its loneliness and blazing heat relieved only by a succession of views of the steel blue lake that were increasingly breathtaking, breathtaken, and hazardous.

"If an augur were to make this pilgrimage every day of his life," Silk asked Oreb, "in all weathers and whether he was well or ill, don't you believe that eventually, perhaps on the final day of his whorldly existence, Surging Scylla would reveal herself to him, rising from the lake? I do, and if I didn't have the manteion to take care of—if the people of our quarter didn't have need of me and it, and if the Outsider hadn't ordered me to save it—I'd be tempted to try the experiment. Even if it failed, one might live a far worse life."

Oreb croaked and muttered in reply, peering this way and that.

"It's Scylla, Pas's eldest child, who selects us to be augurs, after all. Each year arrives like a flotilla laden with young men and women—this is what they tell you at the schola, you understand."

A beetling rock provided a few square cubits of shade;

Silk squatted in it, fanning his dripping face with the wide hat he had bought in Limna.

"Some, drawn to the ideal of holiness, sail very near Scylla indeed; and from those she plucks a number that is neither great nor small, but the necessary number for that year. Others, repelled by the augurial ideals of simplicity and chastity, sail as far from her as they dare; from them, also, she takes a number that is neither great nor small but the necessary number for the year. That is why artists show her with many long arms like whips. She snatched me up with one, you see. It may even be that she snatched you as well, Oreb."

"No see!"

"Nor I," Silk confessed. "I didn't see her either. But I felt her pull. Do you know, I believe all this walking's doing my ankle good? It must've reached the stage at which it needs exercise more than rest. We're coming to another point. What do you say, shall I sacrifice Blood's stick to Lady Scylla?"

"No hit?"

"No hit, I swear."

"Keep it."

"Because someone else might find it and hit you? Don't worry. I'll stand out there and throw it as far as I can."

Silk rose and walked to the point, advancing ever more cautiously until he stood at the very edge of the projecting rock, above a drop of five hundred cubits, jumbled slabs of stone, and breaking waves. "How about it, Oreb? Should we make the offering? An informal sacrifice to Surging Scylla? It must surely have been Scylla who sent that nice couple to us. They told me where they live quite willingly, and some of the questions Doctor Crane had asked them were certainly suggestive."

He paused. Like a gift from the goddess, a sudden gust of cool wind from the lake set his black robe flapping behind him, and dried the sweat that had soaked his tunic.

"Auk and Chenille—and I, too—talked about turning him over to the Guard, Oreb, after we'd taken his money; it bothered me at the time, and it's been bothering me more and more ever since. I'd almost prefer failing the Outsider to doing that."

"Good man."

"Yes." Silk lowered the walking stick, discovered that he had nowhere to rest its ferrule, and took a step backward. "That's precisely the trouble. If I were to find out that someone I knew had gone to a foreign city to spy for Viron, I'd consider him a brave man and a patriot. Doctor Crane is clearly a spy for some other city—his home, whether it's Ur, Urbs, Trivigaunte, Sedes, or Palustria. Well, isn't he a brave man and a patriot, too?"

"Walk now?"

"You're right, I suppose. We ought to be on about our business." Silk remained where he was, nevertheless, gazing down at the lake. "I could say, I suppose, that if Scylla accepted my sacrifice—that is to say, if this stick fell into the water—it would be all right to let Crane go free once the manteion had been saved; he'd have to leave Viron, of course; but we wouldn't hand him and our evidence over to the Guard—roll him over to Hoppy, as Auk would say." He tapped the rock with the tip of the stick. "But it would be pure superstition, unworthy of an augur. What we need is a regular sacrifice, preferably on a Scylsday, with all of the forms strictly observed, before a Sacred Window."

"No cut!"

"Not you. How many times do I have to say that? A ram or something. You know, Oreb, there really is—or was—a science of hydromancy, by which the officiating augur read Scylla's will in the patterns of waves. I suggested it to that nice woman in the Juzgado by purest chance—seeing the lake before we went in probably brought it to mind—but

I wouldn't be surprised if that's what Councillor Lemur had in mind when he built this shrine we're going to. It was practiced up until about a hundred years ago, so when the shrine was built there must still have been thousands of people who remembered it. Perhaps Councillor Lemur hoped to revive it."

The bird did not reply. For another two minutes or more Silk stood staring at the surging waters below him before shifting his attention to the rugged cliffs on his right. "Look, you can see the shrine from here." He pointed with the walking stick. "I believe they've actually shaped the pillars that support the dome like Scylla's arms. See how wavy they are?"

"Man there."

A dim figure moved back and forth in the bluish twilight beneath Scylla's airy chalcedony shell, then vanished as he (presumably) knelt.

"You're quite right," Silk told the bird, "so there is. Someone must have been on the path ahead of us all that time. I wish we'd caught up with him."

He contemplated the otherworldly purity of the distant shrine for some time longer, then turned away. "I suppose we'll meet him on the path. But if we don't, we probably ought to wait until he's completed his own devotions. Now what about the stick? Should I go back and throw it?"

"No throw." Oreb unfolded his wings and seemed minded to fly. "Keep it."

"All right. I suppose my leg may be worse before we get back, so you're probably wise."

"Silk fight."

"With this, Oreb?" He twirled it. "I've got Hyacinth's azoth and her little needler, and either would be a much more effective weapon."

"Fight!" the night chough repeated.

"Fight who? There's no one here."

Oreb whistled, a low note followed by a slightly higher one.

"Is that bird speech for 'who knows?' Well, I certainly don't. And neither do you, Oreb, if you ask me. I'm glad I brought the weapons, because my having them here means that Patera Gulo can't find them, and I'd be willing to bet that by now he's searched my room; but if they were mine instead of Hyacinth's, I'd be inclined to pitch them to the goddess after the stick. Gulo'd never find them then."

"Bad man?"

"Yes, I believe he is." Silk returned to the Pilgrims' Way. "I'm guessing, of course. But if I must guess—and it seems that I must—then my guess is that he's the sort of man who thinks himself good, and that's by far the most dangerous sort of man there is."

"Watch out."

"I'll try," Silk promised, though he was not sure whether the bird was referring to Patera Gulo or the path, which wound along the edge of the cliff here. "So—if I'm right—this Patera Gulo's the exact reverse of Auk, who's a good man who believes himself to be a bad one. You've noticed that, I take it."

"Take it."

"I felt sure you had. Auk's helped in a dozen different ways, without even counting that diamond trinket. Patera Gulo was scandalized sufficiently by that, and the bracelet some other thief gave him. I can't imagine what he'd have done, or said, if he'd found the azoth."

"Man go."

"Do you mean Patera Gulo? Well, I wish I had some means of arranging that, I really do; but for the moment it seems to be beyond my reach."

"Man go," Oreb repeated testily. "No pray."

"Gone from the shrine now, is that what you mean?"

Silk pointed with the walking stick. "He can't have gone, unless he jumped. I didn't see him come out, and it's in full view from here."

Rather to Silk's surprise, Oreb launched himself from his shoulder and managed to struggle up to half again his height before settling again. "No see."

"I'm perfectly willing to believe that you can't see him from here," Silk told the bird, "but he has to be there just the same. Possibly there's a chapel below the shrine, cut into the cliff. The path turns inland again up ahead, but even so we should find out in half an hour or less."

Chapter 7

THE ARMS OF SCYLLA

"May every god be with you this, er, noon, Patera," Remora said as soon as his prothonotary had closed the door behind Gulo. It was extraordinary condescension.

"Even so, may they be with Your Eminence." Gulo bowed nearly to the floor. The bow and conventional phrases gave him time for a final review of the principal items he had come to report. "May Maidenly Molpe, patroness of the day, Great Pas, patron of the whorl, to whom we owe all that we possess, and Scalding Scylla, patroness of this our Sacred City of Viron, be with you always, Your Eminence, every day of your life." In the course of his bow, Gulo had contrived to pat the pocket containing the bracelet and the letter.

Straightening up, he added, "I trust that Your Eminence enjoys the best of good health? That I have not come at an inconvenient moment?"

"No, no," Remora told him. "Um—not at all. I'm—ah—delighted, really quite delighted to see you, Patera. Please sit down. What do you—ah—make of young Silk, eh?"

Gulo lowered his pudgy body to the black velvet seat of the armchair beside Remora's escritoire. "I've had little opportunity to observe his person thus far, Your Eminence. Very little. He left our manteion a moment or two after my arrival, and he had not yet returned when I myself left it in order to make this report to Your Eminence. He will not return before evening, or so he said, so it would seem less than likely that he is there now."

Remora nodded.

"He made an impression on me, however, even though I saw him so briefly, Your Eminence. A distinct one."

"I—ah—see." Remora leaned back in his chair, his long fingers tip to tip. "Would it be—um—convenient for you to describe this, um, momentary interview in detail, hey?"

"As Your Eminence desires. Shortly after I entered the quarter a man had given me this." Patera Gulo pulled the bracelet from his pocket and held it up; Remora pursed his lips.

"I must add, Your Eminence, that several other such men have come to the door of the manse since then. It was my impression—my marked impression, Your Eminence— that they had come to proffer similar gifts. They declined to do so when they learned Patera Silk was not present, however."

"You—ah—pressed them, Patera?"

"As much as I dared, Your Eminence. They weren't men of a kind one would care to press too far."

Remora grunted.

"I was about to say, Your Eminence, that when I showed this to Patera Silk he gave me a similar piece and told me to lock both of them in his cashbox. It was a diamond anklet, Your Eminence. There were two other persons with him at the time, a man and a woman. All three were going to the lake, I think. Something was said to that effect." Gulo gave an apologetic cough. "Possibly, Your Eminence, only Patera and the woman."

"You would appear to feel that Patera ought to have
been more discreet." Remora seemed to sink deeper into
his chair. "Yet unless you have—um—ascertained the
identities of these two, you cannot very well, um, gauge how
indiscreet he may have been. Have you, eh?"

Gulo fidgeted. "He called them Auk and Chenille,
Your Eminence. He introduced them to me."

"Let me see that—ah—bangle." Remora held out his
hand for the bracelet. "It ought scarcely to be—ah—need-
ful for me to say that you yourself, Patera, should have
been, er, very much more discreet than you were. Ah—by
discreet in—ah—this instance, Patera, I, um, intend *forceful*. The word will bear that—ah—interpretation, I am confident. To be discreet, Patera, is to, er, exercise good
judgment, hey? In this present—ah—matter, good judgment would have—ah—prompted a forcible—um—strat-
egy? Approach. Or attitude."

"Yes, Your Eminence."

"You ought to have gracefully and—ah—graciously received any offerings from the faithful, Patera." Remora
held up the bracelet so that it caught the light from the
bull's-eye window behind him, and swung it from side to
side. "I will not—ah—um—desire excuses on that—ah—
score, Patera. Do you follow me? None at all, eh?"

Gulo nodded humbly.

"These—ah—gentlemen may return, hey? Perhaps
when Patera is absent, as he was in the—um—occasion.
You will be—ah—vouchsafed an—um—golden opportunity, when that—ah—hour strikes, with which you may—
ah—um—redeem your credit, eh? Not impossibly. See that
you do, Patera."

Gulo squirmed. "I shall try, Your Eminence. I will be
forceful, I assure you."

"Now then. Your—ah—observations of Silk himself?

You needn't—ah—vex yourself with physical description. I've seen him."

"Yes, Your Eminence." Gulo hesitated, his mouth open, his protuberant eyes vague. "He seemed determined."

"Determined, hum?" Remora laid the bracelet on a stack of papers. "To do which?"

"I don't know, Your Eminence. But his jaw was firm, I thought. His manner was decisive. There was—if I may say it, Your Eminence—a glint as of steel in his eyes, I thought. Perhaps that simile is something overblown, Your Eminence—"

"Perhaps it is," Remora told him severely.

"And yet it at least expresses what I sensed in him. At the schola, Your Eminence, Patera was two years before me."

Remora nodded.

"I noticed him there as anyone would, Your Eminence. I thought him good-looking and studious, but rather slow, if anything. Now, however—"

Remora waved the present aside. "You implied, I think, Patera, that Patera—ah—decamped, eh? With a couple. A married couple? Were they—um—ah—wed, so far as you could judge?"

"I believe they may have been, Your Eminence. The woman had a fine ring."

Remora's long fingers toyed with the jeweled gammadion he wore. "Describe them, eh? Their—ah—appearance."

"The man was tough-looking, Your Eminence, and somewhat older than I, I should say. He had not shaved, yet he was decently dressed and wore a hanger. Straight brown hair, Your Eminence. A reddish beard, and dark and piercing eyes. Quite tall. I took note of his hands, particularly, when he took that," Gulo indicated the bracelet, "from me.

And when he returned it to me, Your Eminence. He had unusually large and powerful ones, Your Eminence. A brawler, I should say. Your Eminence finds me fanciful, I fear."

Remora grunted again. "Go ahead, Patera. Let me hear it. I'll tell you afterward, eh?"

"His hanger, Your Eminence. It was brass-fitted, with a large guard, and to judge from the scabbard it had a longer, broader blade than most, rather sharply curved. It seemed to me that the weapon was like to the man, Your Eminence, if you understand what I mean."

"I—ah—misdoubt that you do yourself, Patera. Yet these details may not be, um, wholly valueless. What of the woman, eh? This Chenille? Be as fanciful as you please."

"Remarkably attractive, Your Eminence. About twenty, tall though not stately. And yet there was an air—"

Remora's uplifted palm halted the younger augur in mid-thought. "Cherry-colored hair?"

"Why, yes, Your Eminence."

"I know her, Patera. I have had a—ah—achates or, um, three out looking for her since last night. So this—ah—fiery vixen was back at Silk's manteion this morning, eh? I will have this and that to say to my, um, adherents, Patera. Let's see that gaud again."

He picked the bracelet up. "I don't suppose you know what this is worth? The green stone, eh? Particularly?"

"Fifty cards, Your Eminence?"

"I have no idea. You haven't had it—um—valuated? No, no, don't. Return it to Silk's box, eh? Tell him—ah—nothing. I'll tell him myself. Tell Incus on your way out that I want to speak with Patera on Tarsday. Have Incus send a note with you, but it's not to mention that you were here, hey? Have him mark the time on my regimen."

Gulo nodded forcefully. "I will, Your Eminence."

"This—ah—woman. Precisely what did she say and do while she was in your presence? Every word, eh?"

"Why nothing, Your Eminence. I don't believe she ever spoke. Let me think."

Remora waved permission. "Take as long as you—ah—consider best. No, um, circumstance too trivial to mention, hey?"

Gulo shut his eyes and bent his head, a hand pressed to his temple. Silence descended upon the large and airy room from which Patera Remora, as coadjutor, conducted the often-tangled affairs of the Chapter. Through four blazing eyes, Twice-headed Pas regarded Gulo's bowed back from a priceless painting by Campion; a Guardsman's restless mount nickered in the street below.

After a minute or two had passed, Remora rose and walked to the bull's-eye window behind his chair. It stood open, and through its circular aperture (whose diameter exceeded his own very considerable height), he could see the gabled roofs and massive towers of the Juzgado at the foot of this, the western and least precipitous slope of the Palatine. High above the tallest, flying from a pole some trick of the glaring sunlight rendered nearly invisible, floated the bright green banner of Viron. Upon it, fitfully animated by the hot and dilatory wind, Scylla's long, white arms appeared to beckon, just as the papillae of certain invertebrates of her lake waved in evident imitation of its surface, searching the clear waters blindly and ceaselessly for bits of carrion and living fish alike.

"Your Eminence? I believe I can tell you everything I saw now."

Remora turned back to Gulo. "Excellent. Ah—capital! Proceed, Patera."

"It was brief, as I said, Your Eminence. If it had been longer I would be less confident. Is Your Eminence familiar with the small garden attached to our manteion?"

Remora shook his head.

"There is such a place, Your Eminence. One can enter it from the manteion proper—that's how I entered it upon my arrival. I had looked in the manteion first, thinking that I might find Patera Silk at prayer."

"The woman, please, Patera. This—ah—Chenille, eh?"

"There's a grape arbor near the center, Your Eminence, with seats under the vines. She was sitting there, almost completely concealed by the dependent foliage. Patera and the layman, Auk, had been talking there with her, I believe. They came to meet me, but she remained seated."

"She—ah—emerged, eventually?"

"Yes, Your Eminence. We spoke for a minute or so, and Patera gave me their names, as I've reported them. Then he said that he was leaving, and his bird—is Your Eminence familiar with his bird?"

Remora nodded again. "The woman, Patera."

"Patera said they would leave, and she left the arbor. He said—these are his precise words, I believe—'This is Patera Gulo, Chenille. We were speaking of him earlier.' She nodded and smiled."

"And then, Patera? What—ah—next transpired, hey?"

"They left together, Your Eminence. The three of them. Patera had said, 'We're off to the lake, you silly bird.' And as they went out of the gate—there's a gate to Sun Street from the garden, Your Eminence—the layman said, 'Hope you get something, only don't go down in the chops if you don't.' But the woman said nothing at all."

"Her dress, Patera?"

"Black, Your Eminence. I remember that for a moment I thought it was a sibyl's habit, but it was actually just a black wool gown, such as fashionable women wear in winter."

"Jewelry? You said she wore a ring, eh?"

"Yes, Your Eminence. And a necklace and earrings, both jade. I noticed her ring particularly because it sparkled as she pushed the grapevines to one side. There was a dark red gem like a carbuncle, quite large, I believe in a simple setting of yellow gold. If Your Eminence would only confide in me . . . ?"

"Tell you why she's—um—central? She may not be." Sighing, Remora pushed his chair away from the escritoire and returned to the window. With his back to Gulo and his hands clasped behind it, he repeated, "She may not be."

Moved by an excess of mannerliness, Gulo stood, too.

"Or yet, she—um—may. You're anxious to minister to the gods, Patera. Or so you declare, eh?"

"Oh, yes, Your Eminence. Extremely anxious."

"And also to rise in the—ah—books of an—er—um— remarkably extensive family, hey? That I have—ah—made note of as well. You have considered that in, um, due course you might eventually become Prolocutor, hey?"

Gulo blushed like a girl. "Oh, no, Your Eminence. That—that is—I—"

"No, no, you have, eh? Every young augur does; I did it myself. Has it struck home yet that by the time you get so much as—um—a whiff of mulberry, those whom you hope to—ah—impress? Overawe. That they will be dead? Gone, eh? Forgotten by everyone except the gods, Patera Gulo my boy. And you, eh? Forgotten by everyone save the gods and yourself. And who can vouch for the gods, eh? Such is the—ah—fact of the matter, I, er, warrant you."

No doubt wisely, Gulo swallowed and remained silent.

"You cannot do it by any stretch, Patera. Eh? By none. Assume the office. If you ever do. Not till I myself have gone, eh? And my successor, likewise. You are—ah—too young at present. Not even if I live long, hey? You know it, eh? Take an idiot not to, hey?"

Poor Gulo nodded, desperately wishing that he might flee instead.

The coadjutor turned to face him. "I cannot—um—speak for him, eh? My successor. Only for myself. Ah—yes. For myself, I—ah—um—meditate a reign longer than old Quetzal's, hey?"

"I would never wish you less, Your Eminence."

"His chambers are over there, Patera." Remora waved his left hand vaguely. "On this very floor of the palace, hey? South side. Faces our garden." He chuckled. "Bigger than Patera Silk's. Much more—ah—extensive, er, doubtless. Fountains—ah—statuary, and big trees. All that."

Gulo nodded. "They're lovely, I know, Your Eminence."

"He's held the office for thirty-three years already, hey? Old Quetzal. There are one hundred and—ah—odd of your generation, Patera. Many better—um—connected. I—ah—proffer a nearer target, an—ah—straighter road for your ambition."

Remora resumed his chair and motioned for Gulo to sit. "An—ah—little game now, eh? A sport, to while away this, um, overheated hour. Choose yourself a city, Patera. Any city you care to name, so long as it is not Viron. I'm perfectly serious. Within the—um—hedge of the game. Consider. Large? Fair? Rich? Which city will you have, eh, Patera?"

"Palustria, Your Eminence?"

"Down amongst the pollywogs, hey? Good enough. Then conceive yourself at the head of the Chapter in Palustria. Perhaps—ah—a decade hence. You will tithe, I should think, to the parent Chapter, here in Viron. You continue subject to the Prolocutor, eh? Whomever he may be. To old Quetzal, or to—ah—myself, as is more probable in ten years time. Do you find it a—um—attractive prospect, Patera?" Remora raised a hand as he had before. "Needn't say so, if it—ah—troubles you."

"Your Eminence—?"

"I have no idea, Patera. None whatsoever, eh? But the drought. You're aware of that, hey? Can't escape it. How fairs your—ah—choice, Patera? How fares Palustria in the drought?"

Gulo swallowed. "I've heard that the rice crop failed, Your Eminence. I know there's no rice in the market here, though traders usually bring it."

Remora nodded. "There is rioting, Patera. There is—um—no starvation. None as yet. But there is the specter of starvation. Soldiers trying to, er, check the—ah—mob. Practically—ah—worn out, some of those soldiers. Uncle a military man, eh?"

Bewildered by the sudden shift in topic, Gulo managed, "Wh—why I—one is, Your Eminence."

"Major in the Second Brigade. Ask him where our army is, Patera. Or perhaps you can tell me now? Heard his—um—table talk? Where is it, eh?"

"In storage, Your Eminence. Underground. Here in Viron the Civil Guard is all we need."

"Precisely. Not so elsewhere though, Patera. We die, eh? Grow old like—ah—His Cognizance. And tread the path to Mainframe. Chems last longer, though. Forever?"

"I hadn't considered the matter, Your Eminence. But I would think—"

A corner of Remora's mouth twitched upward. "But you will, eh? To be sure you will, Patera. Now, eh? Good to know that the—ah—arms of Scylla are good as new, eh? Or—ah—very nearly so. Not like—ah—um—Palustria's, hey? And many others. Soldiers and their—ah—weapons like new or nearly. Think about it, Patera."

Remora straightened up in his chair, resting his elbows

on the escritoire. "What—um—more have you to report
concerning Patera, Patera?"

"Your Eminence mentioned weapons. I found a paper
packet of needles, Your Eminence. Opened."

"A paper of needles, Patera? I fail—"

"Not sewing needles," Gulo added hastily. "Projectiles
for a needler, Your Eminence. In one of Patera's drawers,
under clothing."

"I—ah—must consider that," Remora said slowly.
"I—um—it is of—um—concern. No question. Anything—
ah—further?"

"My final item, Your Eminence. One that I would much
rather not have to report. This letter." Gulo extracted it
from the pocket of his robe. "It's from—"

"You have, er, opened it." Remora favored him with a
gentle smile.

"It's in a feminine hand, Your Eminence, and is heavily
perfumed. Under the circumstances I think that what I did
was justified. I hoped, very sincerely, Your Eminence, that
it would prove to have emanated from a sister or some
other female relation, Your Eminence. However—"

"You are—ah—bold, Patera. That's well, or so I am—
ah—disposed to conclude. Sphigx favors the bold, eh?"
Remora peered at the superscription. "Not from this—
um—lady Chenille, hey? Or you would've said so previously, hum?"

"No, Your Eminence. From another woman."

"Read it to me, Patera. You must have—ah—puzzled
out that—um—contorted scribble. I should, er, choose
not to."

"I fear that you will find, Your Eminence, that Patera
Silk has compromised himself. I wish—"

"I'll be the—ah—judge, eh? Read it, Patera."

Gulo cleared his throat and unfolded the letter. " 'O My
Darling Wee Flea: I call you so not only because of the way

you sprang from my window, but because of the way you hopped into my bed! How your lonely bloss has longed for a note from you!!!' "

"Bloss, Patera?"

"A pretended wife, I believe, Your Eminence."

"I—ah—very well. Proceed, Patera. Is there—ah further revelation?"

"I'm afraid so, Your Eminence. 'You might have sent one by the kind friend who brought you my gift, you know!' "

"Let me—ah—examine that, Patera." Remora extended his hand, and Gulo passed him the much-creased paper.

"Ah—hum."

"Yes, Your Eminence."

"She really does—ah—write like that, hey? Doesn't she? Yes—ah—does she not. I would not have—ah—conceded, er, previously, that a human being could."

Brows knit, Remora bent over the paper. " 'Now you have to tender me your,'—ah—um—'thanks,' I suppose that must be, eh? 'And so much more, when,'—ah—um—'next we meet,' with yet another screamer. 'Don't you know that little,'—um—'place up on the Palatine—' Well, well, well!"

"Yes, Your Eminence."

" 'That little place up on the Palatine where Thelx,' I suppose she—ah—intends Thelxiepeia but doesn't—ah—apprehend the spelling. 'Where Thelx holds up a mirror? *Hieraxday.*' That last—um—underscored. Heavily, eh? Signature, 'Hy.' "

Remora tapped the paper with a long fingernail. "Well—ah—do you, Patera? Where is it, eh? A picture, I—ah—if I may guess at hazard. Not in one of the manteions, hey? I know them all."

Gulo shook his head. "I've never seen a picture like that, Your Eminence."

"In a—ah—house, most likely, Patera. A private—um—residence, I would—um—opine." Remora bawled, *"Incus!"* over Gulo's shoulder, and a small, sly-looking augur with buckteeth looked in so quickly as to suggest that he had been eavesdropping.

"Whereabouts might we—ah—descry Thelxiepeia and a mirror, here on the hill, eh, Incus? You don't know. Make—um—inquiries. I shall expect their result tomorrow at, um, no later than luncheon. Should be a simple matter, eh?" Remora glanced down at the letter's broken seal. "And fetch a seal with a—um—heart or kiss or some such for this." He tossed Hyacinth's letter across the room to Incus.

"Immediately, Your Eminence."

Remora turned back to Gulo. "It won't—um—signify if Patera has seen this one, Patera. She's the sort who'll have a round dozen at fewest, eh? You don't know how to—um—preserve the seal? Incus can show you. A useful art, eh?"

As the latch clicked behind his bowing prothonotary, Remora rose once more. "You take that back to Sun Street with you, eh? When he's through with it. If Patera isn't back, put it on the mantel. If he is, say it was—ah—handed to you as you went out, eh? You haven't glanced at it, hey?"

Gulo nodded glumly. "Naturally, Your Eminence."

Remora leaned closer to peer at him. "Something—um—troubling you, Patera. Out with it."

"Your Eminence, how could an anointed augur, a man of Patera's high promise, compromise himself so? I mean this absurd, filthy woman. And yet a goddess—! I understand now, only too well, why Your Eminence believes Patera must be watched, but—but a theophany!"

Remora sucked his teeth. "It's an—ah—habitual observation of old Quetzal's that the gods don't have laws, Patera. Only preferences."

"I myself can see, Your Eminence—but when the augur in question—"

Remora silenced him with a gesture. "Possibly we will, er, be made privy to the secret, Patera. In due time, eh? Possibly there's none. You've considered Palustria?"

Afraid to trust his voice, Gulo merely nodded.

"Capital." Remora regarded him narrowly. "Now then. What do you know about the—ah—history of the caldés, Patera?"

"The caldés, Your Eminence? Only that the last one died before I was born, and the Ayuntamiento decided that nobody could replace him."

"And replaced him—um—themselves, hey? In effect. You realize that, Patera?"

"I suppose so, Your Eminence."

Remora stalked across the room to a tall bookcase. "I knew him, eh? The last. A loud, tyrannical, tumultuous sort of man. The mob—um—doted upon him, hey? They always love that kind." He extracted a thin volume bound in russet leather and recrossed the room to drop it into Gulo's lap. "The Charter, eh? Written in—ah—deity by Scylla and corrected by Pas. So it—um—asserts. Have a look at clause seven. Quickly, hey? Then tell me what you find—um—outré in it."

Silence settled over the spacious, somberly furnished room once more as the young augur bent over the book. In the street, litter bearers fought like sparrows with much shouting and a few blows; as the minutes ticked by, Remora watched their dispute though the open window.

Gulo looked up. "It provides for the election of new councillors, Your Eminence. Every three years. I assume that this provision has been suspended?"

"Delicately—um—phrased, Patera. You may—ah—attain Palustria yet. What else?"

"And it says the caldé is to hold office for life, and may appoint his successor."

Remora nodded. "Reshelve it, will you? Not done now, eh? No caldé at all. Yet it's still law. You know of the frozen embryo trade, Patera? New breeds of cattle, exotic pets, slaves, too, in places like Trivigaunte, eh? Where do they come from, hey?"

Gulo hurried to the bookcase. "From other cities, Your Eminence?"

"Which say the same, Patera. Seeds and cuttings that grow plants of—um—bizarre form. They die, hey? Or most do. Or, um, thrive beyond nature."

"I've heard of them, Your Eminence."

"Most of the beasts, and men, are—ah—commonplace. Or nearly, eh? A few—um—monstrosities, eh? Pitiful. Or fearful. Extraordinary prices for those. Give ear now, Patera."

"I'm listening, Your Eminence."

Remora stood beside him, a hand on his shoulder, nearly whispering. "This was common knowledge, eh? Fifteen years ago. The caldé's folly, we called it. Forgotten now, hum? And you're not to speak about it to anyone, Patera. Not to stir it up, hey?"

Craning his neck to meet the eyes of the coadjutor, Gulo declared, "Your Eminence can rely upon me absolutely."

"Capital. Before he—ah—collected his reward from the gods, Patera, the caldé paid out a sum of that—um—magnitude, hey? Bought a human embryo. Something—ah—extraordinary."

"I see." Gulo moistened his lips. "I appreciate your confidence in me, Your Eminence."

"A successor, eh? Or an—ah—weapon. Nobody knows,

Patera. The Ayuntamiento's no—ah—wiser than yourself, Patera, now that I've told you."

"If I may inquire, Your Eminence . . . ?"

"What became of it? That is the—ah—crux, Patera. And what could it do? Extraordinary strength, perhaps. Or hear your thoughts, eh? Move things without touching them? There are rumors of such people. Ayuntamiento searched, eh? Never stopped, never gave up."

"Had it been implanted, Your Eminence?"

"No one knew. Still don't, eh?" Remora returned to his escritoire and sat down. "A year passed. Then two, five—ah—ten. They came to us. Wanted us to test every child in every palaestra in the city, and we did it. Memory, eh? Dexterity. All sorts of things. There were a few we—ah—took an interest in. No good, hey? The harder we, er, scrutinized them, the less—ah—outlandish they looked. Early development, eh? A few years and the rest caught up."

Remora shook his head. "Not—ah—um—unforeseen, we said, and the—ah—Lemur, Loris, and the rest likewise. They're not always what they're cracked up to be, these frozen embryos. Die in the womb, more often than not. Everybody forgot it. You follow me?"

Though Gulo was seldom subject to flashes of insight, he had one at that moment. "Y-y-your Eminence has located this person! It's this woman Chenille!"

Remora pursed his lips. "I did not—ah—asseverate anything of the kind, Patera."

"Indeed not, Your Eminence."

"Patera has become an—ah—popular figure, Patera, as I, er, implied to you yesterday. This theophany, to be sure. 'Silk for caldé' daubed upon walls forest-to-lake. Bound to attract all sorts, eh? He must be watched over by an acolyte of—um—sagacity. And large discretion. His associates must be watched likewise. A weighty—um—obligation for one so young. But for the future coadjutor for Palustria, a fitting devoir."

Sensing his dismissal, Gulo rose and bowed. "I will do my best, Your Eminence."

"Capital. See Incus about that letter, and my note to Patera."

Greatly daring, Gulo inquired, "Do you think that Patera himself may have guessed, Your Eminence? Or that this woman may have told him outright?"

Remora nodded gloomily.

Here, at its loftiest point, the cliff jutted into the lake like the prow of a giant's boat. Here, according to a modest bronze plaque let into its side next to the entrance, Lacustral Scylla's most humble petitioner Lemur, Presiding Officer of the Ayuntamiento, had erected to her glory this chaste hemispherical dome of milky, translucent, blue stone, supported on the wavering tips of these (Silk counted them) ten tapering, fragile-looking pillars, themselves resting upon a squat balustrade. There were fine-lined drawings of her exploits, both factual and legendary, traced in bronze on the balustrade. Most impressive of all, there was her representation, with floating hair and bare breasts, inlaid in bronze in the stone floor, with ten coiling arms extended toward the ten pillars.

And there was nothing else.

"There's no one here, Oreb," Silk said. "Yet I know we saw somebody."

The bird only muttered.

Still shaking his head in perplexity, Silk stepped into the deep shadow of the dome. As his dusty black shoe made contact with the floor, he thought he heard a faint groan from the solid rock beneath him.

And very much to Silk's surprise, Oreb flew. He did not fly well or far, merely out between two pillars to alight heavily upon a spur of naked rock eight or ten cubits from the shrine; but fly he did, Crane's little splint a bright blue against his sable plumage.

"What are you afraid of, silly bird? Falling?"

Oreb cocked his sleek head in the direction of Limna. "Fish heads?"

"Yes," Silk promised. "More fish heads just as soon as we get back."

"Watch out!"

Fanning himself with his wide straw hat, Silk turned to admire the lake. A few friendly sails shone here and there, minute triangles of white against the prevailing cobalt. It was cooler here than it had been among the rocks, and would be cooler still, no doubt, in a boat like those he watched. If he preserved the manteion as the Outsider wished, perhaps he might some summer bring a party from the palaestra here, children who had never seen the lake or ridden in a boat or caught a fish. It would be an experience that they would never forget, surely; an adventure they would treasure for the whole length of their lives.

"Watch arm!"

Oreb's voice came on the land breeze, faint but shrill. Silk glanced up automatically at his own left hand, lifted nearly to the low dome as he leaned against one of the bent pillars; it was perfectly safe, of course.

He looked around for Oreb, but the bird seemed to have vanished in the jumble of naked rock inland.

Oreb was returning to the wild now, Silk told himself—to freedom, exactly as he himself had invited him to do on that first night. To think of the once-caged bird happy and free should not have been painful, yet it was.

Scanning the rocks for Oreb, he saw, from the corner of one eye, the delicately curved pillars nearest the entrance drop from the dome. One barred the entrance with a double S. The other reached for him, its sinuous motion seemingly casual and almost careless. He dodged and struck at it with Blood's walking stick.

Effortlessly, the pillar looped about his waist, a noose of stone. Blood's stick shattered at the third blow.

In the floor, Scylla opened stony lips; irresistibly the tentacle carried him toward her gaping mouth, and as he hung struggling above the dark orifice, dropped him into it.

The initial fall was not great; but it was onto carpeted steps, and he tumbled down them, rolling in wild confusion until he sprawled at last on a floor twenty or thirty cubits below the shrine, with sore knees and elbows and a bruised cheek.

"Oh, you gods!"

The sound of his voice brought light; there were large, comfortable-looking armchairs here, upholstered in brown and burnt orange, and a sizable table; but Silk gave them small attention, gripping his injured ankle in one hand while the other lashed the carpet with Crane's wrapping.

As though by a miracle, the circular panel of deep blue that was the farther end of the room irised wide, revealing a towering talus; its ogre's face was of black metal, and the slender black barrels of buzz guns flanked its gleaming fangs. *"You again!"* it roared.

The memory of Blood's blade-crowned wall returned—the still and sweltering night, the gate of thick-set bars, and this shouting giant of brass and steel. Silk shook his head as he replaced the wrapping; though it required an effort to keep his voice steady, he said loudly, "I've never been here before."

"I knew you!" Swiftly, the talus's left arm lengthened, reaching for him.

He scrambled up the carpeted stair. "I didn't want to come here! I wasn't trying to get in."

"I know you!"

A metal hand as large as a shovel closed on Silk's right forearm, clamping the injuries inflicted by the white-headed one; Silk screamed.

"Does this hurt you!"

"Yes," he gasped. "It hurts. Terribly. Please let me go. I'll do whatever you say."

The steel hand shook him. *"You don't care!"*

Silk screamed again, writhing in the grasp of fingers as thick as pipes.

"Musk punished me! Humiliated me!"

The shaking stopped. The enormous mechanical arm lifted Silk, and, as he dangled puppylike in midair, contracted. Through chattering teeth, he gasped, "You're Blood's talus. You stopped me at his gate."

The steel hand opened, and he fell heavily to the floor.

"I was right!"

The azoth he had carried from the city to the lake was no longer in his waistband. Striving to keep his voice from breaking, he said, "May I stand up?" hoping to feel it slip down his trouser leg.

"Musk sent me away!" the talus roared; grotesquely, its vertical upper body angled forward as it addressed him.

Silk stood, but the azoth was gone; it had been in place when he had admired the lake from the shrine, certainly; so it had presumably been lost in his fall, and might still be near the top of the stair.

He risked a cautious step backward. "I'm terribly sorry—really, I am. I don't have any influence with Musk, who dislikes me much more than he could ever dislike you. But I may have some small amount with Blood, and I'll do whatever I can to get you reinstated."

"No! You won't!"

"I will." Silk essayed another small backward step. "I will, I assure you."

"You soft things!" Noiselessly, and apparently without

effort, the talus glided over the carpet on twin dark belts, the crest of its brazen helmet almost scraping the ceiling. *"You look the same because you are the same! Easy to break! No repair! Full of filth!"*

Still edging backward, Silk asked, "Were you in the shrine? Up there?"

"Yes! My processor by interface!"

Both the talus's steel hands reached for him this time, extended so swiftly that he escaped them by no more than the width of a finger. He stumbled backward, desperately pushed a heavy armchair into the path of one hand, and dove beneath the table.

It was lifted, rotated in the air, and slammed down flat to kill him as a man swats a fly; he rolled frantically to one side and felt the edge of its massive top brush the wide sleeve of his robe, the sudden gust as it crashed down.

Something lay on the floor, not a cubit from his face, a green crystal in a silver setting. He snatched it up as the talus snatched him up, holding him this time by the back of his robe, so that he dangled from its hand like a black moth caught by its sooty wings.

"Musk hurt me!" the talus roared. *"Hurt me and made me go! I returned to Potto! He was not pleased!"*

"I had nothing to do with that." Silk's voice was as soothing as he could make it. "I'll help you if I can—I swear it."

"You got inside! I was on guard!" It shook him. *"In the tunnel the red water won't matter!"*

It was backing through the irised wall with him, moving slowly but steadily, its arms retracting to bring him ever closer to its fearsome face.

"I don't want to hurt you," Silk told it. "It's evil—that means very wrong—to destroy chems, as wrong as it is to destroy bios, and you're very nearly a chem."

That halted it momentarily. *"Chems are junk!"*

"Chems are wonderful constructions, a race that we bios created long ago, our own image in metal and synthetics."

"Bios are fish guts!" The backward glide resumed.

Silk held the azoth firmly in his left hand, his thumb on the demon. "Please say that you won't kill me."

"No!"

"Let me return to the surface."

"No!"

"I'll do you no more harm, I swear; and I'll help you if I can."

"I will drop you and crush you!" the talus roared. *"One blow!"* The wall irised closed behind them, leaving them in a long, dim passageway, a little more than twice the talus's width, bored through the solid stone of the cliff.

"Don't you fear the immortal gods, my son?" Silk asked in desperation. "I'm the servant of one god and the friend of another."

"I serve Scylla!"

"As an augur, I receive the protection of all the gods, including hers."

The steel fingers shook him more violently than before, then released his robe; he fell, nearly losing his grip on the azoth as he struck the dark and dirty stone floor. Sprawling, half-blind with pain, he looked up into that ogre's mask of a metal face and glimpsed the steel fist lifted higher than its owner's head.

The wings of Hierax roared in his ears; without time to think, reason, threaten, or equivocate, he pressed the demon.

Stabbing out from the hilt, the azoth blade of universal discontinuity caught the talus below the right eye; jagged scraps of incandescent slag burst from the point it struck. The steel fist smashed down but appeared to lose direction as it descended, hammering the stone floor to his left.

Black smoke and crackling orange flames erupted from the mass of wreckage that had been the talus's head, and with them a deafening roar of rage and anguish. The great steel fists swung wildly, pounding flying chips as sharp as flints from the stone sides of the passageway. Eyeless and ablaze, the talus lurched toward him.

A single slash from the azoth severed both the wide dark belts on which it had moved; they lashed the floor, the walls, and the dying talus itself like whips, then fell limp. There was a muffled explosion; flames shot up from the wagonlike body behind the vertical torso.

Scrambling away from the heat and smoke, Silk released the demon, stood, thrust the azoth back into his waistband, dusted off his black robe, and got out his beads. Swinging their voided cross toward the burning talus, he traced the sign of addition again and again. "I convey to you, my son, the forgiveness of all the gods."

His chant was flat and almost mechanical at first, but as the wonder and magnanimity of divine amnesty filled his mind, his voice grew louder and shook with fervor. "Recall now the words of Pas, who said, 'Do my will, live in peace, multiply, and do not disturb my seal. Thus you shall escape my wrath. Go willingly, and any wrong that you have ever done shall be forgiven you. . . .' "

Incus returned Hyacinth's letter to Gulo with a smirk. Its new seal, similar though not identical to the original one, displayed a leaping flame between cupped hands. "Her full name would be *Hymenocallis,* I expect," Incus remarked. "Very pretty. I've used it a time or two myself."

"I didn't write it," Gulo told him sullenly. "But you're supposed to write to Patera Silk now, telling him to wait upon His Eminence Tarsday. You're to set the hour and mark it on His Eminence's regimen."

The buck-toothed prothonotary nodded. "You'll deliver it for us? I'd rather not have to whistle up another boy just now so old Remora can whip your randy cur to kennel."

Pudgy Patera Gulo advanced on him with clenched fists and reddening cheeks. "Patera Silk's a real man, you manse-wife. Whatever he may've done with this woman, he's worth a dozen of you and three of me. Remember that, and the proportion."

Incus grinned up at him. "Why Gully! You're in *love!*"

Chapter 8

FOOD FOR THE GODS

Patera Silk took two long steps back from the still tightly closed door and eyed it with the disgust he felt for himself and his failure. It opened in some fashion—the talus had opened it, after all. Open, it would give him access to the stair that led up to the floor of the cliff-top shrine, and from there it might be possible (might even be easy) to open the mouth of the image of Scylla graven in the floor above and so climb out into the shrine and return to Limna.

Commissioners, Silk told himself, and—what else had the woman said?—judges and the like came here, clearly to confer with the Ayuntamiento. Before he had killed it with the azoth—

(He had to force himself to face those words, although he had told himself repeatedly and with perfect truth that he had killed only to save his own life.)

Before he had killed it, the talus had said that having been discharged by Musk it had returned here to Potto; and by "Potto" it had intended Councillor Potto, surely.

Thus the figure who had entered the shrine and vanished had no doubt been a commissioner, a judge, or something of the sort. Nor was his disappearance at all mysterious: He had entered and been seen, presumably by the talus; possibly he had shown some sort of tessera; Scylla's mouth had opened for him, and he had descended the stair and been conducted to a location that could not be remote, since the talus had been back at its post a half hour later.

It was all perfectly logical and showed clearly that the Ayuntamiento had offices nearby. The realization bowed Silk's shoulders like a burden. How could he, a citizen and an augur, withhold all that he had learned about Crane's activities, even to save the manteion?

Heartsick, he turned back to the door that had opened so smoothly for the talus, but would not open at all for him. It appeared to have no lock, no handle, and in fact no mechanism of any kind to open it. Its irising plates were so tightly fitted that he could scarcely make out the curving lines between them. He had shouted *open* and a hundred other plausible words at it, without result.

Hoarse and discouraged, he had hewed and stabbed it with the shimmering discontinuity that was the blade of the azoth, scarring and fusing the plates until it was doubtful that even one who knew their secret could cause them to iris as they had for the talus. It had made an earsplitting racket, causing stones enough to drop from the walls and ceiling of the tunnel to have killed him ten times over, and at length it rendered the hilt of the azoth almost too hot to hold—all without opening the door or piercing even a single small hole in one plate.

And now there was, Silk told himself, no alternative but to set off, weary and hungry and bruised though he was, down the tunnel in the faint hope of finding some other place of egress. Ready almost to rage against the Outsider and every other god from sheer frustration, he sat down on the naked rock of the floor and removed Crane's wrapping. Crane, Silk recalled with some bitterness, had instructed

him to beat only smooth surfaces with it, instancing his
hassock or a carpet. No doubt Crane's recommendation
had been intended to preserve the wrapping's soft, leather-
like surface from needless wear; the rough floor hardly
qualified, and he owed something to Crane, not least because he intended to extort the money Blood demanded
from Crane if he could, though Crane had befriended him
more than once.

Sighing, Silk took off his robe, folded it, laid it on the
floor, and lashed the folded cloth until the wrapping felt
hotter than the hilt of the azoth. When it was back in place,
he climbed laboriously to his feet, put on his robe again (its
warmth was welcome in the cool and ever-soughing air)
and set out resolutely, choosing the direction that seemed
most likely to bring him nearer Limna.

He began with the idea of counting his steps, so as to
know how far he had traveled underground; he counted
silently at first, moving his lips and extending a finger from
his clenched fist at each hundred. Soon he found that he
was counting aloud, comforted by the faint echo of his
voice, and that he was no longer certain whether he had
reclosed his fist once for five hundred steps or twice for a
thousand.

The tunnel, which had appeared so unchanging, altered in minor ways as he progressed, and these soon became of such interest that he forgot his count in his hurry
to examine them. In places the native freestone gave way to
shiprock, graduated like a cubit stick by seams at intervals
of twenty-three steps. Here and there the creeping sound-
kindled lights failed entirely, so that he was forced to advance in the dark; and though he realized how foolish such
fears were, he could not entirely dispel the thought that he
might fall into a pit, or that another talus or something
more fearsome still might await him in the dark. Twice he
passed irising doors much like the one that had excluded

him from the room beneath Scylla's shrine, both tightly closed; once the tunnel divided, and he followed the left at random; three times side tunnels, dark and somehow menacing, opened from the one he followed.

And always it seemed to him that it descended ever so slightly, and that its air grew cooler and its walls damper.

He prayed his beads as he walked, then tried to reconcile the distance covered during three recitals with his subsequent count of steps, eventually concluding that he had taken ten thousand, three hundred and seventy—or the equivalent of five complete recitals of his beads and an odd decade. To this, add the original five hundred (or possibly one thousand) making . . .

By that time his ankle was acutely painful; he renewed the wrapping as before and hobbled off down the tunnel again, which oppressed him more with each halting stride.

Frequently he was tormented by an almost uncontrollable urge to turn back. If he had allowed the azoth to cool and attacked the door again, it seemed to him almost certain that it would have given way easily; by now he would have been back in Limna. Auk had recommended eating places there; he tried to recall their names, and those of the ones he had passed while looking for the Juzgado.

No, it had been the driver of the wagon who had recommended eating places. One, he had said, was quite good but expensive; that had been the Rusty Lantern. He had no fewer than seven cards in his pocket, five from Orpine's rites, plus two of the three that Blood had surrendered to him on Phaesday. His dinner with Auk in an uphill eating house had cost Auk eighteen bits. It had seemed an extravagant sum then, but it was a small one compared to seven cards. A sumptuous dinner in Limna at one of the better inns, a comfortable bed, and a fine breakfast would leave him change from a single card. It seemed foolish not to turn back, when all these things were (or might so easily be made) so near. Half a dozen words that might open the door, all untried, occurred to him in quick succession: *free, disengage, separate, loose, dissolve,* and *cleave.*

Far worse was the unfounded feeling that he had already turned back, that he was walking not north toward Limna but south again, that at any minute, around any slight curve or turning, he would catch sight of the dead talus.

Of the talus he had killed; but the talus had, or so it seemed, sent him to the grave. It was dead, he buried. Soon, he felt, he would encounter Orpine, old Patera Pike, and his mother, each in the appropriate state of decay. He and they would lie down together on the floor of the tunnel, perhaps, one place being as good as another here, and they would tell him the many things he would need to know among the dead, just as Patera Pike had instructed him (when he had arrived at Sun Street) concerning the shops and people of the quarter, the necessity of buying one's tunics and turnips from those few shopkeepers who attended sacrifice with some regularity, and the need to beware of certain notorious liars and swindlers. Once he heard a distant tittering, a lunatic laughter without humor or merriment or even humanity: the laughter of a devil devouring its own flesh in the dark.

After what seemed half a day or more of weary, frightened walking, he reached a point at which the floor of the tunnel was covered with water for as far as he could see, the dim reflections of the bleared lights that crept along the ceiling showing plainly that the extent of the flood was by no means inconsiderable. Irresolute at the brink of that clear, still pool, he was forced to admit that it was even possible that the tunnel he had followed so long was, within the next league or two, entirely filled.

He knelt and drank, discovering that he was very thirsty indeed. When he tried to stand, his right ankle protested so vehemently that he sat instead, no longer able to hide from himself how tired he was. He would rest here for an hour; he felt certain that it was dark on the surface. Patera Gulo would no doubt be wondering what had become of him, eager to begin spying in earnest. Maytera Marble might be wondering too; but Auk and Chenille would have gone back to the city some time ago, after having left word for him at the wagon stop.

Silk took off his shoes and rubbed his feet (finding it a delightful exercise), and at last lay down. The rough floor of the tunnel ought certainly to have been uncomfortable, but somehow was not. He had been wise, clearly, to take this opportunity to nap on the seat of Blood's floater. He would be more alert, better able to grasp every advantage that their peculiar relationship conferred, thanks to this brief rest. "Can't float too fast," the driver told him, "not going *this* way!" But quite soon now, as the swift floater sailed over a landscape grown liquid, his mother would come to kiss him good-night; he liked to be awake for it, to say distinctly, "Good night to you, too, Mama," when she left.

He resolved not to sleep until she came.

Weaving and more than half-drunk, Chenille emerged from the door of the Full Sail, caught sight of Auk, and waved. "You there! You, Bucko. Don' I know you?" When he smiled and waved in return, she crossed the street and caught his arm. "You've been to Orchid's place. Sure you have, lots, and I oughta know your name. It'll come to me in a minute. Listen, Buck, I'm not queering a lay for you, am I?"

Auk had learned early in childhood to cooperate in such instances. "Dimber with me. Stand you a glass?" He jerked his thumb toward the Full Sail. "I bet there's a nice quiet corner in there?"

"Oh, Bucko, would you?" Chenille leaned upon his arm, walking so close that her thigh brushed his. "Wha's your name? Mine's Chenille. I oughta know yours too, course I should, only I got this queer head an' we're at the lake, aren't we?" She blew her nose in her fingers. "All that water, I seen it down one of these streets, Bucko, only I ought to get back to Orchid's for dinner an' the big room after that, you know? She'll get Bass to winnow me out if I'm not lucky."

Auk had been watching her eyes from the corner of his own; as they entered the Full Sail, he said, "That's the lily word, ain't it, Jugs? You don't remember."

She nodded dolefully as she sat down, her fiery curls trembling. "An' I'm reedy, too—real reedy. You got a pinch for me?"

Auk shook his head.

"Just a pinch an' all night free?"

"I'd give it to you if I had it," Auk told her, "but I don't."

A frowning barmaid stopped beside their table. "Take her someplace else."

"Red ribbon and water," Chenille told the barmaid, "and don't mix them."

The barmaid shook her head emphatically. "I gave you more than I should've already."

"An' I gave *you* all my money!"

He laid a card on the table. "You start a tab for me, darling. My name's Auk."

The barmaid's frown vanished. "Yes, sir."

"And I'll have a beer, the best. Nothing for her."

Chenille protested.

"I said I'd buy you one in the street. We're not in the street." Auk waved the barmaid away.

"That's your name!" Chenille was triumphant. "Auk. I told you I'd think of it."

He leaned toward her. "Where's Patera?"

She wiped her nose on her forearm.

"Patera Silk. You come out here with him. What'd you do with him?"

"Oh, I remember him. He was at Orchid's when—when Auk, I need a pinch bad. You've got money. Please?"

"In a minute, maybe. I ain't got my beer. Now you pay attention to what I say. You sat in here awhile lapping up red ribbon, didn't you?"

Chenille nodded. "I felt so—"

"Up your flue." He caught her hand and squeezed hard enough to hurt. "Where were you before that?"

She belched softly. "I'll tell you the truth, the whole thing. Only it isn't going to make any sense. If I tell you, will you buy me one?"

His eyes narrowed. "Talk fast. I'll decide after I hear it."

The barmaid set a sweating glass of dark beer in front of him. "The best and the coldest. Anything else, sir?"

He shook his head impatiently.

"I got up shaggy late," Chenille began, " 'cause we'd had a big one last night, you know? Real big. Only you weren't there, Hackum. See, I remember you now. I wished you would have been."

Auk tightened his grip on her hand again. "I know I wasn't. Get naked."

"An' I had to dress up 'cause it was the funeral today an' Orchid wanted everybody to go. 'Sides, I'd told that long augur I would." She belched again. "Wha's his name, Hackum?"

"Silk," Auk said.

"Yeah, that's him. So I got out my good black dress, this one, see? An', you know, fixed up. There was a lot going together, only they'd already gone so I had to go by myself. Can't I have just one li'l sippy of that, Hackum? Please?"

"All right."

Auk pushed the sweating glass across the table to her, and she drank and wiped her mouth on her forearm. "You're not s'posed to mix them, are you? I better be careful."

He took back the glass. "You went to Orpine's funeral. Go on from that."

"That's right. Only I had a big pinch first, the last I had. Really sucked it up. I wish I had it back now."

Auk drank.

"Well, I got to the manteion, an' Orchid and everybody was already there an' they'd started, but I got a place an' sat down, an', an'—"

"And what?" Auk demanded.

"An' then I got up, but they were all gone. I was just looking at the Window, you know? But it was just a Window, and there wasn't anybody else in there hardly at all, only a couple old ladies, an' nobody or nothing anymore." She had started to cry, hot tears spilling down the broad flat cheeks. Auk pulled out a not-very-clean handkerchief and gave it to her. "Thanks." She wiped her eyes. "I was so scared, an' I still am. You think I'm scared of you, but it's just so nice to be with somebody an' have somebody to talk to. You don' know."

Auk scratched his head.

"An' I went outside, see? An' I wasn't in the city at all, not on Sun Street or any other place. I was way down here where we used to go when I was little, an' everybody gone. I found this place where they had awnings an' tables under them an' I had maybe three or four, and then this big black bird came, it kept hopping around and talking almost like a person till I threw this one little glass at it an' they made me get out."

Auk stood. "You hit it with that glass? Shag, no, you didn't. Come on. Show me where this place with the awnings is."

*   *   *

A steep hillside covered with brush barred Silk from the cenoby. He scrambled down it, scratching his hands and face and tearing his clothes on thorns and broken twigs, and went inside. Maytera Mint was in bed, sick, and he was briefly glad of it, having forgotten that no male was supposed to enter the cenoby save an augur to bring the pardon of the gods. He murmured their names again and again, each time sure that he had forgotten one, until a short plump student he never remembered from the schola arrived to tell him that they were all going down the street to call on the Prelate, who was also ill. Maytera Mint got out of bed, saying she would come too, but she was naked under her pink peignoir, her sleek metal body gleaming through it like silver. The peignoir carried the cloying perfume of the blue-glass lamp, and he told her she would have to dress before she could go.

He and the short, plump student left the cenoby. It was raining, a hard, cold, pounding rain that chilled him to the bone. A litter with six bearers was waiting in the street, and they discussed its ownership though he felt certain that it was Maytera Marble's. The bearers were all old, one was blind, and the dripping canopy was old, faded, and torn. He was ashamed to ask the old men to carry them, so they went up the street to a large white structure without walls whose roof was of thin white slats set on edge a hand's breadth apart; in it there was so much white furniture that there was scarcely room to walk. They chose chairs and sat down to wait. When the Prelate came, he was Mucor, Blood's mad daughter.

They sat in the rain with her, shivering, discussing the affairs of the schola. She spoke about a difficulty she could not resolve, blaming him for it.

*   *   *

He sat up cold and stiff, and crossed his arms to put his freezing fingers in his armpits. Mucor told him, "It's drier farther on. Meet me where the bios sleep." She was sitting cross-legged on the water, and like the water, transparent. He wanted to ask her to guide him to the surface; at the sound of his voice she vanished with the rest of his dream, leaving only a shimmer of greenish light like slime on the water.

If that still, clear water had receded while he slept, the change was not apparent. He took off his stockings, tied his shoes together by their laces and hung them around his neck, and stuffed the wrapping into the pocket of his robe. He knotted the corners of his robe about his waist and rolled his trousers legs as high as he could while promising himself that exercise would soon warm him, that he would actually be more comfortable once he entered the water and began to walk.

It was as cold as he had feared, but shallow. It seemed to him that its very frigidity, its icy slapping against his injured ankle, should numb it; each time he put his weight on it, a needle stabbed deep into the bone nevertheless.

The faint splashings of his bare feet woke more lights, enabling him to see a considerable distance down the tunnel, which was flooded as far as the light reached. He did not actually know that water would harm the wrapping, and in fact he did not really believe it likely—people clever enough to build such a device would surely be able to protect it from an occasional wetting. But the wrapping was Crane's and not his, and though he would steal Crane's money if he had to in order to preserve the manteion, he would not risk ruining Crane's wrapping to save himself a little pain.

He had walked some distance when it occurred to him that he could warm himself somewhat by re-energizing the wrapping and returning it to his pocket. He tried the experiment, slapping the wrapping against the wall of the tunnel. The result was eminently satisfactory.

He thought of Blood's lioness-headed walking stick with nostalgia; if he had it now, it would take some weight off his injured ankle. Half a day ago (or a little more, perhaps) he had been ready to throw it away, calling his act of contempt a sacrifice to Scylla. Oreb had been frightened by that, and Oreb had been right; the goddess had engaged and defeated that walking stick (and thus her sister Sphigx) when he had brought it into her shrine.

His feet disturbed a clump of shining riparial worms, which scattered in all directions flashing tidings of fear in pale, luminous yellow. The water was deeper here, the gray shiprock walls dark with damp.

On the other hand, the talus he had killed had professed to serve Scylla; but that boast presumably meant no more than that it served Viron, Scylla's sacred city—as did he, for that matter, since he hoped to end Crane's activities. More realistically, the talus had unquestionably been a servant of the Ayuntamiento. It had been Councillor Lemur who had built the shrine; and thus, almost certainly, it was the councillors who met with commissioners and judges in the room below it. This though they must surely come to the Juzgado (the real one in Viron, as Silk thought of it) from time to time. He had seen a picture of Councillor Loris addressing a crowd from the balcony not long ago.

And the talus had said that it had returned to Potto.

Silk halted, balancing himself on his sound foot, and slapped the wrapping against the wall of the tunnel again.

If, however, the talus served the Ayuntamiento (and so by a permissible exaggeration Scylla), what had it been doing at Blood's villa? Mucor had indicated not only that it was his employee, but that it might be corrupted.

This time Silk wound the wrapping around his chest

under his tunic, finding that it did not constrict sufficiently to make it difficult for him to breathe.

At first Silk thought the flashes of pain from his ankle had somehow affected his hearing. The roar increased, and a pinpoint of light appeared far down the tunnel. There was no place to run, even if he had been capable of running, no place to hide. He flattened himself as much as he could against the wall, Hyacinth's azoth in his hand.

The point of light became a glare. The machine racing toward him held its head low, like that of an angry dog. It roared past, drenching him with icy water, and vanished in the direction from which he had come.

He fled, splashing through water that grew deeper and deeper, and saw the steeply rising side tunnel at the same moment that he heard a roar and clatter behind him.

A hundred long and exquisitely painful strides carried him clear of the water; but he did not sit down to rewrap his ankle and resume his shoes and stockings until distance had taken him out of sight of the tunnel he had left. He heard something—he assumed it was the same machine— roar along it once more and listened fearfully, half-convinced that it would turn down this new tunnel. It did not, and soon its clamor faded away.

Now, he told himself, his luck had changed. Or rather, some gracious god had decided to favor him. Perhaps Scylla had forgiven him for bringing her sister's walking stick into her shrine and for proposing to cast it into the lake as a sacrifice to herself. This tunnel could not go far, rising as it did, before it must necessarily reach the surface; and it seemed certain to do so near Limna, if not actually within the village itself. Furthermore, it was above the level of the water, and seemed likely to remain so.

Having put the azoth back into his waistband, he rolled down his trousers legs and untied his robe.

He was no longer counting steps, but he had not gone far before his nose detected the unmistakable tang of wood smoke. It couldn't really be (he told himself) the odor of sacrifice, the fragrant smoke of cedar blended with the pungent smells of burning flesh, fat, and hair. And yet—he sniffed again—it was uncannily like it, so much so that for a moment or two he wondered whether there might not be an actual sacrifice in progress here in these ancient tunnels.

As he approached the next bleared and greenish light, he noticed footprints on the tunnel floor. The tracks of a man, shod as he was, left in a faint, gray deposit that his fingers easily wiped away.

Was it possible that he had been walking in a circle? He shook his head. This tunnel had been climbing steeply from its beginning; and as he scanned the footprints and compared them to his own, he saw that it could not be true: the steps were shorter than his, this walker had not limped, and the shoes that had made them had been somewhat smaller; nor were their heels badly worn at the outside like his own.

The light by which he studied them appeared to be the last for some distance—the tunnel ahead looked as black as pitch. He searched his mind, then each pocket in turn, for some means of creating light, coughed, and found none. He had Hyacinth's azoth and her needler, the seven cards and a quantity of bits he had never counted, his beads, his old pen case (containing several quills, a small bottle of ink, and two folded sheets of paper) his glasses, his keys, and the gammadion his mother had given him, hanging from his neck on a silver chain.

He sneezed.

The reek of smoke had increased, and now his feet were sinking into some soft, dry substance; moreover he saw, not more than a few steps ahead, a fleck of dull red such as he had only too seldom observed in the firebox of the kitchen stove. It was an ember, he felt sure; when he reached it, went to his knees in the dark invisible softness, and blew gently, he knew that he had been correct. He twisted one of the sheets from his pen case into a spill and applied its end to the brightened ember.

Ashes.

Ashes everywhere. He stood upon the lowest slope of a great gray drift that blocked the tunnel entirely on one side, and on the other rose so high that he would be forced to stoop if he was not to knock his head against the ceiling.

He hurried forward, anxious to pass that narrow opening (as the earlier walker, who had left tracks there, had done) before the feeble yellow flame from the spill flickered out. It was difficult going; he sank in ash nearly to his knees at every step, and the fine haze that his hurrying feet stirred up clutched at his throat.

He sneezed again, and this time his sneeze was answered by an odd, low stridulation, louder and deeper than the noise of even a very large broken clock, yet something akin to it.

The flame of the spill was almost touching his fingers; he shifted his hold on the spill and puffed its flame higher, then dropped it, having seen its glow reflected in four eyes.

He shouted as he sometimes shouted at rats in the manse, snatched the azoth from his waistband, waved its deadly blade in the direction of the eyes, and was rewarded by a shriek of pain. It was quickly followed by the boom of a slug gun and a soft avalanche of ash that left him half buried.

The slug gun spoke again, its hollow report evoking a half-human screech. A strong light pierced swirling clouds of ash, and a creature that seemed half dog and half devil fled past him, stirring up more ash. As soon as he could catch his breath he shouted for help; minutes passed before two soldiers, thick-limbed chems two full heads taller than he, found him and jerked him unceremoniously out of the ash.

"You're under arrest," the first told him, shining his light in Silk's face. It was not a lantern or a candle, or any other portable lighting device with which Silk was familiar; he stared at it, much too interested to be frightened.

"Who are you?" asked the second.

"Patera Silk, from the manteion on Sun Street." Silk sneezed yet again while trying hopelessly to brush the ash from his clothes.

"You come down the chute, Patera? Put your hands where I can see them. Both hands."

He did so, displaying their palms to show that both were empty.

"This is a restricted area. A military area. What are you doing here, Patera?"

"I'm lost. I hoped to speak to the Ayuntamiento about a spy some foreign city has sent into Viron, but I got lost in these tunnels. And then—" Silk paused, at a loss for words. "Then all this."

The first soldier said, "They send for you?" And the second, "Are you armed?"

"They didn't send for me. Yes, I've got a needler in my trousers pocket." Inanely he added, "A very small one."

"You planning to shoot us with it?" The first soldier sounded amused.

"No. I was concerned about the spy I told you about. I believe he may have confederates."

The first soldier said, "Pull out that needler, Patera. We want to see it."

Reluctantly, Silk displayed it.

The soldier turned his light upon his own mottled steel chest. "Shoot me."

"I'm a loyal citizen," Silk protested. "I wouldn't want to
shoot one of our soldiers."

The soldier thrust the gaping muzzle of his slug gun at
Silk's face. "You see this? It shoots a slug of depleted ura-
nium as long as my thumb and just about as big around.
If you won't shoot me, I'm going to shoot you, and mine
will blow your head apart like a powder can. Now shoot."

Silk fired; the crack of the needler seemed loud in the
tunnel. A bright scratch appeared on the soldier's massive
chest.

"Again."

"What would be the point?" Silk dropped the needler
back into his pocket.

"I was giving you another chance, that's all." The first
soldier handed his light to the second. "All right, you've
had your turn. Give it to me."

"So that you can shoot me with it? It would kill me."

"Maybe not. Hand it over, and we'll see."

Silk shook his head. "You said I was under arrest. If I
am, you have to send for an advocate, provided I wish to
engage one. I do. His name is Vulpes, and he has chambers
on Shore Street in Limna, which can't be far from here."

The second soldier chuckled, a curiously inhuman
sound like a steel rule run along the teeth of a rack. "Leave
him alone, corporal. I'm Sergeant Sand, Patera. Who's this
spy you were talking about?"

"I prefer to reserve that unless asked by a member of
the Ayuntamiento."

Sand leveled his slug gun. "Bios like you die all the time
down here, Patera. They wander in and most of them never
get out. I'll show you one in a minute, if you're not dead
yourself. They die and they're eaten, even the bones. Maybe
there's scraps of clothes, maybe not. That's the truth, and
for your sake you'd better believe me."

"I do." Silk rubbed his palms on his thighs to get off as much ash as he could.

"Our standing orders are to kill anybody who endangers Viron. If you know about a spy and won't tell us, that's you, and you're no better than a spy yourself. Do you understand what I'm telling you?"

Silk nodded reluctantly.

"Corporal Hammerstone was playing with you. He wouldn't really have shot you, just roughed you up a little. I'm not playing." Sand pushed off the safety of his slug gun with an audible click. "Name the spy!"

It was difficult for Silk to make himself speak: another moral capitulation in what seemed to be an endless series of such capitulations. "His name is Crane. Doctor Crane."

Hammerstone said, "Maybe he heard it too."

"I doubt it. What time did you come down here, Patera? Any idea?"

Doctor Crane would be arrested, and eventually shot or sent to the pits; Silk recalled how Crane had winked, pointing to the ceiling as he said, "Somebody up there likes you, some infatuated goddess, I should imagine." At which he, Silk, had known that Hyacinth had provided the object Crane had passed to him, and guessed that it was her azoth.

Sand said, "Make a guess if you can't be sure, Patera. This's Molpsday, pretty late. About when was it?"

"Shortly before noon, I believe—perhaps about eleven. I'd ridden the first wagon from Viron, and I must have spent at least an hour in Limna before I started up the Pilgrims' Way to Scylla's shrine."

Hammerstone asked, "Did you use the glass there?"

"No. Is there one? If there is, I didn't see it."

"Under the plaque that tells who built it. You lift it up and there's a glass."

Sand said, "What he's getting at, Patera, is that some news came over our glass at Division Headquarters before we jumped off tonight. It seems like Councillor Lemur caught himself a spy, in person. A doctor called Crane."

"Why, that's wonderful!"

Sand cocked his head. "What is? Finding out that you came down here for nothing?"

"No, no! It's not that." For the first time since Oreb had left him, Silk smiled. "That it won't be my fault. That it isn't. I felt it was my duty to tell somebody everything I'd learned—someone in authority, who could take action. I knew Crane would suffer as a result. That he'd probably die, in fact."

Sand said almost gently, "He's just a bio, Patera. You get built inside each other, so there's millions of you. One more or less doesn't matter." He started back up the hill of ash, sinking deeply at every step but making steady progress in spite of it. "Fetch him along, Corporal."

Hammerstone prodded Silk with the barrel of his slug gun. "Get moving."

One of the doglike creatures lay bleeding in the ash less than a chain from the point at which the soldiers had found Silk, too weak to stand but not too weak to snarl. Silk asked, "What is that?"

"A god. The things that eat you bios down here."

Staring down at the dying animal, Silk shook his head. "The impious harm no one but themselves, my son."

"Get going, Patera. You're an augur, don't you sacrifice to the gods every week?"

"More often, if I can." The ash made it increasingly difficult to walk.

"Uh-huh. What about the leftovers? What do you do with them?"

Silk glanced back at him. "If the victim is edible—as most are—its flesh is distributed to those who have attended the ceremony. Surely you've been to at least one sacrifice, my son."

"Yeah, they made us go." Shifting his slug gun to his left hand, Hammerstone offered Silk his right arm. "Here, hang on. What about the other stuff, Patera? The hide and head and so forth, and the ones you won't eat?"

"They are consumed by the altar fire," Silk told him.

"And that sends them to the gods, right?"

"Symbolically, yes."

Another doglike animal lay dead in the ash; Hammerstone kicked it as he passed. "Your little fires aren't really up to it, Patera. They're not big enough or hot enough to burn up the bones of a big animal. Sometimes they don't even burn up all the meat. All that stuff gets dumped down here with the ashes. When they build a manteion, they try to put it on top of one of these old tunnels, so there's a place to get rid of the ashes. There's a manteion in Limna, see? We're right under it. Up around the city, there's a lot more places like this, and a lot more gods."

Silk swallowed. "I see."

"Remember those we chased off? They'll be back as soon as we're out of here. We'll hear them laughing and fighting over the good parts."

Sand had halted some distance ahead. He called, "Hurry it up, Corporal."

Silk, who was already walking as fast as he could, tried to go faster still; Hammerstone murmured, "Don't worry about that, he does it all day. That's how you get stripes."

They had almost reached Sand before Silk realized that the shapeless gray bundle at Sand's feet was a human being. Sand pointed with his slug gun. "Have a look, Patera. Maybe you knew him."

Silk knelt beside the body and lifted one mangled hand, then tried to scrape the caked ash away from the place where a face should have been; there were only shreds of flesh and splinters of bone beneath it. "It's gone!" he exclaimed.

"Gods can do that. They tear the whole thing off with one bite, the way I'd pull off my faceplate, or maybe you'd bite into a . . . What do you call those things?"

Silk rose, rubbing his hands in a desperate effort to get them clean. "I'm afraid I don't know what you mean."

"The round red things from the trees. Apples, that's it. Aren't you going to bless him or something?"

"Bring him the Pardon of Pas, you mean. We can do that only before death is complete—before the last cells of the body die, technically. Did you kill him?"

Sand shook his head. "I won't lie to you, Patera. If we'd seen him and yelled for him to halt, and he had run, we would've shot him. But we didn't. He had a lantern, it's over there someplace. And a needler. I've got that now. So he probably figured he'd be all right. But there must have been gods hanging around here like there always are. It's always pretty dark here, too, because ash gets on the lights. Maybe his lantern blew out, or maybe the gods got extra hungry and rushed him."

Hammerstone grunted his assent. "This isn't a good place for bios, Patera, like the sergeant said."

"He should be buried at least," Silk told them. "I'll do it, if you'll let me."

"If you were to bury him in these ashes, the gods would dig him up as soon as we were gone," Sand said.

"You could carry him. I've heard that you soldiers are a great deal stronger than we are."

"I could make you carry him, too," Sand told Silk, "but I'm not going to do that, either." He turned and strode away.

Hammerstone followed him, calling over his shoulder, "Get going, Patera. You can't help her now, and neither can we."

Suddenly fearful of being left behind, Silk broke into a limping trot. "Didn't you say it was a man?"

"The sergeant did, maybe. I went through her pockets, and she seemed like a woman in man's clothes."

Half to himself, Silk said, "There was someone in front of me on the Pilgrims' Way, only about half an hour ahead of me then. I stopped and slept awhile—I really can't say how long. She didn't, I suppose."

Hammerstone threw back his head in a grin. "My last nap was seventy-four years, they tell me. Back at Division, I could show you a couple hundred replacements that haven't ever been awake. Some of you bios, too."

Recalling the words Mucor had spoken in his dream, Silk said, "Please do. I'd like very much to see them, my son."

"Get a move on, then. The major may want to lock you up. We'll see."

Silk nodded, but stopped for a moment to look behind him. The nameless corpse was merely a shapeless bundle again, its identity—even its identity as the mortal remains of a human being—lost in the darkness that had rushed back even faster than the misshapen animals the soldiers called gods. Silk thought of Patera Pike's death, alone in the bedroom next to his own, an old man's peaceful death, a silent and uncontested cessation of breath. Even that had seemed terrible; how much worse, how unspeakably horrible, to die in this buried maze of darkness and decay, these wormholes in the whorl.

Chapter 9

IN DREAMS LIKE DEATH

"Patera Silk went this way?" Auk asked the night chough on his shoulder.

"Yes, yes!" Oreb fluttered urgently. "From here! Go shrine!"

"Well, I'm not going," Chenille told them.

An old woman who happened to be passing the first white stone that marked the Pilgrims' Way ventured timidly, "Hardly anyone goes out there after dark, dear, and it will be dark soon."

"Dark good," Oreb announced with unshakable conviction. "Day bad. Sleep."

The old woman tittered.

"A friend of ours went out to the shrine earlier," Auk explained. "He hasn't come back."

"Oh, my!"

Chenille asked, "Is there something out there that eats people? This crazy bird says the shrine ate him."

The old woman smiled, her face breaking into a thousand cheerful creases. "Oh, no, dear. But you can fall. People do almost every year."

"See?" Chenille shrilled. "You can hike half to shaggy Hierax through those godforsaken rocks if you want to. I'm going back to Orchid's."

Auk caught her wrist and twisted her arm until she fell to her knees.

Awed, Silk stared up at the banked racks of gray steel. Half, perhaps, were empty; the remainder held soldiers, each lying on his back with his arms at his sides, as if sleeping or dead.

"Back when this place was built, it was under the lake," Corporal Hammerstone told Silk conversationally. "No going straight down if somebody wanted to take it, see? And pretty tough to figure out exactly where it was. They'd have to come quite a ways through the tunnels, and there's places where twenty tinpots could stand off an army."

Silk nodded absently, still mesmerized by the recumbent soldiers.

"You'd think the water'd leak inside here, but it didn't. There's lots of solid rock up there. We got four big pumps to send it back if it did, and three of them haven't ever run. I was pretty surprised to find out the lake had gone over the hill on us when I woke up, but it'd still be a dirty job to take this place. I wouldn't want to be one of them."

"You slept here like this for seventy-five years?" Silk asked him.

"Seventy-four, the last time. All these been awake some time, like me. But if you want to keep going, I'll show you some that never was yet. Come on."

Silk followed him. "There must be thousands."

"About seven thousand of us left now. The way he set it up, see, when we come here from the Short Sun, was for all the cities to be independent. Pas figured that if somebody had too much territory, he'd try to take over Mainframe, the superbrain that astrogates and runs the ship."

Somewhat confused, Silk asked, "Do you mean the whole whorl?"

"Yeah, right. The *Whorl.* So what he did, see—if you ask

me, this was pretty smart—was to give every city a heavy infantry division, twelve thousand tinpots. For a big offensive you want armor and air and armored infantry and all that junk. But for defense, heavy infantry and lots of it. Bust the *Whorl* up into a couple of hundred cities, give each of them a division to defend it, and the whole thing ought to stay put, no matter what some crazy caldé someplace tries to do. So far it's held for three hundred years, and like I said, we've still got over half our strength fit for duty."

Silk was happy to be able to contribute some information of his own. "Viron doesn't have a caldé anymore."

"Yeah, right." Hammerstone sounded uneasy. "I heard. It's kind of a shag-up, because standing orders say that's who we're supposed to get our orders from. The major says we got to obey the Ayuntamiento for now, but nobody really likes it much. You know about standing orders, Patera?"

"Not really." Silk had lagged behind him to count the levels in a rack: twenty. "Sand said something about them, I think."

"You've got them too," Hammerstone told him. "Watch this."

He aimed a vicious left cross at Silk's face. Silk's hands flew up to protect it, but the oversized steel fist stopped a finger's width short of them.

"See that? Your standing orders say your hands got to protect your clock, just like ours say we've got to protect Viron. You can't change them or get rid of them, even if maybe somebody else could do it by messing around inside of your head."

"A need to worship is another of those standing orders," Silk told the soldier slowly. "It is innate in man that he cannot help wanting to thank the immortal gods, who give him all that he possesses, even life. You and your sergeant saw fit to disparage our sacrifices, and I will very willingly grant that they're pitifully inadequate. Yet they satisfy, to a considerable degree, that otherwise unmet need, for the community as well as for many individuals."

Hammerstone shook his head. "It's pretty hard for me to picture Pas biting into a dead goat, Patera."

"But is it hard for you to picture him being made happy, in a very minor fashion, by that concrete evidence that we have not forgotten him? That we—even the people of my own quarter, who are so poor—are eager to share such food as we have with him?"

"No, I can see that all right."

"Then we have nothing to argue about," Silk told him, "because that is what I see, too, applied not only to Pas but to all the other gods, the remaining gods of the Nine, the Outsider, and all the minor deities."

Hammerstone stopped and turned to face Silk, his massive body practically blocking the aisle. "You know what I think you're doing now, Patera?"

Silk, who had finished speaking before he fully realized what he had said—that he had just refused to number the Outsider among the minor gods—felt certain he was about to be charged with heresy. He could only mumble, "No. I've no idea."

"I think you're practicing what you're going to tell the brass on me. How you're going to try to get them to let you go. Maybe you don't know it, but I think that's what it is."

"Perhaps I was trying to justify myself," Silk conceded with an immense sense of relief, "but that doesn't show what I said to be false, nor does it prove me insincere in saying it."

"I guess not."

"Do you believe that they will?"

"I dunno, Patera. Neither does Sand." Hammerstone threw back his head in a grin. "That's why he's letting me show you around like this, see? If he'd of been sure the brass would turn you loose, he'd of turned you loose himself and not said nothing. Or if he was sure they'd lock you up, he'd have you locked up right now, sitting in the dark in a certain room we got, with maybe a swell bottle of water 'cause he likes you. But you were talking about how we had to send for your advocate, and Sand's not sure what the major's going to say, so he let you clean up a little and he's treating you nice while I keep an eye on you."

"He allowed me to keep my needler as well—or rather, the one a kind friend lent me, which was very good of him." Silk hesitated, and when he spoke again did so only because his conscience demanded it. "Perhaps I shouldn't say this, my son, but haven't you told me a great deal that a spy would wish to know? I'm not a spy but a loyal citizen, as I said earlier; and because I am, it disturbs me that an actual spy could learn some of the things I have. That our army numbers seven thousand, for example."

Hammerstone leaned against a rack. "Don't overheat. If I was just some dummy, you think I'd be awake pulling C.Q.? All that I've told you is that taking this place would be holy corrosion. Let the spies go back home and tell their bosses that. Viron don't care. And I've not just told you, I'm flat *showing* you, that Viron's got seven thousand tinpots it can call on any day of the week. No other city in this part of the *Whorl*'s got more than half that, from what we hear. So they better leave Viron alone, and if Viron says spit oil, they better spit far."

"Then the things you've told me should not endanger me further?" Silk asked.

"Not a drip. Still want to see the replacements?"

"Certainly, if you're still willing to show them to me. May I ask why you're concerned about spies at all, when you don't object to someone who might be a spy—I repeat that I am not—touring this facility?"

"Because this isn't what the spies are looking for. If it

was, we'd just trot them around and send them back. What they want to know is where our government's got to."

Silk looked at him inquiringly. "Where the Ayuntamiento meets?"

"For now, yeah."

"It would seem to me that it would be even more heavily defended than this headquarters is. If so, what would be the point?"

"It is," Hammerstone told him, "only not the same way. If it was, that would make it easy to spot. You've seen me and you've seen the sergeant. You figure we're real tough metal, Patera?"

"Very much so."

Hammerstone lifted a most impressive fist. "Think you might whip me?"

"Of course not. I'm well aware that you could kill me very quickly, if you wished."

"Maybe you know a bio that you think could do it?"

Silk shook his head. "The most formidable bio I know is my friend Auk. Auk's somewhat taller than I am, and a good deal more strongly built. He's an experienced fighter, too; but you would defeat him with ease, I'm sure."

"In a fistfight? You bet I would. I'd break his jaw with my first punch. And you remember this." Hammerstone pointed to the bright scratch left by Hyacinth's needler on his camouflaged chest. "But what about if we both had slug guns?"

Diplomatically, Silk ventured, "I don't believe that Auk owns one."

"Supposing Viron hands him one with a box of ammo."

"In that case, I would imagine that it would be largely a matter of luck."

"Does this Auk that you know have many friends besides you, Patera?"

"I'm sure he must. There's a man named Gib—a larger man even than Auk, now that I come to think of it. And one of our sibyls is certainly Auk's friend."

"We'll leave her out. Suppose I had to fight you and Auk and this other bio Gib, and all three of you had slug guns."

Still anxious not to offend, Silk said, "I would think that any outcome would be possible."

Hammerstone straightened up and took a step toward Silk, looming above him. "You're right. Maybe I'd kill all three of you, or maybe you'd kill me and never get a scratch doing it. But what would you say's most likely? I'm telling you right now that if you lie to me, I'm not going to be as nice to you as I been up till now, and you best think some about that before you answer. So what about it? The three of you against me, and we've all got guns."

Silk shrugged. "If you wish. I certainly don't know a great deal about fighting, but it would seem to me probable that you would kill one or two of us, but that you would be killed yourself—in the process, so to speak."

Hammerstone threw back his head in another grin. "You don't scare easy, do you, Patera?"

"On the contrary, I'm a rather timid man. I was quite frightened when I said that—as I still am—but it was what you had asked me for, the truth."

"How many bios in Viron, Patera?"

"I don't know." Silk paused, stroking his cheek. "What an interesting question! I've never actually thought about it."

"You're a smart man, I've seen that already, and it's been a long time since I spent much time in the city. How many would you say?"

Silk continued to stroke his cheek. "Ideally we—the Chapter, I mean—would like to have a manteion for each five thousand residents, and these days nearly all of those residents would be bios—there are a few chems left, of course, but the number is probably less than one in twenty. I believe that there are a hundred and seventeen manteions in current operation. That was the figure, at least, when I was at the schola."

"Five hundred and fifty-five thousand, seven hundred and fifty," Hammerstone told him.

"But the actual ratio is much higher. Certainly over six thousand, and perhaps as high as eight or nine."

"All right, let's say six thousand bios," Hammerstone decided, "since you sound pretty sure it's more than that. That's seven hundred and two thousand bios. Suppose that half are sprats, all right? And half the rest are females, and not enough of them will fight to make much difference. That leaves a hundred and seventy-five thousand five hundred males. Say half those are too old or too sick, or they run off. That's eighty-seven thousand seven hundred and fifty. You see what I'm getting at, Patera?"

Bewildered by the deluge of figures, Silk shook his head.

"You and me said three to one would probably end up with me dead. All right, eighty-seven thousand seven hundred and fifty against thirty-five hundred tinpots, which is about what we think Wick's got, just to grab a for instance, makes it about twenty-five to one."

"I believe I'm beginning to understand," Silk said.

Hammerstone aimed a finger as thick as a crowbar at his face. "That's everybody that'll fight. Take just the Guard. Five brigades?"

"They're forming a new one," Silk told him, "a reserve brigade, which will make six."

"Six brigades, with four or maybe five thousand troopers in each of them. So what matters if there's a new war soon, Patera? Us tinpots, or the Ayuntamiento, that gives the Guard its orders and could pass out slug guns to half the bios in Viron if it wanted to?"

Lost in thought, Silk did not reply.

"You know now, Patera, and so do we. These days we're an elite corps, where we used to be the whole show. Come on, I want to show you those replacements."

At the back of that wide and lofty arsenal, in the racks nearest the rear wall, lay soldiers swaddled in dirty sheets of polymer, their limbs smeared with some glutinous brownish black preservative. Full of wonder, Silk stooped to examine the nearest, blowing at the dust and cobwebs, and (when that proved insufficient) wiping them away with his sleeve.

"One company," Hammerstone announced with casual pride, "still exactly like they came out of Final Assembly."

"He's never spoken a word, or . . . or sat up and looked around? Not in three hundred years?"

"A little longer than that. They were stockpiling us for maybe twenty years before we ever went on board."

This man had come into being at about the same time as Maytera Marble, Silk reflected—had come to be at the same time that Hammerstone himself had, for that matter. Now she was old and worn and not far from death; but Hammerstone was still young and strong, and this man still unborn.

"We could wake him up right now," Hammerstone explained, "just yell in his ear a little and beat on his chest. Don't do it though."

"I won't." Silk straightened up. "That would start his mental processes?"

"They're started already, Patera. They had to do that at Final Assembly to make sure everything worked. So they just left them on. Only turned way down, if you know what I mean, so there's practically no reduction in parts life at all. He knows we're here, kind of. He's listening to us talking, but it doesn't mean a lot to him and he won't think about it. The good thing is that if there's ever an emergency like a fire in here, he'd wake up, and he'd have his Standing Orders."

"There's a question about all those things you told me earlier that I'm anxious to ask you," Silk said. "Several questions, really, and I hope very much that you won't be angry, although you may consider them impolite; but before I do, is it the same for all these other soldiers sleeping in these racks?"

"Not exactly." Hammerstone sounded troubled, reminding Silk of his dissatisfaction with the Ayuntamiento. "When you've been awake for a while it's harder to shut down. I guess because there's so much more that's got started up. You know what I mean?"

Silk nodded. "I think so."

"At first it just seems to you like you're just lying there. You think something's wrong and you're not going to sleep at all and you might as well get up. You never quite do, but that's how you think. So then you think, well, I got nothing better to do, so I'll just go over some the best stuff that happened, like the time Schist got the shell in backwards. And it goes on like that, except that after a while it's not quite the way it really happened, and maybe you're somebody else." Hammerstone made an odd, unfinished gesture. "I can't really explain it."

"On the contrary," Silk told him, "I would say you've explained it very well indeed."

"And it keeps getting darker. There's something else I wanted to show you, Patera. Come on, we got to follow this back wall a ways to see it."

"Just a moment, please, my son." Silk put his right foot on the lowest transverse bar of the rack and unwound Crane's wrapping. "May I ask those questions I mentioned while I take care of this?"

"Sure. Shoot."

"Some time ago, you mentioned a major who would decide whether to put me under arrest. I assume that he's the highest-ranking officer awake?"

Hammerstone nodded. "He's the real C.Q., the Officer in Charge of Quarters. The sergeant and me and all the rest of us are really the O.C.Q.'s detail. But we say we're on C.Q. It's just the way everybody talks about it."

"I understand. My question is why is this major—or any officer—an officer, while you're a corporal? Why is Sand a sergeant, for that matter? It seems to me that all of you soldiers should be interchangeable."

Hammerstone stood silent and motionless for so long that Silk became embarrassed. "I apologize, my son. I was afraid that was going to sound insulting, although it wasn't intended to be, and it emerged worse even than I had feared. I withdraw the question."

"It isn't that, Patera. It's just that I was thinking everything over before I shot off my mouth. It's not like there was only the one answer."

"I don't even require one," Silk assured him. "It was an idle and ill-advised question, one that I should never have asked."

"To start with, you're right. Just about all the basic hardware's the same, but the software's different. There's a lot that a corporal has to know that a major doesn't need, and probably the other way 'round, too. You ever notice the way I talk? I don't sound exactly like you do, do I? But we're both of us speaking the same shaggy language, begging your pardon, Patera."

Silk said carefully, "I haven't noticed your diction as being in any way odd or unusual, but now that you've called my attention to it, you're undoubtedly correct."

"See? You talk kind of like an officer, and they don't talk as good as privates and corporals do, or even as good as sergeants. They use a lot more words, and longer words, and nothing's ever said as clear as a corporal would say it. Why is that? All right, next time there's a war, Sand and me are going to be doing this and that with Guards, privates, corporals, and sergeants, won't we? Maybe showing them where we want their buzz guns set up and things like that. So we got to talk like they do, so they'll understand and so we'll both be fighting the enemy and not each other. For the major, it's the same thing with officers, so he has to talk like them. And he does. You ever tried to talk like I do, Patera?"

Silk nodded, shamefaced. "It was a lamentable failure, I'm afraid."

"Right. Well, the major can't talk like me either, and I can't talk like him. For either of us to do it, we'd have to have software for both speech patterns. Trouble is, our heads won't hold all the crap that's floating around, see? We only got so much room up there, just like you do, so we can't spare the extra space. Out where the iron flies, that means the major wouldn't make as good a corporal as me, and I wouldn't make as good a major as him."

Silk nodded. "Thank you. I feel better now about the way I speak."

"Why's that?"

"It's troubled me up until now that the people of our quarter don't speak as I do, and that I can't speak as they do. After hearing you, I realize that all is as it should be. They live—if I may put it so—where the iron flies. They cannot afford to waste a moment, and though they need not deal with the complexities of abstract thought, they dare not be misunderstood. I, however, am their legate— their envoy to the wealthier levels of our society, where lives are more leisured, but where the need to deal with complexities and abstractions is far more frequent and the penalties for being misunderstood are not nearly so great.

Thus I speak as I must if I am to serve the people that I represent."

Hammerstone nodded. "I think I get you, Patera. And I think you get me. All right, there's other stuff, too, like A.I. You know about that? What it means?"

"I'm afraid I've never heard the term." Silk had been slapping Crane's wrapping against one of the rack's upright members. He put his foot on the transverse beam again and rewound the wrapping.

"It's just fancy talk for learning stuff. Everything I do, I learn a little better from doing it. Suppose I take a shot at one of those gods. If I miss it, I learn something from missing. If I hit it, I learn from that, too. So my shooting gets better all the time, and I don't waste shells firing at stuff I'm not going to hit except from dumb luck. You do the same thing."

"Of course."

"Nope! That's where you're wrong, Patera." Hammerstone waggled his big steel forefinger in Silk's face. "There's a lot that don't. Take a floater. It knows about not going too fast south, but it never does learn what it can float over and what it can't. The driver's got to learn about that for it. Or take a cat now. You ever try to teach a cat anything?"

"No," Silk admitted. "However I have—I ought to say I had—a bird that certainly appeared to learn. He learned my name and his own, for example."

"I'm talking cats particularly. Back in the second year against Urbs, I found this kitty in a knocked-out farmhouse, and I kept her awhile just so's to have something to talk to and scrounge for. It was kind of nice, sometimes."

"I know precisely what you mean, my son."

"Well, we had a big toss gun sighted in up on a hilltop that summer, and when the battle got going we were firing it as fast as you ever seen anything like that done in your life, and the lieutenant hollering all the time for us to go faster. A couple times we had eight or nine rounds in the air at once. You ever man a toss gun, Patera?"

Silk shook his head.

"All right, suppose you just go up to one and open up the breech, cold, and shove a H.E. round in there, and shoot it off. Then you open the breech again and out comes the casing, see? And it'll be pretty hot."

"I should imagine."

"But when you're keeping six, seven, eight rounds in the air all at once, that breech'll get so hot itself that it'll practically cook off a fresh round before you can pull the lanyard. And when that casing pops out, well, you could see it in the dark.

"So we're shooting and shooting and shooting, and hiking up more ammo and tossing it around and shooting some more till we were about ready to light up ourselves, and we got a pile of empty casings about so high off to the side, and here comes that poor little kitty and decides to sit down someplace where she can watch us, and she picks out that pile of casings and jumps right up. Naturally the ones at the top of the pile was hot enough to solder with."

Silk nodded sympathetically.

"She gives a whoop and off she scoots, and I didn't see her again for two-three days."

"She did return, though?" Silk felt somewhat heartened by the implication that Oreb might return as well.

"She did, but she wouldn't get anywheres near to one of those casings after that. I could show it to her, and maybe push a paw or her nose up against it to prove it was stone-cold, and it wouldn't make one m.o.a.'s difference. She'd learned those casings were hot, see, Patera? After that, she couldn't ever learn that one wasn't, no matter how plain I showed it. She didn't have A.I., and there's people that's the same way, too, plenty of them."

Silk nodded again. "A theodidact once wrote that the wise learn from the experiences of others. Fools, he said, could learn only from experiences of their own, while the great mass of men never learn at all. By which I imagine that he meant that the great mass had no A.I."

"You're right on target, Patera. But if you've got it, then the more experience somebody's got, the higher up you want him. So Sand's a sergeant, I'm a corporal, and Schist is a private. You said you had a couple questions. What's the other one?"

"Since we have a walk ahead of us, perhaps we'd better begin it now," Silk suggested; and they set off together, walking side-by-side down the wide aisle between the wall and the rearmost row of racks. "I wanted to ask you about Pas's provision to keep the cities independent. When you described it to me, it seemed eminently sound; I felt sure that it would function precisely as Pas intended."

"It has," Hammerstone confirmed. "I said I thought it was pretty smart, and I still do."

"But afterward, we spoke of a soldier such as yourself engaging three bios with slug guns like his own, and about the Civil Guard, and so forth. And it struck me that the arrangement you'd described, admirable as it may once have been, can hardly prevail now. If Wick has three thousand five hundred soldiers and our own city seven thousand, our city is twice as strong only if soldiers are the only men of value in war. If Guardsmen to the number of ten or twenty thousand are to fight as well—to say nothing of hundreds of thousands of ordinary citizens—then may Wick not be as strong, overall, as Viron? Or stronger? What becomes of Pas's arrangement under such circumstances as these?"

Hammerstone nodded. "That's something that's worrying everybody quite a bit. The way I see it, Pas was thinking mostly about the first two hundred years. Maybe the first two hundred and fifty. I think maybe he figured after that we'd have learned to live with each other or kill each other off, which isn't so dumb either. See, Patera, there weren't anywheres near so many bios at first, and they weren't big on making stuff. The cities were all there when they come, paved streets and shiprock buildings, mostly. Growing food was the big thing. So when they made stuff, it was mostly tools and clothes, and mud bricks so they could put up more buildings where Pas hadn't put any but they felt like they needed some.

"Stop right here, Patera, and I'll show you in a minute."

Hammerstone halted before a pair of wide double doors, standing with his broad body in front of the line at which they met, clearly to block Silk's view of some object. ;

"Like I was saying, back three hundred years ago there wasn't all that many bios. A lot of the work was done by chems. Us soldiers did some, but mostly it was civilians. Maybe you know some. They don't have armor and they've got different software."

"They're largely gone now, I'm sorry to say," Silk told him.

"Yeah, and that's one place where I feel like old Pas sort of slipped up. Me and a fem-chem could make a sprat. You know about that?"

"Certainly."

"Each of us is hardwired with half the plans. But the thing is, it might take us a year or so if we're lucky, maybe twenty if we weren't, where you bios can do the main business any night after work."

"Believe me," Silk told him, "I wish with all my heart that you were more like us, and we more like you. I have never been more sincere in my life."

"Thanks. Well, anyhow, after a while there got to be more bios and the tools were better, mostly 'cause there was still a lot of chems around to make them. Also, there was quite a few slug guns floating around in all the cities that'd had wars, 'cause the soldiers that had owned them were dead. A slug gun isn't all that tough to make, really. You got to have some bar stock and a lathe for the barrel, and a milling machine's nice. But there's nothing a milling machine can do that somebody careful can't do about as good with a set of files and a hand drill, if he's got the time."

Hammerstone included the entire armory in a gesture. "So here we are. Not near as steady as we used to be, and all set to lay the blame on poor old Pas the first time we lose."

"It seems a pity," Silk said pensively.

"Chin up, Patera. Right here's the best thing I got to show you, you being a augur, so I saved it for the last, or almost the last, anyway. Have you ever heard of what they call Pas's seal?"

Silk's eyes went wide with astonishment. "Certainly I have. It's mentioned in the Pardon. 'Do my will, live in peace, multiply, and do not disturb my seal. Thus you shall escape my wrath.' "

Hammerstone threw back his head in another grin. "Have you ever seen it?"

"Why no. Pas's seal is—to the best of my knowledge at any rate—largely a metaphor. If I were to shrive you, for example, anything I learned during your shriving would be under the seal of Pas, never to be divulged to a third party without your express permission."

"Well, have a look," Hammerstone said, and stepped to one side.

Waist-high on the line where the double doors met, they were joined by a broad daub of dark synthetic. Silk dropped to one knee to read the letters and numbers pressed into it.

$$5553 \quad 8783 \quad 4223 \quad 9700 \quad 34$$
$$2221 \quad 0401 \quad 1101 \quad 7276 \quad 56$$

SEALED FOR THE MONARCH

"There it is," Hammerstone told Silk. "It's been there ever since we came on board, and whenever people talk about Pas's seal, that thing you're looking at's what they're talking about. There used to be a lot more of them."

"If this imprint is truly what is intended by the seal of Pas," Silk whispered, "it is a priceless relic." Bowing reverently, he traced the sign of addition in the air before the seal and murmured a prayer.

"If we could take it off and carry it up to one of those big manteions it would be, maybe. The thing is, you can't. If you were to try to get it off of those doors, that black stuff would bust into a million pieces. We broke a bunch after we got here, and what's left isn't a whole lot bigger than H-Six Powder."

"And no one knows what lies beyond it?" Silk inquired. "In the next room?"

"Oh, no. We know what's in there all right. It's pretty much like this one, a whole lot of people in the rack. Only in there it's bios. Want to see them?"

"Bios?" Silk repeated. At the word, his dream of a few hours earlier returned to the forefront of his mind with an urgency and immediacy that were wholly new: the bramble-covered hillside, Maytera Marble (absurdly) sick in bed, the oversweet scent of Maytera Rose's blue-glass lamp, and Mucor seated upon the still water when the dream in which she had played her part had vanished. *"It's drier farther on. Meet me where the bios sleep."*

"Sure," Hammerstone confirmed, "bios just like you. See, this one we're in right now had extra soldiers, and this next one, with the seal still on the doors, has extra bios. Old Pas must of been scared there might be some kind of a disease, or maybe a famine, and Viron would have to have more bios to get started again. They don't get to lie down like us, though. They're all standing up. Want to see them?"

"Certainly," Silk told him, "if it can be done without breaking Pas's seal."

"Don't worry. I've done this probably a couple dozen times." Hammerstone's steel knuckles rang against one of the doors. "That's not so somebody'll come and let us in, see. I got to stir up the lights inside, or you won't be able to see anything."

Silk nodded.

"I doubt your hands are strong enough, so I'll have to do it for you." He wedged chisel-like fingernails into the crevice between the doors. "There's a button underneath of the seal and it's got them latched shut. That's the way a lot of them were when we first come aboard. So Pas's seal won't break even when I pull as hard as I can. But I can get this top part far enough apart for you to peek inside if you put your eye to the crack. Have a look."

There was a faint thrumming from Hammerstone's thorax as he spoke, and the dark line where the edges of the doors met became a thread of greenish light. "You'll have to sort of wiggle between me and the door to see in, but you got to get your eye up close to see anything anyhow."

With his body pressed against the hard, smooth surfaces of the doors, Silk managed to peer through the crevice. He was looking at a thin section of what appeared to be a wide and brilliantly illuminated hall. Here, too, stood racks of gray-painted steel; but the motionless bios in the row nearest the floor (in line with the crevice through which he peered) were nearly upright. Each was contained in what appeared to be a cylinder of the thinnest glass, glass rendered visible only by a coating of dust. With his vision constricted by the narrow opening between the doors, he could make out only three of these sleepers clearly: a woman and two men. All three were naked and were (in appearance at least) of approximately his own age. All three stared straight ahead, with open eyes in empty, untroubled faces.

"Lights on enough?" Hammerstone asked; he leaned forward to peer through the crevice himself, the tip of his chin well above the top of Silk's head.

"Someone's in there," Silk informed him. "Someone who's not asleep."

"Inside?" There was a metallic clang as Hammerstone's forehead struck the doors.

"Look at how bright it is. Every light in the room must be blazing. A few taps on the door cannot possibly have done that."

"There can't be anybody in there!"

"Of course there can," Silk told him. "There's another way in, that's all."

Slowly—so slowly that at first Silk was not sure he was seeing them move at all—the woman in the lowest row lifted her hands to press against the crystalline wall that confined her.

"Corporal of the guard!" Hammerstone blared. "Back of Personnel Storage!" Faintly, a distant sentry took up the cry.

Before Silk could protest, Hammerstone had slammed the butt of his slug gun against the seal, which shattered into coarse black dust. As Silk recoiled in horror, Hammerstone jerked open both doors and charged into the enormous hall beyond them.

Silk knelt, collected as much of the black dust as he could, and, lacking any more suitable receptacle, folded it into his remaining sheet of paper and deposited it in his pen case.

By the time that he had closed the case and returned it to the pocket of his robe, the imprisoned woman's hands were clutching her throat and her eyes starting from her head. He scrambled to his feet, hobbled into the brilliantly lit hall, and wasted precious seconds trying to discover some means of broaching the transparent cylinder that confined her before snatching Hyacinth's needler from his pocket and striking the almost invisible crystal with its butt.

It shattered at the first blow. At once the atmosphere within it darkened to the blue-black of ripe grapes, swirling and spiraling as it mixed with air, then vanished as abruptly as Mucor in the aftermath of his dream. With somnambulistic slowness the naked woman's hands returned to her sides.

She gasped for breath.

Silk averted his eyes and untied the bands of his robe. "Will you put this on, please?"

"We'll be lovers," the woman told him loudly, her voice breaking at the penultimate syllable. Her hair was as black as Hyacinth's, her eyes a startling blue deeper than Silk's own.

"Do you know this place?" Silk asked her urgently. "Is there another way out?"

"Everything." Moving almost normally, she stepped from the rack.

"I must get away." Silk spoke as quickly as he could, wondering whether she would understand him even if he had spoken as slowly as he would have to a child. "There must be another way out, because there was someone in here who hadn't come through these doors. Show me, please."

"That way."

He risked a glance at her face, careful not to let his gaze stray below her long and graceful neck; there was something familiar—something horrible that he struggled to deny—in her smile. With cautious hands, he draped his robe about her shoulders. "You'll have to hold it closed in front."

"Tie it for me?"

He hesitated. "It would be better . . ."

"I don't know how."

She stepped toward him. "Please?" Her voice was under better control now, and almost familiar.

He fumbled the bands; it seemed unfair that something he did automatically each morning should be so difficult to do for someone else.

"Now I can fly!" With outstretched arms she spread the robe wide, running slowly and clumsily down the aisle until she nearly disappeared from view at the distant wall. There she turned and dashed back, sprinting without wasted motion. "I—really—can!" She gulped for air, breasts heaving. "But—you—can't—see—me—then." Still gasping, she smiled proudly, her head thrown back like Hammerstone's; and in her smile, the grinning rictus of a corpse, Silk knew her.

"You have no right to this woman, Mucor!" He traced the sign of addition. "In the name of Pas, Master of the Whorl, be gone!"

"I—am—a—woman. Oh—yes!"

"In the name of Lady Echidna, be gone!"

"I—know—her. She—likes—me."

"In the names of Scylla and Sphigx! In the most sacred name of the Outsider!"

She was no longer paying attention. "Do you—know why this—place is—so high?" She gestured toward the domed ceiling. "So that fliers—could fly—over it without—having to—walk." She pointed to a jumbled heap of bones, hair, and blackened flesh at the bottom of a cylinder on the second level. "I was her—once. She—remembered."

"To me you're the devil who possessed that poor woman's daughter," Silk told her angrily. "The devil who possessed Orpine." He saw a flash of fear in her eyes. "I am a bad man, granted—a lawless man, and often less than pious. Yet I am a holy augur, consecrated and blessed. Is there no name that you respect?"

"I will not be afraid, Silk." She backed away from him as she spoke.

"In the name of Phaea, go! In the name of Thelxiepeia, go! In the name of Molpe, whose day this is, and in those of Scylla and Sphigx. Be gone in the names of these gods!"

"I wanted to help. . . ."

"Be gone in the names of Tartaros and Hierax!"

She raised her hands, as he had to ward off Hammerstone's blow; and Silk, seeing her fear, remembered that *Hierax* had been the name that Musk had given the whiteheaded one, the griffon vulture on Blood's roof. With that memory, Phaesday night returned: his frantic dash across Blood's lawn in the shadow of a racing cloud; the thump of his forked branch on the roof of the conservatory; and the blade of his hatchet wedged between the casement of Mucor's window and its frame, the window that had supplied the threat he had used the next day to banish her from Orchid's.

Almost kindly he told her, "I will close your window, Mucor, so that it can never be opened again, if you don't leave me alone. Go."

As though she had never been present, she abandoned the tall, raven-haired woman who faced him; he had seen nothing and heard nothing, but he knew it as surely as if there had been a flash of fire or a gale of wind.

The woman blinked twice, her eyes unfocused and without comprehension. "Go? Where?" She drew his robe about her.

"Praise Great Hierax, the Son of Death, the New Death, whose mercy is terminal and infinite," Silk said feelingly. "Are you all right, my daughter?"

She stared at him, a hand between her breasts. "My— heart?"

"It's still racing from Mucor's exertions, I'm sure; but your pulse should slow in a few minutes."

She trembled, saying nothing. In the silence he heard the pounding of steel feet.

He closed the double doors that Hammerstone had opened, reflecting that Hammerstone had specified the back of the armory. It might be some time before the hurrying soldiers realized that he had actually meant to summon them to this vast hall beyond it. "Perhaps if we walk a little," he suggested. "We may be able to find a place of comfort, where you can sit down. Do you know a way out?"

The woman said nothing but offered no objection as Silk led her along an aisle he chose at random. The bases of the crystal cylinders, as he now saw, were black with print. By rising on his toes, he was able to examine one on the second tier, reading the name (Olive) of the woman in the cylinder, her age (twenty-four), and what he took to be a précis of her education.

"I ought to have read yours." He spoke to her as he had to Oreb, to give form to his thoughts. "But we'd better not go back. If I had when I had the opportunity, I'd know your name, at least."

"Mamelta."

He looked at her curiously. "Is that your name?" It was one that he had never heard.

"I think so. I can't . . ."

"Remember?" he suggested gently.

She nodded.

"It's certainly not a common name." The greenish lights overhead were dimming now; in the twilight that remained, he glimpsed Hammerstone running down an intersecting aisle half the hall away and asked, "Can you walk just a little faster, Mamelta?"

She did not reply.

"I'd like to avoid him," he explained, "for reasons of my own. You don't have to be afraid of him, however—he won't hurt you or me."

Mamelta nodded, although he could not be sure that she understood.

"He won't find what he's searching for, I'm afraid, poor fellow. He wants to find the person who energized all these lights, but I'm reasonably sure that it was Mucor, and she's gone."

"Mucor?" Mamelta indicated herself, both hands at her face.

"No," Silk told her, "you are not Mucor, although Mucor possessed you for a short time. It woke you, I think, while you were still in your glass tube. I don't believe that was supposed to happen. Can we walk a bit faster now?"

"All right."

"It wouldn't do to run. He might hear, and it would make him suspicious, I'm sure; but if we walk, we may be able to get away from him. If we don't, and he finds us, he'll think you energized the lights, no doubt. That should satisfy him, and we'll have lost nothing." Under his breath Silk added, "I hope."

"Who is Mucor?"

He looked at Mamelta in some surprise. "You're feeling better now, aren't you?"

She stared straight ahead, her gaze fixed on the distant wall, and did not appear to have heard his question.

"I suppose—no, I know—that you're morally entitled to an answer, the best I can provide; but I'm afraid I can't provide a very good one. I don't know nearly as much about her as I'd like, and at least two of the things I think I know are conjectural. She is a young woman who can leave her body—or to put it another way, send forth her spirit. She's not well mentally, or at least I felt that she wasn't on the one occasion when I met her face-to-face.

Now that I've had time to think about her, I believe she may be less disturbed than I assumed. She must see the whorl very differently from the way that most of us see it."

"I feel I am Mucor. . . ."

He nodded. "This morning—though I suppose it may be yesterday morning by now—I conferred with—" Words failed him. "With someone I'll call an extraordinary woman. We were talking about possession, and she said something that I didn't give as much attention as I should have. But I was thinking about our conversation as I walked out to the shrine—I'll tell you about that later, perhaps—and I realized that it might be extremely important. She had said, 'Even then, there would be something left behind, as there always is.' Or words to that effect. If I understood her, Mucor must leave a part of her spirit behind when she leaves a person, and must take a small part of that person's spirit with her when she goes. We usually think of spirits as indivisible, I'm afraid; but the Writings compare them to winds again and again. Winds aren't indivisible. Winds are air in motion, and air is divided each time we shut a door or draw a breath."

Mamelta whispered, "So many dead." She was looking at a crystalline cylinder that held only bones, what appeared to be black soil, and a few strands of hair.

"Some of that must be Mucor's doing, I'm afraid." Silk fell silent for a moment, tortured by conscience. "I said I'd tell you about her, but I haven't told you one of the most important things—to me, at any rate. It is that I betrayed her. She's the daughter of a man named Blood, a powerful man who treats her abominably. When I talked with her, I told her that whenever I had a chance to see her father I'd remonstrate with him. Later I had a lengthy conversation with him, but I never brought up his treatment of his daughter. I was afraid he'd punish her if he knew she'd spoken to me; but now I feel it was a betrayal nonetheless. If she were shown that others value her, she might—"

"*Patera!*" It was Hammerstone's voice.

Silk looked around for him. "Yes, my son?"

"Over this way. Couple rows, maybe. You all right?"

"Oh, yes, I'm fine," Silk told him. "I've been, well, more or less touring this fascinating warehouse or whatever you call it, and looking at some of the people."

"Who were you talking to?"

"To tell you the truth, to one of these women. I've been lecturing her, I'm afraid."

Hammerstone chuckled, the same dry, inhuman sound Silk had heard from Sergeant Sand in the tunnel. "You see anybody?"

"Intruders? No, no one."

"All right. The guard detail ought to be here now, but they haven't showed. I'm going to find out what's keeping them. Meet me over at the door where we came in." Without waiting for Silk's reply, Hammerstone clattered away.

"I must get back into the tunnels," Silk told Mamelta. "I left something valuable there; it isn't mine, and even if that soldier's officer allows me to leave, he's sure to see that I'm escorted back to Limna."

"This way," she said, and pointed, though Silk was not sure at what.

He nodded and set off. "I can't run, I'm afraid. Not like you. I'd run now, if I could."

For the first time, she seemed to see him. "You have a bruise on your face, and you're lame."

He nodded. "I've had various accidents. I was dropped down a flight of stairs, for one thing. My bruises will heal though, quite quickly. I was going to tell you about Mucor, who I'm afraid will not. Are you sure we're going the right way? If we go back—"

Mamelta pointed again, and this time he saw that she

was indicating a green line in the floor. "We follow that."

He smiled. "I should have realized that there must be a system of some kind."

The green line ended before a cubical structure faced with a panel of many small plates. Mamelta pressed its center, and the plates shuddered and squealed, turned pale, and eventually creaked into motion, first reminding Silk of the irising door that had defied his efforts, then of the unfolding of a blush rose. "It's beautiful," he told Mamelta. "But this can't be the way out. It looks like . . . a toolshed, perhaps."

The square room, revealed as the rose door opened, was dim and dirty; there were bits of broken glass on its floor, and its corners held heaps of the gray-painted steel. Mamelta sat on one, educing a minute puff of dust. "Will this take us to the lifter?"

Although she had looked at him as she spoke, Silk felt it was not his face that she had seen. "This won't take us anywhere, I'm afraid," he told her as the door folded again. "But I suppose that we might hide here for a time. If the soldiers have gone when we come out, I may be able to find my way back to the tunnels."

"We want to go back. Sit down."

He sat, feeling unaccountably that the stacked steel—that the whole storeroom in fact—was sinking beneath him. "What is the lifter, Mamelta?"

"The *Loganstone,* the ship that will take us up to the starcrosser *Whorl.*"

"I think—" Silk wrestled briefly with the unfamiliar term. "I mean, don't you—haven't you considered—that, that perhaps this boat that was to take you wherever it was, that it may have been a long time ago? A very long time?"

She was staring straight ahead; he was conscious of the tightness of her jaw.

"I was going to tell you about Mucor. Perhaps I ought

to finish that; then we can go on to other things. I realize all this must be very unsettling to you."

Mamelta nodded almost imperceptibly.

"I was going to say that it has bothered me a great deal that her father appears to be unaware of what she does. She goes forth in spirit, as I told you. She possesses people, as she possessed you. She appeared to me, bodiless, in my manse, and later—today, actually—in the tunnels after I dreamed of her. Furthermore, the ghost of a very dear friend—of my teacher and advisor, I should have said—appeared to me at almost the same time that she did. I believe her appearance must have made his possible in some fashion, though I really know much less than I should about such matters."

"Am I a ghost?"

"No, certainly not. You're very much alive—a living woman, and a very attractive one. Nor was Mucor a ghost when she appeared to me. It was a spirit of the living that I saw, in other words, and not that of someone who had died. When she spoke, what I heard was actual sound, I feel certain, and she must have shouted or broken something in the room outside to make the lights so bright." Silk bit his lips; some sixth sense told him (though clearly falsely) that he was falling, falling forever, the stack of gray steel and the glass-strewn floor itself dropping perpetually from under him and pulling him down with them.

"I was going to say that when Mucor possessed some women at a house in our city, her father never appeared to suspect that the devil they complained of was his own daughter; that puzzled me all day. I believe I've hit upon the answer, and I'd like you to tell me, if you can, whether I'm correct. If Mucor left a small part of her spirit with you, it's possible you know. Has she ever undergone a surgical procedure? An operation on her head?"

There was a long pause. "I'm not sure."

"Because her father and I talked about physicians, among many other things. He has a resident physician, and he told me that an earlier one had been a brain surgeon." Silk waited for Mamelta's reaction, but there was none.

"That seemed strange to me until it occurred to me that the brain surgeon might have been employed to meet a specific need. Suppose that Mucor had been a normal child in every respect except for her ability to possess others. She would have possessed those closest to her, or so I'd think, and they can hardly have enjoyed it. Blood probably consulted several physicians—treating her phenomenal ability as a disease, since he is by no means religious. Eventually he must have found one who told him that he could 'cure' her by removing a tumor or something of that kind from her brain. Or perhaps even by removing a part of the brain itself, though that is such a horrible thought that I wish there were some way to avoid it."

Mamelta nodded.

Encouraged, Silk continued, "Blood must have believed that the operation had been a complete success. He didn't suspect it was his own daughter who was possessing the women because he firmly believed, as he presumably had for years, that she was no longer able to possess anyone. I think it's probable that the operation did in fact interfere with her ability until she was older, just as it seems to have damaged her thought processes. But in time, as that part of her brain regenerated, her ability returned; and having been granted a second chance, she was prudent enough to go farther afield, and in general to conceal her restored ability; although it would seem that she followed her father or some other member of the household to the place where the women lived, as she undoubtedly followed me later. Does any of this sound at all familiar to you, Mamelta? Can you tell me anything about it?"

"The operation was before I went on the ship."

"I see," Silk said, although he did not. "And then . . . ?"

"It came. I remember now. They strapped us in."

"Was it a slave boat? We don't have them in Viron, but I know that some other cities do, and that there are slave boats on the Amnis that raid the fishing villages. I would be sorry to learn that there are slave boats beyond the whorl as well."

"Yes," Mamelta said.

Silk rose and pressed the center of the door as Mamelta had, but the door did not open.

"Not yet. It will open automatically, soon."

He sat down again, feeling unaccountably that the whole room was slipping left and falling too. "The boat came?"

"We had to volunteer. They were—you couldn't say no."

"Do you recall being outside, Mamelta? Grass and trees and sky and so on?"

"Yes." A smile lifted the corners of her mouth. "Yes, with my brothers." Her face became animated. "Playing ball in the patio. Mama wouldn't let me go out in the street the way they did. There was a fountain, and we'd throw the ball through the water so that whoever caught it would get wet."

"Could you see the sun? Was it long or short?"

"I don't understand."

Silk searched his memory for everything Maytera Marble had ever said relating to the Short Sun. "Here," he began carefully, "our sun is long and straight, a line of burning gold fencing our lands from the skylands. Was it like that for you? Or was it a disk in the center of the sky?"

Her face crumpled, while tears overflowed her eyes. "And never come back. Hold me. Oh, hold me!"

He did so, awkward as a boy and acutely conscious of the soft, warm flesh beneath the worn black twill of the robe he had lent her.

Chapter 10

ON THE BELLY OF THE
WHORL

Auk leaned across the squat balustrade of Scylla's shrine to study the jagged slabs of gray rock at the foot of the cliff. Their disordered, acutely angled surfaces gleamed ghostly pale in the skylight, but the clefts and fissures between them were as black as pitch.

"Here, here!" Oreb pecked enthusiastically at Scylla's lips. "Shrine eat!"

"I'm not going back with you," Chenille told Auk. "You made me walk all the way out here in my good wool dress for nothing. All right. You hit me and kicked me—all right, too. But if you want me to go back with you, you're going to have to carry me. Try it. Smack me a couple more times and give me a good hard kick. See if I get up."

"You can't stay here all night," Auk growled.

"I can't? Watch me."

Oreb pecked again. "Here Auk!"

"Here yourself." Auk caught him. "Now you listen up. I'm going to pitch you over like I pitched you off the path back there. You look for Patera Silk like you did before. If you find him, sing out."

With weary indifference, Chenille warned, "He won't come back this time."

"Sure he will. Get set, bird. Here you go." He tossed Oreb over the balustrade and watched as he glided down.

Chenille said, "There's a hundred places where that long butcher could have fallen."

"Eight or ten, maybe. I was looking."

She stretched out on the stone floor. "Oh, Molpe, I'm so tired!"

Auk turned to face her. "You really going to stay here all night?"

If she nodded, it was too dark beneath the dome of the shrine for him to see her.

"Somebody could come out here."

"Somebody worse than you?"

He grunted.

"That's so funny. I'd bet everything I've got that if you checked out every last cull in that godforsaken little town you couldn't find a single—"

"Shut up!"

For a time she did, whether from fear or sheer fatigue she could not herself have said. In the silence, she could hear the lapping of the waves at the foot of the cliff, the sob of the wind through the strangely twisted pillars of the shrine, the surge of blood in her own ears, and the rhythmic thumping of her heart.

Rust would have made everything all right. Recalling the empty vial she had left on her bed at Orchid's, she imagined one twenty times larger, a vial bigger than a bottle, filled with rust. She would sniff a pinch, and drop a big one in her lip, and walk back with Auk till they reached that bit where you felt like you were hanging in air, then push him off, down and down, until he fell into the lake below.

But there was no such vial, there never would be, and the half bottle of red she had drunk had died in her long ago; she pressed her fingers to her throbbing temples.

Auk bawled, *"Bird!* You down there? Sing out!"

If Oreb heard him, he did not reply.

Argumentatively, Auk inquired, "Why would he come way out here?"

Chenille rolled her head from side to side. "You asked me that before. I don't know. I remember us riding in some kind of cart or something, all right? Horses. Only somebody else was in charge then, and I wish she'd come back." She bit her knuckle, herself astonished by what she had said. Wearily she added, "She did a better job of it than I do. A better job than you're doing, too."

"Shut up. Listen, I'm going to climb down a ways. As far as I can go without falling. You rest. I should be back pretty soon."

"We'll have a parade," Chenille told him. Some minutes afterward she added, "A big one, right up the Alameda. With bands."

Then she slept and entered a great, shining room full of men in black-and-white and jeweled women. A three-sun admiral in full dress walked beside her holding her arm and did not count in the least. She walked proudly, smiling, and her wide collar was entirely of diamonds, and diamonds cascaded from her ears and flashed like the lights in the night sky from her wrists; and every eye was on her.

Then Auk was shaking her shoulder. "I'm going. You want to come or not?"

"No."

"There's good places to eat in Limna. I'll buy dinner and rent a room, and we can head back to the city tomorrow. You want to come?"

By now she was awake enough to say, "You don't listen, do you? No. Go away."

"All right. If some cull gets to you out here, don't blame me. I did the best I could for you."

She closed her eyes again. "If some cully wants to rape

me, that's dimber with me, just as long as he's not you and he doesn't want me to wiggle around while he's doing it. If he'd like to vent my pipe, that'll be dimber, too." She sighed. "Long as he doesn't want me to help."

Distinctly, she heard the scraping of Auk's boots as he left the shrine, and after what seemed to her a very short time she struggled to her feet. The night was clear; eerie skylight glimmered on the rolling lake and illuminated every harsh, bare point of rock. On the horizon, distant cities wrapped with Viron in the night appeared as tiny smears of fox fire, not half so desirable as the icy sparkles that had deserted her wrists.

"Hackum?" she called, lifting her voice. "Hackum?"

Almost at once he emerged from the shadows of the rocks to stand upon that very outthrust point of rock from which Silk had watched the spy vanish from the shrine, and from which she had imagined herself pushing him. "Jugs? Are you all right?"

Something invisible tightened around her throat. "No. But I will be. Hackum?"

"What is it?" The flooding skylight that rendered every bush and outcrop far and fey prevented her from reading his posture (she was good at that, although she was unaware of it), even while it revealed it; and his tone was flat and devoid of emotion, though perhaps it was only made to sound so by distance.

"I'd like to start over. I thought maybe you'd like to start over, too."

He was silent while she counted seven thuddings of her pulse. At last: "You want me to come back?"

"No," she called, and he seemed to have become minutely smaller. "What I mean is . . . I want you to come to Orchid's some night. All right?"

"All right." It was not the echo.

"Maybe next week. And I don't know you. And you don't know me. Start over."

"All right," he called again. And then, "Sometime I'd like to meet you."

She intended to say *we will*, but the words stuck in her throat; she waved instead, and then, realizing that he could not see her, stepped from under the dome so that she too was in the clear, soft skylight and waved again, and watched him disappear where the Pilgrims' Way bent inland.

That was it, she thought.

She was tired and her feet hurt, and for some reason she did not want to step back under the dome again; she sat down on the smooth, flat rock outside the entrance to the shrine instead, kicked off her shoes, and comforted her blisters.

It was funny how you knew. That was it, and this's him, and I never knew till he said that: *Someday I'd like to meet you.*

He'd want her to leave Orchid's, and quite unexpectedly she realized she'd be glad to leave shaggy Orchid's to live anywhere, even under a bridge, with him.

Funny.

There was a brass plate thing let into the smooth stone of the shrine; she fingered its letters idly, naming the ones she knew. The plate seemed to move, ever so slightly, as if it was not solidly fastened but hinged at the top. She got her nails under it, lifted it, and saw swirling colors: reds and blues and pinks and yellows and golden browns and greens and greenish blacks and others for which she had no names.

"Immediately, Your Eminence," Incus said, bowing again. "I understand entirely, Your Eminence, and I shall be on the scene within the hour. You can trust in me absolutely, Your Eminence. As always."

He shut the door slowly and almost noiselessly, bowing

all the while, and made certain that the latchbar had dropped before he spat. The Circle was to convene after a dinner at Fulmar's, and Bittersweet had promised to show everyone the wonders she claimed to have achieved with an old porter, who would—as she reportedly had confided to Patera Tussah—adore her as Echidna, Scylla, Molpe, Thelxiepeia, Phaea, or Sphigx on command, all of it supposedly executed in compiler. Incus had wanted (never more than now) to see that. He had wanted very much to see the porter with his skullplate and faceplate removed. He had been (as he told himself angrily) more than merely anxious to witness at first hand an actual demonstration of Bittersweet's technique in order that he might compare it to his own.

Was it actually possible for anyone to download—or was the whole thing, perhaps, a great deal simpler than he had imagined? Ideally, one subverted the art of the Short Sun programmers, utilizing it to one's own advantage, as an expert wrestler threw an opponent too heavy to lift by enlisting his opponent's strength in his own cause.

Clenching his teeth and slamming his small fist into his palm, Incus sought to convince himself that there would be a raid tonight and that some well-disposed god had maddened old Remora so that he might be spared; but it was nonsense, and he knew it. He was *entitled* to go tonight. The Circle would not meet again until next month, and no one had toiled harder at black mechanics than he—no one had shared all that he had learned more willingly, earning this night a dozen times over. There was no fairness, no justice in the whorl. The gods did not care—or rather, were inimical. Beyond question, they were inimical to him.

Dropping angrily into his chair, he jammed the nearest quill into the inkwell.

My Dear Friend Fulmar:
    It is with deep regret that I must tell you that the old

fool has cooked up another perfectly ridiculous piece of busywork for me. I am to go to Limna tonight, and no other night will do. I am to consort with fishermen in search of a woman (yes, I write <u>a woman</u>) I have never seen, who may not be there at all, all because his worthless spies have failed him again.

So grieve, my dear friend, for your poor coworker <u>Myself</u>, who would be with you this night if he could.

Myself standing for *I,* as even that fool Fulmar could not help but understand. Briefly but satisfyingly, Incus reread, admired, amended mentally, and at last approved the note before ripping it in two, wadding it up, and flinging the wad into the incineratium. The chances that old Remora would ever see what he had written and identify him as the writer were slight, but not so slight that prudence did not forbid him to write his mind in any such fashion. A fresh sheet, in that case, and more ink—with the quill grasped wrongly.

My Dear Friend,
    Pressing duties constrain me to forebear the pleasant social meal to which you were so very kind as to invite me tonight.

His characteristic spiky *M* had been replaced by a new character remarkably like a double *E* upside down. Good— good!

You know, my friend, yet it might more thoughtfully be said that you cannot know, how much I have been looking forward to a <u>plain firsthand account</u> of the marvelous adventures of our mutual acquaintance Bee. Bee himself

No, it would not do. Fulmar would be utterly thrown off the scent by the male pronoun; it would be necessary to stop at his house and leave a clear, straightforward message with his valet. Nor would the trouble and loss of time go entirely unrecompensed; he, Incus, would at least have the satisfaction of inquiring just how long it had been since the unfortunate valet had received his wages, and observing the chem's baffled incomprehension. The valet had been a most creditable little project, and one Fulmar could never have brought to its wholly successful conclusion without his help.

Rising from his chair, Incus whistled shrilly and told the fat and worried-looking boy who answered his summons, "I need a *fast* litter with eight bearers to take me to the lake. Some fool woman— Never mind. His Eminence won't authorize renting a floater, although he insists upon speed. Tell the men that there will be only one passenger, myself. You might well describe me, I'm not weighty. They'll receive *double pay* at Limna and be dismissed there. Do the best you can, but hurry. Meanwhile I've got a hundred urgencies that must— Go, I say! Hurry! Is your bottom still sore? I'll make it sorer if you don't fly."

"Yes, Patera. At once, Patera. Immediately." Bowing, the fat boy shut the door, made sure the latchbar had dropped, and spat expertly into a corner.

Fascinated, Silk watched as the door opened in a swirl of petals, seeming to create the lofty green corridor beyond it. "It took me a while to identify the sensation," he confided to Mamelta, "but I placed it eventually. It was the feeling I'd had as a small boy when my mother had been holding me and put me down." He paused, musing.

"And now we're in another place altogether, much deeper underground. Truly extraordinary! Is there a way to prevent Hammerstone's following us down in this thing?"

Mamelta shook her head, whether in negation or merely to clear it, Silk could not have said. "So strange . . . Is this another dream?"

"No," he assured her. He rose from his seat. "No, it isn't. Put that thought from your mind entirely. Did you dream much, up there?"

"I don't know how long it was. Suppose I dreamed once each hundred years . . . ?"

Silk stepped out into the corridor. There was a well in it not far from the petaled door: a twilit shaft descended by spiraling steps. He set off down the corridor to examine it, felt something through the worn sole of one shoe, and stopped to pick it up.

It was a card.

"Look at this, Mamelta!" He held it up. "Money! My luck's certainly changed since I met you. Some god smiles on you, and smiles on me, too, because I'm with you."

"That is not money."

"Yes, it is," he told her. "Did you have money of some other kind on the Short Sun Whorl? This is the sort we use in Viron, and traders from foreign cities accept it, so I suppose they must use cards, too. This would buy a nice goat for Pas, for example—even a white ewe, if the market were depressed. Chop it into a hundred pieces, and every piece is one bit. A bit will buy two large cabbages or half a dozen eggs. Aren't you going to come out? I don't believe that the moving room is going to sink any farther."

She rose and followed him into the corridor.

"Maytera Marble remembers the Short Sun. I'll try to introduce you to her. You'll have a great deal in common, I'm sure."

When Mamelta did not reply, he asked, "Do you want to tell me about your dreams? That might help. What did you dream about?"

"People like you."

Silk leaned over the coping of the shaft to peer down. The first six steps bore six words:

HE WHO DESCENDS SERVES PAS BEST

"Look at this," he said; she did not, and he asked, "Who were these people in your dreams?"

She was silent so long that he thought she was not going to reply; he went through a gap in the coping and down to the first step. "There's writing on all of these," he told her. "The next series says, 'I will teach my children how I carried out the Plan of Pas.' There must be a shrine of Pas's at the bottom. Would you care to see it?"

"I am trying to . . . think of a way to tell you. We did not speak. Words. I have to remember to speak words now. I say something. But you do not hear me unless I move my lips. To move my lips and my tongue . . . while I make this noise in my throat."

"You're doing very well," Silk told her warmly. "Soon we'll have to go back up again, but not in that same little room since I'd assume it would take us to the place we left. I have to get back into the tunnels under Limna, however, and find the ashes from the manteion there. I'm not at all sure that we ought to take the time to look around this shrine and recite prayers and so forth. What do you think?"

"I . . ." Mamelta fell silent, staring.

"Patera Pike—my predecessor, and a most devout man—used to call out in dreams," Silk told her. "Sometimes he'd wake me in the next room. I think you may be afraid to speak, believing that this, too, is a dream; and that you might wake other sleepers. It isn't, so you will not."

She nodded, the movement of her head barely perceptible. "I may have called out in the beginning. One was small, the Monarch's second daughter. The one you used to see dance."

"Molpe?" Silk suggested.

"I remember seeing her often at home, dancing through my dreams. She was a wonderful dancer, but we cheered because we were afraid. You saw the hunger in her face for the kind of cheers the others got."

"It may be Pas who favors you," Silk decided. "Indeed it probably is, since the moving room carried us straight to this shrine of his. If so, he'll certainly be offended if we don't visit it, after all that he's done for us. Won't you come with me?"

She joined him on the uppermost step, and side-by-side they descended the spiral, seeing the footprints of those who had preceded them in the thin dust on the treads, and shivering in the cool air of the shaft, which narrowed and grew darker as they descended.

They were less than halfway down when a faint odor of decay set Silk's nostrils twitching; it was as though an altar had not been properly cleansed and purified, and he (assuming that the shrine he anticipated included such an altar) resolved to purify it himself if need be.

Mamelta, who had lagged behind him by a few steps, now touched his arm. "Is that a hammerstone?"

Silk looked back at her. "Hammerstone? Where?"

"Down there." She indicated the bottom of the shaft by a vague gesture. "Moaning? Something is moaning."

Silk stopped to listen; the sound was so faint that he could not be certain he did not imagine it, an eerie keening, rising and falling, always at the edge of his hearing, and often threatening to fade away altogether.

It was no louder at the bottom, where the soldier lay. Silk gripped the dead man's left arm and rolled him over, in the process discovering that he was no longer as strong as he had been. There was a ragged hole the size of his thumb in the dead man's blue-painted chest.

When he had recovered breath he said, "You'd better

stand back, Mamelta. Chems seldom explode once the moment of death is past, but there's always a risk." Squatting, he employed one of the steel gammas forming the voided cross he wore to remove the dead man's faceplate. When bridging connections with the gamma produced no arc, he shook his head.

"How . . . ? Mamelta is my name, and I told you. Have you told me yours?"

"Patera Silk." He straightened up. "Call me Patera, please. Were you about to ask how this man died?"

"He is a machine." She was looking at the dead man's wound. "A robot?"

"A soldier," Silk told her, "though I've never seen a blue one before. Ours are mottled—green, brown, and black—so I suppose he must have come from another city. In any case he's been dead a long time, while someone in the shrine is alive and in pain."

A massive door in the side of the shaft stood ajar. Silk opened it and stepped into the shrine, finding himself (to his astonishment) in a circular room a full thirty cubits high, with padded divans and glasses and multicolored readouts on its ceiling, its floor, and its curving wall. Every glass was energized, and in them all bobbed a tattered, skull-like thing that was no longer a face, wailing.

He clapped his hands. "Monitor!"

Gabbling sounds issued from the face. An irregular hole opened and closed; the sounds rose to a piercing shriek and a trapdoor in the center of the room flew back.

"It wants you to go into the nose," Mamelta said.

Silk crossed to the opening in the floor and stared down. At its bottom, fifty cubits away, swam three bright pinpricks that moved as one; irresistibly reminded of similar lights at the bottom of a grave he had dreamed was Orpine's, he watched until they vanished, replaced by a single spark. "I'm going down there."

"Yes. That is what it wants."

"The monitor? Could you understand him?"

She shook her head, a minute motion. "I have seen this. Going to the ship that would lift us off the *Whorl.*"

"This can't be any sort of boat," Silk protested. "This entire shrine must be embedded in solid rock."

"That is its berth," she murmured, but he had dropped to the floor already and swung his legs into the circular opening revealed by the trapdoor. Rungs set in the wall permitted him to climb down to a lucent bubble through which he looked across a benighted plain of naked rock. As he stared at it, a nameless mental mechanism adjusted, and the sparks swarming under the concave crystal floor were not merely distant but infinitely remote, the lamps and fires of new skylands.

"Great Pas . . ."

The divine name sounded empty and foolish here, though he had employed it with no doubts of its validity all his life; Great Pas was not so great as this, nor was Pas a god here, outside.

Silk swallowed, dry-mouthed and swallowing nothing, then traced the sign of addition with the gammadion he wore about his neck. "This is what you showed me, isn't it? The same thing I saw in the ball court, the black velvet and colored sparks below my feet."

There was, or so it seemed to him, an assent that was not a spoken word.

It steadied him as nothing else could have. One at a time, he removed his sweating hands from the icy rungs of the ladder and wiped them on his tunic.

"If you wish for me to die, then I'll die, I know; and I wouldn't have it otherwise. But after you showed me this in the ball court, you asked me to save our manteion, so please let me go back to—to the whorl I know. I'll offer you a white bull, I swear, as soon as I can afford it."

This time there was no response.

He stared about him; some of the pinpricks of light were red, some yellow as topaz, some violet, many like diamonds. Here and there he saw what appeared to be mists or clouds of light—whole cities, surely. The somber plain was pitted like the cheeks of a child who had survived the pox, and far more barren than the sheer cliffs of the Pilgrims' Way; no tree, no flower, no least weed or dot of moss sprouted from its rock.

Silk remained where he was, staring down at the gleaming dark, until Mamelta, from a higher rung, touched the top of his head to get his attention; then he started, peered up at her in surprise, and looked away, dismayed by his glimpse of her unclothed loins.

"What you found? I have found where it belongs. Give it to me."

"I'll bring it," he told her. When he tried to climb, he discovered that his hands were cold and stiff. "You mean the card?"

She did not reply.

All the rooms were small, though the widest was lined with innumerable divans and was higher than the principal tower of the Grand Manteion, facing the Prolocutor's palace on the Palatine. In a room above that very tall cylindrical room, Silk's heel slipped on a small white rotted thing, and he learned where the pervasive odor of decay originated. A dozen such flecks of dead flesh were scattered over the floor. He asked Mamelta what they were, and she bent to examine one and said, "Human."

Crouching to look at another, he recognized the coarse black dust in which it lay; the polished metal cabinet that had presumably held thousands or tens of thousands originally had, like the room in which Mamelta and so many other bios had stood sleeping, been sealed with the Seal of Pas; that seal had been broken, and the embryos flung wantonly about. At the schola, Silk had been taught to regard the mere misuse of any divine name as blasphemous. If that was true, what was this? Shuddering, he hurried after Mamelta.

In a compartment so small that he could not help brushing against her, she pointed to a frame and dangling wires. "This is the place. You won't know how to tag it. Let me."

Curious, and still half-stunned by the looting of Pas's treasures, he gave her a card. She attached three clips, then studied a glass overhead. "This is a different kind," she said. Stooping, she inserted it in the frame at ankle height. "Let me see them all."

He did; and she tested each as she had the first, working slowly and appearing unsure of her decisions at times, but always making the correct one. As she worked, a broken gray face took shape in the glass. "Is it time?" the face inquired—and again: "Is it time?" Silk shook his head, but the face continued to inquire.

Mamelta told Silk, "If you have more, you must give them to me."

"I don't. There were seven left after Orpine's rites, two left from Blood's sacrifice, and the one that you saw me find. I've given them all to you to repair this poor monitor. I never knew that money . . ."

"We must have more," Mamelta said.

He nodded. "More if I'm to save my manteion, certainly. Far more than ten. Yet if I take back those ten cards, he'll be as he was when we arrived." Exhausted, Silk leaned against the wall, and would have sat if he could.

"Have you eaten? There is food on board."

"I must go back down." He sternly repressed the sudden pleasure her concern gave him. "I have to see it again. The monitor— Is this really a kind of boat?"

"Not like the *Loganstone*. This is smaller."

"Its monitor was correct, in any event—what I saw from the bow was something I was meant to see. But you're correct as well. I should eat first. I haven't eaten since— since the morning of the day we went to the lake; I suppose that was yesterday now. I ate half a pear then, very quickly before we said our morning prayers. No wonder I'm so tired."

Small dishes swathed in a clouded film that Mamelta ate with obvious enjoyment grew almost too hot to hold as soon as the film was peeled away, and proved to be pressed from hard, crisp biscuit. Still shivering and grateful for the warmth, they devoured the dishes themselves as well as their contents, sitting side-by-side on one of the many divans; all the while, the monitor inquired, "Is it time? Is it time?" until Silk, at least, ceased to hear it. Mamelta presented him with a deep green twining vegetable whose taste reminded him of the gray goose he had offered to all the gods on the day he had come to Sun Street; he gave her a little dusky-gold cake in return, though she appeared to feel that it was too much.

"Now I'm going to go down into the bow again," he told her. "I may never return to this place, and I couldn't bear it if I hadn't gone again to prove to myself forever that I saw what I saw."

"The belly of the *Whorl?*"

He nodded. "If that's what you wish to call it, yes—and what lies beyond the belly. You can rest up here if you need to, or leave if you'd rather not wait for me. You're welcome to my robe, but please leave my pen case here if you go. It's in the pocket."

A little food remained, with some of the crisp dish; but he found that he did not want either. He stood up, brushing crumbs from his ash-smeared tunic. "When I come back, we—I alone, if you don't want to come—will have to return to the tunnels to recover the azoth I left there when

I met the soldiers. It will be very dangerous, I warn you. There are terrible animals."

Mamelta said, "If you have no more cards, there may be other repairs I can make." He turned to go, but she had not finished speaking. "This is my work, or at least a part of my work."

The ladder was the same, the pinpricks of unimaginably distant light the same, yet new. This otherwhorldly boat was a shrine after all, Silk decided, and smiled to himself. Or rather, it was the doorway to a shrine bigger than the whole whorl, the shrine of a god greater even than Great Pas.

There were four divans in the bubble below the end of the ladder. While eating with Mamelta, he had noticed thick woven straps dangling from the divan on which they sat; these divans had identical straps; seeing them, he thought again of slaves, and of the slavers said to ply the rivers that fed Lake Limna.

Reflecting that straps stout enough to hold slaves would hold him as well, he dropped to the upper end of the nearest divan and buckled its uppermost strap so that he could stand on it, virtually at the center of the bubble, while grasping the last rung.

By the time he looked out again, something wholly new was happening. The plain of rock had blanched unwatched, and was streaked with sable. Craning his neck to look behind him, he saw a thin crescent of blinding light at the utmost reach of the plain. At that moment it seemed to him that the Outsider had grasped the entire whorl as a man might grasp a stick—grasped it in a hand immensely greater, of which no more than the tip of the nail on a single finger had appeared.

Terrified, he fled up the ladder.

Chapter 11

SOME SUMMATIONS

"Auk? Have you forgotten me?"

He had thought himself utterly alone on the windswept Pilgrims' Way, trudging back to Limna. Twice before he had stopped to rest, sitting on white stones to scan the skylands. Auk was frequently outdoors and alone nightside, and it was something he enjoyed doing when he had the time: tracing the silver threads of rivers from which he would never drink, and exploring mentally the innumerable unknown cities in which the pickings were (as he liked to imagine) considerably better. Despite Chenille's insistence, he had not believed that she would actually remain in Scylla's shrine all night; but he had never supposed that she might overtake him. He pictured her as she had been when they reached it, footsore and exhausted, her face shining with sweat, her raspberry curls a mass of sodden tangles, her voluptuous body drooping like a bouquet on a grave.

Yet he felt sure it had been her voice that had sounded behind him. "Chenille!" he called. "Is that you?"

"No."

He rose, nonplussed, and shouted, "Chenille?"

The syllables of her name echoed from the rocks.

"I won't wait for you, Chenille."

Much nearer: *"Then I'll wait for you at the next stone."*

The faint pattering might have been rain; he glanced up at the cloudless sky again. The sound grew louder— running feet on the Pilgrims' Way behind him. As his eyes had traced the rivers, they followed its winding path across the barren, jutting cliff.

The clear skylight revealed her almost at once, nearer than he had supposed, her skirt hiked to her thighs and her arms and legs pumping. Abruptly she vanished in the shadow of a beetling rock, only to emerge like a stone from a sling and shoot toward him. For an instant he felt that she was running faster and faster with every stride, and would never slow or stop, or even stop gaining speed. Gaping, he stood aside.

She passed like a whirlwind, mouth wide, teeth gleaming, eyes starting from their sockets. A moment more and she was lost among stunted trees.

He drew his needler, checked the breech and pushed off the safety, and advanced cautiously, the needler in his hand ready to fire. The moaning wind brought the sound of tearing cloth, and her hoarse respirations.

"Chenille?"

Again, there was no reply.

"Chenille, I'm sorry."

He felt that some monstrous beast awaited him among the shadows; and although he called himself a fool, he could not free himself from the presentiment.

"I'm sorry," he repeated. "It was a rotten thing to do. I should have stayed there with you."

Half a chain farther, and the shadows closed about him. The beast still waited, nearer now. He mopped his sweating face with his bandanna; and as he wadded it into his pocket, he caught sight of her, quite naked, sitting on one of the white stones in a patch of skylight. Her black dress and pale undergarments were heaped at her feet, and her tongue lolled from her mouth so far that she appeared to lick her breasts.

He halted, tightening his grip on the needler.

She stood and strode toward him. He backed into deeper shadow and leveled the needler; she passed him without a word, stalking through the leafless spinney straight to the edge of the cliff. For a second or two she paused there, her arms above her head.

She dove, and after what seemed too long an interval he heard the faint splash.

He was halfway to the edge before he pushed the safety back up and restored the needler to his waistband. Heights held no fear for him; still, he knew fear as he stood at the brink of the cliff and stared down, a hundred cubits or more, into the skylit water.

She was not there. Wind-driven combers charged at the tumbled rocks like a herd of white-maned horses, but she was not among them.

"Chenille?"

He was about to turn away when her head burst through from a wave. *"I'll meet you,"* she called, *"there."* An arm that for an instant seemed but one of many pointed down the rocky beach toward the scattered lights of Limna.

"Arms?"

The question was Oreb's, and had come from a clump of straggling bushes to Auk's right.

He sighed, glad of any company and ashamed to be glad. "Yeah. Too many arms." He mopped his sweating face again. "No, that's gammon. It was like in a mirror, see? Chenille held her arms up out of the water, and it reflected 'em so it looked like there was more underneath, that's all. You find Patera?"

"Shrine eat."

"Sure. Come over and I'll give you a lift to Limna."

"Like bird?"

"I guess. I won't hurt you if that's what you mean, but you're Patera's, and I'm going to give you back to him if we ever find him."

Oreb fluttered up from the bushes to a landing on Auk's shoulder. "Girl like? Now like?"

"Chenille? Sure." Auk paused. "You're right. That's not her, is it?"

"No, no!"

"Yeah, right." Auk nodded to himself. "It's some kind of devil that only looks like Chenille. Shag, I don't know whether it likes birds or not. If I had to guess, I'd say it probably likes 'em for breakfast and lunch, but maybe it'd like something a little more solid for dinner. Anyhow, we'll dodge it if we can."

Worn out though he was, it seemed to him that his lagging feet flew over the next hill and all the rest, when he would have preferred that entire months be consumed in climbing and descending each. An hour passed in weary walking seemed less than a minute to him; and though Oreb kept him company on his shoulder, he had seldom felt so alone.

"I've found it!" Chenille's voice sounded practically at his ear; he jumped and Oreb squawked. "Can you swim? Are you carrying valuables that would be damaged by water?"

"A little," Auk admitted. He had stopped in his tracks to look for her; it was difficult to keep his hand away from his needler. When he spoke again, he was afraid that he might stammer. "Yeah, I am. Couple things."

"Then we must have a boat." Like mist from the lake, she rose between him and the rocky beach—he had been looking in the wrong direction. "You don't comprehend the littlest part of this, do you? I'm Scylla."

It was, to Auk's mind, an assertion of such preeminent

significance that no being of which he could conceive
would have the audacity to make it falsely. He fell to his
knees and mumbled a prayer.

"It's 'lovely Scylla,' " his deity told him, " *'wonderful* of
waters', not *'woman* of *the water.'* If you must mouth that
nonsense, do it correctly."

"Yes, Scylla."

She caught him by the hair. "Straighten up! And stop
whining. You're a burglar and a thug, so you may be useful.
But only if you do precisely as I direct." For a moment she
glared at him, her eyes burning into his. "You still don't
understand. Where can we find a boat? Around that village,
I suppose. Do you know?"

Standing, he was a head taller than she, and felt that he
ought to cower. "There's boats there for rent, lovely Scylla.
I've got some money."

"Don't try to make me laugh. It will do you no good, I
warn you. Follow me."

"Yes, Scylla."

"I don't care for birds." She did not trouble to look
back at Oreb as she spoke. "They belonged to Daddy, and
now to Molpe and ones like that to little Hierax. I don't
even like having my people named for them. You know I'm
oldest?"

"Yes, I sure do, lovely Scylla." Auk's voice had been an
octave too high; he cleared his throat and made an effort
to regain his self-possession. "That's the way Patera Pike
always told it at the palaestra."

"Pike?" She glanced back at him. "That's good. Is he
particularly devoted to me?"

"Yes, lovely Scylla. Or anyhow he was. He's dead."

"It doesn't matter."

Already they had reached the beginning of the Pilgrims' Way; the glowing windows of cookshops and taverns
illuminated the street; late diners bound for rented beds

stared rudely at Chenille's nakedness, or resolutely did not stare.

"Six children after me! Daddy had this thing about a male heir, and this other thing about not dying." A drunken carter tried to tweak her nipple; she gouged his eyes with both thumbs and left him keening in the gutter. "Molpe was just another girl, but you would have thought Tartaros would do it. Oh, no. So along came little Hierax, but even Hierax wasn't enough. So then three more girls, and after that—I suppose you already knew we could take you over like this?"

Oreb croaked, "Girl?" But if she heard him she gave no sign of it.

Auk muttered, "I didn't know it could still happen now, lovely Scylla."

"It's our right, but most of us have to have a glass or a Window. That's what you call them. A terminal. But this whole lake's my terminal, which gives me lots of power around here."

She was not looking at him, but Auk nodded.

"I haven't been here for a while, though. This woman's a whore. No wonder Kypris went for her."

Auk nodded again, weakly.

"In the beginning we chose up, with Daddy to be the god of everything—that's what his name meant—and boss over everybody. You see? Where are the boats?"

"If we turn the next corner and go down a ways we might find some, lovely Scylla."

"He's dead now, though. We wiped him out of core thirty years ago. Anyway, Mama got to pick next, and she grabbed the whole inner surface. I knew she'd stay on land, mostly, so I took the water. I was doing lots of diving back then. Molpe took the arts, like you'd expect." As Chenille rounded the corner, she caught sight of a fishing boat moored at the end of the alley; she pointed. "That one's already got a man on it. Two, and one's an augur. Perfect! Can you sail? I can."

Pas was dead! Auk could think of nothing else.

"No? Then don't kill them. I was going to say that we took new names that would fit. Daddy was Typhon the First, back home. What none of us knew was that he'd let *her* choose, too. So she picked love, what a surprise. And got sex and everything dirty with it. She didn't meddle very much in the beginning, knowing that—"

Hearing her voice, Patera Incus had looked up.

"You! Augur! Prepare to cast off." Chenille herself was off like a sprinter, disappearing in the dense shadow of a salting shed. A moment later Auk saw her leap—flying in a way that he knew would have been impossible had she not been possessed—to land with a roll upon the deck of the fishing boat.

"I said prepare to cast off. Are you deaf?"

She struck the augur with her left hand and the fisherman with her right, and the sounds of the blows might almost have been the slamming of double doors. Auk drew his needler and hurried after her.

Another hot—another scorching—morning. Maytera Marble fanned herself with a pamphlet. There were coils in her cheeks; their plan no longer appeared at her call, but she was almost sure of it. Her main coils were in her legs, with an auxiliary coil in each cheek; there the fluid that carried such strength as she still possessed was brought (or at least ought to have been brought) into intimate contact with her titanium faceplate, which was in turn in intimate contact with the air of the kitchen.

And the air was supposed to be cooler.

But no, that couldn't be right. She had once looked— she was almost sure she had looked—distinctly like a bio. Her cheeks had been overlaid with . . . with some material that would very likely have impeded the transfer of heat. What had she told dear Patera Silk the other day? Three centuries? Three hundred years? The decimal had slipped, must certainly have slipped to the left.

It had to have. She had looked like a bio then—like a bio girl, with black hair and red cheeks. Like a somewhat older Dahlia in fact, and Dahlia had always been so bad at arithmetic, forever mixing up her decimals, multiplying two decimal numbers and getting one with two decimal points, mere scrambled digits that meant not even His Cognizance could have said what.

With her free hand, Maytera Marble stirred the porridge. It was done, nearly overcooked. She lifted it from the stove and fanned herself again. In the refectory on the other side of the doorway, little Maytera Mint waited for her breakfast with exemplary patience. Maytera Marble told her, "Perhaps you'd better eat now, sib. Maytera Rose may be ill."

"All right, sib."

"That was obedience, wasn't it?" The pamphlet drifted past Maytera Marble's face; it bore a watery picture of Scylla frolicking with sunfish and sturgeon, but carried no cooling. Deep within Maytera Marble, an almost-forgotten sensor stirred dangerously. "You don't have to obey me, sib."

"You're senior, sib." Normally the words would have been nearly inaudible; this morning they were firm and clear.

Maytera Marble was too hot to notice. "I won't make you eat now if you don't want to, but I've got to take it off the stove."

"I want what you want, sib."

"I'm going to go upstairs. Maytera may require my help." Maytera Marble had an inspiration. "I'll take her bowl up on a tray." That would make it possible for Maytera Mint to eat her breakfast without waiting for the eldest sibyl. "First I'm going to give you porridge, and you must eat it all."

"If that's what you wish, sib."

Maytera Marble opened the cupboard and got Maytera Rose's bowl and the old, chipped bowl that Maytera Mint professed to prefer. Climbing the stair would overheat her; but she had not thought of that in time, so she would have to climb. She ladled out porridge until the ladle dissolved into a cloud of digits, then stared at it. She had always taught her classes that solid objects were composed of swarming atoms, but she had been wrong; every solid object, each solid thought, was swarming numbers. Shutting her eyes, she forced herself to dip up more porridge, to drop the pamphlet and find the lip of a bowl with her fingers and dump more porridge in.

The stair was not as onerous as she had feared, but the second story of the cenoby had vanished, replaced by neat rows of wilting herbs, by straggling vines. Someone had chalked up a message: SILK FOR CALDE!

"Sib?" It was Maytera Mint, her voice faint and far. "Are you all right, sib?"

The crude letters and the shiprock wall fell into digits. "Sib?"

"Yes. Yes, I was going upstairs, wasn't I? To look in on Maytera Betel." It would not do to worry timorous little Maytera Mint. "I only stepped out here for a minute to cool down."

"I'm afraid Maytera Betel's left us, sib. To look in on Maytera Rose."

"Yes, sib. To be sure." These dancing bands of numbers were steps, she felt. But steps leading to the door or to an upper floor? "I must have become confused, Maytera. It's so hot."

"Be brave, sib." A hand touched her shoulder. "Perhaps you'd like to call me that? We're sisters, you and I."

Now and again she saw actual stairs, the strip of brown carpet with its pattern worn away that she had swept so often. Maytera Rose's door ended the short corridor: the corner room. Maytera Marble knocked and found that her knuckles had smashed the panel; through the splintered wood she glimpsed Maytera Rose still in bed, her mouth and eyes open and her face dotted with flies.

She entered, ripped Maytera Rose's threadbare nightgown from neck to hem, and opened Maytera Rose's chest; then she pulled off her habit, hung it neatly over a chair, and opened her own. Almost reluctantly, she began to exchange components with her dead sib, testing each as it went into place, and rejecting a few. This is Tarsday, she reminded herself, but Maytera's gone, so this can't be theft.

I won't need these any more.

The glass on the north wall showed a fishing boat under full sail; a naked woman standing beside the helmsman wore a flashing ring. Maytera, naked herself, averted her eyes.

Silk's head throbbed, and his eyes seemed glued shut. Short and fat yet somehow huge, Councillor Potto loomed over him, fists cocked, waiting for his eyes to open. Somewhere—somewhere there had been peace. Turn the key the other way, and the dancers would dance backward, the music play backward, vanished nights reappear . . .

Darkness and a steady thudding, infinitely reassuring. Knees drawn up, arms bent in prayer. Wordless contemplation, free of the need to eat or drink or breathe.

The tunnel, dark and warm but ever colder. Anguished cries, Mamelta beside him, her hand in his and Hyacinth's tiny needler yapping like a terrier.

How much did they give you? Blows that rocked him.

Ashes, unseen but choking.

"This is the place."

How much did you tell Blood?

A shower of fire. Morning prayers in a manteion in Limna that was perhaps thirty cubits, yet a thousand leagues away.

"Behind you! Behind you!" Whirl and shoot.

The dead woman's lantern, its candle three-quarters consumed. Mamelta blowing on a glowing coal to light it.

"I am a loyal cit—"

"Councillor, I am a loyal cit—"

Spitting blood.

"Those who harm an augur—"

How much—

Silk's right eye opened, saw a wall as gray as ash, and closed again.

He tried to count his shots—and found himself in the eating house again. "Well, Patera, for one thing mine holds a lot more needles. . . . All of them good and thick, this was the Alambrera in the old days." The door opened and Potto came in with their dinners on a tray, Sergeant Sand behind him with the box and the terrible rods.

Back! Back!

Kneeling in the ashes, digging with his hands. A god who took five needles and still stood at the edge of the lantern light, snarling, blood and slaver running from its mouth. The boom of a slug gun, loud in the tunnel and very near.

. . . did you give him?

Metal rods jammed into his groin, Sand's arm spinning the crank, his expressionless face washed away by unbearable pain.

He bought your manteion.

"Yes. I'm a—"
Indefinitely? He let you stay indefinitely?
"Yes."
Indefinitely.
"Yes. I don't know . . ."
(Back, oh, back, but the current is too strong.)

Silk's left eye opened. Painted steel, gray as ash. He rubbed his eyes and sat up, his head aching and his stomach queasy. He was in a gray-walled room of modest size, without windows. He shivered. He had been lying on a low, hard, and very narrow cot.

A voice from the edge of memory said, "Ah, you're awake. I need somebody to talk to."

He gasped and blinked. It was Doctor Crane, one hand raised, eyes sparkling. "How many fingers?"

"You? I dreamed . . ."

"You got caught, Silk. So did I. How many fingers do you see?"

"Three."

"Good. What day is it?"

Silk had to consider; it was an effort to remember. At last he said, "Tarsday? Orpine's obsequies were on Scylsday; we went to the lake on Molpsday, and I went down . . ."

"Yes?"

"Into these tunnels. I've been down here a long time. It might even be Hieraxday by now."

"Good enough, but we're not in the tunnels."

"The Alambrera?"

Crane shook his head. "I'll tell you, but it'll take some explaining, and I ought to warn you first that they've probably locked us up together hoping we may say something useful. You may not want to oblige them."

Silk nodded and found it a mistake. "I wish I had some water."

"It's all around us. But you'll have to wait till they give us some, if they ever do."

"Councillor Potto hit me with his fist." Silk caressed the swelling on the side of his head gingerly. "That's the last thing that I remember. When you say *they*, do you mean our Ayuntamiento?"

"That's right." Crane sat down on the cot beside him. "I hope you don't mind. I was sitting on the floor while you were unconscious, and it's cold and hard on the buttocks. Why did you go out to the lake? Mind telling me?"

"I can't remember."

Crane nodded approvingly. "That's probably the best line to take."

"It isn't a line at all. I've—I've had very strange dreams." Silk pushed away terrifying memories of Potto and Sand. "One about a naked woman who had strange dreams too."

"Tch, tch!"

"I talked with a—it doesn't matter. And I vanquished a devil. You won't believe that, Doctor."

"I don't," Crane told him cheerfully.

"But I did. I called on the gods in turn. Only Hierax frightened her."

"A female devil. Did she look like this?" Crane bared his teeth.

"Yes, a little." Silk paused, rubbing his head. "And it wasn't a dream—it's not fading. You know her. You must."

Crane lifted an eyebrow. "I know the devil you drove away? My circle of acquaintants is wide, I admit, but—"

"She's Mucor, Blood's daughter. She can possess people, and she possessed the woman I was with."

Suddenly serious, Crane whistled softly.

"Was it you who operated on her?"

Crane shook his head. "Blood told you?"

"He told me he'd had a brain surgeon in the house before you. When I learned what Mucor could do, I understood—or at least, I think I do. Will you tell me about it?"

Crane fingered his beard, then shrugged. "Can't hurt, I suppose. The Ayuntamiento knows all the important points anyhow, and we've got to pass the time some way. If I do, will you answer a few questions of mine? Honest, complete answers, unless it's something that you don't want them to know?"

"I know nothing that I wouldn't want the Ayuntamiento to learn," Silk declared, "and I've already answered a great many questions for Councillor Potto. I'll tell you anything concerning myself, and anything I know about other people that wasn't learned under the seal."

Crane grinned. "In that case I'll start with the most basic one. Who are you working for?"

"I should have said that I'll answer after you answer my own questions about Mucor. That was the agreement, and I'd like to help her if I can."

The eyebrow went up again. "Including my first one?"

"Yes," Silk said. "Very much including that one. That one first of all. Is Mucor really Blood's daughter? That's what she told me."

"Legally. His adopted daughter. Unmarried men aren't usually allowed to adopt, but Blood's been working for the Ayuntamiento. Were you aware of that?"

Silk remembered in the nick of time not to shake his head. "No. Nor do I believe it now. He's a criminal."

"They don't pay him so many cards, you understand. They let him operate without interference as long as there's no serious trouble at any of his places, and do him favors. This seems to have been one of them. A word to the judge from any of the councillors would have been more than enough, and by adopting her he could control her up to the age of consent."

"I see. Who are her real parents?"

Crane shrugged again. "She doesn't have any. Not in our whorl, anyhow. And whoever they were, they probably met in a petri dish. She was a frozen embryo. Blood paid a good deal for it, I imagine. I know he paid a small fortune to get that brain man you mentioned."

Recalling the bare and filthy room in which he had first encountered Mucor, Silk said bitterly, "A fortune to destroy what he had given so much to get."

"Not really. It was supposed to make her pliable. She was a holy terror, from what I've heard. But when the brain man—he came from Palustria, by the way, which is how we found out what was going on. When he opened up her cranium, he got hit with a new organ." Crane chuckled. "I've read his report. It's in the medical file back at the villa."

"A new organ? What was it?"

"I didn't mean that it wasn't a brain. It was. But it wasn't like anything the brain man had worked on before. It wasn't a human brain for medical purposes, or an animal's brain, either. He had to go by guess and good gods, as they say. And in the end he made a botch of it. He as much as admitted it."

Silk wiped his eyes.

"Oh, come now. It was ten years ago, and we spies are supposed to be of sterner stuff."

"Has anybody ever cried for her, Doctor?" Silk asked. "You, or Blood, or Musk, or the brain surgeon? Anyone at all?"

"Not that I know of."

"Then let me cry for her. Let her have that at least."

"I wouldn't think of trying to stop you. You haven't asked why Blood didn't get rid of her."

"She's his daughter, according to what you just told me—his daughter legally, at least."

"That wouldn't stop him. It was because the brain man said her subrogative abilities could regenerate some time after she'd healed. It was only a guess, but judging from your story about a devil, they have. And the Ayuntamiento knows it now, thanks to you. It's going to make Viron more dangerous than ever."

Silk daubed at his eyes again with a corner of his robe and wiped his nose. "More formidable, you mean. That may trouble your government in Palustria, but it doesn't bother me."

"I see." Crane slid backward on the cot until he could prop his spine against the steel wall. "You promised you'd tell me who you were working for, if I told you about Mucor. Now you're going to say you're working for His Cognizance the Prolocutor, or something like that. Is that it? Hardly what I'd call fair play."

"No. Or perhaps, in a way, I am. It's a nice ethical point. Certainly I'm doing what His Cognizance would wish me to do, but I haven't told him—haven't informed the Chapter formally, I should say. I really haven't had time, the old excuse. Would you have believed me if I'd said I was a spy for His Cognizance?"

"I wouldn't and I don't. Your Prolocutor's got spies, plenty of them. But they aren't holy augurs. He's not so foolish as that. Who is it?"

"The Outsider."

"The god?"

"Yes." Silk sensed that Crane's eyebrow had been raised again, though he was not looking at Crane's face; he filled his lungs and expelled the air through his mouth. "No one believes me—except for Maytera Marble, a little—so I don't expect you to, either, Doctor. You least of all. But I've already told Councillor Potto, and I'll tell you. The Outsider spoke to me last Phaesday, on the ballcourt at our palaestra." He waited for Crane's snort of contempt.

"Now that's interesting. We ought to be able to talk about that for a long time. Did you see him?"

Silk considered the question. "Not in the way I see you now, and in fact I feel sure it's impossible to see him like that. All visual representations of the gods are ultimately false, as I told Blood a few days ago; they're more or less appropriate, not more or less like. But the Outsider showed himself to me—his spirit, if one can speak of the spirit of a god—by showing me innumerable things he had done and made, people and animals and plants and myriad other things that he cares very much about, not all of them beautiful or lovable things to you, Doctor, or to me. Huge fires outside the whorl, a beetle that looked like a piece of jewelry but laid its eggs in dung, and a boy who can't speak and lives—well, like a wild beast.

"There was a naked criminal on a scaffold, and we came back to that when he died, and again when his body was taken down. His mother was watching with a group of his friends, and when someone said he had incited sedition, she said that she didn't think he had ever been really bad, and that she would always love him. There was a dead woman who had been left in an alley, and Patera Pike, and it was all connected, as if they were pieces of something larger." Silk paused, remembering.

"Let's get back to the god. Could you hear his voice?"

"Voices," Silk said. "One spoke into each ear most of the time. One was very masculine—not falsely deep, but solid, as if a mountain of stone were speaking. The other was feminine, a sort of gentle cooing; yet both voices were his. When my enlightenment was over, I understood far, far better than I ever had before why artists show Pas with two heads, though I believe, too, that the Outsider had a great many more voices as well. I could hear them in back of me at times, although indistinctly. It was as if a crowd were waiting behind me while its leaders whispered in my ears; but as if the crowd was actually all one person, somehow: the Outsider. Do you want to comment?"

Crane shook his head. "When both voices spoke at once, could you understand what they said?"

"Oh, yes. Even when they were saying quite different things, as they usually did. The difficult thing for me to understand, even now—one of the difficult things, anyway—is that all of this took place in an instant. I think I told someone later that it seemed to last hundreds of years, but the truth is that it didn't occupy any amount of time at all. It took place during something else that wasn't time, something I've never known at any other time. That's badly expressed, but perhaps you understand what I mean."

Crane nodded.

"One of the boys—Horn, the best player we have—was reaching for a catch. He had his fingers almost on the ball, and then this took place outside of time. It was as if the Outsider had been standing in back of me all my life, but had never spoken until it was necessary. He showed me who he was and how he felt about everything he had made. Then how he felt about me, and what he wanted me to do. He warned me that he wouldn't help me. . . ." The words faded away; Silk pressed his palm to his forehead.

Crane chuckled. "That wasn't very nice of him."

"I don't believe it's a question of niceness," Silk said slowly. "It's a matter of logic. If I was to be his agent, as he asked—he never demanded anything. I ought to have emphasized that.

"But if I was to be his agent, then he was doing it; he was preserving our manteion, because that was what he wanted me to do. He is preserving it through me. I'm the help he sent, you see; and you don't rescue the rescuer, just as you don't scrub a bar of soap or buy plums to hang on

your plum tree. I said I'd try to do it, of course. I said I'd
try to do whatever he wanted me to."

"So then you sallied forth to save that run-down manteion on Sun Street? And that little house where you live, and
the rest of it?"

"Yes." Silk nodded, wished he had not, and added,
"Not necessarily the buildings that are there now. If they
could be replaced with new and larger buildings—Patera
Remora, the coadjutor, hinted at that the other night—it
would be even better. But that answers your question. That
tells you whom I'm working for. Spying for, if you like,
because I was spying on you."

"For a minor god called the Outsider."

"Yes. Correct. We were going—I was going to tell you
that I knew you were a spy, the next time you came to treat
my ankle. That I'd talked to people who'd provided you
with information without realizing why you wanted it,
who'd carried messages for you and to you; and I'd seen a
pattern in those things—I see it more clearly now, but I had
seen it even then."

Crane smiled and shook his head in mock despair. "So
did Councillor Lemur, unfortunately."

"I see other things, too," Silk told him. "Why you were
at Blood's, for example; and why I encountered Blood's
talus here in the tunnels."

"We're not in the tunnels," Crane said absently, "didn't
you hear me say that there's water all around us? We're in
a sunken ship in the lake. Or to be a little more exact, in
a ship that was built to sink, and to float to the surface on
the captain's order. To swim underwater like a fish, if you
can believe that. This is the secret capital of Viron. I'd be
a wealthy man as well as a hero, if only I could get that
information to my superiors back home."

Silk slid from the cot and crossed the room to its steel
door. It was locked, as he had expected, and there was no

pane of glass or peephole through which he could look out. Suddenly conscious of the odor of his body and the smears of ash on his clothing, he asked, "Isn't there any way we can wash here?"

Crane shook his head again. "There's a slop jar under the cot, if you want that."

"No. Not now."

"Then tell me why you cared whether I was a spy or not, if you weren't going to hand me over to the Ayuntamiento."

"I was," Silk said simply, "if you wouldn't help me save our manteion from Blood. I was going to say that if you did that, I'd let you leave the city."

He sat down in the corner farthest from the cot, finding the steel floor as cold and as hard as Crane had said. "But if you wouldn't, I planned to roll you over to the hoppies. That's the way the people of our quarter would say it, and I was working for them as well as for the Outsider, who wanted to save our manteion because he cares so deeply about them."

He pulled off his shoes. "By 'hoppies' they mean the troopers of our Civil Guard. They say that the Guardsmen look like frogs, because of their green uniforms."

"I know. Why did you go into the tunnels? Because I'd asked some people about them?"

Silk was peeling off his stockings as he replied. "Not really. I didn't intend to enter the tunnels, although I'd heard of them vaguely—circles of black mechanics meeting there and so on, which they told us at the schola was a lot of nonsense. You and this wrapping you lent me had made it possible for me to walk out to Scylla's shrine on the lake. I went out there because Commissioner Simuliid had; and the person who told me that said you'd been interested to learn of it."

"Chenille."

"No." Silk shook his head, knowing that it would hurt, but eager to make his answer as negative as possible.

"You know it was. Not that it matters. I was listening outside while you shrove her, by the way. I couldn't hear a lot, but I wish I'd heard that."

"You couldn't have heard it, because it was never said. Chenille acknowledged her own transgressions, not yours." Silk removed the wrapping.

"Have it your way. Did Blood's talus turn you over to Potto?"

"It was more complicated than that," Silk hesitated. "I suppose it's imprudent for me to say it; but if Councillor Potto has someone listening to us, all the better—I want to get this off my conscience. I killed Blood's talus. I had to in order to preserve my own life; but I didn't like it, and I haven't come to like it any better since it happened."

"With . . . ?"

Silk nodded. "With an azoth I happened to have upon my person. It was later taken from me."

"I've got you. Maybe we'd better not say anything else about that."

"Then let's talk about this," Silk said, and held up the wrapping. "You very generously lent me this, and I've been as ungrateful as I could possibly be. You know my excuse, which is that I was hoping to do what the Outsider had asked—to justify his faith in me, who in twenty-three years had never paid him even trifling honors. It wouldn't be right for me to keep this, and I'm grateful for this opportunity to return it."

"I won't accept it. Is it cold now? It must be. Do you want me to recharge it for you?"

"I want you to take it, Doctor. I would have extorted the money I need from you if I could. I deserve no favors from you."

"You've never gotten any, either." Crane drew his legs

onto the cot to sit cross-legged. "I didn't invent you, but I wish I had, because I'd like to take credit for you. You're exactly what we've needed. You're a rallying point for the underclass in Viron, and a city divided is a city too weak to attack its neighbors. Now recharge that thing and put it back on your ankle."

"I never wished to weaken Viron," Silk told him. "That was no part of my task."

"Don't blame yourself. The Ayuntamiento did the damage when they assassinated the caldé and governed in defiance of your Charter and their people—which won't save your life when Lemur's finished with you. He'll kill you just like he'll kill me."

Silk nodded ruefully. "Councillor Potto said something of the sort. I hoped—I still hope that it was no more than a threat. That he will no more kill me, despite his threat, than Blood would."

"The situation is entirely different. You'd gone out to Blood's, and it seemed likely that others knew about it. If his talus caught you and dragged you into the tunnels, it's not likely that anybody else knows the Ayuntamiento has you. Not even the talus, since you say you killed it."

"Only Mamelta, the woman who was captured with me."

"What's more," Crane said, "killing you would have made Blood much less secure. Killing you would make Lemur and the rest *more* secure. In fact, I'm surprised they haven't done it already. Who's Mamelta, by the way? One of those holy women?"

"One of the people whom Pas put into the whorl when he had finished it. Did you know that some of them are still alive, though sleeping?"

Crane shook his head. "Did he tell you that? Pas?"

"No, she did. I had been captured by soldiers—I left the azoth behind when that happened, because I knew I'd be searched. A drift of ashes almost filled that tunnel, and I left it buried in them when the soldiers pulled me out."

Crane grinned. "Shrewd enough."

"It wasn't. Not really. I was going to say that one of the soldiers showed me the sleeping people and told me they had been there since the time of the first settlers. Mucor woke one, Mamelta, and I exorcised Mucor, as I told you."

"Yes."

"Mamelta and I got away from the soldiers—Hammerstone will be punished for that, I'm afraid—but we were arrested again when we went back for the azoth. They locked me up in a place worse than this one, and after a while they brought me my robe. Mamelta had been wearing it, so they must have given her proper clothing; at least, I hope they did." Silk paused, gnawing his lower lip. "I could have resisted the soldiers with the azoth, I suppose; it's quite possible that I would have killed them both. But I couldn't bring myself to do it."

"Very creditable. But by the time you were rearrested Potto was there?"

"Yes."

"And he soon realized who you were."

"I told him," Silk admitted. "That is to say, he asked my name, and I gave it. I would do it again. I'm a loyal citizen, as I assured him repeatedly."

"I wonder if it's possible to be loyal while dead. But that's your bailiwick. The thing that interests me is that you escaped the first time, with this woman. Mind telling me how you reconciled that with your loyalty?"

"I had an urgent matter to attend to," Silk said. "I won't go into detail now, but I did; and because I had done nothing wrong, I was morally justified in leaving when the opportunity presented itself."

"But now you have? Are you a criminal deserving of death?"

"No. My conscience isn't entirely clear, but the worst thing on it is that I've failed the Outsider. If I could get away again in some fashion—though that appears impossible now—it's conceivable that I might succeed after all."

"Then you'd be willing to escape if we could?"

"From an iron room with a locked door?" Silk ran his fingers through his untidy thatch of yellow hair. "How do you propose to do it, Doctor?"

"We may not be here forever. Would you be willing?"

"Yes. Certainly."

"Then recharge your wrapping. We may have to run, and I hope we will. Go ahead, kick it or wallop the floor with it."

Silk did as he had been told, flailing the steel plates. "If there's even the slightest chance to fulfill my pledge to the Outsider, I must take it; and I will. He'll surely bless you, as I do, for your magnanimity."

"I won't bank on it." Crane smiled, and for a moment actually appeared cheerful. "You had a cerebral accident, that's all. Most likely a tiny vein burst as a result of your exertions during the game. When that happens in the right spot, delusions like yours aren't at all uncommon. Wernicke's area, it's called." He touched his own head to indicate the place.

Chapter 12

LEMUR

Silk knelt in silent prayer, his face to the gray-painted wall of the compartment.

Marvelous Molpe, be not angry with me, who have always honored you. Music is yours. Am I never to hear it again? Recall my music box, Molpe, how many hours I spent with it when I was a child. It is in my closet now, Molpe, and if only you will free me I will oil the dancers and its works as well, and play it each night. I have searched my conscience, Molpe, to discover that in which I have displeased you. I find this: that I dealt overharshly with Mucor when she possessed Mamelta. Those whose wits are disordered and those who, though grown, remain as children are, are yours, I know, Molpe, and for your sake I should have been more gentle with her. Nor should I have called her a devil, for she is none. I renounce my pride, and I will separate Mucor from Blood if I can, and treat her as I would my own child. This I swear. A singing bird to you, Molpe, if you will but—

Crane asked, "You don't think that stuff really helps, do you?"

A singing bird to you, Molpe, if you will but set us free.

Tenebrous Tartaros, be not angry with me, who have always honored you. Theft is yours, murder, and foul deeds done in darkness. Am I never again to walk freely the dark streets of my native city? Recall how I walked there with Auk, like me a thief. When I surmounted Blood's wall, you favored me, and I gladly paid the black lamb and the cock I swore. Recall that it was I who brought the Pardon of Pas to Kalan, and allow me to steal away now, Tartaros, and Doctor Crane with me. I will never forget, Tartaros, that thieves are yours and I am one. I have searched my conscience, Tartaros, to discover that in which I have displeased you. I find this: that I detested your darksome tunnels with all my heart, never thinking in my pride that you had sent me there, nor that they were a most proper place for such as I. I renounce my pride; if ever you send me there again, I will strive to be grateful, recalling your favors. This I swear. A score of black rats to you, Tartaros, if you will but set us free.

Highest Hierax, be not angry with me, who have always honored you. Death is yours. Am I never to comfort the dying again? Recall my kindnesses to Pricklythrift, Shrub, Flax, Orpine, Bharal, Kalan, and Exmoor, Hierax. Recall how Exmoor blessed me with his dying breath, and forget not that it was I who slew the bird to whom blasphemers had given your name. If only you will free us, I will bring pardon to the dying all my life, and burial to the dead. I have searched my conscience, Hierax, to discover that in which I have displeased you. I find this: that—

"I thought you fellows used beads."

"Potto took them, as I told you," Silk said dispiritedly. "He took everything, even my glasses."

"I didn't know you wore glasses."

That when I beheld those who had died in the sleep into which Pas had cast them, I did not propose their burial, or so much as offer a prayer for them; and when Mamelta and I found the bones of she who had carried a lantern, I in my pride took her lantern without interring her bones. I renounce my pride and will be ever mindful of the dead. This I swear. A black he-goat to you, Hierax, if you will but set us free.

Enchanting Thelxiepeia, be not angry with me, who have always honored you. Prophesy and magic are yours. Am I never to cast the Thelxday lots again, nor to descry in the entrails of sacrifice the records of days to come? Recall that of the many sacrifices I offered for Orpine, for Auk, and for myself on Scylsday past, I read all save the birds. I have searched my conscience, Thelxiepeia, to discover that in which I have displeased—

Abruptly the room was plunged in such darkness as Silk had never known, not even in the ash-choked tunnel, a darkness palpable and suffocating, without the smallest spark or hint of light.

Crane whispered urgently, "It's Lemur! Cover your head."

Despondent, not knowing why he should cover it or what he might cover it with, Silk did not.

I find this: that I sought no charm—

The door opened; Silk turned at the sound in time to see someone who nearly filled the doorway enter. The door closed again with a solid thud, but no snick from the bolt.

"Stand up, Patera." Councillor Lemur's voice was deep and rich, a resonant baritone. "I want both of you. Doctor, take this."

A thump.

"Pick it up."

Crane's voice: "This is my medical bag. How did you get it?"

Lemur laughed. (Silk, rising, felt an irrational longing to join in that laughter, so compellingly agreeable and good-natured was it.) "You think we're in the middle of the lake? We're still in the cave, but we'll be putting out shortly. I spoke to Blood and one of his drivers brought it, that's all.

"Patera, I have some little presents for you, too. Take them, they're yours."

Silk held out both hands and received his prayer beads and the gammadion and silver chain his mother had given him, the beads and chain in a single, tangled mass. "Thank you," he said.

"You're a bold man, Patera. An extremely bold man, for an augur. Do you consider that you and the doctor, acting in concert, might overpower me?"

"I don't know."

"But not so bold now that you've lost your god. Doctor, what about you? You and the augur, together?"

Crane's voice, from the direction of the cot, "No." As he spoke, Silk heard the soft snap of a catch.

"I have your needler in my waistband. And yours, Patera. It's in my sleeve. In a moment I'm going to give them back to you. With your needlers back in your possession, do you think you and your friend the doctor could kill me in the dark?"

Silk said, "May all the gods forbid that I should ever kill you, or anyone, or even wish to."

Lemur laughed again, softly. "You wanted to kill Potto, didn't you, Patera? He questioned you for hours, according to what he told me. I've known Potto all my life, and there is no more objectionable man in the whorl, even when he's trying to ingratiate himself."

"It is true that I could not like him." Silk chose his words. "Yet I respected him as a member of the Ayuntamiento, and thus one of the legitimate rulers of our city. Certainly I did not wish to harm him."

"He hit you repeatedly, and eventually so hard that you were in a coma for hours. The whorl would be well rid of my cousin Potto. Don't you want your needler back?"

"Yes. Very much." Silk extended his hand blindly.

"And you'll try to kill me?"

"Hammerstone challenged me in the same way," Silk said. "I told Councillor Potto about it, and he must have told you; but you're not a soldier."

"I'm not even a chem."

Crane's voice: "He's never seen you."

"In that case, look at me now, Patera."

A faint glow, a nebulous splotch of white phosphorescence near the ceiling, appeared to relieve the utter darkness. As Silk stared in fascination, the closely shaven face of a man of sixty or thereabouts appeared. It was a noble face, with a lofty brow surmounted by a mane of silver hair, an aquiline nose, and a wide mobile-looking mouth; staring up at it, Silk realized that Councillor Lemur had to be taller even than Gib.

The face spoke: "Aren't you going to ask how I do this? My skin is self-luminescent. Even my eyes. Watch."

Two more faintly glowing splotches appeared and became Lemur's hands. One held a needler as large as Auk's by the barrel. "Take it, Doctor. It's your own."

Crane's voice, from the darkness beyond Lemur's hands: "Silk's not impressed."

Leaving Lemur, the needler vanished.

"He's a man of the spirit." Crane chuckled.

"As am I, Patera. Very much so. You've lost your god. May I propose another?"

"Tartaros? I was praying to him before you came in."

"Because of the dark, you mean." Lemur's face and hands faded, replaced by a blackness that now seemed blacker still.

"And because it's his day," Silk said. "At least, I'd assume that it's Tarsday by now."

"Tartaros and the rest are only ghosts, Patera. They've never been anything more, and ghosts fade. With the passing of three hundred years, Pas, Echidna, Tartaros, Scylla, and the rest have faded almost to invisibility. The Prolocutor knows it, and since you're going to succeed him, you should know it, too."

"Since I—" Silk fell silent, suddenly glad that the room was dark.

Lemur laughed again; and Silk—heartsick and terrified—nearly laughed with him, and found that he was smiling. "If only you could see yourself, Patera! Or have your likeness taken."

"You . . ."

"You're a trained augur, I'm told. You graduated from the schola with honors. So tell me, can Tartaros see in the dark?"

Silk nodded, and by that automatic motion discovered that he had already accepted the implication that Lemur could see in the dark as well. "Certainly. All gods can, actually."

Crane's voice: "That's what you were taught, anyhow."

Lemur's baritone, so resonant that it made Crane sound thin and scratchy in comparison. "I can, too, no less than they. By waves of energy too long for your eyes, I'm seeing you now. And I hear and see in places where I am not. When you woke, Doctor Crane held up his fingers and required you to count them. Now it's your turn. Any number you choose."

Silk raised his right hand.

"All five. Again."

Silk complied.

"Three. Crane held up three for you. Again."

"I believe you," Silk said.

"Six. You believed Crane as well, when he told you that I plan to kill you both. It's quite untrue, as you've heard. We mean to elevate and honor you both."

"Thank you," Silk said.

"First I shall tell you the story of the gods. Doctor Crane knows it already, or guesses if he does not know. A certain ruler, a man who had the strength to rule alone and so called himself the monarch, built our whorl, Patera. It was to be a message from himself to the universe. You have seen some of the people he put on board it, and in fact you have walked and talked with one."

Silk nodded, then (conscious of Crane) said, "Yes. Her name is Mamelta."

"You talked about Mucor. The monarch's doctors tinkered with the minds of the men and women he put into the whorl as Blood's surgeon did with hers. But more skillfully, erasing as much as they dared of their patients' personal lives."

Silk said, "Mamelta told me she had been operated upon before she was lifted up to this whorl."

"There you have it. The surgeons found, however, that their patients' memories of their ruler, his family, and some of his officials were too deeply entrenched to be eliminated altogether. To obscure the record, they renamed them. Their ruler, the man who called himself the monarch, became Pas, the shrew he had married Echidna, and so on. She had borne him seven children. We call them Scylla, Molpe, Tartaros, Hierax, Thelxiepeia, Phaea, and Sphigx."

In the darkness, Silk traced the sign of addition.

"The monarch had wanted a son to succeed him. Scylla was as strong-willed as the monarch himself, but female. It is a law of nature, as concerns our race, that females are subject to males. Her father allowed her to found our city, however, and many others. She founded your Chapter as well, a parody of the state religion of her own whorl. She was hardly more than a child, you understand, and the rest younger even than she."

Silk swallowed and said nothing.

"His queen bore the monarch another, but she was worse yet, a fine dancer and a skilled musician, but female, too, and subject to fits of insanity. We call her Molpe."

There was a soft click.

"Nothing useful in your bag, Doctor? We searched it, naturally.

"To continue. Their third child was male, but no better

than the first two, because he was born blind. He became that Tartaros to whom you were recommending yourself, Patera. You believe he can see without light. The truth is that he cannot see by daylight. Am I boring you?"

"That wouldn't matter, but you're risking the displeasure of the gods, and endangering your own spirit."

Crane's dry chuckle came out of the darkness.

"I'll continue to do it. Echidna conceived again and bore another male, a boy who inherited his father's virile indifference to the physical sensations of others to the point of mania. You must know, Patera, as we all do, the exquisite pleasure of inflicting pain upon those we dislike. He allowed himself to be seduced by it, to the point that he came to care for nothing else and while still a child slaughtered thousands for his amusement. We call him Hierax now, the god of death.

"Shall I go on? There are three more, all girls, but you know them as well as I. Thelxiepeia with her spells and drugs and poisons, fat Phaea, and Sphigx, who combined her father's fortitude with her mother's vile temper. In a family such as hers, she would be forced to cultivate those qualities or die, unquestionably."

Silk coughed. "You indicated that you intended to return my needler, Councillor. I'd like very much to have it back."

This time the uncanny light wrapped Lemur's entire body, strong enough to glow faintly through his tunic and trousers. "Watch," he said, and held out his right arm. A dark smudge beneath the embroidered satin of his sleeve crept down his arm to the elbow, then down his forearm until Hyacinth's gold-plated needler slid into his open hand. "Here you are."

"How did you do that?" Silk inquired.

"There are thousands of minute circuits in my arms. By flexing certain muscles, I can create a magnetic field, and by tightening them in sequence while relaxing others, I can move the field. Watch."

Hyacinth's needler crept from Lemur's hand to his wrist, and disappeared into his sleeve. "You say you'd like to have it back?"

"Yes, very much."

"And you, Doctor Crane? I have already given you yours, and I plan to make use of your services. Will you count your needler as your fee, paid in advance?"

The light that streamed from Lemur was now so bright that Silk could make out Crane, seated on the cot, as he drew his needler and held it out. "You can have it back, if you want. But give Silk his, and I'll accept that."

"Doctor Crane has already tried to shoot me, you see." Lemur's shining face smiled. "He's playing a cruel trick on you, Patera."

"No, he's being the same kind friend he has been to me since we first met. There are men who are ashamed of their best impulses, because they have come to associate goodness with weakness. Give it to me, please."

It was not Hyacinth's needler but her azoth that crawled like a silver spider into Lemur's open hand. Silk reached for it, but the hand closed about it; Lemur laughed, and they were plunged in darkness again.

Crane's voice: "Silk tells me you captured a woman with him. If you've hurt her badly, I want to see her."

"I could squeeze this hard enough to crush it," Lemur told them. "That would be dangerous even for me."

Silk had succeeded in untangling the silver chain; he put it about his neck and adjusted the position of Pas's gammadion as he spoke. "Then I advise you not to do it."

"I won't. Before I told you the truth about your gods, Patera, I hinted that I'd propose a new god to you, a living god to whom the wisest might kneel. I meant myself, as you must have realized. Are you ready to worship me?"

"I'm afraid we lack an appropriate victim for sacrifice."

Lemur's eyes glowed. "You're wasting your tact, Patera. Don't you want to be Prolocutor? When I happened to mention it, I expected you to kiss my rump for the thought. Instead you're acting as if you didn't hear me."

"After the first moment or two, I assumed you intended a subtle torture. To speak frankly, I still do."

"Not at all. I'm completely serious. The doctor said he wished he'd invented you. So do I. If you're what he and his masters required, you suit my purposes even better."

Silk felt as though he were choking. "You want me to tell people that you're a god, Councillor? That you are to be paid divine honors?"

Warm and rich and friendly, Lemur's voice boomed out of the darkness. "More than that. The present Prolocutor could do that, and would in a moment if I told him to. Or I could replace him with any of a hundred augurs who would."

Silk shook his head. "I doubt it. But even if you're correct, they would not be believed."

"Precisely. But you would be. His Cognizance is old. His Cognizance will die, tomorrow perhaps. In a surprising but hugely popular development, it will be discovered that he has named you as his successor, and you will explain to the people that Pas has withheld his rains out of consideration for me. They need only pay me proper honors to be forgiven. Eventually they will come to understand that I am, as I am, a greater god than Pas. After all that I've told you, do you retain some loyalty to him? And Echidna and their brats?"

Silk sighed. "I realized as you spoke how little I have ever had. Your blasphemies ought to have outraged me. I was merely shocked instead, like a maiden aunt who overhears her cook swearing; but you see, I've encountered a real god, the Outsider—"

Crane whooped with laughter.

"And Kypris, a real goddess. Thus I know what divinity is, the look and the sound and the true texture of it. You said something else that I ignored, Councillor."

For the first time, Lemur sounded dangerous and even deadly. "Which was . . . ?"

"You said that you were not a chem. I'm not one of those ignorant and prejudiced bios who consider themselves superior to chems, but I know—"

"You lie!" Doubly terrifying in the darkness, the blade of the azoth tore the plane of existence like so much paper, shooting past Silk's ear, manifest to every cell in his body, and horrible as nothing the universe contained could be.

From the other side of the room, Crane shouted, "You'll sink us!" and the vessel lurched and shook as he spoke. Chips of burning paint and flakes of incandescent steel showered Silk with fire; he backed away in horror.

"One born a biological man did that, Patera. A man who has become more." Something rang in the darkness as a hammer rings against an anvil. "I *am* a biological man *and* a god." The harrowing discontinuity that had wounded the very fabric of the universe was gone.

"Thank you," Silk said. He gasped for breath. "Thank you every much. Please don't do that again."

As the violence of the vessel's motion abated to steady thrumming, Lemur's luminous arm reappeared; his hand opened, and the hilt of the azoth slid smoothly into its sleeve.

There was a thump as Crane dropped his medical bag. "Are you inside there?"

Lemur's voice was warm again. "Why do you ask?"

"Just curious. I was wondering if it might not be like conflict armor, but better."

"Which would be of some interest to your masters in the government of . . . ?"

"Palustria."

"No. Not Palustria. We have eliminated certain cities, and that is one of them. Like Patera Silk, you'll soon come to serve Viron, and when you do, you must be more forthright. Meanwhile, let it be enough for you that I am in another part of this boat. Perhaps I'll show you when we're done with the business at hand."

"Serve you, you mean."

"We gods have many names.

"Patera, you needn't concern yourself about your paramour from the past. She's nursing Doctor Crane's patient even as I speak, and worrying about you."

Crane's voice: "You use some old-fashioned words. How old are you, Councillor?"

"How old would you say I am?" Lemur extended his shining hand. "You doctors like to speak of pronounced tremors. Can you pronounce upon that one?"

"You've held office under two caldés, and for twenty-two years since the death of the last. Naturally we wondered."

"In Palustria. Yes, in Palustria, naturally you did. When you see me elsewhere you can formulate an estimate of your own, and I'll be interested to learn it.

"Patera, doesn't all this astound you?"

"I can understand how you could be a bio with prosthetic parts; our Maytera Rose is like that." Silk discovered that his own hands were trembling and pushed them into his pockets. "Not how you could be in another part of this boat."

"In the same way that a glass conveys to you the image of a room at the opposite end of the city. In the same way that your Sacred Window showed you the tricked-out image of a woman dead three hundred years and convinced you that you had spoken with a minor goddess." Lemur chuckled. "But I've wasted too much time already, while Doctor Crane's patient lies dying. I trust he'll forgive me, I was enjoying myself." The luminous hand held up Hyacinth's needler. "Here's Doctor Crane's fee, as specified by him. Doctor, I wish you to look at a patient. To earn this fee, you need only examine him and tell him the truth. Is it a violation of medical ethics to tell a patient the truth?"

"No."

"There have been times when I've thought that it must be. This fourth prisoner of mine's a spy, too. Will you do it? He's badly injured."

"After which you'll kill Silk and me." Crane snorted. "All right, I've lived as a quacksalver. Since I've got to die, I'll die as one, too."

"Both of you will live," Lemur told him, "because you will both become admirably cooperative. I could have you so now, if I wished, but for the present you serve me better as opponents. I will not say foes. You see, I have told this fourth prisoner that the doctor who will examine him and the augur who will shrive him are no friends of mine. That they have, in fact, seen fit to intrigue against the government I direct."

The luminosity of Lemur's hand and arm brightened, and Hyacinth's engraved, gold-plated, little needler slithered like a living animal into his open palm. "Your Cognizance? Here you are." He handed the needler to Silk. "Will you, as an anointed augur, administer the Pardon of Pas to Doctor Crane's patient, if Crane judges him in imminent danger of death?"

"Of course," Silk said.

"Then let's go. I know you'll find this interesting." Lemur threw open the door. Blinking and wiping their eyes, they followed him along a narrow corridor floored with steel grating, and down a flight of steel stairs almost as steep as a ladder.

"I'm taking you all the way down to the keel," Lemur

told them. "I hope you weren't expecting this boat to rock, by the way. We've put out—I gave the order while we were playing with that azoth—and we're cruising beneath the surface now, where there's no wave action."

He led them to a heavy door set into the floor, spun two handwheels, and threw it back. "Down here. I'm about to show you the hole in our bottom."

Silk went first. The vibration that had shaken the boat since Lemur had threatened him with the azoth was stronger here, almost an audible sound; there was a cool freshness to the air, and the iron railing of the steps he descended felt damp beneath his hand. Green lights that seemed imitations of the ancient lights provided the first settlers by Pas, and an indefinable odor that might have been no more than the absence of any other, made him feel for the first time that he was actually beneath the waters of Lake Limna.

The flier's broken wings were the first things he saw. They had been laid out, with scraps of the nearly invisible fabric that had covered them, on the transparent canopy of a sizable yawl—shattered spars of a material that might have been polished bone, less thick than his forefinger.

"Wait there a moment, Your Cognizance," Lemur called. "I want to show you these. You and Doctor Crane both. It will be well worth your while."

"You got one after all," Crane said. "You've brought down a flier."

There was a note of defeat in his voice that made Silk turn to stare back at him.

"They'd all gone," Crane explained. "Blood and his thugs and most of the male servants. I thought this might be it, but I hoped . . ." He left the sentence incomplete and shrugged.

Lemur had picked up an oddly curved, almost teardrop-shaped grid of the cream-colored material. "We have, Doctor. And this is the secret. Simple, yet infinitely precious. Don't you want to examine it? Wouldn't you like to provide your masters with the secret of flight? The key that opens the sky? This is its shape. Pick it up if you wish. See how light it is. Run your fingers over it, Doctor."

Crane shook his head.

"Then you, Your Cognizance. When your followers have installed you as caldé, it could prove a most useful thing to know."

"I'll never be caldé," Silk told him, "and I have never wished to be." He accepted the almost weightless grid, and stared at its fluid lines. "This is what lets a flier fly? This shape?"

Lemur nodded. "With the material from which it's made. Tarsier's analyzing that. When you broke into Blood's villa Phaesday night—I know all about that, you see. When you broke in, didn't you wonder why Crane's city had sent him to watch Blood?"

"I didn't realize he was a spy then," Silk explained. He put down the grid and fingered the swelling that Potto's fist had left on the side of his head. He felt weak and a little dizzy.

"To keep his masters appraised of Blood's progress with the eagle," Lemur told him. "More than twenty-five years ago, I realized the possibilities of flight. I saw that if our troopers could fly as fliers did, enemy troop movements would be revealed at once, that picked bodies of men could land behind an enemy's lines to disrupt communications, and all the rest of it. As soon as I was free to act, I backed various experimenters whose work appeared promising. None developed a device capable of carrying a child, much less a trooper."

Recalling Hammerstone, Silk asked, "Why not a soldier?"

Crane grunted. "They're too heavy. Lemur there weighs four times as much as you and me together."

"Ah!" Lemur turned to Crane. "You've looked into the matter, I see."

Crane nodded. "Fliers are actually a bit smaller than most troopers. I'm small, as everybody keeps reminding me. But I'm bigger than most fliers."

"You sound as though you've seen some close up."

"Through a telescope," Crane said. "Want to object that I had nothing to compare them to?"

"To oblige you, yes."

"I didn't need anything. A small man isn't proportioned like a big one, and as a small physician I'm very much aware of that. A small man's head is bigger in proportion to his shoulders, for instance."

Silk fidgeted. "If someone may be dying . . ."

"That someone could be you, Your Cognizance." Lemur laid a heavy hand upon Silk's shoulder. "Purely as an hypothesis, let's say that I plan to pull your head off as soon as you've conveyed the Pardon of Pas to this unfortunate. If that were the case, shortening our discussion would materially shorten your life."

"As a citizen I'm entitled to a public trial, and to an advocate. As an augur—"

The pressure of Lemur's fingers increased. "It's too bad you're not an advocate yourself, Your Cognizance. If you were you'd realize that there's a further, unwritten provision. It is that the urgent needs of Viron must be served. As we speak a mendacious and malcontented radical faction is attempting to overthrow our lawfully constituted Ayuntamiento and substitute for it the rule of one inexperienced—but deep, and I admit that freely—augur, stirring up the populace by alleging a lot of superstitious taradiddle about enlightenment and the supposed favor of the gods. Am I crushing your shoulder?"

"It is certainly very painful."

"It can easily become more so. Did you really speak to a goddess in a house of ill repute? Say no, or I'll crush it."

"A goddess in the sense that the god who enlightened me is a god? Doctor Crane insists that there is no such being. Whether he's right or not, I'm inclined to doubt that there are any more such gods."

Lemur tightened his grip, so that Silk would have fallen to his knees if he could. "I want to tell you in some detail, Your Cognizance, how I hit upon the notion of using a bird of prey to bring down a flier for our examination. How I saw a hawk take a merganser at twilight and conceived the idea. How I combed Viron, with the utmost secrecy, for the right man to carry it out. And how I found him."

Silk moaned, and Crane said, "And so on and so forth. Let him go, and I'll tell you how we learned of it."

"*Let him go!*" It was Mamelta, dashing out of the dimness and throwing herself on Silk. "*You damned robot! You THING!*" She was naked save for a blood-smeared rag knotted about her waist, her full breasts and rounded thighs trembling, her bare skin the color of old ivory.

Lemur released Silk and cuffed her almost casually; white bone gleamed where his long nails had torn her forehead, until blood streamed forth to cover it.

Crane crouched beside her and snapped open his brown bag.

"Very good, Doctor," Lemur said. "Patch her up by all means. But not here." He threw her over his shoulder and stalked away.

"Come on." Agilely for a man of his age, Crane mounted the steps to the trapdoor Lemur had opened for them and tugged at one of its wheels.

"We can't leave her," Silk said. He moved his shoulder experimentally and decided no bones had been broken.

"We can't help her while we're prisoners ourselves."

Lemur's mocking voice echoed from the other end of the hold. "A man is dying, and this woman is bleeding like a stuck pig. Don't either of you care?"

"I do," Silk called, and hobbled in the direction of the voice.

Beyond the bow of the yawl, the flier lay on a blanket spread on the steel floor, his sun-browned face twisted in agony. Beside him stretched a second trapdoor, far larger than the one through which they had come—large enough, as Silk realized with some astonishment, to admit the yawl. An instrument panel stood against the bulkhead at the end of the compartment.

Lemur dropped Mamelta next to the flier. In a deafening roar that reminded Silk of the talus, he called, *"Rejoin us, Doctor. You can't open that hatch."* To Silk he added, "I tightened those locking screws, you see. And I'm a great deal stronger than both of you together, as well as a great deal heavier."

Silk had already knelt at the flier's head. "I convey to you, my son, the forgiveness of all the gods. Recall now the words of Pas, who—"

"That's enough." Lemur took him by the shoulder again. "We want the doctor first, I think. If he won't come, you must bring him."

"I'm here," Crane announced.

"This is our flier," Lemur said. "His name's Iolar. He has told us a little, you see, though nothing of value, not even the name of his city. I would have to agree that he's scarcely taller than you, and he may well be a trifle lighter. Yet he is flier enough, or almost enough."

Crane did not reply. After a moment he took scissors from his bag and began to cut away the flightsuit. Silk tore a strip from his robe, wound it twice about Mamelta's head, and tied it.

Lemur nodded approvingly. "She will live to be grateful

for your efforts, I'm sure, Patera. So will Iolar, I hope. Are you listening, Doctor Crane?"

Crane nodded without looking up. "I'm going to have to roll you over. Put your arms above your head. Don't try to roll yourself. Let me do it."

"You see," Lemur continued conversationally, "Iolar came down right here, in the lake. In one way, that was extremely convenient for us. We sent our little boat to the surface and scooped up him and his wings without help from the Civil Guard. Or from Blood, I should add, and very much to the discomfiture of them both." Lemur chuckled.

"That was early yesterday morning. As it chanced, I was ashore at the time, so Loris directed the recovery. Whether I could've managed things better, I can't say. Loris is not Lemur, but then who is? In any event one vital part was not retrieved, although the flier himself was, with most of the wings and harness and so on that permitted him to fly. He calls it a propulsion module, or PM. Isn't that so, Iolar?"

Crane glanced up at Lemur, then looked quickly back to his patient.

"Precisely so, Doctor. Without the device, our troopers will still be able to fly in a manner of speaking. But only to glide, as a gull does when it rides the breeze without moving its wings. It should be possible for such a trooper to launch himself from a cliff or a tower and fly a great distance, given a strong and favoring wind. Only under the most extraordinary conditions, however, could he take off from a level field. Under no conceivable conditions could he fly into the eye of any wind, even the weakest. Is this too technical for you, Patera? Doctor Crane's following me, I believe."

Silk said, "So am I, I think."

"At first the deficiency appeared only temporary. Iolar had a propulsion module—he admitted as much. Presumably it was torn free by the impact when he struck the water. We could fish it up, which we tried to do all that day, or he could tell us how to make them. This last, I am sorry to say, he refuses to do."

Crane said, "You must have some sort of medical facility on this boat. Something better than this."

"Oh, we do," Lemur assured him. "In fact, we had him there for a while. But he didn't repay our kindness, so we brought him back here. Is he conscious?"

"Didn't you hear me talking to him a minute ago? Of course he is."

"Fine. Iolar, listen to me. I'm Councillor Lemur, and I am speaking to you. I may never do this again, and what I'm about to say will be more important to you than anything you've ever heard before, or that you're ever apt to hear. Do you hear me now? Say something or move your head."

The flier lay face down, his face turned toward the long steel hatch in the deck. His voice, when it came, was weak and strangely accented. "I hear."

Lemur smiled and nodded. "You've found me to be a man of my word, haven't you? Very well, I'm giving you my word that everything I'm about to say is true. I'm not going to try to trick you again, and I'm not inclined to be patient with you any longer. These are the men Potto and I told you about. This doctor is an admitted spy, just like you. Not a spy of ours, you may be sure. A spy from Palustria, or so he says. This augur is the leader of the faction that has been trying to seize control of our city. If Doctor Crane says you're going to die, you've won our argument. I'll let the augur bring you Pas's Pardon, and that's that. But if Doctor Crane says you'll live, you'll be surrendering your life if you continue to refuse. Have I made myself clear? I'm not going to waste any more of my time, or Potto's, in trying to force the facts we need from you. We're building new equipment to find your propulsion module on the bottom. We'll get it, and you'll have died for nothing. If we don't find it, we still have the eagle. She knows her business now, and all we'll have to do to get a propulsion module is send her after the next flier we see."

Lemur pointed a finger at Crane. "No threats, Doctor. No promises. Truth will cost you nothing, and a lie gain you nothing. Is he going to live?"

"I don't know," Crane said levelly. "He's got a couple of broken ribs—they haven't punctured the lung, or he might be dead already. At least four thoracic vertebrae are in pretty bad shape. There's damage to the spinal cord, but I don't think it's been severed, although I can't be sure. Given proper care and a first-rate surgeon, I'd say he might have a good chance."

Lemur looked sceptical. "A complete recovery?"

"I doubt it. He might be able to walk."

"Now then." Lemur's voice dropped to a whisper. "Which will it be? In two or three hours we could have you ashore. Those black canisters all of you wear—how do they work?"

Silence filled the hold. Silk, bent over Mamelta, saw her eyelids flutter, and clasped her hand. Crane shrugged and snapped his bag shut, the sound as abrupt and final as the report of Auk's needler in the Cock.

"I didn't think you would," Lemur told the flier almost conversationally. "That's why I put out. Patera, you can start your rigmarole, if you want to. I don't care. He'll be dead almost before you finish it."

"What are you going to do?" Crane asked.

"Put him off the boat." Lemur strode to the instrument panel. "As a man of science you might be interested in this, Doctor. This compartment is at the bottom of our boat, as I told you. It's tightly sealed, as you discovered a few minutes ago when you tried to open the hatch. At present," he glanced at one of the gauges, "we're seventy cubits below the surface. At this depth, the water pressure around our hull is roughly three atmospheres. Has anyone explained to you how we rise and sink?"

"No," Crane said. "I've wondered." He glanced at Silk as though to see whether he, too, was curious; but Silk was chanting and swinging his beads over the head of the injured flier.

"We do it with compressed air. If we want to go deeper, we open one of our ballast tanks. That lets lake water in, so we lose buoyancy and sink. When we want to surface, we valve compressed air into that tank to force the water out. The tank becomes a float, so we gain buoyancy. Simple but effective. When I open this valve, more air will flow into this compartment." Lemur turned it, producing a loud hiss.

"If I were to let it in fast, you'd find it painful, so I've only cracked the valve. Swallow if your ears hurt."

Silk, who had been giving Lemur some small fraction of his attention, paused in his chant to swallow. As he did, the injured flier whispered, "The sun . . ." His eyes, which had been half-shut, opened wide, and he struggled to turn his face toward Silk. "Tell your people!"

No audible response was permitted until the liturgy was complete, but Silk nodded, swinging his beads in the sign of subtraction. "You are blessed." While bobbing his head nine times, as the ritual demanded, he made the sign of addition.

"When the pressure here reaches three atmospheres, as it soon will, we can open that boat hole without flooding the compartment." Lemur chuckled. "I'll loosen up the fittings now."

Crane started to protest, then clamped his jaw.

"We're losing control," the flier whispered to Silk, and his eyes closed.

With his free hand, Silk stroked the flier's temple to

indicate that he had heard. "I pray you to forgive us, the living." Another sign of addition. "I and many another have wronged you often, my son, committing terrible crimes and numerous offenses against you. Do not hold them in your heart, but begin the life that follows life in innocence, all these wrongs forgiven." With his beads, he traced the sign of subtraction again.

Mamelta's hand found Silk's again and closed upon it. "He . . . Am I dreaming?"

Silk shook his head. "I speak here for Great Pas, for Divine Echidna, for Scalding Scylla, for Marvelous Molpe, for Tenebrous Tartaros, for Highest Hierax, for Thoughtful Thelxiepeia, for Fierce Phaea, and for Strong Sphigx. Also for all lesser gods." Lowering his voice, Silk added, "The Outsider likewise forgives you, my son, for I speak here for him."

"He's going to die?"

Silk put a finger to his lips. In a surprisingly gentle tone, Crane said, "Lemur's going to kill him. He's opted for it. So would I."

"So do I." Mamelta touched the black cloth with which Silk had bandaged her head. "They said we were going to a wonderful world of peace and plenty, where it would be noon all day. We knew they lied. When I die, I'll go home. My mother and brothers . . . Chiquito on his perch in the patio."

Crane took out his scissors again. He was cutting away the cloth when Lemur threw open the hatch.

It was—to Silk the thought was irresistible—as if the Outsider himself had entered the hold. Where the dark steel hatch had been a moment before, there was a rectangle of liquid light, translucent and coolly lambent. The light of the Long Sun, penetrating the clear water of Lake Limna even to a depth of seventy cubits, was refracted and diffused, filling the opening that Lemur had so suddenly revealed and invading the hold with a supernal dawn of celestial blue. For a few seconds, Silk could scarcely believe that the ethereal substance was water. Leaning across the flier with his right hand (still grasping his beads) braced upon the coaming, he dipped his fingers into it.

Crane said, "A little air escaped. Did you feel it?"

Staring down into the crystal water, Silk shook his head. A school of slender silver fish materialized at one end of the hatchway, and in the space of a breath appeared to drift to the other, ten cubits or more beneath the steel plate on which he knelt.

Lemur said, "Move, Patera," and picked up the flier.

Crane shouted, "Watch out! Don't hold him like that!"

"Afraid I'll damage him further, Doctor?" Lemur smiled and lifted the flier effortlessly above his head. "It won't matter.

"What about it, Iolar? Anything to say? This is the last chance."

"Thank the woman," the flier gasped. "The men. Strong wings."

Lemur threw him down. The lambent water that filled the hatchway erupted in Silk's face, drenching and momentarily blinding him. By the time he could see again, the flier had nearly passed out of sight. A brief glimpse of his agonized face, his startled eyes and open mouth, from which bubbles like spheres of thin glass streamed, and he was gone.

Lemur slammed down the hatch with a deafening crash and tightened its fastenings. "When I open the one that we came through, the pressure here will equalize with the pressure in the rest of the ship. Keep your mouths open, or it may blow out your eardrums."

He led them up a different companionway this time, and along a broader corridor (in which they passed Councillors Galago and Potto deep in conversation), and at last through a doorway guarded by two soldiers. "This is what you were looking for, Doctor," he told Crane, "although you may not have known it. In this stateroom you will behold our true, biological selves. I'm over there."

He pointed toward a circle of gleaming machines; Crane hurried toward it. Silk, limping and supporting Mamelta, followed more slowly.

Councillor Lemur's bio body lay upon an immaculate white pallet, an equally immaculate white sheet drawn to his chin. His eyes were closed, his cheeks sunken; his chest rose and fell gently and slowly; the faint wheeze of his breath was barely audible. A wisp of white hair escaped the circlet of black synthetic and network of multicolored wires that bound his brows. Snakelike tubes from a dozen machines (clear, straw-yellow, and darkly crimson) ducked beneath the sheet.

"No treacherous bios in here," Lemur told them. "We're nursed by devoted chems, and the machines that maintain us in life are maintained by chems. They love us, and we love them. We promise them immortality, and we will deliver it: a never-ending supply of replacement parts. They repay us with infinite prolongation of our merely mortal lives."

Crane was inspecting one of the machines. "Your life-support equipment seems very impressive. I wish I had it."

"My kidneys and liver have failed. So we have devices to perform those functions. There's a booster on my heart that's capable of taking over its function completely whenever that becomes necessary. Pulses of oxygen, of course."

Crane sucked his teeth and shook his head.

Mamelta said softly, "This is the first time I haven't been cold."

"The air in here is completely reprocessed every seventy seconds. It is filtered, irradiated to destroy bacteria and viruses, and maintained at a relative humidity of thirty-five

percent, within a quarter degree of the normal temperature of the bio body."

Looking down at the recumbent councillor, Silk told
him, "I'd never have thought I'd feel sorry for you. But
I do."

"I'm seldom conscious of lying here. This is me."
Lemur struck his chest, and the sound was that of the
ringing hammer Silk had heard in the dark. "Vigorous and
alert, with perfect hearing and vision. All that I lack is good
digestion. And at times," Lemur paused significantly, "patience."

Crane was bending over the recumbent figure; before
Lemur could move to stop him, he pushed up one gray
eyelid with his thumb. "This man is dead."

"Don't be absurd!" Lemur started toward him, but Silk,
acting immediately upon an impulse of which he was
scarcely aware, stepped into his path. And Lemur, perhaps
responding to some childhood injunction to respect an
augur's habit, stopped short.

"Look." Crane reached with thumb and forefinger into
the empty socket and drew out a pinch of black detritus
that might almost have been a mixture of earth and tar.
After exhibiting it to Lemur, he dropped it on the pristine
sheet, where it lay like so much filth, and wiped his fingers
on the thin white pillow, leaving dingy, mephitic streaks.

Lemur made a sound, not loud, that Silk had never
heard before (though Silk had already, young as he was,
heard so much grief). It was a snuffling, and in it a whine
like the cry of a small shaft driven faster and faster—the
sound of a drill that has struck a nail, and, impelled by a
madman, spins on harder and harder and faster and faster
until it smokes, destroying itself by its own boundless, un-
governed energy. Some hours later, Silk would think of that
sound and recall the clockwork universe the Outsider had
shown him on the Phaesday before in the ballcourt; for it

was the sound of that universe dying, or rather of a part of it dying, or rather (he would decide sleepily) of the whole of it dying for someone.

Lemur crouched, slowly and unsteadily, as he sounded the note that would stay with Silk until night; his hands moved haplessly, as though of their own volition, not pawing or clawing or indeed doing anything at all, but writhing as the dead flier's hands were moving (perhaps) even then, in the cold waters of the lake as they awaited the onset of that stiffening which follows death and endures for half a day. (Or a day, or a day and a half, depending upon a variety of circumstances, and always subject to some dispute.) As he crouched, Lemur's eyes never left the mummified councillor on the snowy pallet; and at length, when one knee was on the green-tiled floor, and it seemed that Lemur could not crouch further, his arms fell.

Then the silver azoth that Silk had taken from a drawer in Hyacinth's dressing table, on the night of the same day that the Outsider had revealed to Silk the essence of the universe in which he existed, fell from Lemur's tapestried sleeve and skittered across the floor.

And Crane dove for it, bumping hard against one of the medical machines that surrounded the dead councillor's bed and sending it crashing down on its side; but quickly and deftly, gray-bearded though he was, he snatched up the azoth.

Its terrible beam shot forth, and Lemur exploded in a ball of flame. Silk and Mamelta staggered back, covering their faces with their arms.

Crane dashed past them and was out the door by the time that Silk could see again.

Mamelta screamed.

Silk held her arm and dragged her behind him, conscious that he should silence her but conscious also that it would probably prove impossible and that there was not a second to waste in any event.

The soldiers at the door were firing when Silk opened it. Before he could draw back, they charged down the broad corridor, running at thrice the speed even a fleet boy like Horn could have managed and ten times the best that Silk, handicapped by his ankle and the shrieking Mamelta, could hope to achieve; the two of them had not covered half the distance when there was a flash from the companionway and a double explosion—horribly painful, though not loud to ears still shocked and ringing from Lemur's detonation.

"We must get there before he shuts the hatch," Silk told Mamelta, and then, when she still would not run, he (to his own later amazement) picked her up bodily, and throwing her over one shoulder like a rolled mattress or a sack of flour, ran himself, stumbling and staggering, once crashing into a bulkhead and nearly falling headlong down the companionway. Someone was shouting, *"Wait! Wait!"* and he had reached the hatch before he realized that it was himself.

It was shut, but he dropped Mamelta and wrenched around the handwheels. A roaring wind from below lifted it as he did.

"Doctor!"

"Help me!" Crane shouted. "We can get away in the boat."

Half a dozen slug guns boomed in the corridor as Silk and Mamelta stumbled down the short companionway into the boat hold, and a slug slammed the hatch like a sledge-hammer as he retightened its fastenings.

When he reached Crane, the little physician was heaving at the longer hatch that covered the boat hole. The three of them threw it back, with chill lake water gushing in after it, helping to lift it as air pressure had opened the

much smaller hatch above. For a moment Silk was conscious of floundering in rising water. He spat, managed to
get his face clear, and gasped for breath.

The flood slacked, then held steady for a second or two
that seemed a minute at least; he was conscious of the
full-throated hoot of the air valve, and of someone
(whether it was Mamelta or Crane he could not be sure)
struggling and splashing nearby.

The flow reversed. Slowly at first, then swifter and
swifter, sweeping him along, the flood that had practically
filled the compartment rushed back to Lake Limna. Help-
less as a doll in a maelstrom, he spun in a dizzy whorl of
blue light, slowed (his lungs ready to burst), and caught
sight of another figure suspended like himself with splayed
limbs and drifting hair.

And then, dimly, of a monstrous mottled face—black,
red, and gold—far larger than any wall of the manse, and
a gaping mouth that closed upon the splayed figure he had
seen. It passed below him as a floater rushing down some
reeling mountain meadow might pass a floating thistle
seed, and the turbulence of its wake sent him spinning.

Chapter 13

THE CALDÉ SURRENDERS

"Patera? Oh, Patera!"

Maytera Marble was waving from the front steps of the old manteion on Sun Street. Two troopers in armor stood beside her; their officer, in dress greens, indulgently exhibited his sword to little Maytera Mint. Gulo hurried forward.

The officer glanced up. "Patera Silk? You are under arrest." Gulo shook his head and explained.

Maytera Marble sniffed, a sniff of such devastating power and contempt that it burned to dust all the pleasure the young officer had enjoyed from Maytera Mint's wide-eyed admiration. "Take Patera Silk away? You can't! Such a holy—"

A soft snarl came from the crowd that had been clustered about Gulo. Gulo was not an imaginative man, yet it seemed to him that an unseen lion was awakening; and the prayers he had chanted each Sphigxday were not nonsensical after all.

"Don't fight!" Maytera Mint returned the officer's sword and raised her hands. "Please! There's no need."

A stone flew, striking the helmet of one of the troopers. A second whizzed past Maytera Marble's head to thump the door, and the trooper who had been hit fired, his shot followed by a scream. Maytera Mint dashed down the steps into the crowd.

The trooper fired again, and his officer slapped down the muzzle of his slug gun. "Open these," the officer told Gulo. "We had better go inside." More stones flew as they fled into the manteion. The trooper who had been hit fired twice more as Maytera Marble and the other trooper swung its heavy door shut, his shots so closely spaced that they might almost have been one. There was an answering rattle of stones.

"It is the heat." The officer spoke confidently and even smiled. "They will forget now that we are out of sight." He sheathed his sword. "This Patera Silk is popular."

Maytera Marble nodded. And then, *"Patera!"*

"I have to go." Gulo was sliding back the bolt. "I—I shouldn't have gone in here at all." He struggled to remember the other sibyl's name, failed, and concluded lamely, "She was right."

The officer snatched at his robe an instant too late as Gulo slipped out; angry yells invaded the manteion, then muted as the troopers shut the door and bolted it again. Faintly, the officer could hear Gulo shouting, *"People! People!"*

"They won't hurt him, Maytera." He paused to listen, his head cocked. "I do not like arresting . . ."

He let the apology trail away, having realized that he no longer had her attention. Her metal face mirrored faint hues: lemon, pink, and sorrel. Following the direction of her gaze, he saw the swirling color of the Sacred Window and knelt. The dancing hues created patterns he could not quite distinguish, glyphs, figures, and landscapes half formed, a face that swam, melted, and coalesced before the goddess spoke in a tongue he almost understood, a language that he too had known in a long-past life in an unimaginable place at an inconceivable time. In this, he was a maggot; her utterance proclaimed that he had once been a man, though the memories she woke were perhaps no more than the dead thoughts of the man he devoured.

I will, Great Goddess. I will. He will be safe with us.

Behind and above him he heard the chem talking to the fat augur. "A god came while you were outside, Patera. Honored us without a sacrifice. There was no one to interpret. I'm so terribly sorry you missed it—" And the augur, "I didn't, Maytera. Not all of it."

The officer willed them to be quiet. Her divine voice still strummed in his ears, far and sweet; and he knew what she desired him to do.

To breach the surface of the lake as Silk did, to rise from suffocation and see afresh the thin, bright streak of the sun and draw one's first breath, was to be reborn. He was not a strong swimmer, and indeed was hardly a swimmer at all; yet exhausted as he was, he managed to stay afloat on the long, slow swell, kicking spasmodically, dimly fearful that each kick might draw the attention of the huge fish.

There was a distant shout, followed by the clamor of a pan wildly beaten; he ignored both until the swell heaved him high enough to see the worn brown sails.

Three half-naked fishermen pulled him onto their boat. "There's someone else," he gasped. "We've got to find him."

"They already have!" And Crane was grinning at him.

The tallest and most grizzled of the fishermen slapped him on the back. "Gods look out for augurs. That's what my paw used to tell, Patera."

Crane nodded sagely. "Augurs and fools."

"Yes, sir. Them, too. Next time you go sailin', you take a sailor. Let's hope we can find your woman."

The thought of the great fish filled Silk's mind, and he

shuddered. "It's good of you to look, but I'm afraid . . ."

"Couldn't reach her, Patera?"

"No, but— No."

"Well, we'll haul her out if we see her."

Silk stood; at once the rolling of the boat cost him his footing, and he found himself sitting on piled nets.

"Stay where you are and rest," Crane muttered. "You've been through a lot. So've I. But we've gotten a thorough washing, and that's good. Lots of isotopes released when a chem blows." He held up a gleaming card. "Captain, could you find us something to eat? Or a little wine?"

"Let me put her about, sir, and I'll see what's left."

"Money belt," Crane whispered, noticing Silk's puzzled look. "Lemur made me turn out my pockets but never patted me down. I promised them a card to take us back to Limna."

"That poor woman," Silk said to no one in particular, "three hundred years, for that." A black bird was perched in the rigging of a distant boat; seeing it, Silk recalled Oreb, smiled, and reproached himself for smiling.

Guiltily he glanced about him, hoping that his unseemly levity had passed unnoticed. Crane was watching the captain, and the captain, the largest sail. One sailor stood in the bow with a foot upon the bowsprit. The other, grasping a rope connected to the long stick (Silk could not recall its name, if he had ever known it) that spread the sail, appeared to be waiting for a signal from the captain—the back of his head seemed uncannily familiar. As Silk altered his position to get a better view of it, he realized that the nets on which he sat were dry.

Crane had bought Silk a red tunic, brown trousers, and brown shoes to replace the black ones he had kicked off in the lake. He changed in a deserted alley, throwing his robe, his torn tunic, and his old trousers behind a pile of refuse. "I got Hyacinth's needler back," he said, "and my gammadion and my beads; but not my glasses or any of my other possessions. Perhaps that's a sign."

Crane shrugged. "They were probably in Lemur's pocket." He had a new tunic and new trousers, too, and he had bought a razor. Glancing toward the mouth of the alley, he added, "Keep your voice down."

"What did you see?"

"Couple of Guardsmen."

"The Ayuntamiento will surely think we're dead," Silk objected. "Until they learn otherwise, we have no reason to fear the Guard."

Crane shook his head.

"If they thought we might have survived, they could have come to the surface and looked for us, couldn't they?"

"Not without telling everybody on the lake about their underwater boat. How do those fit?"

"They're a trifle large." Silk looked down at himself, wishing that he had a mirror. "Their boat must have come to the surface to collect poor Iolar."

"You're thin," Crane told him. "No, they sent up that little one we saw. They couldn't send it after us because that compartment down in the keel would've flooded again as soon as they undogged the hatch."

"It flooded when we opened the one in the floor," Silk murmured.

"That's right. I'd opened the air valve as far as it would go, but it hadn't had much time to build up pressure after you and the woman vented it coming down. Naturally a lot of water came in. It cut down the air space and pushed the pressure up to the water pressure, so the water flowed out again almost right away."

Silk hesitated, then nodded. "But if they open the

upper hatch—the one in the corridor—the compartment will flood again, won't it?"

"Sure. Water would rise into the rest of the boat, too. Which is why they couldn't send their little boat after us. I can't imagine how they'll shut the boat door when they can't get into the compartment to do it, but no doubt they'll figure out something."

Silk leaned against a wall and removed Crane's wrapping from his ankle. "I'm not a sailor, but if it were up to me, I'd go far out in the lake, where there wasn't much chance of being seen—or perhaps into the cave Lemur mentioned when you asked how he had gotten your bag."

"I wish I hadn't lost that." Crane fingered his beard. "I'd had it twenty years."

Recalling his pen case, Silk said, "I know how you must feel, Doctor." He flogged the wall with the wrapping.

"Suppose they did go back into their cave. They'd still have the problem. That underwater boat's too big to drag up on shore."

"But they could tilt it," Silk said. "Shift everything to one side and force all the water out of the floats on the other. They might even be able to pull it over with a cable attached to the side of the cave."

Crane nodded, still watching the mouth of the alley. "I suppose so. Are you ready?"

When Crane had gone, Silk opened the window. Their room was on the third floor of the Rusty Lantern, and provided a magnificent view of the lake, as well as a refreshing breeze. Leaning across the sill, Silk looked down into Dock Street. Crane had wanted to get out of sight, or so he had said; but he had called for pen and paper as soon as they had taken this room, and gone out into the street again, leaving Silk behind, after scribbling a not very lengthy note. Looking up and down Dock Street now, Silk decided that if it did no harm for Crane to go out again, it could surely do none for him to study the street from a window this high.

Limna was peaceful, the innkeeper had said; but there had been rioting in the city the night before, rioting put down harshly by the Guard. "Silk's men," the innkeeper had told them wisely. "They're the ones stirring it up, if you ask me."

Silk's men.

Who were they? Deep in thought, Silk stroked his cheek, feeling two days' beard beneath his fingertips. The men who had chalked up his name, no doubt. There were some in the quarter who would do that and more, beyond doubt, and even assert that they were acting under his direction. Not for the first time, it occurred to him that some of them might be the men who had knelt in Sun Street for his blessing when he had told Blood he had been enlight-ened—men so desperate that they would accept any leader who appeared to have the favor of the gods.

Even himself.

Two Guardsmen in mottled green conflict armor were coming up Dock Street with slug guns at the ready. They were showing themselves, clearly, in the hope that the sight of them by day would prevent disturbances tonight—would prevent men with clubs and stones, and hangers like Auk's and a few needlers, from fighting troopers in armor, armed with slug guns. For a moment Silk considered calling out to them, telling them that he was Patera Silk, and that he was ready to give himself up if that would end the fighting. The Ayuntamiento could hardly kill him without a trial if he surrendered publicly; it would have to try him, and even if he could not prove his innocence he would have the satisfaction of declaring it.

The manteion was not yet safe, however. He had prom-ised to save it if he could, and it was in more danger than ever now. Musk had given him how long? A week? Yes, one week from Scylsday. But had Musk really been speaking for Blood as he had claimed, or for himself? Legally, the manteion was Musk's: to give himself up now would be to turn his manteion over to Musk.

Something deep in Silk's being recoiled at the thought. To Blood, perhaps, if it could not be helped. But never, surely never, to someone—to . . . Why, the very possibility had moved the Outsider to enlighten him in order to prevent it. He would kill Musk if—

If there was no other way, and he could bring himself to do it.

He turned away from the window and stretched himself on his bed, recalling Councillor Lemur and the way Lemur had died. As Presiding Officer of the Ayuntamiento, Lemur had been caldé, in fact if not in name; and Crane had killed him. It had been Crane's right to do that, perhaps, since Lemur had intended to execute Crane without a trial.

And yet a trial would have been a mere formality. Crane was a spy and had admitted it—a spy from Palustria. Had Crane then really had the right to kill Lemur? And did that matter?

Belatedly, it struck Silk that the note that Crane had written so hurriedly had almost certainly been a message to the government of his city—to the caldé of Palustria, or whatever they called him. To the prince-president. Crane would have described the Ayuntamiento's underwater boat (Crane had considered it extremely important) and the peculiar teardrop shape that was the cross section of a wing that could fly.

There were steps in the hall outside, and Silk held his breath. Crane had told him to unbar the door only to three quick taps, but it did not matter. The Guard would come, would search this inn and every other inn, beyond question, as soon as the Ayuntamiento chose a new Presiding Officer and that Presiding Officer decided there was a chance that he and Crane (and even poor Mamelta, for the new Presiding Officer could not be sure that Mamelta was dead either) might have survived. Crane had defended the cost of this room in the best inn in Limna by saying that the Guard would be less ready to disturb them if they appeared rich; but spurred by urgent orders from the Ayuntamiento, the Guard would not hesitate to disturb anyone, no matter how rich.

The steps faded away and were gone.

Silk had sat up and pulled off his new red tunic before he fully realized that he had resolved to shave. Rising, he jerked the bellpull vigorously and was rewarded by a distant drumroll on the stairs. Two days' beard might disguise him, but it would also mark him as someone requiring a disguise, and the Outsider could not reasonably object to his shaving, something that he did every day. If he were arrested, well and good. There would be no further rioting and loss of life; and he would be arrested as himself—as Silk, the man others called caldé, and not as some skulking fugitive.

"Soap, towels, and a basin of hot water," he told the deferential maid who answered his ring. "I'm going to get rid of all this right now." She had brought the aroma of the kitchen with her, and one whiff of it woke his hunger. "I'll have a sandwich or something, too. Whatever you can prepare quickly. Maté or tea. Put everything on our bill."

Crane had rung for more towels and fresh shaving water as soon as he bustled in. "I'll bet you thought I'd deserted you," he said as he arranged them on the washstand.

Silk shook his head and, finding the action practically painless, fingered the lump left by Potto's fist. "If you hadn't returned, I'd have known you were under arrest. Do you intend to shave off your beard? I hope you don't mind my borrowing your razor."

"No, not a bit." Crane eyed himself in the luxuriously large mirror. "I think I'd better whack away the best part of it, anyhow."

"Most men in your position would have shaved first and sent their report afterward. Do you think those fishermen who rescued us will tell the Guard, if they're questioned?"

"Uh-huh." Crane slipped out of his tunic.

"Then the Guard will know enough to look for us here, in Limna."

"They'd look here anyhow. This is the most likely spot, if we lived."

"I suppose so. You gave those fishermen a card? A card must be a great deal of money to a fisherman."

"They saved our lives. Besides, the captain will go to Viron to buy something, and his sailors will get drunk. If they're drunk enough, they won't be questioned."

Silk nodded again, knowing that Crane could see him in the mirror. "I can't tell you how surprised I was to find that the driver who had taken me home from Blood's was one of the crew. He's become a fisherman, it seems."

Crane turned to stare at Silk, his face lathered and the razor in his hand. "I keep underestimating you. Every time I do, I tell myself that's the last time." He waited for a reply, then turned back to the mirror. "Thanks for keeping it to yourself until we were alone."

"I thought he seemed familiar, but we were in the harbor before I placed him. He tried to keep his face turned away from me, and it gave me a good view of the back of his head; and that had been what I'd seen, mostly, when he took me to my manteion. I'd been sitting behind him."

Crane dabbed at one sideburn with the razor. "Then you knew."

"I didn't really understand until just now, when I was thinking about what a good spy you are—how valuable you must be to your city."

Crane chuckled. "We're soaping each other's beards, it seems."

"I didn't really understand about the fishing boat until we changed clothes in that alley," Silk told him. "Before that I was simply mystified; but someone aboard that fishing boat, the captain or more plausibly the driver who had taken me home, had given you several cards."

"You saw there was no money belt. I've been kicking myself ever since and hoping you hadn't noticed."

"When Chenille told you about that commissioner . . ."

"Simuliid."

"Yes, Simuliid. When Chenille told you he'd gone to the lake to meet with members of the Ayuntamiento, you came here yourself to investigate. I know you did, because I spoke to a young couple you befriended. If you didn't have somebody here already, you decided then that you should have someone all the time; and you hired the captain and his boat. I'd imagine they were to keep an eye on the Pilgrims' Way. The path runs along the edge of the cliffs in places, and anyone on it could be seen easily from a boat on that part of the lake. I won't inform on him or you now, of course; yet I'm curious. Is the captain Vironese?"

"Yes," Crane told him. "Not that it matters."

"You're not shaving. I didn't intend to interrupt you."

Crane turned to face him again. "I'd rather give you my complete attention. I hope you realize I've been working for you as well as for my city. Working to put you in power because it might head off a war."

"I don't want power," Silk told him, "but it would be iniquitous not to thank you for everything you've done—

for saving my life, too, when it would have been safer for you to have left me in the water."

"If you really feel like that, are you willing to formalize our alliance? Viron's Ayuntamiento's going to kill us if it gets hold of us again. I'm a spy, and you've become a major threat to its power. You realize that, don't you?"

Reluctantly, Silk nodded.

"Then we'd better stand back to back, or we'll lie side by side. Tell me everything you know, and I'll tell you anything else you want to know. My word on it. You've got no particular reason to trust it, but it's better than you think. What do you say?"

"It's hardly fair to you, Doctor. The things that I've guessed will be of no particular value to you; but you may have information that will be extremely valuable to me."

"There's more. You do everything you can to see to it that my people and I aren't picked up, and to free us if we are. I promise we'll do nothing to injure your city. You realize, don't you, that you may have to run if you want to keep breathing? If we can't make you caldé, we'll at least give you a place to go. Not because we're overflowing with kindness, but because you'll be a focus for discontent as long as you're alive. You need us now, and you may need us a lot more in a few days."

"You'll answer all my questions openly and honestly?"

"I said so, didn't I? Yes. You've got my word on all of it. We'll put you in power if we can, and you'll keep the peace when we do and not go after us. Now I want your word. Have I got it?"

Slowly, Silk nodded. He extended his hand. Crane laid aside his razor, and he and Silk joined hands.

"Now tell me what you learned about my operation."

"Very little, really. Hyacinth's working for you, of course. Isn't she?"

Crane nodded.

"That's why I'm doing this." Silk had taken his beads from his pocket; he pulled them through his fingers as he spoke. "Turning against my city, I mean. That burst vein in my brain—I don't feel up to arguing with you about it, you see. Not yet, because it might make us enemies again. It wants me to save the manteion, and so I must if I can; but I myself want to save Hyacinth. You must think that's foolish, too."

"I'm trying to save her myself," Crane told him. "And the men on the fishing boat who saved us both from drowning. All of them are my people. I feel responsible for them. By Tartaros, I *am* responsible for them. If it wasn't for that, I'd have told you about the boat when we picked you up. But what if you were caught and talked? Those three men would be killed, and they're mine."

Silk nodded again. "I feel like that about the people who come to sacrifice at our manteion. You would probably say that they're only porters and thieves and washerwomen, but they are our manteion, really. The buildings and even our Sacred Window could be replaced, just as I could; they can't." He stood and went to the window.

"As I said, Doctor, I was thinking about how important you were, and how silly I'd been not to realize it earlier. You must be fifty at least."

Crane turned back to the mirror and washed the dried foam from his beard. "Fifty-six."

"Thank you. So you've been a spy for a long time, and you're likely to be of high rank. Besides you're a doctor, and that in itself would make you important to your city's government. They wouldn't just send you off to Blood's by yourself. Hyacinth's Vironese. I know that because I've spoken with someone who knew her when she was younger. But my driver is from your own city, or so I would guess. Was he your second in command?"

"That's right." Crane was lathering his beard for the

second time, plying the big boar's-hair brush with sweeping strokes.

"Blood told Musk to have a driver bring a floater around for me; but you had anticipated that, and when you left us you told your second in command to be ready. You'd brought me the azoth, of course, and there was a chance that whoever drove me might see it."

"You're right." Crane scraped a little hair from one cheek. "I also wanted him to get a look at you and become acquainted. I thought it might be useful later. I could say now that it has been."

"I suppose I ought to be flattered." Silk leaned out of the window, peering upward. "The important point, I'd say, is that in order to act as he did—I mean today—your second in command must have known not only that you had been captured, but that you had been taken to the lake. It would even appear that he knew precisely where the Ayuntamiento's underwater boat was when we were swept out of it, since he had your fishing boat so accurately positioned that he and the fishermen were able to pick you up as soon as you came to the surface. You can't have gotten out of the underwater boat much before I did; nor can you have reached the surface much faster. I wasn't in the water very long, yet you were already in the boat when I was rescued, and there had been time for your second in command to pass you some money. He would have been prepared for that, because he would've known that your possessions had been taken from you. Even if he was the person who brought your medical bag to Lemur—"

"He wasn't. He'd left Blood's earlier. In a way that was too bad. He might've been able to slip something useful past them."

"I was about to say that even if he had learned that you were at the lake because he brought your bag, or overheard the order that another driver do it, he had to have had some further means of locating you. I've been trying to imagine what that means might be, and the only things I can think of are that he can send forth his spirit like Mucor, or that you're carrying a very small glass, or at least some device of that kind. You promised to answer my questions. Will you tell me whether I'm correct, and how they failed to find it?"

"Because it's in here." Crane tapped his chest. "Eight years ago I had bypass surgery. We took the opportunity to implant a gadget that sends a half-second signal every two minutes. It tells anyone who's listening how my heart's doing, and the direction of the signal lets them find me. So if you're ever in need of rescue again, just kill me."

He grinned. "While I'm still among the living, can I ask why you're so interested in that window?"

"I've been wondering whether we could get out of here if we had to—if the Guard began breaking down the door, for example. I could reach the edge of the roof and pull myself up, I believe."

"I couldn't. When I was your age I might have." Crane went back to his shaving.

"Can't you fly?"

Crane chuckled. "I wish I could."

"But that's what you reported to the prince-president, isn't it? That shape Lemur showed us? How fliers fly?"

"You're wrong there. I didn't."

Silk turned away from the window. "A secret with so much military value? Why not?"

"I wish I could tell you, I really do. But I can't. It wasn't included in our agreement. I hope you realize that. I swore I'd tell you everything you wanted to know about my organization and our operation. I can tell you what *was* in my report. My report was a part of the operation, I admit."

"Go on."

"But it didn't go to the prince-president of Palustria.

Did you really think I'd tell that maniac Lemur the truth? You did, I know. But I'm not you."

"I hope you're not about to say that you're not a spy at all, Doctor."

"No, I'm a spy all right. What do you think of this? Or should I shave it all off?"

"I'd remove it all."

"I was afraid you were going to say that." Reluctantly, Crane pared away another patch of beard. "Aren't you going to ask who I spy for? It's Trivigaunte."

"The women?"

Crane chuckled again. "In Trivigaunte they'd say, 'The *men?*' Viron's dominated by men, like most other cities. Do you think the Ayuntamiento's got no female spies? It's got all it wants, I guarantee you."

"Naturally our women are loyal."

"Admirable." Crane turned to face Silk, gesturing with his razor. "So are men in Trivigaunte. We're not slaves. If anything we're better off than your women are here."

"Is this the truth?"

"Absolutely. The truth, and nothing over."

"Then tell me what was in your report."

"I will," Crane wiped his razor. "It was pretty short. You saw me write it so you know that already, or you ought to. I reported that the Ayuntamiento was onto me, that I'd been picked up and had killed Councillor Lemur while making my escape. That they'd brought down a flier but lost the PM in the lake. That I'd found their headquarters, a boat in Lake Limna that sails under the water. I claimed the reward our Rani's offered for that."

Grinning more broadly than ever, Crane continued, "And I'll get it, too. When I go back to Trivigaunte I'll be a rich man. But I said I wasn't going to leave yet because I thought there was a good chance that Silk might unseat the Ayuntamiento. I'd rescued him from them, he had reason to be grateful to me, and I thought a change in government here was worth any risk."

"I am grateful to you," Silk said. "Very much so, as I've told you already. Was that all?"

Crane nodded. "That's the lot, pretty much exactly as I wrote it down. Now I want you to explain to me how you knew Hyacinth was working for me. Did she say so?"

"No. I looked at the engraving on this needler." Silk took it from his pocket. "It has hyacinths all over it, but here on the top there's a tall bird—a heron, I thought— standing in a pool; when I realized that it could be a crane instead of a heron, I knew you must have had it engraved for her." He opened the breech. "I hope that the water hasn't ruined it."

"Let it dry out before you try to shoot. Oil it first, and it should be all right. But the fact that I presented Hy with a fancy needler can't have been the only thing that tipped you off. Any old fool with a crush on a beautiful woman might have given her something like that."

"That's true, of course; but she kept the azoth in the same drawer. Do you still have it, by the way?"

Crane nodded.

"So it seemed likely that it had been given her by the same person, since she wouldn't want you to see it if you hadn't given it to her. An azoth's worth several thousand cards; thus if you'd given her one, you were clearly more than you seemed. Furthermore, you passed it to me while you were examining me in Blood's presence. I didn't believe the man you were pretending to be would have dared to do that."

Crane chuckled again. "You're so shrewd, I'm beginning to doubt your innocence. Sure you're not of my trade?"

"You're confusing innocence with ignorance, though I'm ignorant in many ways as well. Innocence is something one chooses, and something one chooses for the same reason one chooses any other thing—because it seems best."

"I'll have to think about that. Anyhow, you're wrong about me giving Hy the azoth. Somebody'd searched my room a couple of days before. They didn't find it, but I asked Hy to keep it for me to be on the safe side."

"When you put it in my waistband—"

"I said that there was a goddess up there who liked you, sure. She brought it to me and said we had to figure out a way of getting it to you, because she thought Blood was going to have Musk kill you. When she came in she thought she'd find me patching you up, but I'd finished with you and sent you in to Blood. Musk came to get me while we were talking it over, so I tipped Hy a wink and took the azoth with me, figuring I'd have a chance to slip it to you."

"But she came to you and asked you to do it?"

"That's right," Crane said, "and if that makes you feel good, I don't blame you. When I was your age, it would've had me swinging on the rafters."

"It does. I don't deny it." Silk gnawed his lip. "As a favor—a very great favor—may I see the azoth again, please? Just for a minute or two? I don't intend to harm you with it, or even project the blade, and I'll return it the moment you ask. I just want to look at it again, and hold it."

Crane took the azoth from his waistband and handed it to him.

"Thank you. While I had it, it bothered me that there were no hyacinths on it; but I understand that now. This demon, is it a bloodstone?"

"That's right. It was meant to be a present for Blood. Our Rani gave me a nice bit of money in case it looked like we ought to buy him, and one of our khanums threw in that azoth for an extra goodwill gift. He's got a couple already, but back then we hadn't found that out yet."

"Thank you." Silk revolved the azoth in his hands. "If I'd known that this was yours and not Hyacinth's, I wouldn't have returned with Mamelta to search those devilish tunnels for it. She and I would not have been overtaken by Lemur's soldiers, and she wouldn't have died."

"If you hadn't gone back, you might have been picked up anyhow," Crane told him. "But Lemur wouldn't have had that azoth, and without it I couldn't have killed him. By this time you and I would both be dead. Your woman friend, too, most likely."

"I suppose so." For what he believed to be the final time, Silk pressed his lips to the gleaming silver hilt. "I feel that it's brought me only bad luck; yet if I hadn't had it, the talus would have killed me." With some reluctance, he handed it back to Crane.

That night, as Silk lay in his rented bed whispering to a strange ceiling, the tunnels involved themselves in all his thoughts, their dim, tangled strands looping underneath everything. Was that lofty chamber in which the sleepers waited in their fragile tubes beneath him now, as he waited for sleep? It seemed entirely possible, since that chamber had not been far from the ash-choked tunnel, and its ashes had fallen from the manteion here in Limna. No doubt his own manteion on Sun Street was above just such a tunnel, as Hammerstone had implied.

How horribly cramped those tunnels had seemed, always about to close in and crush him! The Ayuntamiento hadn't built them—could not have built them. The tunnels were far older, and workmen digging new foundations struck them now and then, and wisely reclosed the holes in tunnel walls that they had made by accident.

But who had made the tunnels, and what had been

their purpose? Maytera Marble recalled the Short Sun. Did she remember the tunnels, the digging of the tunnels, and the uses of the tunnels as well?

Their room, which should have been cool, was over-warm—hotter than his bedroom in the manse, which was always too warm, always baking, though both its windows, the Silver Street window and the garden window, stood wide open, their thin white curtains flapping in a hot wind that did nothing to cool the room. All the while Doctor Crane waited outside with Maytera Marble, throwing chips of shiprock from the tunnels through his window to tell him that he must go back for Hyacinth's silver azoth.

Like smoke, he rose and drifted to the window. The dead flier floated there, his last breath bubbling from nose and mouth. Everyone drew a final breath eventually, not knowing it for the last. Was that what the flier had been trying to say?

The door burst open. It was Lemur. Behind him waited the monstrous black, red, and gold face of the fish that had devoured the woman who slept in the glass tube, the tube in which he himself now slept beside Chenille, who was Kypris, who was Hyacinth, who was Mamelta, with Hyacinth's jet-black hair, which the fish had and would devour, snap, snap, snap, snapping monstrous jaws. . . .

Silk sat up. The room was wide and dark and silent, its warm, humid air retaining the memory of the sound that had awakened him. Crane stirred in the other bed.

It came again, a faint tapping, a knock like the rapid ticking of the little clock in his room in the manse.

"The Guard." Silk could not have explained how he knew.

Crane muttered, "Probably just a maid wanting to change the beds."

"It's still dark. The middle of the night." Silk swung his legs to the floor.

The tapping resumed.

An armored Guardsman with a slug gun stood in the middle of Dock Street, scarcely visible in the cloud-dimmed sunlight. He waved as he caught sight of Silk at the window, then came to attention and saluted.

"It is the Guard," Silk said. By an effort of will, he kept his tone conversational. "I'm afraid they have us."

Crane sat up. "That's not a Guardsman's knock."

"There's one outside, watching our window." Silk slid back the bolt and swung the door wide. A uniformed captain of the Civil Guard saluted, the click of polished boot heels as sharp as the snap of the great fish's jaws. Behind the captain, another armored trooper saluted like the first, his flattened hand across the barrel of his slug gun.

"May every god favor you," Silk said, not knowing what else to say. He stood aside. "Would you like to come in?"

"Thank you, My Caldé."

Silk blinked.

They stepped over the threshold, the captain negligently elegant in his tailored uniform, the trooper immaculate in waxed green armor.

Crane yawned. "You haven't come to arrest us?"

"No, no!" the captain said. "By no means. I've come to warn you—to warn our caldé particularly—that there are others who *will* arrest him. Others who are searching for him even as we speak. I take it that you are Doctor Crane, sir? There are warrants for you both. You stand in urgent need of protection, and I have arrived. I am sorry to have disturbed your sleep, but delighted that I found you before the others did."

Silk said slowly, "This is happening because of an ill-considered remark of Councillor Lemur's, I believe."

"I know nothing of that, My Caldé."

"Some god overheard him—I believe I can guess which. What time is it, Captain?"

"Three forty-five, My Caldé."

"Too early to start back to the city, then. Sit—no, first bring the trooper who's watching our window inside. Then I want you to sit down, all three of you, and tell us what's been happening in Viron."

"It might be better to leave him where he is, My Caldé, if we wish the others to believe I am arresting you."

"And now you've made the arrest." Silk picked up his trousers and sat on the bed to put them on. "Doctor Crane and I have been subdued and disarmed, so the man outside is no longer needed. Bring him in."

The captain motioned to the trooper, who strode to the window and gestured; the captain himself took a chair.

Silk slapped Crane's wrapping against the bedpost. "You addressed me as caldé. Why did you do that?"

"Everyone knows, My Caldé, that there is supposed to be a caldé. The Charter, written by Our Patroness and Lord Pas himself, says so plainly—yet there has been no caldé in twenty years."

Crane said, "But everything's gone along pretty well, hasn't it? The city's quiet?"

The captain shook his head. "Not really, Doctor." He glanced toward his trooper, then shrugged. "There was more rioting last night, and houses and shops were burned. An entire brigade was scarcely enough to defend the Palatine. Unbelievable! It gets a little worse each year. The heat has made things very bad this year, and the high prices in the market . . ." He shrugged again. "If the Ayuntamiento had asked my opinion, I would have advised buying up staples—corn and beans, the foods of the poor—and re-selling them below cost. They did not ask, and I shall write my opinion in their blood."

Unexpectedly, the trooper said, "A goddess spoke to us, Caldé."

The captain smoothed his thin mustache. "That is so,

My Caldé. We were signally honored yesterday at your manteion, where now the gods speak again."

Silk wound the wrapping about his ankle. "One of you understood her?"

"We all did, My Caldé. Not in the way that I understand you, and not in the way that you yourself would beyond doubt have understood her. Yet she told us plainly that what we had been ordered to do was blasphemy, that you are accounted sacred. By the favor of the goddess, your acolyte returned as she spoke. He can relate her message in her own words. The substance was that the immortal gods are displeased with our unhappy city, that they have chosen you to be our caldé, and that all who resist you must perish. My own men—"

As if on cue, there was a knock at the door; the trooper opened it to admit his comrade.

"These men," the captain continued, "were ready to kill me if I insisted we carry out our orders, My Caldé. I had no intention of doing so, however, you may be sure."

Silk received this in silence. When the captain had finished speaking, Silk pulled on his red tunic.

The trooper who had just come in glanced at his captain; he nodded, and the trooper said, "Everybody can see there's something wrong. Pas is holding back the rain, and there's all this heat. One crop after another's failing. My father had a good big pond, but we pumped it dry to water the corn. Now it's stayed dry all summer, and he was lucky to get ten quintals."

The captain cocked his head toward the trooper who had spoken as if to say *you see the difficulties with which I must deal.* "There is talk of digging canals from the lake, My Caldé, but it will take years. Meanwhile the skies are locked against us, and every manteion in the city is silent except yours. Long before the goddess spoke, it was clear that the gods are displeased with us. Many of us feel that it is equally

obvious why. Are you aware, My Caldé, that people all over
the city have been chalking 'Silk for Caldé' on walls?"

Silk nodded.

"Tonight my men and I have been doing a bit of chalking of our own. We write, 'Silk *is* Caldé.' "

Crane chuckled dryly. "They mean the same thing,
don't they, Captain? 'Silk will be killed if caught.' "

"Let us be grateful that it has not occurred, Doctor."

"I'm grateful, I can tell you that." Crane threw aside his
sweat-soaked sheet. "But gratitude won't get the caldé into
the Juzgado. Can you suggest a place where we could hide
until that's attended to?"

"I'm not going to hide," Silk told him. "I'm going back
to my manteion."

Crane's eyebrow went up, and the captain stared.

"In the first place, because I want to consult the gods.
In the second, because I have to tell everyone that we must
overthrow the Ayuntamiento by peaceful means, if we
can."

The captain stood up. "But you agree that it must be
overthrown, don't you, My Caldé? Peacefully if it can be
done peacefully, but by force if force is required?"

Silk hesitated.

"Remember Iolar," Crane muttered.

"All right," Silk said at last. "New councillors must
replace those presently in the Ayuntamiento, but it's to be
accomplished without bloodshed if possible. You three
have indicated that you're ready to fight for me. Are you
ready to accompany me to my manteion as well? If someone comes to arrest me, you can tell them I'm under arrest
already, just as you were going to do here. You might say
you returned me to my manteion so I could collect my
belongings. A courtesy like that, extended to an augur,
wouldn't be out of place, would it?"

"It will be very dangerous, My Caldé," the captain said grimly.

"Anything we do will be dangerous, Captain. What about you, Doctor?"

"Here I shaved my beard, and you're going to go back to the quarter where everybody knows you."

"You can begin on a new one today."

"Then how could I refuse?" Crane grinned. "There's no way to get rid of me, Caldé. You couldn't scrape me off of your shoes."

"I was hoping you'd say something like that. Captain, have you been searching for me all night? That's what it sounded like."

"Since the goddess favored us, My Caldé. First in the city, then here because your acolyte said you'd gone here."

"Then all three of you ought to have something to eat before we leave, and so should Doctor Crane and I. Could you send one of your troopers down to wake up the inn-keeper? Tell him we'll pay for everything, but we must eat and go as soon as possible."

A look sent one of the troopers hurrying out.

Crane asked, "Do you have a floater?"

The captain's face fell. "Only horses. One must be a colonel at least to authorize a floater. My Caldé, it might be possible to commandeer a floater for you here. I will make the attempt."

Silk said, "Don't be ridiculous. A floater for your pris-oner! I'll walk in front of your horse with my hands tied. Isn't that how you do it?"

Reluctantly, the captain nodded. "However—"

Crane sputtered, "He's lame! You must've noticed it. He has a broken ankle. He can't possibly walk from here to Viron."

"There is a Guard post here, My Caldé. I could procure an additional horse there, perhaps."

Recalling his ride to Blood's villa with Auk, Silk said, "Donkeys. It must be possible to rent donkeys here, and I can have Horn or one of the other boys bring them back. An augur and a man of the doctor's age might be permitted to ride donkeys, I'd think."

The first gray light of shadeup had filled the streets of Limna before they were ready to leave. Silk was still murmuring the morning prayer to High Hierax as he mounted the young white donkey one of the troopers held for him, and put his hands behind his back for the other to tie.

"I'll make this real loose, Caldé," the trooper told him apologetically. "Loose enough so it won't hurt, and you can shake it off whenever you want to."

Silk nodded without interrupting his prayer. It seemed strange to pray now in a red tunic, though he had frequently prayed in colored clothes before he entered the schola. He would change at the manse, he told himself; he would put on a clean tunic and his best robe. He was a poor speaker (in his own estimation), and people would make fun of him if he wasn't habited like an augur.

There would have to be a lot of people, too. As many as he and the three sibyls—and, yes, of course, the students from the palaestra—could get together. When he spoke . . . In the manteion or outside? When he spoke, he—

The captain had mounted his prancing charger. "If you are ready, My Caldé?"

Silk nodded. "It's occurred to me that you might easily turn this pretended arrest into a real one, Captain. If you do, you'll have nothing to fear from me—or from the gods, I believe."

"Hierax have my bones if I intend any such treachery, My Caldé. You may take the reins whenever you wish."

Though Silk could not recall kicking it, his donkey was ambling forward. After a moment's reflection, he con-

cluded that the trooper who had tied his hands had probably prodded it from behind.

Crane was studying the black cloud banks rolling across
the lake. "Going to be a dark day." He urged his donkey
forward to keep up with Silk's. "The first one in quite a
while. At least we won't have to fry on these things in the
sun."

Silk asked how long he thought the ride would take.

"On these? Four hours, minimum. Don't donkeys ever
run?"

"I saw one run across a meadow when I was a boy," Silk
said. "Of course it had no man on its back."

"That fellow just finished tying my hands, and my nose
itches already."

They trotted up Shore Street, past the Juzgado in which
the helpful woman who had admired Oreb had mentioned
Scylla's shrine and the Pilgrims' Way, past Advocate
Vulpes's gaudy signboard with its scarlet fox. Vulpes would
wonder why he had not given the captain his card, Silk
thought—assuming that Vulpes saw him and recognized
him in his new clothes. Vulpes would protest that criminals
arrested in Limna should not be returned to the city to
deprive them of his services.

Vulpes's card had been lost with so many other things
when he had been searched—with his keys to the manteion, now that he came to think of them. Possibly Lemur,
who had gotten Hyacinth's needler, the azoth, and his
gammadion and beads from Councillor Potto, had taken
Vulpes's card as well, though it would do Lemur no good
in the court to which he had gone. . . .

Silk looked up, and Limna had vanished behind them.
The road wound among low, sandy hills that must have
been islets and shallows even when the lake was much
larger. He turned in his saddle for a final glimpse of the

village, but behind the captain and the two troopers on their horses saw only the steely blue waters of the lake.

"This must be about the time Chenille used to arrive as a child," he told Crane. "She used to look for the water at shadeup. Did she ever tell you about it?"

"That would have been earlier than this."

A falling drop of water darkened the hair of the white donkey's neck; another splashed Silk's own rather less tidy hair, wet but astonishingly warm.

"Good thing this didn't come a little earlier," Crane said, "not that I like it anytime."

Silk heard the rattle of shots an instant after he saw Crane stiffen. Behind him, the captain shouted, "Get down!" and something else, words drowned by the boom of a trooper's slug gun.

The rope about Silk's wrists, which had been about to fall off a moment before, seemed to tighten as soon as he tried to free his hands from it.

"*Caldé! Get down!*"

He dove from the saddle into the dust of the road. By a seeming miracle, one hand was free. The roar of a floater was followed by a longer coarse, dry rattle, the sound of an immense child hurrying a lath along the bars of a cage.

He scrambled to his feet. Crane's hands were free, too; he put them about Silk's neck as Silk helped him off his donkey. More shots. The captain's charger screamed—a horrible sound—reared and plunged into them, knocking them both into the ditch.

"My left lung," Crane muttered. Blood trickled from his mouth.

"All right." Silk pushed up Crane's tunic and tore it in a single motion.

"Azoth."

The booms of slug guns were followed by the greater

boom of thunder, as if the gods were firing and dying too. Pale drops the size of pigeons' eggs splattered the dust.

"I'm going to bandage you," Silk said. "I don't think it's fatal. You're going to be all right."

"No good." Crane spat blood. And then, "Pretend you're my father." A torrent of rain engulfed them like a wave.

"I *am* your father, Doctor." Silk pushed a wadded rag into the hot and pulsing cavity that was Crane's wound and tore a long strip from Crane's tunic to hold it in place.

"Caldé. Take the azoth." Crane put it into his hands, and died.

"All right."

Bent above him, the useless strip of rag in his hands, Silk watched him go, saw the shudder that convulsed him and the upward rolling of his eyes, felt the final stiffening of his limbs and the relaxation that followed, and knew that life had gone, that the great and invisible vulture that was Hierax at such moments had swooped through the driving rain to seize Crane's spirit and tear it free from Crane's body—that he himself, kneeling in the mud, knelt in the divine substance of the unseen god. As he watched, Crane's wound ceased to throb with blood; in a second or two, the rain had washed it white.

He put Crane's azoth into his own waistband and took out his beads. "I convey to you, Doctor Crane, the forgiveness of all the gods. Recall now the words of Pas, who said, 'Do my will, live in peace, multiply, and do not disturb my seal. Thus you shall escape my wrath.' "

Yet Pas's seal had been disturbed many times; he himself had scraped up the remains of one such seal. Embryos, mere flecks of rotten flesh, had lain among the remains of another. Was Pas's seal to be valued more than the things it had been intended to protect? (Thunder crashed.) Pas's wrath had been loosed upon the whorl.

" 'Go willingly,' " (Where?) " 'and any wrong that you have ever done shall be forgiven.' "

The floater was nearer, the roar of its blowers audible above the roaring of the storm.

"O Doctor Crane, my son, know that this Pas and all the lesser gods have empowered me to forgive you in their names. And I do forgive you, remitting every crime and wrong. They are expunged." Streaming water, Silk's beads traced the sign of subtraction. "You are blessed."

There was no more shooting. Presumably the captain and both troopers were dead. Would the Guard let him bring them the Pardon of Pas before he was taken away?

"I pray you to forgive us, the living." Silk spoke as quickly as he could, racing words his teachers at the schola would never have approved. "I and many another have wronged you often, Doctor, committing terrible crimes against you. Do not hold them in your heart, but begin the life that follows life in all innocence, all these wrongs forgiven."

A slug gun boomed three times in rapid succession, very near. The buzz gun rattled again, and mud erupted a hand's breadth from Crane's head.

The effectual point: "In the name of all the gods you are forgiven forever, Doctor Crane. I speak here for Great Pas—" So many in the Nine, each with an honorific. Silk was seized by the feeling that none of them really mattered, not even Hierax, though Hierax was surely present. "And for the Outsider and all lesser gods."

He stood.

A muddy figure crouching behind a dead horse shouted, "Run, My Caldé! Save yourself!" then turned to fire again at the Guard floater bearing down on them.

Silk raised his hands, the rope that had not bound him still dangling from one wrist. "I surrender!" The azoth in his waistband seemed a lump of lead. He limped forward as fast as he could, slipping and sliding in the mud while rain pelted his face. "I'm Caldé Silk!" Lightning flared across the sky, and for an instant the advancing floater seemed a talus with tusks and staring, painted eyes. "If you have to shoot someone, shoot me!"

The mud-smeared figure dropped its slug gun and raised its hands as well.

The floater halted, the air blasting from its blowers raising a secondary rain of muddy water.

"They fired upon us from ambush, My Caldé." As though by a trick, the muddy figure spoke with the captain's voice. "We die for you and for Viron."

A hatch below the turret opened, and an officer whose uniform was instantly soaked with rain vaulted out.

"I know," Silk said. "I'll never forget you." He tried to recall the captain's name, but if he had ever heard it, it was gone, like the name of the trooper with the long, serious brown face, the one whose father's pond had gone dry.

The officer strode toward them, halted, and drew his sword with a flourish. Heels together and head erect, he saluted with it as though upon the drill field, holding it vertically before his face. "Caldé! Thank Hierax and all the gods that I was able to rescue you!"